Pathos of

A

Wilting ROSE

EJINE OKOROAFOR-EZEDIARO

Pathos of a Wilting Rose

From the Author of acclaimed,

A Rose in Bloom

ISBN 978-0-6152-2193-3

For

Damanze Akaraka Agorua Justlyn Okoroafor,

My dearest Papa

Prologue

Ever reflected back on an event and wished you could re-enact the exact moment when the realization had hit you. Your intent is not so much to pinpoint the precise location or your preoccupation at the time but only an optimistic quest for that desirable intermission before the muck hit the fan. Your thoughts are far from wishing to recreate or re-live that moment; however your bid is to attempt to freeze your reverie prior to the period when it all went awry and eternally repress it.

Try as she might to recreate this, Nkiru couldn't. Instead she tried to envisage that fateful day, 2 and more years ago as it would have been. She must have woken up as usual but it was no ordinary dawn. She must have tarried to get out of bed that morning because there would have been no need to hurry. She must have been cheerful or even hummed a melody underneath her breath, the possibilities were endless.

One certainty though was her then general state of mind because she was undoubtedly happy, just happy?   No, ecstatic would be a more appropriate descriptive term.

She and her betrothed, Obinna had just concluded their 'iku aka' or knocking ceremony the previous day and the formal traditional wedding ceremony was billed to follow suit and subsequently church or white wedding. Who wouldn't have been happy? She queried rhetorically. To cap their rosy future together, they were also intended to depart soon afterwards to start a new life in the USA.

There possibly couldn't have been a happier couple in the whole town of Ubi. None!

Her residual memory of the exact moment when her world was overturned was however a blur.   What remained vivid in her mind was the fall, not a physical fall. You know just like the rug had been pulled from under your feet and you whirl in a free fall. She remembered watching herself declining rapidly as she tumbled down an apparently endless pit. Bizarrely, she also stood atop the gaping hole while her other self tumbled down. There was two of her, each image more factual than the other. An out of body experience it is called.

She recalled plummeting incessantly, thumping down an endless cascade of stairs, her body flailing like a lifeless doll as it went

7

thump, thump from one step to the next. Her eyes ached from watching the spectacle of her simultaneous endless drift while her observer body stood numb and standstill. She had felt drained, hapless, helpless and incapable of movement or reaching out to rescue her counterpart battered ostensibly inert body rattling along in quick descent down the ditch. She couldn't recall when or how the fall broke, much less when or how the two images finally merged back into one.

She was subsequently engulfed by blankness and transported into a hollow shell devoid of pain or emotions. She found herself encased in limbo and suspended in time. Inside her pristine cocoon, she refused to feel or acknowledge the prickly thorns that encircled her head. Maybe if she stayed motionless for long enough, the events will upend. For when she finally rises, time would have reset itself back to her pre-plunge period. It wasn't, couldn't and shouldn't be true. She had mentally shut herself down, denying and refusing to acknowledge that Obinna was gone. In her then thwarted troubled mind, she argued that the rest of the world was mistaken.

It was only a bad dream and the nightmare would be over as soon as she wakes up. She stayed in bed hoping that when she finally decides to wake up, it would have been a mere fluke, none of it real.

Alas, if only wishes were horses because she did wake up but it was not a dream. When she emerged from her cocoon, it was no pretty sight. She finally had to confront her reality. The impervious cocoon that she had encased herself in hoping that when she creeps out that life would be normal again, had only but offered her a temporary refuge. Her desire to rewind time or restart from her previous comfort zone was just wishful thinking. Life was far from a slate that she could wipe clean and rewrite. It is a master of its own fate; her part is to arbitrate with destiny.

She still longed for a clean slate to rewrite her residual life and plug with only laughter, very little of S's but no T's of life. However, more than two years later and the numbness were yet to fully dissipate. The entire period is interposed by pure anguish.

Her heart threatened to burst out of its seams with sorrow as she re-contemplated her recent past. She had refused to cry throughout the initial trial period. Her eyes were wide open but blind, ears receptive of sounds but she was deaf. She learnt how to cry with a smile while her smile was transformed into a smirk. She had clutched her cell phone to chest, clung to it as if her dear life depended on it. She had grasped so tightly that the veins at the back of her hand were visibly outlined and threatening to pop. She willed the phone to ring and waited expectantly to hear his voice at the other end.

"Hello Baby, it's me." She'd have heard him say because those were his usual opening line like she could mistake him for any other. She was failed by the phone which refused to ring with his name reflected on the interface. Why? Why? She had queried repeatedly in anguish. Had they not suffered enough? Their strife with her parents and kinsmen weren't enough penalties? Had they not propitiated the gods enough?

A myriad of recriminations, doubts, anger and various other emotions clogged flittingly through her mind, flickering like the embers of a dying candle through her tormented soul. This was followed by another series of unrelenting queries flashing one after the other across her mind like the pages of a book left flustering in the face of the wind. She still didn't have all the answers but was healing and trying to fully embrace the realms of her tragedy.

It was against the tenets of her religion to doubt God, query her fate or the power above. She was supposed to stay complacent to destiny after all the Almighty Savour was crucified to atone for her sins, yet never bemoaned his trials. Which sacrifice is greater than that? He never uttered a single word of complaint. She recounted penitently. She was no god but we are supposed to embrace his sacrifice.

So why should she still be complaining? She might well embrace her lot and get a grip but it was just too much. God, unbearable! She suppurated in anguish, albeit no tears or words escaped from her lips, just the blank stare that kept forcing her mother back on her knees clutching and praying rosary beads while pleading for absolution and beseeching the Lord to intercede before her daughter loses her sanity.

But…but…why? She still soliloquised in vain, knowing no straight answers were forthcoming. A conflict of emotions raced through her tormented soul offering no relief as powerless rage crushingly engulfed her once again. Time was supposed to be the greatest healer yet her pain was persistent and raw, harsher than the sharp painful sting of a tincture of iodine applied to fresh wound.

She usually flourished on staying upbeat in the face of adversity but not anymore. Life had dealt her too heavy a hand. As if Obinna's tragedy was not enough, she had to contend with others too. Her reoccurring trials beggared the aphorism 'when it rains, it rains in torrents' as a relentless torrent of mishaps had dogged her very existence in the last two years, end-to-end.

Where does she start to recount her inveterate heartbreaks? She lamented repeatedly, bemoaning the culmination of events that had rocked the root of her equilibrium nearly forcing her senses to desert her. She was still trying to rein herself in but as of yet was en-route to recovery.

Her eyes brimmed with tears as memories of her beloved Obinna came flooding back. They trickled down her cheeks as she gazed up at the ceiling half blindly and momentarily fixed her gaze on the shoddy chandelier at the centre of her bed-sit. She noticed a tiny spider dangling precariously at the edge of a stringy web extending from the chandelier. She watched the tiny creature spinning energetically and erratically while rapidly transforming a webby mesh into a globe around the chandelier.

Lucky spider, at least you spin your own world, she pondered enviously, mesmerized by its adroitness at work. She soon turned away to take in the rest of her nearly bare typical student digs. Nothing mattered anymore, she sighed.

What was it with life anyway? Her rage rose again in indiscriminate anger. Life was what you make of it, came a devilish reprimand from her subconscious. I never asked for misfortune to befall me, she canted back. She had frequently found herself engaging in a tacit exchange with her chi but dared not confide this to anyone. Enough swirl of insanity already.

Winter was setting in after her first month of settling in. Her mother had left a few days earlier to return home, reassured now that her daughter was psychologically strong enough to take on the world again. Both of her parents reckoned a new start in a different environment would be the best option for her. A change of scene and a Masters program in tow to help her heal. They were optimistic that this new environment could prove to be the catalyst to reignite her waned interest in life and surroundings. They had almost arrived at the end of their tether before coming to the conclusion that uprooting her from the shores of her home country; Nigeria might well overturn her recent misfortune. Nkiru on her part was personally past caring because nothing seemed to matter anymore. She was virtually a living dead encased in an empty shell. She was convinced that without Obinna, she was only but a robotic moving, walking, talking zombie. That was all that was left of her.

The memory of her first official meeting with Obinna was stirred up again. She could still visualize the day like it was just yesterday because the memory was indelibly encased on her mind. It wasn't actually their first meeting per se but the day that they became officially acquainted. This was around her third year semester exam period. She had left the lecture rooms after a prolonged revision session and briskly making her way back to her hostel. Obinna had approached and offered to accompany her back. She had pretended to be reluctant to let him while pleased deep down for his offer since she dreaded the solitary walk. It was pitch dark and pretty late. She and Obinna struck up minor conversation as he walked her back and consequently became firm friends, transcending into lovers and naturally contemplating marriage.

Her beloved Obinna was a considerably good natured fellow. He also possessed an uncanny knack for upending adversity into good fortune, no matter how awful the situation that he happens to find himself in. He had even proposed marriage to her the following morning following his rescue from the hands of a formidable gang of kidnappers. It is difficult to imagine how he could have pulled that off now given their respective dispositions a few hours earlier. They had both been in a quadroon, he was terrified and held captive by imprudent kidnappers whereas she was frantic with worry and haunted by an extraordinary premonitory fear for his safety. He had been scheduled to return ashore from an offshore duty assignment the previous evening and she had waited at her base for a call from him confirming his safe arrival but to no avail. She was increasingly apprehensive by nightfall when he failed to contact her or answer his perpetually switched off phone when she dialled his number. Her gut instinct foresaw he was in danger and she feared for his safety. Her hunch was later confirmed after she solicited the help of their mutual friend Sanni, who lived in the same city as Obinna to verify his exact whereabouts.

Sanni on arriving at Obinna's digs met with his absence but on further enquiries from his next door colleagues learnt the distressing truth. Obinna's boat was hijacked and he was kidnapped. The kidnappers uncannily enough contacted Sanni with a demand for ransom while he was still over at Obinna's residence ascertaining his whereabouts. Nkiru and Sanni subsequently rallied Sanni's father's immense support to ensure Obinna's successful rescue. Sanni's father was a very influential business tycoon. He didn't disappoint by pulling all the right strings to guarantee a wide scale police search that led to the successful rescuing of Obinna but sadly his fellow co-worker, Mike kidnapped alongside him was not successfully rescued or found.

Nkiru's family as was customary in their culture after she and Obinna announced their engagement proceeded on a reconnaissance of his extraction prior to sanctioning the proposed union, more so because Obinna hailed from a different town. They unexpectedly unravelled that Obinna was an OSU in the course of their investigation, thereby literally opening up The Pandora's Box.

Her parents immediately prohibited her from associating with or marrying Obinna since it was taboo for a freeborn to marry an OSU. She however refused to heed to their advice. A major rift developed threatening to cause a major discord not only within her immediate but also amongst her extended family members. She and Obinna remained pretty unwavering in their decision to wed, refusing to keel under the pressure from her family members who were vehemently agitating for their break up. She and Obinna did ultimately succeed in winning her parents over, especially after they had enlisted the help of the Parish priest to persuade them to change their minds.

Nkiru's father had unpredictably contrived a cleansing ritual after they considered the whole matter settled. This was believed to help appease and assuage the wrath of the angry gods that would arise from desecrating the OSU taboo.

OSU diatribe was a cankerworm that ate deep into the fabrics of her culture and people. An individual is designated OSU, slave, untouchable, and non freeborn, or such analogous terminology depending on a wide range of factors. These are supposed descendants of forefathers or ancestors who had been consecrated to peculiar gods as sacrificial lambs either as captives from intertribal wars or had worshipped and served at shrines of deities in the their day amongst others. The subsequent lineages of such consecrated fellows automatically inherit the OSU legacy and have to endure a peculiar segregation. They are erroneously perceived as untouchable, inferior to the freeborn and meet with constant discrimination from the rest of the society.

Obinna hadn't been aware of his OSU legacy prior to Nkiru's family discovery of his iniquitous legacy rendering his situation more complex. His father had concealed their OSU heritage from his brood. He was under the misguided notion that by so doing, he was protecting them from similar discrimination and ridicule that he had encountered in his youth. He went to a great length to conceal their legacy by resettling far from his birthplace in hopes that his new neighbours wouldn't fixate on their cumbersome heritage. He subsequently embarked on petty trade and hardly ever revisited his birthplace. In place of notifying them of their legacy, Obinna's father thrived on nurturing and equipping them adequately to counter any future strife. He was of the opinion that their future would be more secured if they obtained ample education, which would be their eventual weapon against the unkind world. They didn't disappoint him either. Obinna was a first class brain and had graduated with a first class degree in Petroleum Engineering while his younger brother was nearly completing his medical degree program. Their much younger siblings also exhibit a similar academic prowess and promise.

The whole brouhaha arising from the proposed nuptial between herself and Obinna was finally resolved after the cleansing ritual was accomplished. The preliminary knocking ceremony finally held with a mini jamboree attended by both arms of their respective close family members. They formally congregated at her home to dine and wine together thereby officially indicating accord on both sides for the nuptials to proceed.

Alongside the endorsed nuptials plans scheduled to hold in next to no time, Obinna had also received a new transfer posting notification to the United States. Both of them were therefore aligned to relocate abroad to the USA after the conclusion of both traditional and church wedding ceremonies. There was a huge sigh of relief on all sides and for all intents and purposes, their initial run of hitches seemed to be behind them.

The next day though, her world was suddenly collapsed like a pack of cards. Man proposes but God disposes, she deigned once again. She frequently wished to be suspended in the realm of that last evening when their beloved ones and family members had assembled for their knocking ceremony and to rejoice and celebrate her engagement to Obinna. She also wished to capture and freeze Obinna in his most delightful moment when he had broken the news of his transfer posting to her after keeping the secret for days to surprise her.

They were so happy and reckoned things were finally falling back into place until … … ….

The beginning of the end, that fateful Saturday- 2 years ago when the dark clouds set ... ...

One

Obinna and his family had set off from Nkiru's household in Ubi town. The *iku-aka* or *knocking ceremony* had concluded fairly late in the evening and they were embarking on the 4 hours or so return trip back to their home at Obah.

'Hello Mrs. Ejike-to-be, how are you doing?' he enquired jokily when he called to chat with his betrothed yet again. His cab was unfortunately stranded halfway through their home-bound trip. They were stuck between a fleet of other stalled vehicles travelling in the same direction on the major highway.

'Fine and how's my future husband?' Nkiru returned with similar flippancy. She had just re-entered her room and was lounging in bed browsing through an old magazine when his next call came through. 'How's the traffic?' She asked without waiting for a reply to her initial query after overhearing noisy impatient motorists blasting their car horns in the background.

'Still congested,' he reported, having intimated her earlier of the prolonged traffic jam. 'Who could have foreseen a similar delay given the time of the night? You can't believe it but we've barely gone more than 5km in the last hour,' he complained. 'This jam is said to extend to River Ajaba. Apparently a trailer derailed earlier this afternoon leaving a trail of catastrophe behind. More than ten vehicles in total are rumoured to be involved in the subsequent chain reaction of multiple crashes. Some of the injured passengers are still waiting to be evacuated besides the huge wreckage blocking the freeway.'

'Oh my God, that sounds like absolute horror.' Nkiru declared and sat up at once. She was rattled by the news. 'I hope most of the victims' survive.' She prayed. 'You know it had occurred to me that an accident was causing the delay as soon as you mentioned a hold up so that explains it then. I hope the road clears soon. It's rather late to be out on the road though.' She fretted for his safety. 'Are you sure it won't be safer for you guys to return here and travel in the morning instead.'

'You know I'd love nothing better than that but we're already half way home besides knowing my parents, I'm sure they'd prefer for us to return home instead. My younger ones are home alone and expecting us back too. Hopefully it shouldn't be too long before the jam clears. So what have you been up to anyway?'

'Daydreaming about our impending wedding of course, I was just discussing with Mum and she had suggested we might have to postpone the London sojourn given our now impending USA trip.'

'Okay but that means you'll have to purchase your wedding gown here, at home.' Obinna emphasized, knowing her prior fervent desire to purchase one overseas.

'I suppose so but then I can place an order online through one of my numerous cousins abroad or better still get one of them to help me buy one. I've spoken to Idu already and she promised to dispatch wedding catalogues and magazines ASAP through Nkechi so I can see if there's any I would like there.' Nkiru gushed. 'We'll see what happens after I speak to dad tomorrow. He mightn't be averse to sponsoring us for a quick trip.' She contemplated.

'Fine then, you do whatever you think is best.'

'Thanks for the vote of confidence. Did I mention that is one of the reasons why I love you so much?'

'No you didn't so what are the others?'

'I'll tell you if you remain good.' She teased.

'I thought I'm perfect.' He joked.

'Yeah right!' She scorned in jest.

'I love you, babes.'

'I love you too. We'd better stop now or Zube will start to think we are acting like two silly kids.'

'Never mind him; he's indicating his disgust by a shake of head.'

'Bye.' Nkiru bid him still giggling.

'Bye love.' He echoed back.

They were both chuckling as they momentarily cut off. An hour and half later, Obinna called to report they were still stuck in the traffic jam. The two lovebirds updated each other repeatedly and the hold up didn't dampen their high spirits. They exchanged ideas for their impending wedding and travel abroad without forgetting to express their devotion and love.

When she called him anew a few hours later, Obinna was beginning to sound worried and exhausted. 'We've been stuck in this horrible jam for well over 5 hours my dear,' he complained. 'The only consolation is that the police have finally succeeded in securing a crane to haul the trailer out of the road and clear the wreckage obstructing our path.' He added to reassure her

'You sound very tired honey,' she commented sympathetically. 'How are your parents coping with the ordeal?' She enquired with great concern.

'They are holding up well for now. We had quit our cars earlier to congregate and mingle with other stranded passengers in groups. You could've easily mistaken the set-up for a convention of sorts because of the camaraderie displayed. We were conversing, joking and even sharing food supplies like we were old friends just to keep our spirits up.' He told her. 'Chatting with you too sure made the situation more tolerable because the period seems so much shorter but now I'm tired. Almost five hours has elapsed and counting.' He calculated off a quick glance at his watch. 'I'm worried about Uncle Lekwa and my relatives headed for Ogbani. I know that they had departed earlier so I'm fervently hoping that they aren't stuck in this traffic jam or they'd be so irritated.'

'I can well imagine. Their route diverts before Ajaba River so hopefully they should have reached home by now.'

'I hope so too. Any way babes let me not hold you up on your beauty sleep, we'll chat tomorrow.'

'Let me know when the jam eases so I can sleep easier or I'll remain worried. My parents were also suggesting that it might be safer and a better idea for you to come back and travel in the morning instead.' She offered anxiously.

'We'll be fine.' He assured her. 'And speaking of the devil but the traffic has started to move.' He announced joyfully as he clambered back into the waiting taxi. His driver hurriedly rejoined the fleet of stalled cars starting to depart at snail-speed. 'Don't worry we'll be fine.' He repeated loudly as the din of resuscitated traffic and blaring horns grew louder around him. 'Try to catch some sleep and we'll talk tomorrow.'

'Goodnight and safe trip.'

'Goodnight, love you babes.'

'Love you too.'

The traffic progressively picked up velocity as the jam gradually eased off as they approached the River Ajaba Bridge. As they drove slowly past the accident site, Obinna and his fellow passengers including his brother Zube, his father's friend, Ijem as well as the cab driver gleaned the gruesome aftermath from the wreckages deposited at the roadside. The huge petrol tanker that spawned the tragic accident was keeled over across one side of the road. A mangled and

17

charred beyond recognition heap of what could only be some of the other vehicles involved in the accident laid on the opposite side of the bridge.

'This huge trailer truck initially collided into a fully loaded bus with forty or more passengers travelling from Isako to the East after tumbling and swerving off its course for no apparent reason. The vehicles following behind them also ended up crashing into one another causing a chain reaction of multiple accidents.' Obinna recounted as he and his fellow passengers rehashed the tragic details and pieced the stories that they had gathered earlier together.

'Yes, more than 10 cars in total were involved, a very horrific crash indeed.' Uncle Ijem surmised with a mournful shake of head

'Isn't it a sheer miracle how this whole surrounding region was not engulfed in a massive inferno given the scale of the multiple crashes?' Zube marvelled envisioning the disaster and the fact that a petrol tanker was involved.

'It's only by a lucky stroke of luck.' Uncle Ijem furnished. 'I think God works overtime protecting us given our multitude of limitations. The minor fire that was said to have emanated from the crash had miraculously fizzled out. One can only imagine what would have happened if trailer tank wasn't empty and on its way for a refill or else the resulting calamity would have been unfathomable. It is not farfetched that the whole of Ajaba would've been razed.'

'I agree it was nothing short of a pure miracle.' Obinna's concurred. 'I can't even begin to imagine what could have obtained if the fire had escalated since there are no suitable fire brigades or fighters who could have helped to curb a spreading inferno.'

'True.' They agreed and pensively offered a minute's silence in addition to prayers for the wounded and departed.

'Look at those shameless vultures.' Zube muttered pointing disgustingly at human outlines scavenging and rummaging through the ruins obviously in search of valuables to steal even at the odd late hour.

'What did you expect? That is their way.' Obinna stated, unfazed by the spectacle.

'They are on a fruitless search anyway given that the accident occurred almost ten hours ago.' Zube summated.

'Yes,' Obinna replied. 'It had occurred around 3 pm.'

'My main concern lies solely with the unfortunate victims. I pray that most of them survive.'

18

'My driver friend say he been witness the evacuation of passengers involved in the crash,' the cab driver chipped in. 'Him alone been count up to fifty dead bodies but he swear say they plenty pass fifty. Even self, some passengers been lose arms or legs as they dey yank them out from the rubble. He said blood full everywhere. Women, children and even men wey dey around dey wail. People wey dey help rescue the wounded or the dead before the fire catch them, dey weep also. Those wey just stand dey watch, dey cry too so much so that they no even sabi who they cry for pain or who just dey cry. He say the set-up been remind him of war zone but this one be worst. For war at least you know say people dey in combat **korokoro** (*plainly*) and are dying for a cause.' The cab driver related gory details.

Obinna developed goose pimples as he envisaged the horror as narrated by the cab driver.

'I hear also say some doctors wey they been carry some of the victims to no agree commence treatment unless someone been guarantee their fees first.' The cab driver continued. 'Some even demand huge deposits before they go as much as examine the patients. The unlucky ones wey no find guarantor or didn't have the deposit to pay steadily bled to death. Some of the wounded passengers been die as well-wishers dey ferry them from one hospital to another seeking for doctor or hospital wey go get sympathy initiate treatment as they no find anybody to sign on their behalf or money on them straight up.'

'That is true and only a few fared any better. Those are the few fortunate victims with minor injuries and could survive the hour or so trip to Mkpala Teaching Hospital. The doctors over there were offering immediate treatment to save lives without insisting on mandatory deposits or guarantors.' Zube related.

'It irks me to no end to think that we live in a so called modern society and contemporary time, yet lives are lost senselessly and on innumerable occasions too. We are failed by our misguided leaders who fail to institute appropriate measures to combat such calamities or provide basic amenities for the populace. No contingency plans are laid in place to secure lives especially during related emergency situations like this one. It is more painful given that we have the resources to implement these basic amenities if nothing else yet those criminals or our so called leaders at the helm are only interested in self enrichment or siphoning money into secret accounts overseas.' Obinna seethed grimly. 'Sometimes I'm forced to wonder if we're a cursed lot.' he cogitated retrospectively.

'Cursed as in Nigerians, Africans or Blacks?' Zube wanted to clarify.

'Any of those categories will do me really.' Obinna declared. 'Let's explore my notion baring any sentiments. I'm personally convinced that the black race is the most disadvantaged in the general scheme of life for that matter. I must also admit that the bulk of our misfortunes are of our own making in some cases. It sometimes looks to me that God himself might have set us up for failure, just think about it.' Obinna opined, strengthening up in his seat at the back of the cab to brace his audience counterattack.

'I have to agree with you to a certain extent,' Zube, his younger brother sitting beside him concurred. 'But I wouldn't necessarily call us a cursed race. We might be unlucky in more ways than one but not necessarily cursed.' He attested more diplomatically.

'Well,' Uncle Ijem turned from his front passenger's seat to wade into the dialogue. 'I agree with Zube, cursed is too harsh a description besides I don't believe any god will be so ruthless as to set his own children up for failure. We are unfortunate especially because our evolution is continuously retarded and thwarted by so called Westerners. I'd also confess that we had lent them the rope with which to hang us. The immaturity and gluttony of most of our leaders is constantly exploited to retard our growth.'

'You're right.' Zube agreed with Uncle Ijem. 'Our insecurities are exploited and a plain example is the erstwhile brazen apartheid leader who had purported that Blacks cannot rule themselves and that if handed guns, would use them to kill themselves? How preposterous is that statement? I'll deliberately ignore the rest of his supposed spiteful speech but my point is that such injudicious statements help to prove how our race is deliberately maligned and manipulated. Colonization, apartheid, slave trade and the rest of them have all played a great part in retarding our evolution.' He enumerated.

'Very true but we're taking baby steps nonetheless. I have no doubts that we would overcome and surely become a force to be reckoned with in the nearest future. I must remind you that these so-called First World nations never grappled with similar tribulations. And if it is any comfort, Rome was not built in a day so surely our day will come.' Uncle Ijem declared passionately.

'Well, I think that is all well and true for patriotism but if I may put a little damp on that, all races or Gods creations basically evolved at the same epoch then have we ever pondered why our progress and evolution are so retarded in comparison to the rest of the world?' Obinna countered ardently.

'**Nna**, guys you don dey go too deep.' The cab driver protested, inadvertently diffusing the sombre discussion. 'I never read book reach that one but if you ask me, I say na our leaders fail us tire.'

'Yes, I agree with you but it would also unreasonable to heap the total blame on just our leaders, government or any specific one group. We are all culpable in some way. Our handicap is most certainly far reaching; even the grassroots can not be exonerated.'

'What is grassroots, abeg?' The befuddled cab driver enquired.

'Obinna is referring to the common man or our root source.' Zube explained. 'I agree that our incompetence stems directly from our homes, pedigree, extended families, villages, peer pressure and so on and so forth.'

'Na now you start to dey talk. I no know book too much oh but I just dey marvel at our people. Your son go just carry car land for village **kpam**.' He slammed his hand at the steering wheel to ram home his point. 'But no one bothers to ask am how he get the car, even him own papa turn blind eye. He *sabi* (knows) say his son dey out of job for the last six months so how he come get car out of the blues. Everybody just dey jolly with am, pat him head giving accolade. Next, he go take title and everyone dey hail am 'chief'. Him papa happy say he bring car, bring cash. He even encourage am, tell am in confidence say how others dey do am, make him self go do am. The day before he be apprentice wey dey serve under somebody. When and how wey he become oga overnight.'

The rest guffawed in amusement at his hilarious tirade.

'Na true wey I dey talk.' He cab driver griped.

'Of course, we are not disputing them. Your words rightly hit the nail right on the head. We have culturally managed to establish a peculiar decadence from the top to bottom with our misplaced priorities and ill conceived morals. Where does one really start to catalogue the atrocities that we have allowed to eat into the very fabric of our lives and society? We surely do require a major shake up. Attitudes need to be changed right from the nitty-gritty to the top. Our present perspective needs a major overhaul. First, we should start by preaching morally correct principles and stressing the need for simple truth to our children; we need to de-emphasize the current belief that wealth or affluence is the be all and end all. We should reward hard work and diligence and highlight integrity. We should deviate from

21

the current trend of lauding unscrupulous fellows and their ill gotten riches and try the leaders who misappropriate government funds.' Obinna enumerated.

'I no lie you shaa, my next world? I go be rich man.' The cab driver surprisingly backtracked. 'I go learn book well, well and use am make money.'

'I'm glad you inferred that one needs to strive hard to make the money. Similar virtues and aspirations are necessary for us all to imbibe. Don't get me wrong, I personally have no aversion to affluence but I believe one has to work for and earn it unless one wins the lottery of course.' Zube added jokingly.

The traffic jam had completely eased off a few kilometres after they drove past the bridge as they continued their repartee and journey. They soon turned unto the freeway to Obah before following the cue of the cab ahead of them to stop at the junction leading to the residential area. The cab was conveying Obinna's parents and Aunty Mary. The group had originally planned to return to Obinna's father's residence as a group but due to the ungodly hours of their actual arrival, had to change the plans.

Aunty Mary, Obinna's father's younger sister joined Uncle Ijem's cab for the rest of the journey home with the entertaining cab driver. Obinna and Zube on the other hand exited to join their parents' cab to expedite their respective group's journey home. Uncle Ijem's and Aunty Mary's abodes were not too far from each other but at a different section of Obah from them. It made more sense for them to reshuffle.

Obinna and his group continued towards their residence. Their cabdriver had turned a corner a few blocks away from their destination when they were suddenly confronted by a temporary road block. The road was barricaded with three huge drums aligning the breadth of the narrow street and in between them; spiky platforms layered with multiple sharp nail tooth ends. The nails had been tacked from behind exposing a dangerous array of sharp nail spikes on the exterior. The driver was therefore debarred and discouraged from trying to evade this block as the sharp nails would definitely deflate his car tyres if he were to try to be audacious. They could also distinguish three figures clad in police uniform standing behind the block illuminated by their dimmed car headlamps.

One of the men stepped over the block as they slowly crawled to a stop. He was waving his torchlight vigorously in an up and down motion beckoning them to a complete stop. The cab driver drew to a halt a few inches away from him and turned off his engine.

'A road block at this time of the night?' Obinna muttered aloud as they waited.

'It no pass bribe. Na only money they want.' The driver predicted.

'Oya come down, step out. Where are your particulars?' The policeman demanded sternly as he stepped up to the driver's side. He also stuck his head through to shine his torchlight at the rest of the passengers including Obinna, Zube and their parents. They watched and waited meditatively.

The driver quickly extracted his documents promptly and handed them over to the policeman but he vaguely shone his torchlight across the documents, scarcely verifying any.

'Who you carry and wetin you carry? Why una dey travel so late for night?' The policeman demanded curtly and impatiently.

'We been attend knocking ceremony. Na the accident wey happen for near Ajaba River wey delay us.' The cab driver explained.

'Okay, make una come out, all of you. Quick, quick and identify yourselves.' The policemen barked opening the back passenger's door at the same time for Obinna, and his parents to emerge. Zube also stepped down from the front passenger's seat.

'Please my son, we're returning from my son's knocking ceremony. It was the traffic that delayed us. I'm sure you must have heard about the terrible accident that occurred near Ajaba River.' Obinna's father explained without prompt after they alighted.

'Old man, shut up. Make you no talk if I no refer to you.' The policeman snapped and roughly shoved him aside, nearly pushing him down in the process.

Obinna and Zube were infuriated. Their mother quickly grabbed Zube by the arm to stop him as he made to advance angrily towards the police man. Obinna on his part timely held and broke his father's fall as he staggered back unto him on his way to the floor. He managed to steady his father and himself.

'*Rapu nwam*, Leave it alone, my son.' Ego, Obinna's mother whispered to Zube while maintaining a strong hold on his elbow. She knew that he'll only be aggravating the situation by confronting the uncouth policeman. Zube was more forceful by nature than Obinna.

The other two policemen who had been observing the situation all the while from behind the road block emerged to unite with their colleague on observing Zube's attempted angry advance towards him.

'Make una line up with your hands above una heads.' The policemen commanded, geared to quell any act of rebellion on Obinna and his family's part as well as assert their brutal clout. They proceeded to march and inspect them, tendering their baton in hand as the family and driver aligned in a single file.

'Why are you doing this?' The usually laidback Obinna demanded, exasperated by their undue show of callousness and jungle justice.

'This people no dey hear word.' The first policeman alerted his cohorts. He then stopped at Obinna's front. 'I say make you shut up and no utter a word unless I speak to you directly.' He barked at Obinna's face, spraying him with saliva escaping from his mouth at the same time.

Obinna didn't utter another word or bother to wipe the saliva off his face for fear of aggravating the fellow further.

The police man was increasingly enraged even so and swung at Obinna's forehead with his baton to ram home his exasperation.

Obinna felt an instant sore bump developing at the spot but resisted the urge to feel the area for obvious reasons.

'*Nwam ndo*, I *apologize my son*. Sorry. We didn't mean to offend you. We are very tired from our prolonged trip and just want to return home.' Obinna's father pleaded in a bid to placate him. He was hoping that they'd possibly respect his elderly counsel to let them off.

'Okay, you people no dey obey simple command at all.' The incensed policeman raged before exchanging his baton for a gun that he swiftly extracted from the sling around his waist. He proceeded to butt Obinna's father head with the end of his gun.

Obinna and Zube could no longer contain their outrage or remain inactive while their old man was visibly assaulted in their presence. They guardedly encircled their father to shield him than attack the policeman directly.

The policeman seemed to go berserk by virtues of their action and uncorked his rifle. His red-hot eyes were obtrusive as he aimed to shoot at the hapless family.

His first bullet hit Obinna point blank on the forehead and he staggered backward, knocking his father down with him. They both landed with a heavy thud on the side of the hard tarred roadside with Obinna's body atop his father's. The next bullet struck Obinna's father's forehead as he tried to shift his son's dead weight to confront the fellow. His disbelief was obvious from his open wide eyes as he contorted convulsively after the bullet hit him and gave up the ghost.

Obinna's mother was screaming hysterically at the implausible sight. One of the other policemen promptly shot into her mouth to silence her hysterics and she collapsed to the ground too.

The driver was shell shocked and stood rooted to his exact position in the line up. He was frozen and incapable of movement or flight. He involuntarily wet himself as he stood with mouth agape and arms in the air observing the horror that had unfolded before him. The enraged policeman callously shot at him too.

Zube on his part scuttled from attending to his brother's and father's bodies to rushing across to his mother as she was felled. The shocking drama had unfolded in a quick flash. He barely had enough time to reflect on the situation before for some mystifying reason; he stood up and took to his heels. His legs felt strangely stiff as he struggled to sprint away from the monstrous site.

The men on noticing his quick dart simultaneously pointed their guns at his escaping figure, firing and pummelling two successive shots apiece from their guns. Zube was instantly knocked down by the looming blitz and momentum of the numerous bullets piercing into different parts of his backside at the same time. He fell a few paces away from the rest of his family members and cab driver. The swift onslaught of bullets ceased as abruptly as it had began after he had collapsed to the ground with a heavy thump. A portentous silence followed.

'What have we done?' Zube vaguely overheard one ask the others even as he lay on a pool of blood on the floor.

'Now no be the time. Quick, quick, make we search their car, Okongwu search their pockets and grab any valuable you fit find fast.' The unrepentant policeman who had initiated the carnage ordered briskly.

Zube could still perceive the sound of their car engine starting through his agony before the men rapidly zoomed off abandoning them and the road block. He felt weak and was in excruciating pain. He tried to scream for help but only managed a feeble whimper as a gush of blood spluttered out of his mouth instead. He didn't require his extensive font of medical knowledge to decipher his predicament or possible imminent death if he didn't receive express medical attention. He could hardly dwell on the monstrosity that was perpetrated before him because his major concern was his younger siblings and their looming plight if none of them survives. One of the major arteries in his body or femoral artery was badly severed and he had also received multiple other wounds. The escape wounds in his abdomen from the bullets which had virtually pierced through from his back caused his entrails to gush out. He clutched at them and made to stand to go seek for help. He only was able to crouch on one knee while dragging his other leg behind him as he attempted to agonizingly crawl away from the scene for help. He barely managed a few steps before buckling back unto the floor. A transient wave of chilliness engulfed him, subsequently followed by an overpowering soothing calmness as he shuddered violently and gave up the ghost.

The corpses were still littered on the street as a crowd gathered to view the monstrous spectacle with great shock and disbelief at the crack of dawn.

Two

Mr. Ejike had his wife's hands entwined in his as they soulfully journeyed to meet their maker. So this is how the cookie crumbles; he factually cogitated as he tenderly drew his wife closer to his side. If it were any consolation, they were together in death as they have been in life.

Ahead of them, Obinna strode steadily flanked by a solemn crowd of departed souls ascending towards heaven. The couple glanced back simultaneously as if on cue to observe Zube following closely behind them. What will become of the rest of our living brood? They exchanged wordlessly as their eyes met while steadily on the ascent.

It is said that the god that gives kids, usually provides for their upkeep and so shall it be with our brood. Mr. Ejike rationalized as he responded reassuringly to the haunting query in his beloved wife's flittingly dejected eyes. He subsequently squeezed her hand to indicate that all was well. Matters have coincidentally been taken right out of their hands but they had always endeavoured in life and encouraged their children too to tread a righteous course. As they soared up the skies and geared to defend their conduct on earth, they were optimistic that they would receive commendation and absolution in place of an unlikely condemnation. They were absolved also by the fact that their lives have been untimely terminated by criminals.

Obinna waited for the rest of his family members to catch up with him at the doorstep of paradise so they could make a united entrance into heaven. They were one family and even in death will remain one. They jointly offered prayers for their brethren left behind before knocking on heaven's door. Just before they crossed over, Mr. Ejike evoked the memories of his remaining live kids.

There were three of them left. Ngozi was the eldest girl and twelve years old. She was reserved but had always exhibited a maturity ways beyond her age. He was sure she could be entrusted with taking proper care of her younger ones. Chidinma was the second girl and ten years old, bubbly and outspoken. One could always expect a quick reply or retort from her. He reminisced with an indulgent smile. She was also good-natured and would provide a much needed balance. The last but not the least was Ifedi, better known as the baby of the family and five years old. Unlike the rest of his siblings, the age gap between him and his immediate elder one was more extensive. While his elder siblings shared a two years age gap apiece, he was however five years younger than his preceding elder. He was the much pampered junior of the family.

Mr. Ejike feared for him most. Ifedi required a firm hand to guide and nurture him which only an adult or parent would have been able to provide.

Both he and his wife had met and married in their late thirties. Ego, his lovable wife was a humble servant in her youth and was compelled to wed late because her Master had refused to discharge her early from servitude. They had believed their family was complete after Chidinma, his last daughter was born. Moreover, Ego presumed her menopause had commenced after her period became ever so irregular shortly after she delivered Chidinma. That was until the morning she began to suffer from severe gripping lower-abdominal pains which she initially attributed to the unsavoury **moi-moi** (*bean cake*) supper that she had consumed the previous afternoon. The pain remained unabated in spite of an overnight fast and he was forced to rush her to the hospital the following day. The doctors had discovered she was on the verge of a miscarriage but they hadn't even suspected she was heavy with child before then. It was a sheer miracle that his adored wife was pregnant in her fifties and a rather difficult pregnancy ensued but as luck would have it, both she and baby Ifedi survived.

Mr. Ejike drew his beloved wife, Ego protectively closer once again and held her snugly to his side as he momentarily reminisced their past. He was avowed to protecting and caring for her for the rest of his life. Death couldn't debar him from keeping that promise, not after her horrific youth. He gazed at her lovingly and adoringly, remembering her poignant beginnings.

* * * * * * * *

Ego settled for the night in her undersized bed, tucked underneath a wrapper after turning off the light in her equally cramped room. She had only just concluded her chores for the day. It was already past midnight. She had been cleaning up after the last of master's guests had departed. The other members of her household including Master and his wife had retired to bed hours ago. It was a wonder that it was so quiet now, given the racket while the guests had been around, she deliberated. She reclined in bed wide awake and unable to doze off immediately. She was nervously pinning her ears back and praying that Master wouldn't materialize. To eavesdrop on his footsteps marching down the corridor to her room filled her with dread. She tugged her wrapper more tightly for more comfort at the thought.

They lived in a five bedroom bungalow with detached backyard attachment enclosing another three medium sized rooms. The main house consisted of a spacious, overly furnished living room situated adjacent to the master bedroom and two other rooms in one section. Master and his wife naturally shared the outsized master bedroom while their kids' who were away presently owned the other two rooms. There was a corridor demarcating that section from the remaining two rooms, kitchen and a guest toilet. Ego's room was the smallest in the complex and located at the far end of the corridor leading to the kitchen and general toilet as well as the exit to the backyard.

She was still dreading the sound of Master's footsteps shuffling down the corridor to her room as she lay wide-eyed in bed. She had noticed him guzzling many shots of alcoholic beverage while entertaining his friends at dinnertime. That was a portentous sign and she was afraid that he'll call on her later that night in his drunken stupor.

She had lived in this household for as long as she could possibly remember but her core origin was still a haze. She had no inkling as to where she hailed from originally, who her real parents were nor was she aware of any live siblings or blood relatives. Her earliest memories revolved mainly around her arrival at Master's household as a maid at about the tender age of six or eight. Not even Master could authenticate her actual age at the time. She could barely recollect her prior existence before arriving at this household because her earlier memories were somewhat distorted. She however has a legacy of a recurring dream of water and fish. This particular vision was more vivid and frequent in her youth but she has hardly been able to explain its import. The same static picture of glimmering blue water and a basket of fish at the shore is endlessly depicted in her dream most nights. The apparition isn't alarming or nightmarish but disturbed her because of its frequency and perseverance. She could well deduce the basic fact that fish derives from water but why this particular vision was perpetually depicted or dominating her dreams, she couldn't fathom out for the life of her.

Her father or possibly parents must be fishermen, she had decided. Her resolution made ways before Master explained that she was found abandoned beside the seaside by an undisclosed fisherman. That kind of explained her apparition to an extent but nevertheless why was no human image, say for instance this said fisherman or her genuine parents superimposed in the recurrent vision that perpetually haunted the realm of her subconscious. She regularly found herself pondering on this enduring riddle and intermittently fantasized about a magical underwater life. She would conjure an image of her cast as an underwater princess or '*mammy water*' surrounded by a serving school of fish and other creatures. She was always bemused by her strange rumination though because of her private insight into the absurdity of her fantasy. She was also occasionally aggrieved, incensed with anger at the thought that her real parents had abandoned her and no relative ever came to ask after her. Maybe she was really from underwater, she'd counter insolently but then would have expected the tides to overflow or zigzag through the expanse of the earth to seek her out or didn't the sea creatures miss her either?

A load of house helps were in the household when she initially arrived to assume residency here ages ago. The family lived in the capital city of Isoka in the western region of the country.

Ego vaguely recalled departing from a village and embarking on the eye opening trip to Isoka in the company of a stranger. He had arrived that morning to take her away from her then current home which she could barely recall now. She had only lived there for a few days and remembered weeping incessantly as the strange fellow bundled her away again. She'd since learnt he's Master's brother-in-law.

Aunty Ify was another prominent figure in her memoirs. She was an older maid in Master's home and had taken her straight under her wings when she arrived newly. She helped her settle in, allaying her fears and nurturing her. Ego could still remember the countless occasions when she had sat in the kitchen listening to Aunty Ify while washing a continuous supply of dirty plates and utensils with great fondness. Aunty Ify consistently prepared a variety of dishes that were subsequently transported to Madam's pepper soup joint. It was ages ago but those were her fondest memories. Madam's joint had closed down a couple of years ago.

Master or Chief Nnameze is an affluent business man and runs two sizeable supermarkets. His wife, Madam Chinelo used to run a pepper soup joint which was since derelict. She now helps with managing the supermarket accounts. The couple travels out to Cotonou, the economic capital of the neighbouring Benin Republic to purchase stock and other essentials to sell in their supermarkets. They owned another home there and were contemplating opening an outlet of their thriving supermarket business over there.

Master and his wife were fully integrated into the elite society in their region of Isoka, predominately inhabited by fellow Easterners. They loved to throw extravagant parties like that of the previous night when they had hosted a special committee of The People's Club, an elitist organisation. Madam was dead keen on maintaining their status quo or high social ranking and made sure to don the latest fashion trends. She also possessed an array of gold and diamond jewellery pieces bedecking her neck on any festive occasions.

Ego reflected on the passage of several servants in her ongoing tenure in the Nnameze household including her favourite, Aunty Ify. She was the first person to show her any special affection. She had passed on a few survival tips including how best to stay in madam's good books. She unfortunately departed to her home village shortly to wed a suitable suitor. A number of other servants had come and gone since then, most of them had helped out in the supermarkets or Madam's restaurant when it was still active.

Ego's routine was dissimilar to those of the others because she was specifically assigned to tender to the home front plus helping to rear Madam's kids when they came along. She basically kept home while the other servants departed early in the morning and returned late at night. While they were also granted a half-day off on Sundays, she was constantly on duty. Madam attested that she gets enough off times as it was, staying at home all day but in reality, she barely received any reprieve from the chores. Ego looked back indulgently on the memories of fellow servants who had transited same household but variable tenures of service. A number of them had only lasted a few weeks before either quitting voluntarily, complaining about the gruelling nature of the job, or else were discharged for laziness. Only a handful had managed to persevere for longer periods but family commitments had necessitated their early release. Aunty Ify, for one had left after her parents secured a suitable and reliable suitor for her. Only a minor handful lasted the distance to complete full stewardship and as such reaping good rewards. Chief Nnameze awarded those cash to set up individual trades. A good number were fired for pilfering from the businesses.

Ego recognized her divergent circumstance from the rest at a fairly early stage. Whereas the others could walk away or quit at will and also owned alternative homes or relatives to return to, she on the reverse was afforded no such liberties.

She had been recurrently yanked from one home to the next from infancy. She vaguely remembered transferring from one home to another before she could as much as form any tangible memories of the place or the people that she had lived with before relocating to the next. That was the norm until she finally settled here. This household was her first stable home and she was ever grateful for the stability it had afforded her. She was indebted to Master and Madam for offering her both stability and comfort, or did they let her forget either.

Ego has always tried to piece details of her roots together over the years but not quite successfully. She wasn't disillusioned in the least on learning Chief Nnameze and his wife were not her real parents because she had always knew that for a fact. She had however assumed that they were her distant relatives. Master had dispelled that notion lately after admitting he had procured her service in exchange for a piece of land and unspecified cash. She had no identifiable blood relatives or alternative home to return to even if she had wished to quit the Nnameze household. Master alleges that he doesn't have a clue as to who her real parents were and the fellow who had endorsed her transfer to his care via the help of his in-law was not her actual relative either. The fellow was purported to have procured her from another stranger, who had in turn inherited her under doubtful circumstances.

Ego observed her small room again as her eyes become fully adjusted to the dim light. It was a tiny space but she had adored it. There was just enough space for her narrow spring bed and equally modest set of drawers. The room was originally a storage space until Master decreed that she could move in. Her ramshackle suitcase and sizeable holdall bag rescued from the bin after Madam had discarded it lay under her bed secured with a long scarf to hold its two separate parts together as well as a battered pair of sandals. The suitcase held her few garments or meagre life belongings so to say. It included her very coveted pink flowered elegant ankle length ready-made gown. Madam had ordered it for herself but it had shrunk after the first wash. Ego was incredibly surprised when Madam said she could have it for Christmas. Ego was beside herself with joy to have such a pretty piece. It fitted her perfectly when she tried it on and the other maids were envious. She was never going to wash it so wrapped it in paper before placing it in a plastic bag. It lay right at the bottom of her suitcase, secluded from the rest of her drab hand-downs from Madam and minor knick knacks. Her most precious possession beside her precious gown was an authentic 14 carat gold chain with a crucifix pendant. She rarely wore the piece or Madam would have her head if she should find it on her. It nestled underneath the seams of the pocket in her only handbag. It was a gift from James, one of the most audacious male servants that had lived with them. He had wooed her a few years back before Madam swiftly dismissed him after she learnt of the budding romance. Madam disapproved of relationships amongst the helps. James was also street smart and had pilfered a lot of stuff from the stores to impress her. Ego suspected the pricey ornament come from a similar source but was too charmed to query him or return the gift. James made her laugh but he was too brash for her liking. She usually wore both the dress and chain and would stand admiring herself in front of Madam's bedroom mirror when no one else was home. Madam for all her paranoia hadn't been able to locate her priceless gem during her numerous impromptu inspections to ascertain whether she was hiding a secret stash. She had it firmly secured and slipped through a hole in the inside pocket of her handbag and sewed up. Her reverie was unrelenting since it was impossible for her to doze off. She marvelled at the elapsed interlude since her arrival at Master's home. Twenty odd years, she enumerated wordlessly and couldn't believe how swiftly that period had elapsed.

Ego could still remember how overjoyed she was when she was assigned a room of her own. It was a huge upgrade signifying and fulfilling her perpetual crave for legitimacy and acceptance into the family but little did she know. She had consistently shared rooms in the backyard with various other maids before Master's intervention. No house help had shared the main house proper prior to her. She was now the longest serving maid and knew the workings of the household like the back of her palm.

The years had also transited predictably with Master's kids becoming adults and leaving home for further studies abroad. The family had ceased to entertain as frequently as in the past but intermittently hosted an occasional soiree like the previous night.

Ego was particularly exhausted tonight from cooking, serving and cleaning up after everybody else. She had over the years evolved into maid, cook, and butler all rolled into one besides helping to raise Master's kids. Their first offspring was ironically just a decade younger than her when they were born. Ego wound her wrapper more tightly around her wishing that she could drift off to sleep instead of her protracted nostalgia. The possibility of Master's sudden appearance was niggling at her especially as he had downed too many shots of strong spirit. Master only visited in an inebriated state and would fondle and grope at her in his drunken stupor. He never straddles her but sits by her thus forcing her to crouch against the wall due to the undersized bed. He'd also lean so close to her face on occasions that she could smell his loud heavy stinky breath reeking of his favourite tipple, *Hennessey*. He had done many shots that evening which formed the basis for her enduring apprehension. She had long learnt to suffer his assault with tightly shut eyes, pretending to be detached from the situation or imagining the ordeal was happening to someone else. The prospect of his appearance was nonetheless a frightening prospect.

She couldn't usually dare to move or protest when Master unceremoniously shoves her tattered underpants aside and dips his fingers into her while holding his exposed manhood with the other. She occasionally peers at him while he gingerly moves both hands; one in her while concurrently masturbating himself.

His movement would become increasingly erratic and forceful as his excitement heightens or until she opens her eyes to witness milky discharge oozing from him as he jerks off. She must have been twelve years old when the sexual abuse commenced. Her breast had just sprouted out and Master had seemed more enamoured by them than her. He groped them at any chance but never in the presence of Madam or anyone else for that matter. He also threateningly warned her never to tell anyone about their private secret. He had started to secretly creep up to her room at midnight after she moved into this room a few years back, away from the scrutiny of the other helps. He orders her to keep calm while he cups her breast and touches her womanhood. It was a natural act; he had reassured her and their special secret but in same breath threatens to have her out in the streets if she ever tells anyone. It wasn't like she had any confidante or alternative home to return to if Master were to eject her so she kept the secret and continued to endure the assault over the years.

Ego could always tell when Master was about to conclude because his fingers will start to wrench roughly and uncaringly inside of her. She was subsequently left with a mixture of hurt, self loath and thrill at the same time. She deemed herself lucky in that his visits were infrequent because afterwards on occasions, he'd have hurt her so badly that she bled. She then has to adopt a funny walk with legs spread apart or forced to go without underpants for a few days because any slight movement or friction was torture and aggravated her agony. Madam would obviously notice and nag at her unusual awkwardness because she'll start to tarry with normal chores due to the excruciating pain between her legs.

Master on his part will regard her the next morning while she serves his breakfast with a blank and indifferent stare as if he hadn't been jerking off on her the previous night. He'll sometimes overlook her misery and revisit to molest her on consecutive days while in full knowledge that he was culpable for her distress or aggravating her woes. He'd also vigorously hush up her protestations and in his passive aggressive comportment threaten to subdue her physically if she wouldn't let him have his way. She daren't protest or try to stop him. She loathed her helplessness and inability to stop him but he practically owned her. She'd find herself homeless if she didn't let him have his way anyhow.

Ego felt ashamed to openly admit Master's assault when tempted to tell others. Master had warned her to keep the matter secret in any case and she was scared of the thought of becoming homeless. It was her fault somehow, she believed and who would believe her anyway if she were to expose him? Madam would surely beat her mercilessly for false accusations if she were to disclose her husband's secret exploit.

Master sneakily visited only when his wife was away but had become more audacious lately, calling on her a few times when Madam was in residence. How he was able to explain his absence from their matrimonial bed at the middle of the night to Madam was beyond Ego. Were the two in cahoots? She had wondered incredulously on occasions.

Ego soon nodded off to sleep without overhearing Master's telling footsteps. The picture of the basket of fish beside the shores was once again reflected in her dream.

'Ego, Ego.' She heard Madam yell while she was bustling around in the kitchen the next morning. She was waiting for the water to boil so she could pour it into the flask and complete the setting of the table. She had woken up an hour earlier than the rest of the household as usual to commence morning chores. She had already swept the front yard with a special rake, cleaned and dusted the furniture in the sitting room before commencing preparations for breakfast.

'Yes Ma.' Ego answered and hurriedly abandoned her chores to heed Madam's call or incur her wrath for an unnecessary delay.

Madam Chinelo was in the parlour and sitting on the middle settee with the centre table drawn nearer to her. Ego hadn't heard her enter the sitting room while she was in the kitchen. Madam looked like she was balancing the books from the supermarket accounts from the previous week which was her usual routine at the start of the week. Ego predicted she'd subsequently proceed to the bank later in the day to deposit cash if the accounts tally or else, a few heads will roll. Madam was decidedly waging a running war against the lot of dishonest staff that they've consistently contended with in conducting their supermarket business.

'Good morning, Ma.'

'Ego, you must find a tailor.' Madam ordered, peering down from beneath her glasses to spare her a brief glance. 'We need a change of curtains.' She indicated the sitting room drapes.

There was nothing wrong with the lot, at least not as far as Ego could tell. She had washed, ironed and hung them back again a few days ago in lieu of the Christmas festive period.

'I don't want Cecilia to think that we're too broke to afford a change of curtains in two years.' She added, uncharacteristically offering an explanation.

'Yes Madam.' Ego agreed and turned to leave.

'Serve breakfast before you leave.' Madam snapped before turning back to her books. She had only completed Secondary School but was streetwise. Master entrusted the finances with her.

'Yes Madam.' Ego replied before fugitively peeking at her face before leaving. She noticed that Madam was growing chubbier by the day but her naturally pretty face was evident regardless of her double chin. Madam always states that her escalating weight gain was a sign of good health and affluence. Her first name was Chinelo but no one except for Master addressed her as such. She insists on being addressed to as Madam or if you must, Madam *'Odozi Aku'* i.e. *one who arranges her husband's wealth*. She was now forty and Master, fifteen or more years older than her. Madam was also fiery and domineering. She insisted on maintaining their prestigious social standing and imposed a boundary between her and the less fortunate via her insufferable attitude. Her ghastly attitude endeared her to very few but Ego found her fascinating.

36

Madam never encourages pointless chitchats and only ever deigns to speak to her when arrogating orders. As such Ego wouldn't ordinarily dare to start a conversation unless Madam initiates one. "Ladies are to be seen, not heard; madam would misquote to chastise her if dares to initiate an unsolicited banter. Ego was nonetheless enchanted by Madam's referral to her as a lady than the obvious snub.

Ego returned to the kitchen to find the water in the kettle whistling to a boil. She gingerly lifted the kettle from the fire and poured the hot water into a ready flask. She subsequently cut onions and sizzled in hot vegetable oil until slightly brown before pouring in her egg mix for an omelette. She placed slices of bread and the fried eggs at the centre of the table. She also set mugs for Madam's favourite cocoa beverage, Ovaltine and tea bags for Master in addition to placing a tin of Carnation milk and margarine on the table. She stood back and inspected the table, ascertaining that everything was in place just like Madam loved to have them.

'I'm leaving now, Ma. Breakfast is ready.' She reported back to her but Madam neither replied nor bothered raising her head to acknowledge her report. She departed after a short pause anyhow, knowing Madam would have indicated if she required her to run another errand prior to her exit.

As she embarked on the long trek to the market to find a tailor, Ego was reminded of Madam Cecilia whom Madam had mentioned was visiting. Madam Cecilia and her family must be coming to visit from Cotonou where they had relocated a few years back then. She had eavesdropped on Madam narrating to another friend of hers how well Madam Cecilia and her family had settled down there. She even suggested that she and Master were considering a similar move if the country became unstable.

Cecilia was Madam's best friend. Both were birds of the same feather but rivals at the same time. They juggled a peculiar love-hate dynamics that Ego deemed rather odd. They were fiercely competitive and tried to out do each other in terms of whose family unit was more affluent, who owned more jewellery pieces, whose home held more modern gadgets to their kids and their respective accomplishments, nothing was spared in their misguided bid to out do each other.

Madam should have offered to give her a bus fare to the market instead of allowing her trek the extensive distance, Ego bemoaned. It was a pretty long walk, she lamented again while negotiating through the busy noisy streets and darting out of the way every so often to escape being hit by impatient motorists and hasty cyclists sharing the busy narrow roads as well as avoiding collision with other passers-by. There was nothing wrong with the drapes in the sitting room but for Madam Cecilia's coming. She briefly contemplated if she should have offered to sew the curtains for Madam and saved herself the tedious walk. She had purposely learnt how to sew by practicing on Madam's sewing machine. Madam actually bought the beautiful 'Singer' standing sewing machine on a whim and left it untouched at the guest room. Ego had seized the oppourtunity when home alone to learn to pedal and operate the machine, sewing rags or old garments together until she became fairly adept at the task. She was however reluctant to admit this to Madam for fear of terrible repercussions.

'You want us to make curtains at this time of the year?' One tailor repeated sceptically after the other as Ego went stall to stall canvassing for a tailor to make new curtains. It was two days away from Christmas so they were otherwise inundated with orders to sew fresh garments for their customers to don for the festive occasion.

'Please do the favour for my Madam. I promise she'll pay you well.' Ego plea bargained.

'You're from Madam *`Odozi Aku`* right?' Another tried to ascertain before disdainfully declaring. 'She never pays any one well. She arranges wealth for only herself. I could consider squeezing in an order for anyone else but your Madam.'

Ego knew her Madam's reputation preceded her. She was renowned in the neighbourhood and beyond for her legendary stinginess in spite of her husband's affluence. Ego was therefore unsuccessful in her quest to find or persuade any of the tailors to take the job. She became exhausted and decided to return home, albeit dreading Madam's reaction. She prayed that Madam would've departed by the time she arrives back home. Ego was however disappointed to find Madam was home on arrival. She was absorbed in the chore of sorting through bales of clothes materials spread all over the spacious living room. Ego guessed the traders must have dropped them off. Madam always mandated that they dropped off their trade at her home so she could peruse and pick at leisure than haggle in an overcrowded market place. Madam was an enigma sometimes because as stingy as she was reputed to be, she was nevertheless a big spender when it came to the appropriate fashion to parade her social standing.

'I don't understand how you couldn't have found a single tailor to sew curtains.' Madam objected after Ego had reported her failure to find one. 'It's not like we're asking them to sew curtains for free. These tailors can be unnecessarily difficult but you must go back and locate one.' She ordered. 'We'll offer them a little more than the going price. I said a little before you'll offer them the world as if I have money to burn.'

'Yes Madam.' Ego agreed slightly disheartened. She'd already bargained with them pledging a substantive fee to no avail. She knew that she'd be no more successful if she were to return. Her best bet was to try a more distant market. She was well aware that Madam wouldn't offer her bus fare nor would she dare to ask. Any such demand on her part might goad a slap. Madam's reputation did precede her and she'll find faults with service providers at the end of a job so as to avoid paying the full fee.

'Come back here,' Madam shouted as Ego made to depart again. 'Should I beg you to clear the table?' She demanded, glaring angrily at her.

'I'm sorry Madam; I'll take care of it immediately.' Ego apologised and proceeded to clear the dining table. The untidy table had escaped her attention. She could overhear Master showering in the background as she cleared up. Both of her bosses were unusually tardy in leaving home today, she mused. They would ordinarily have left home early in the morning save for Sundays. She guessed Master's tardiness was a result of his hangover from the previous night. He had been drinking more than usual lately and to her detriment too but he hadn't shown up at her room last night. Thank God for little mercies, Ego accredited.

The thought of another futile long trek to a faraway market finally spurred Ego into confessing to Madam. 'I'm sorry Ma, but I think I can sew the curtains.' She admitted sheepishly and held her breath for Madam's predictable outburst.

'How come you can sew?'

'I learnt on the sewing machine in the guest room.' Ego replied, bracing for a slap.

'What did you say?' Madam screeched angrily and sprang to her feet. She was enraged at the thought of Ego training on her sewing machine without prior permission and struck her sharply across the face at the same time.

'I'm sorry Madam. I should have asked for your permission first.' Ego apologised.

'And so you should have, how dare you touch anything in this house without my permission?' Madam raged. 'So because you've grown breast now, you've started to assume that you can take the laws into your own hands. You are growing into a madam in her own right now; tell me if that is not the case?' Madam spurted venomously, panting with rage as she struck Ego repeatedly across her face.

'I'm sorry Madam, please forgive me. I'm very sorry.' Ego apologized while brandishing her forearm across her eyes to protect them.

'You'd better make excellent curtains or I swear I'll throw you out of this house. Get out of my sight now, ingrate.' Madam cursed at her.

'I'm sorry Madam.' Ego repeated before skulking away lest Madam would change her mind and beat her some more. She quickly lugged the material Madam had indicated was for the new curtains with her as she left the room. That her fate was now dependent on her sewing skill didn't escape her as she ferried them to the guest room. She was yet to make any design from the scratch but was damned if she'll fail to make good enough drapes for Madam to save her board. She pulled down one of the old curtains and copied the pattern to reproduce a new set. She sewed through the night and the next day as well as contending with her usual chores and by the end of the next day had produced a fresh pile of neatly sewn curtains. She waited apprehensively as Madam inspected them after she had hung them up in place of the old ones.

'Well done, these are well made.' Madam conceded while inspecting the new curtains. She was for once commended Ego's efforts and her earlier rage seemed to have dissipated.

Ego was delirious at Madam's praise. It was practically the first time that Madam had openly applauded her.

'Well then, you have to sew my wrappers.' Madam pronounced factually. Those words were like music to Ego's ears and she was optimistic that both Madam and Master might soon help her set up a trade on the strength of her newly acquired craft especially since their last child had left for further studies abroad following in the footsteps of Madam Cecilia's kids. That particular Christmas turned out to be her most memorable since Madam's attitude towards her seemed to have undergone an overnight transformation. She had even showed Ego off to Cecilia and her family, praising her sewing skills.

Ego had always craved Madam's seal of approval which she always strove hard to achieve until now. She had used to torture herself before contemplating ways of achieving this besides her speculation on the extent of Madam's actual awareness of Master's infrequent visits to her room. Was Madam really in the know and refused to act? That would have been odd, knowing her. Or maybe Madam was angry with her for enticing her husband, she contrived in the absence of any plausible explanations. It must be her fault that Master sexually abused her, she concluded once again not contending that he abused her against her will. She wished he would stop him or that she could stop him but Master owned her. He would eject her from his home if it ever came out.

So now that she had finally gained Madam's much desired approval, Ego was determined to sustain the endorsement. Madam became a saint in her eyes. Madam's wish was her command, same as Master's. She had always deemed Madam's aloofness more hurtful than the physical abuse that she endured from her or sexual abuse from her husband. Yet Madam's coldness when she would ignore her for days on end, barely acknowledging her very existence until she was ready to arrogate new chores for her to carry out was most hurtful. Their kids, Juliet and John had also strangely adopted a similar nonchalant attitude towards her in their early teens.

Her relationship with them wasn't always frosty. They were adorable as toddlers and she had completely adored them, suckling them to her non- lactating breast and pretending they were hers in their infancy. She had practically raised them while their parents were immersed in their demanding business ventures. Madam must have poisoned their minds against her; Ego guessed but for what purpose? She initially found it hard to come to terms or accept their sudden change of attitude towards her. She could actually pinpoint the genesis of their rebuff which she attributed to the period when they had returned home from boarding school the only time Madam went to fetch them home. They were rapidly transformed from respectfully loving kids towards her to ordering her around like their mother did. They would demand a different dish after she'd served their meal even when Madam's menu stipulated another such that she was forced to discard the meal and prepare a new dish afresh. They tormented her deliberately and incessantly especially Juliet who usually coerced John, her younger brother along. Their unpredicted rebuff reached new heights after they left home to study abroad and would refuse to respond to her candid queries after their welfare.

Madam's rare and long-awaited commendation therefore filled her heart with so much joy and she was psyched to literally bend over backwards to accomplish any difficult chores in order to sustain the amity. A few nights later, Master attended her room after she had already dozed off and hadn't expected him to call. She could no longer foretell his visits with her prior precision but he was predictably drunk. He proceeded to masturbate with his other hand implanted in her and jerking recklessly. He didn't rise to leave immediately but rested his head on the pillow next to her for a short interlude.

Ego quickly seized the chance to query him about her origins again. She had deduced he was more receptive to her queries while in bed with her but even then could still act unpredictably. 'Chief Sir, please can you tell me more about my parents?' She pled in a small voice fearing he might scold or decline to answer her. She was long reconciled to her fate and life as an enduring maid in Master's household but couldn't help but try to gather a few more details every now and then, especially when the opportunity presented itself. Master was her only chance at discerning her roots since Madam wouldn't grant her the time of the day for similar queries.

'Again?' He muttered, partly exasperated but amused at her growing boldness. He decided to humour her all the same. 'I've told you everything that I know already. I don't know who your parents are, Ego.'

Ego was encouraged by Master's mild-tempered response to ask more questions. She was never certain of what reaction to expect from him. He was erratically moody, placid, brisk or impatient depending on the day. She just had to trust her instinct and hope to catch him in the right state of mind or mood.

'Please Sir; tell me how I had come to live here.' She implored bravely.

'It was a long time ago.' He recounted tolerantly. 'My wife's uncle helped us find you. He knew a farmer who was in desperate need for cash to resuscitate his trade and proposed we exchanged our piece of land in the village for your service. The farmer wasn't someone I knew or from our village.' He narrated the familiar tale.

'You're sure that he is not my real father?' Ego enquired; as if it was the first time that she was hearing the tale or that she had asked that particular question. She was always optimistic that Master will counter his earlier account and assert that the farmer is her father so she could finally find closure or learn enough details about him to help her in locating him or other blood relatives.

'No, he is certainly not. He had inherited you from another relative of his; none of them are your real relatives. From what we were told, your parents had abandoned you at birth and a fisherman had found you beside a river. I'm not sure of the full details but his wife refused for him to keep you at his home. She suspected that you were really a product of a secret affair her husband was covering up while passing you off as an abandoned baby he had recovered. She gave him the ultimatum of choosing between her and you so he was forced to reluctantly give you away. You were subsequently passed off to anyone who was willing to accommodate you until we gave up our land to have you. So you see we saved you and you belong to us.' Master concluded with a wicked smirk and so saying, strengthened up and zipped up his trousers before shuffling away.

Ego was disappointed irrespective of knowing Master wouldn't provide any fresh details. She had countless unanswered queries to ask him; how could she locate this farmer or even the fisherman? Which village were they from... ... but Master had exited as hastily as he had appeared. She was left stuck in the same darkness.

To his defence, Master recounted same tale consistently but she couldn't help but hope that every time she cross-questioned him that he'd offer her an alternative story or else provides more details to help her retrace her roots. She fervently wished he could be more helpful or finally consent to helping her to retrace her roots.

Ego was continually haunted by an superseding feeling of incompleteness. She inadvertently felt like a limb or a part of her body was lost but who wouldn't be if they were completely clueless as to their origins. She however laid her inner turmoil to rest while continuing to serve Master and his family to the best of her capabilities. She was also resigned to the idea that she might never find a man or a suitable suitor to wed.

Neither Master nor his wife offered to discharge or help her set up a sewing trade as she had envisaged. She on her part was too timid to demand discharge or mustered enough courage to quit their home on her own accord. She was secretly apprehensive of a future without them because they were all that was known to her. Moreover, who was going to marry the little servant girl that Master had procured her lifelong servitude in exchange for a piece of land?

The eruption of a Civil War in the country between the Nigerian and their Biafran counterpart changed everything. The conflict arose from a series of mainly economic and ethnic tensions existing amongst the diverse ethnicities. A dynamic Igbo Colonel proclaimed the largely Igbo-dominated Eastern / Southeastern Region of the country as the new Republic of Biafra. The central Nigerian government counter-launched a war against the secessionist Biafran territory.

Master and his wife immediately escaped to Cotonou as soon as the threat of a civil war loomed. Some unknown vandals raided their supermarket helping to impel them to flee earlier than they had intended. They placed Ego in charge of the household assuring them of their imminent return once the conflict settles while absconding for safety.

Ego initially refused to vacate the house alongside the other helps who had fled following their bosses' hasty getaway. Some of them had invited her to accompany them back to their respective hometowns promising to accommodate her but she declined. She was more inclined to staying behind and tending to Master's home. She strove to keep the place as meticulously neat as when the family was in residence in the ensuing weeks. She also hopelessly anticipated that the conflict will be resolved sooner than later and Master and his family would return shortly and commend her efforts.

As the warfare unfolded, her tribal entity or Igbo's scattered in areas now denoted as non-Biafran soil were being forcibly ejected or mandated to vacate their previous safe havens. They were compelled to vacate the new Nigerian territory to return to their new Republic or original native hometowns at the wake of the growing conflict. They were otherwise pronounced dissidents and observed with great animosity if they chose to stay behind. Most of them evacuated hastily reluctant to face the wrath of their newly declared enemies.

A group of so called currently bona fide Nigerian citizens in the face of the calamity embarked on sporadic looting sessions or widely agitated to reclaim private assets and landed properties from the new dissidents.

Their erstwhile friendly neighbours of Isoka origin were no different. To Nkiru's surprise, some of the impetuous youths followed the bandwagon and were agitating to take over Master's home. They charged that Chief Nnameze had no right to own landed property on

Nigerian soil since he was Biafran by birth. Ego was ultimately forced to flee for her dear life one afternoon after she learnt that the incensed villains were on a pillaging spree of similar homes in their neighbourhood armed with machetes and other arsenal before they reached her home.

She had been defiant and reluctant to flee against advice until she overheard their chants approaching steadily and growing louder as the group plundered a supposed Biafran citizen home after the other. She didn't need any further warnings to run for her dear life and headed for the nearest motor park. A large number of her tribesmen who found themselves in a similar plight were speedily boarding buses to ferry them to the safety of their new Biafran homeland. Most of the buses were crammed to full capacity as can well be imagined when she arrived. Equally frantic passengers were jostling for spaces in jam-packed buses at the bus station. The same irate civilian nationalists who had wilfully initiated the rampage and ethnic cleansing were rumoured to be heading towards the bus station next.

Ego was lucky to secure a seat in an overcrowded bus after an elderly lady shifted to let her squeeze in between her and others. She was really more anxious of the fact that she had no preceding knowledge of this new homeland that she was supposedly fleeing to. She appraised the faces of her fellow passengers searching for a familiar face but they were all strangers to her. The animated frenzy on the bus while they jostled for space and seats died down as the bus commenced its outward journey to Obah. Most of the passengers seemed more engrossed in relishing their luck of securing a space and guaranteed getaway than the ensuing hairy ride. They included men, women and children of different sizes and shapes strewn across every accessible space and on the floor too. A few obstinate passengers managed to smuggle in cockerels against the conductor's advice. Their crackling noises soon subsided as if they sensed the danger was over and a Billy goat with a pervading odour at another corner mustered only a weakened bleat.

The jam-packed bus heaved dangerously under the strain of its excessive cargo. It was also swaying precariously from one side of the road to the other as its lowered engine crunched harshly against the uneven road surface. None of the passengers dared to complain or reprimanded the driver or his conductor to slow down. They held on tightly to any support they could reach while bracing the rough ride. They were keener to escape the hostile throng than upsetting the bus crew. Ego surveyed the sea of crestfallen faces clutching varied bundles of their current life possessions around her. Some clutched bags or parcels wrapped in lone 'abada' wrappers to bosom. A lucky few ones lugged small suitcases along but a large number had been compelled to abandon their homes without a single possession in hand. The bus driver and conductor allotted minimal individual space and baggage spaces in order to accommodate the throng and maximize profits.

Ego envied those with any substantial amount of luggage whatsoever because if they had been in her peculiar haste might only have been able to grab the next available thing handy to them. She had barely managed to retrieve her handbag with her precious ornament and life savings of fifty shillings which she had scrimped together over the years before blindly reaching to retrieve her suitcase from underneath the bed. She unintentionally snatched a pair of shoes in its place but scarcely noticed in her swift bid to escape. She had subsequently absconded to safety and the motor park. She only had the chance to review her gear a few minutes ago only to notice that she had grabbed entirely two separate legs of different shoes. She still held on to them despite their apparent worthlessness knowing they were her only assets at this stage besides the clothes on her body and the sandals on her feet. Her glorious readymade gown was left behind.

The rest of the passengers were collectively forlorn and far from chitty chatty while taking in the rest of the gloomy faces around them. They soberly endured the hairy ride as the overcrowded bus ferried them home and eastbound.

'We're embarking on '*oso agha*' already.' A middle-aged female passenger intoned sombrely and loudly with a shake of head as if she was just coming into the realization. She was echoing the thought on most of their minds as they were forced to desert their homes and livelihood for an emergency 'war evacuation' as well as to escape the wrath of irate Nigerian civilians.

'My name is Mary, Mary Ejike.' The woman sitting next to Ego introduced herself initiating a conversation halfway through the journey. She was the same middle-aged affable looking lady who had helped her secure a sitting space. Ego thought she wasn't as flustered as the rest of the passengers.

'I'm Ego.' Ego returned simply.

'This is a huge mess. I wonder when and how this conflict would end.' Aunty Mary continued in a muted tone.

46

'I know. My main worry is that I really have no clue as to where we're headed.' Ego whispered, confiding her core fears to the affable lady.

'How come, are you not from the bosom of Igbo land? Which is your village, where does your family live?' Aunty Mary queried successively.

'I've lived in Isoka for as long as I can remember. Chief Nnameze, my master and his wife whom I used to live with travelled abroad. I don't have or know any one else.' Ego explained.

'But you must have family somewhere, where is your master from.' Aunty Mary insisted, sceptical of her explanation.

'Ajaba but I've never been there. Master said someone had given me up in exchange for a piece of land but this person wasn't even my real father. No family member had come asking for me in all the years that I've lived with Master's family.'

'And your master says he just accepted a kid from someone without asking proper questions as to where you came from?' Aunty Mary queried doubtfully, thinking her story didn't quite sound right.

'He really doesn't know or he would have told me but they did me a favour really. They required a reliable maid and someone offered me up in exchange. They had wanted someone they could trust with their kids' upbringing while they ran their business.' Ego was quick to defend her bosses.

'So how long did you live with this your Master and his family?'

'Almost twenty years.'

'Didn't you try to leave or to locate your family in all that time?' Aunty Mary was baffled at her easy acquiescence.

'There were really not that many options at my disposal.' Ego admitted. 'I wouldn't have known where or how to go about trying to locate my original family. I forgot to say that a fisherman is supposed to have found me abandoned by my parents originally or so the story goes.'

'Your story is stranger than fiction; I've never heard any similar tale. So which village were these people from again, I mean this farmer or fisherman? They must have originated from a place at least.' Aunty Mary persisted impatiently; keen to get to the bottom of the story.

'I had queried Master repeatedly but he didn't know much. He was too preoccupied to help me locate any of my people.' Ego admitted defensively, determined not to come across as apportioning blame on either Master or Madam. They offered her shelter whereas her real parents had abandoned her.

'I don't know why you are bent on defending these people who seem to have enjoyed keeping you in the dark for their own personal reasons.'

'They're not bad folk. I'm sure they would've helped me find my family if they had any more information.'

'My child, you're too naïve but never mind about that. What about you, what do you intend to do now?'

'I'm not sure but I'll decide when we arrive at our destination.' Ego replied simply, albeit completely clueless as to how to proceed.

'I hear our people are setting up refugee camps already for people in your shoes.' Aunty Mary informed her.

'I suppose I'll go to one then.'

'Never mind, you can stay with me. I have no children and my husband left to join the Biafran army with his Oga. I suppose I can accommodate you until you decide what you want to do with your life.' Aunty Mary offered impulsively.

'Thank you. I can call you Aunty Mary, Thank you very much.' Ego thanked her tearfully. She was moved by the kindness of this stranger that she had only just met.

'Never mind, we Ibos are one and together now. With the ongoing madness, all we have left is helping and supporting one another,' Aunty Mary declared, instantaneously adopting a solidarity stance. She had only gone to Isoka to purchase materials to sell alongside her sewing business not envisaging that she'll get embroiled in the unfolding mayhem. She was one of the lucky few returning to her actual home than fleeing from the big city. Her husband had enlisted with the Biafran army to serve under his former boss who was a top ranking officer in the new Republic.

She regarded Ego again sideways, scrutinizing her deceptively plain looks. The lady possessed a freshness and innocence to her; Aunty Mary surmised and was motivated to adopt this sweet guileless immature young lady beside her if that will construe her own contribution to the Biafran side. She still found it hard to believe that anyone could be so gullible but hoped she wouldn't come to regret her impulsive offer. She reappraised Ego again from head to toe refocusing on her candid unaffected face and corn row braids; her slightly oversized gown and faded brown sandals. She looked transparently vulnerable and Aunty Mary didn't want to leave her unprotected. She pondered once more that she wouldn't come to regret her impulsive kindness.

Obah was a far cry from Isoka, Ego immediately noticed as she plodded after Aunty Mary as she took in her new environ after they arrived. Whereas her home in Isoka was situated in a largely residential area, Obah on its part was a jumble of residences, shops, schools and factories all located at close proximity to each other and all jumbled up together. She lugged one of Aunty Mary's baggages as they trekked along the un-tarred foot path leading to her home. It was an undeniably big city but in a state of panic. They trudged past newly emigrated mass of half sprinting panicked pedestrians with variably sized luggage hurrying along to and fro the streets and fugitively surveying their new environ. There were groups of stately men rallied in groups either glued to radios for updates or could be distinctively overheard exalting the benefits of a new Biafran Republic and their expected immediate triumph over the Nigerians.

Aunty Mary explained that Obah was definitely more congested than ever due to the influx of returning Ibo kinsmen. Her home was situated in a nearby sizeable yard, a short distance from the motor park. She shared the residence with a multitude of other tenants. She ushered Ego through a major entrance gate into the compound and led the way to her place, comprising of a room and sitting room. Ego will sleep in the sitting room; she motioned but will store her meagre belongings in the bedroom.

Aunty Mary was a very simple lady and didn't stand on ceremonies. She interacted with Ego both as a mother and bigger sister rolled into one. Although Aunty Mary's home was far more modest in comparison to Master's home, Ego was just as happy settling into her new modest abode. She was shortly introduced to Aunty Mary's younger brother the next day after he came to visit. He was taller and heavier built than Aunty Mary. He could be handsome if he would only loosen up; she noted and was immediately struck by his stern resolve and grit when they first met.

'Welcome,' Okechukwu greeted again after his elder sister explained the circumstances of their meeting.

'Thank you very much.' Ego returned. She was struck by the fact that he said very little. He really was a man of few words and didn't smile much either. She met his dark impassive eyes as they observed each other. What lurks behind those eyes, she speculated.

Aunty Mary later revealed her brother was training as an apprentice, learning the tools of trading in building materials. Ego thought that was a bit odd because he looked far too advanced in age to be an ordinary trainee. He was younger than Aunty Mary but definitely older than her, possibly in his thirties, she guessed. Aunty Mary had also disclosed that he was on the verge of setting up his own stall baring the onset of war.

Okechukwu visited his sister's home frequently. He was always polite, enquiring after Ego's welfare before focussing on his particular mission. He brought them foodstuff or other products. More so as there was a dearth and steep price tags on most good as a result of the raging war.

Ego was baffled at Okechukwu's lack of personal interest in her. He never sought her out for a private chat or showed any curiosity regarding her rather intriguing circumstance. She occasionally imagined that his eyes bore into her back when he must have thought that her attention was diverted elsewhere but he didn't proposition her for friendship. He attended his sister's home alone or occasionally accompanied by his friend, Ijem but never presented a wife or girlfriend.

Aunty Mary divulged that he had neither girlfriend nor wife, yet he never showed any special interest in her. Ego was secretly miffed at his indifference. She continuously speculated on his staidness or why he didn't show any interest in her. She'd never been in a proper relationship and was naïve in the matters of the heart. She found herself inadvertently falling in love with this brooding fellow. Her thoughts were frequently fixated on him and what could be between them.

Unfortunately he soon left to join the Biafran army as soon as all age appropriate males were enforced to draft into the army with or against their wills and to defend their Biafran side. The enemy or Nigerian side with a superior armoury and international support were capturing Biafran strongholds leaving devastating tragedy and ruins behind as well as advancing steadily into the heart of Biafra.

Aunty Mary was coincidentally a seamstress and Ego endeavoured to hone her sewing skills under her tutelage amidst the surrounding turmoil.

'*Ewo- oh* what am I going to do now?' Ego heard Aunty Mary's distinctive voice wailing as she stepped into the yard headed for their lodging. She had left her a few hours ago for the deserted marketplace to hunt for any palatable food product to purchase. Food and other basic commodities were hard to come by in addition to bearing very steep price tags if one could manage to locate any. Ego had been in luck that morning and had succeeded in purchasing two loaves of corn meal bread from a lone seller who had appeared at the same time as she had arrived at the market. She had quickly grabbed the loaves as the rest of the public rushed for them. It was sheer survival of the fittest because some of the women were geared to wrestle if that was required in order to secure a loaf.

Ego cradled her bounty proudly and couldn't wait to get home to show Aunty Mary, only to hear her disturbing bawl as she approached their doorstep.

What could possibly cause Aunty Mary to wail in such a distressed manner? Ego wondered with great concern as she hurried to reach her. There must be a fundamental problem or else Aunty Mary wouldn't be howling aloud for an unjustifiable reason. Someone or something must have upset her greatly.

'What's the matter, Aunty Mary? What happened?' Ego enquired worriedly on finding Aunty Mary sitting on the bare floor. Two other female neighbours of theirs were also present in the room and holding Aunty Mary by the arms. Ego quickly rushed to her side as the women gave way.

'It's Ibe, my husband Ibe has left us. Ego my sister tell me, what does he want me to do now?' Aunty Mary wept despondently while reaching out to enfold Ego who had knelt down beside her. Aunty Mary insinuated her husband was dead.

'How is that Aunty Mary, are you sure it is true?'

'How can it not be true? They just left; his uncle sent word. Ibe is dead. My good husband has left me without any warning.'

'Please stop Aunty Mary or you are going to hurt yourself.' Ego pleaded and held her tightly so as to restrain her as she started to flay about on the floor again. The other women lent a hand too.

'Tears are the only things I have left. Ibe my good husband has left me nothing but tears. Tears are all I have left.' She wailed pitifully.

'Run for cover, air raid, air raid!' Aunty Mary, Ego and their neighbours heard the distressed call simultaneously. This was accompanied by alarming shrill screams from across the streets followed by what could only be termed as a near pandemonium. People were obviously making a run for it. The women didn't require further prompt to scamper along. They quickly sped outside to join the initial chaos within their yard as fellow jostled through their narrow main exit to the street.

The street was filled with panic-stricken folks screaming and running like headless chickens, desperately seeking a suitable hiding place to duck. Aunty Mary quickly grabbed Ego by the hand to ensure that they stayed together. They darted along with a group into an underground trench just in time to escape the sudden blaze of overpowering banging, booming deafening explosions of the enemy bombs on the attack. The enemy was finally and indisputably laying siege on Obah.

None of the indigenes of Obah town had any proper forewarning or might have been better prepared. There had been numerous false rumours and alarms but none of them could have envisaged the ensuing bedlam that was unleashed.

Aunty Mary, Ego and their group lay trembling with great trepidation underneath the cramped ditch, hours after the hubbub settled. They and other lucky survivors could hardly believe their eyes when they emerged from the underground trenches hours later.

Obah town has been razed to the ground and in complete ruins. They could hardly identify any specific homes or infrastructures within the vicinity in the ensuing rubble. They had suffered a massive devastation and destruction from the attack.

Loud hysterical cries, recriminations, prayers and howls of disbelief emanated from different corners while a few numb spectators stood horrified, dumbfounded and speechless at the sight of the horror. Many had lost spouses, children, brethren, or friends while a number wept in excruciating agony from sustained injuries. The few that were seemingly unscathed expressed their consternation at the horrific sight and rallied to help the multiple casualties.

On the whole, they could only stop momentarily, barely afforded enough time to survey the ruins or contemplate their losses before hurriedly evacuating on another enforced **"oso agha"** en route to adjoining villages. They had no homes to return to even if they had wanted to stay back. Obah was now a phantom of its old self. None of the survivals could ever have envisaged the massive devastation or extent of damage wrought by the enemy bombs. With little or no time to reflect or lament on their mammoth losses, they shepherded off for fear of a return assault by the enemy. Only but a handful bothered to rummage through the rubble that remained of their previous homes or town before fleeing.

Aunty Mary's shocking news of her husband's death paled in significance to the current chaos. She wasn't afforded any time to grieve properly or arrange for the burial ceremony of her beloved husband. Ego sympathized with her and lamented the lost chance of meeting Aunty Mary's beloved spouse that she had never tired of recounting. He had ironically died from explosives made by their Biafran side during initial trials. The two women tagged along the rest of the stunned indigenes of Obah seeking refuge elsewhere. They retreated further afield in a bid to escape the advancing Nigerian army troops and their horrific shells.

Her entire Ibo tribe or Easterners/South easterners collectively bore and suffered the brunt as well as the rigors of the ongoing warfare. None of them could have anticipated the ferociousness of the ensuing combat between their seceding Biafran side and Nigerian counterparts or the devastating aftermath. They were initially imbued by the courage and resilience exhibited by their side in mounting counter attacks and resistance in the face of a multitude of handicaps. They were ultimately forced to surrender.

Ego and Aunty Mary were amongst the lucky survivors at the end of the ill fated war and returned to Obah to pick up the remnants of their overturned lives. They needed to start afresh in trying to rebuild their upturned existence after their Biafran side conceded a devastating defeat.

A few weeks later after they were helping to fetch the materials towards rebuilding their old abode, Aunty Mary excitedly pointed out a figure to Ego. 'See that looks like my Okechukwu. Hurry let's find out if he is really the one.'

Ego gazed at the gaunt looking figure backing them from a distance. He was oddly familiar and must be Okechukwu, she agreed.

He was standing by the roadside and gazing at the ruins of what would have been his old home. The two women hurriedly left their chores to catch up with him.

'Okechukwu my brother, it is you. You are here.' Aunty Mary repeated effusively, unable to believe that he was real. He had practically risen from the dead as far as she was concerned. She hugged him repeatedly and outlined his face with the palm of her hands to Ego's amusement as if she was ascertaining that he was live and intact.

Okechukwu bore minor injuries and was severely emaciated but real. Ego could well understand Aunty Mary's fuss because they had both given him up for the dead. They had on their return received no word or message from him or been able to confirm from other returning soldiers of his possible whereabouts or indication that he had survived the devastating war. Ego was therefore overjoyed to see his stern looking face too, albeit looking grimmer than she could recall from the past. She hugged him briefly, drawing away hastily because she was afraid that he'd sense the thrill that shot through her loins at the brief contact. 'Welcome home.' She offered in rushed perplexity.

Okechukwu declined to discuss or detail his experience in the army or war as he rushed through the hasty meal Aunty Mary had rustled up for him. He only commented on the tedious trip back home to Obah but seemed more interested in their escapade.   As they regaled him with their harrowing experiences and lucky escapes, Ego noted that Okechukwu was still as reticent as ever. She guessed that he must have undergone a very traumatic experience. None of them had really been spared the rigors of the war in any case. They had collectively suffered immensely but in diverse degrees from hunger, homelessness, overcrowding, various illnesses and trepidation of and from bomb attacks to the tragedy of losing loved ones or tending to injured or disabled relatives, friends and others in the process. Her solace lay in the reality of survival and being able to recount the story but most importantly that they still had each other. They might seem to be physically unscathed but were mentally traumatised to a huge extent.   War was never a good option or solution, she concluded. She relished Okechukwu's return and watched him recover his strength and accustomed sprint. She felt safer for his presence because for some inexplicable reason it gave her a peculiar sense of security and comfort.

Aunty Mary who had been heartbroken from the prospect of losing both her husband and only brother to the tragic war was greatly relieved and overjoyed to have her younger brother home. She had been contemplating funeral ceremonies for both before Okechukwu's surprise reappearance.

A few months later after their lives had returned to normalcy of sorts, Okechukwu finally set up his stall and commenced building materials trade. He had borrowed money from a local Sherlock to achieve his lifelong dream.

Ego made no moves to return back to Isoka where she had lived and served under Master and his family after the war ended. They didn't send word either searching or asking for her to return, assuming that they had returned from Cotonou. She was also occasionally wistful after settling down for good in Obah especially when she overhears other women singing and dancing to a particular song eulogizing '*nma nwanyi bu di*' i.e. *the beauty of a woman is in a husband.* She longed for same exclusiveness and a soul mate or companion to share the rest of her life, some one to protect and take care of her. She felt vulnerable and lonesome on occasions and infrequently ached for Master's fingers between her legs. Her throbbing loins will however contract in disgust when she recalls his dirty cigarette charred finger nails plunging in, out and deeper into her, causing her pain and pleasure at same time.

She became fully resettled in Obah and months later opted to venture out of Aunty Mary's home to embark on a single life for the first time. She also contracted a stall after scrimping and saving to buy a small table sewing machine to commence her sewing trade. She and Aunty Mary however continued to maintain their close bond.

'Which day are you visiting again?' Donatus, a trader in her market accosted her with a rather lewd expression on his face.

Ego couldn't recall a prior conversation during which she had promised to visit him. 'Soon,' she replied deciding to humour him but knowing that was never going to happen.

'You know my patience will run out soon so you better visit soonest.' He jokingly threatened, chuckling derisively at same time.

Ego chose not to dignify his words with any further reply. She frequently received similar uncouth chat up lines since her independent status. It seemed like these unlikely Lotharios' had been initially kept at bay by Aunty Mary's presence but it was a different story now. They weren't wooing her in the conventional mode but made no secrets as to their dishonourable intent. None tabled a marriage proposal but she could well see where they were coming from as well as pardon them in her usual altruism. She was personally resolved to holding out for a proper suitor but her chances were very slim. She was fairly advanced in age compared to other spinsters to strengthen the conjecture that she'll be easily agreeable to one night stands or becoming a mistress. She disliked her contemptible situation but secretly savoured the attention from the opposite sex for what it was worth. They found her attractive enough to court even if with less than a noble intent in mind. A handful of her acquaintances complained they barely received any compliments whatsoever from same men. She found the gossips from fellow females more discontenting. Those spread all sorts of rumours regarding her roots and single status.

'I hope you've acquired plenty of customers at the moment.' Aunty Mary voiced optimistically on one of the occasions when Ego came to visit.

'I'm taking each day as it come but I must admit that it's getting better by the day.' she confided.

'That's as it should be. I promise that you'll soon receive more orders than you can handle.'

'I can't wait for that moment.' Ego agreed buying into Aunty Mary's optimism.

'It will happen.' Aunty Mary assured her. 'Mark my words.'

'I pray it does.' Ego entreated prayerfully.

'It would, any suitable suitors yet?'

'Aunty Mary, I don't know if it is my fault or these fellows but all I hear is, are you coming to visit us in an annoyingly suggestive tone,' Ego complained. 'There is no shame anymore. These fellows are direct to the point of being rude and disrespectful.'

'Don't worry too much, have patience. Your preordained husband shall come and like my Ibe would be heaven-sent.' Aunty Mary counselled and became momentarily pensive.

Ego knew that Aunty Mary missed her late husband a lot, although she rarely mentioned it.

'Thank you, Aunty Mary. I hope he shows up before I'm old and wrinkly.'

'That wouldn't happen. You deserve better.' Aunty Mary stated both categorically and reassuringly.

'Thank you, Aunty Mary. You never fail to restore my confidence.'

The two women spent the rest of the evening together before Ego left for her place later that evening.

Okechukwu attended her stall practically out of the blues a few days later and she was sure he came at Aunty Mary's behest. She wondered what Aunty Mary must have said to persuade her younger brother to visit her stall. She hadn't exactly expected Aunty Mary to recount her confidence to him. She wasn't exactly open with Aunty Mary regarding her secret crush on Okechukwu or the fact that she was peeved by his persistent apathy. In retrospect though, it seemed like she was more transparent than she had assumed. She was gradually becoming reconciled to the fact that she was in love with a man who might never reciprocate her feelings in her usual affable acceptance of destiny mode. Yet here he was taking a purposeful stance towards her.

'I want us to wed.' He frankly proposed or rather stated after they were done with initial pleasantries. Ego observed that he was as taciturn as usual and not one to beat about the bush.

'Eh …eh…' She stammered, considerably taken aback. She hadn't known what to expect when he showed up but was simultaneously pleased and confused at his proposal. This was a man that she had known for ages now but rarely shared any meaningful conversation with. Yet, here he was proposing to her. He was the first man to ever to proposition her even if without the usual fanfare.

She was slightly unnerved by the abruptness of his proposal and worse still that he stood waiting for an immediate reply. He seemed more factual than cocky but she would have preferred he begged or at least asked for her hand in marriage in such a manner as to indicate he was fearful and unsure of what her reply would be. She would have wished he would court her in the conventional way and given her time to ponder his proposal before she'll give him an answer, rather than this brash manner of his.

The truth however was that deep down in her mind she absolutely adored him. She always sensed that there was an eerie bond between them. He possessed a certain self assurance and grit that convinced her that she'd never want for anything if they were to be together. He was the exact man of her dreams.

She regarded his expressionless face and against her accustomed accommodating nature called his bluff. 'I'm not sure I want to do that.' She was surprised at her own boldness while anticipating that he might walk away. This was the bravest statement that she had ever made in her whole life and she waited; watching him with almost bated breath and heart thumping so loudly that she feared he could hear her galloping pulse and pulsating heartbeat.

She started to panic inwardly, fearful that if he chooses to walk away. He would certainly never return; much less reiterate his offer for her hand in marriage.

'What I'm trying to say is that maybe we should try to get to know one another better before we decide on marriage.' She explained, knowing she needed to stop him from walking away somehow.

'Okay, we'll do that.' He agreed readily to her immense surprise and relief. He not only agreed to her suggestion but stayed with for a bit.

He sat at a corner dutifully waiting for her to finish for the day before walking her home.

She prepared dinner for them and subsequently caught a glimpse into the real nature of the man who soon became her husband and what made him tick.

He opened up to her regarding his OSU heritage and narrated the humiliating trials he had faced in his youth. He unreservedly shared his life history, innermost thoughts and dreams with her. She was amazed at how chatty he could be if he set his mind to it. He related his future hopes of marrying and begetting kids and detailed his future plans for them. He narrated how he'd nurture his future kids to become outstanding citizens as well as shield them from the wickedness of the world. He'll ensure that they fared better than him and were also better equipped to face the society so that they'll be spared a comparable humiliation as he had encountered growing up.

Ego was elated as she listened to Okechukwu's deep baritone confident voice opening up to her, confiding in her in the manner that she had always hoped she would relate to a life partner someday. She hung on to both his spoken words and the unspoken innuendo in between knowing that he spoke directly from his heart. His expression of deep emotional turmoil mirrored hers as he let loose words and feelings that he had kept bottled up inside of him for long.

Ego imagined that this was exactly how she would have hoped to mesh with a soul mate whereby they would exchange their deepest fears and dreams without holding any thing back. She listened, mesmerized by his words and gazing at him in earnest. She watched his face soften and flicker with different emotions in accompaniment to his narration. She suddenly began to see him in a different light as he slowly unfolded before her eyes like a blooming budded flower whose petals was blossoming to sunlight and early morning dew at springtime, gradually exposing its hereto hidden beauty.

His voice and attitude commanded anything but pity as he stated raw details of his youthful plight in his measured definitive tone while she took in his narration.

She listened absorbedly as he verbalized her thoughts and aspirations, his words echoing her very thoughts. His dreams and aspirations replicated hers, more so as he was rephrasing her words better than if she had dared to articulate them herself.

She, in turn narrated her poignant memoirs to him after he concluded his wistful tale. He listened to her attentively. He never took his eyes off of her for even a single second as she narrated her private tribulation and poured her heart out to him. She knew instinctively that he empathized with her tale. She saw plain understanding depicted in his eyes, no recrimination or judgment. He only flinched during her narration of Master's fumble. She could tell his repulsion was not directed at her but at Master. She was convinced that only the power of Almighty Saviour himself would have been able to extricate Master from Okechukwu's wrath or his bare strong hands clenched tightly as if invincibly wrung around Master's neck. The veins on his hand were visibly outlined and strained as she related the gory details. They barely slept that night as they swapped stories of their unfortunate childhoods and background as well as mutual dreams.

The next day, Okechukwu stopped by her stall at about closing time and they returned to her place together. They chatted through the night once again.

The first time that they made love was pure heaven for her. She was apprehensive because of the hurtful nature of Master's fingering but Okechukwu was nothing like Master. He was gentle and caring and most importantly sensitive to her needs and desires.   She was shaking like a leaf bellowing in the wind when he first straddled her; tense with fear because he was the first man to mount her but he understood the very basis of her trepidation and allayed her apprehension. He stroked her face gently and caressed her reassuringly. When she felt his hard throbbing manhood between her loins as he gently penetrated her, sending an exquisitely painful but simultaneously sweet jolt through her loins and a fresh gush of her moistness engulfed him inside of her. She had no doubts that he was the one.

They made a pact never to recap the tragic circumstances of their respective childhood to anyone else including future offspring. The horrific chapters of their respective youths were sealed, never to be revisited anytime soon or in the future. They sealed their pact with an abiding promise to each other. They were married soon afterwards without extra fanfare and Obinna was their first child. They strove to raise their brood with an abundance of love, imbibing self worth and inculcating the importance of education in them so that they would be suitably equipped to make their own way in life. Ego quit her sewing at the start of their marriage to dedicate her full time to nurturing their kids along their desired lines while her husband strove to provide for them. They were not rich but were very contented. She had finally found the happiness and peace that had eluded her for most of her earlier life and her recurrent dream of the river and basket of fish gradually vanished.

*   *   *   *   *   *   *   *

So here they were embarking on their final journey but Mr and Mrs Ejike at the epic of their saga were linked and united in the same peaceful harmony.

Death didn't do them part.

Three

Obinna's three younger siblings awaited the return of their parents and elder brothers' as nightfall approached to no avail. Ngozi tried to rustle up dinner since they were hungry and tired of waiting.

'Ifedi, please move away or the oil will spill on you.' She admonished, quickly shoving her kid brother away from the spurting oil from the frying pan. She was hovering near the stove at the improvised kitchen corner their bedroom. The stove was laid atop the surface of a small cupboard where they generally stored food products.

She watched the palm oil thaw and spurt. The thick tawny mould was fast melting into deep red smoky liquid oil and was starting to gather flame before she lifted the frying pan off the stove. Chidinma was holding a kerosene lantern up and beside her, helping to illuminate the corner. There was electricity power outage.

The three siblings stood crammed in the kitchen corner while Ngozi made dinner. Their mother had converted that space within their room into a mini kitchen than have them share the central communal kitchen in the yard. A sizeable plastic drum with a matching lid was stationed beside the cupboard. It served for water storage and the kids were duty bound to fill it up daily for their major water supply. An improvised shelf stood at the opposite end with plates, utensils and a basket containing non-perishable food commodities. The girls slept on the small bed occupying the remaining space beneath the small window in the room.

They had expected their family members to arrive home long before now but they hadn't shown up yet.

'What is the matter with you today?' Chidinma queried as she lumbered along brandishing the lantern after Ngozi and facilitating adequate illumination. She was exasperated by her younger brother's uncanny crankiness.

Ifedi had been unusually clingy and cranky the whole evening, refusing to be left alone for a single minute. He ignored Chidinma's query but continued to tag at the hem of Ngozi's skirt.

'The food is ready, come and sit down beside me.' Ngozi invited after pouring the thawed warm oil into a plate and spicing with a little salt and pepper. She fetched the plate through the door into the sitting room while Chidinma followed carrying a bowl of boiled yam and the

61

lantern. They drew the centre table towards them and sank into the cushions on top of their wooden bouncy sofa to have dinner.

Ifedi sat over the other end of the centre table pulling up another chair to the table as he couldn't quite reach the dish from his sisters' side. They dipped slices of boiled yam into the palm oil sauce to eat.

'It's too hot.' Ifedi complained after his first bite and spat out the piece of yam in his mouth back into the plate.

'What did you do that for?' Chidinma reproached angrily and disposed of the fragments he had spat out immediately.

'He is a young.' Ngozi reminded Chidinma. 'Let me blow it cold for you.' She offered and gently blew air at a morsel of yam before dipping into the oil and offering to Ifedi.

'You are just a spoilt child.' Chidinma pronounced disgustingly.

'Ngo, tell Chi to leave me alone.' Ifedi complained between mouthfuls.

'Please leave him alone, Chi.' Ngozi begged Chidinma. 'Never mind Ifedi, Mama them will be home soon.' She continued to try to cajole him.

After they finished their meal and washing up, they retired to bed since it was relatively late. Ifedi refused to sleep in either his parent's or elder brothers' room where he usually slept. He huddled between his two sisters on the small bed reluctant to be left alone for even a brief moment.

'I wonder what is keeping them for so long.' Chidinma wondered aloud again, expressing her concern for the continued absence of their parents and elder brothers. It was almost midnight. Their family members had promised to return early in the evening.

'I guess it must be the traffic or an accident must have occurred on the road and is causing delay.' Ngozi hazarded a guess.

'I wish we had travelled with them but Papa had said it was more appropriate for us to attend the proper wedding ceremony. This knocking ceremony is only a preliminary step.' Chidinma recounted.

'I wish we had gone with them too but the proper wedding is bound to be much more fun.'

'We've never travelled outside of Obah and I've always looked forward to seeing what lies beyond Obah.' Chidinma revealed.

'We had travelled to Ogbani a few times when we were younger but I suppose you were too young to remember now. Never mind though; we'll be attending the wedding ceremony and you'll have enough sightseeing soon. Aunty Nkiru said we can come to stay with them too when they are married.'

'I think Aunty Nkiru is nice and very pretty. I like her.' Chidinma announced. They had met Nkiru, their brother's fiancée recently after she had come to visit at their home.

'Me too,' Ifedi added his vote of confidence. 'She gave me biscuits and sweets when she came to visit.'

His two sisters couldn't help but be amused at his immaturity, he was five. They continued to discuss and hope for their family's imminent return as their usually noisy yard gradually turned jarringly silent. They also recognized that their delay must be imperative or else they would have come home early as they had promised. There was no home or mobile cell phone for that matter in their home so it was impossible for them to reach them to ascertain what was causing the delay or vice versa.

It was the second time that they had been left alone without at least an elder in attendance. The only other occasion was when something terrible had happened to Brother Obinna at Mekede. He had been kidnapped by criminals. Their parents had left in a rush to travel to his base but arrived back the next day to reassure them that he was rescued and safe.

The three siblings lay in bed, anticipating the key to turn in the knob of the front door to their quarters indicating their family members were home but nothing of the sort happened. They innocently nodded off to sleep exhausted from the long wait. It wasn't long before they were awakened in the middle of the night petrified on hearing a distinctive rapid pop, pop succession of gunshots shattering the silence of the night. There was no mistaking the sound of gunshots, similar but less deafening than the familiar booming shots from mortar. They were more conversant with mortar shots because they were usually fired into the air in gun salute for the dead and in commemoration of the arrival and/or lying in state of an eminent personality's corpse during funeral ceremonies.

'Shush...Shush...,' Ngozi hushed Ifedi by forcefully placing her hand across his mouth to stifle his frightened howl. 'Please stop making noise.'

Their neighbourhood was not ideal but gunshots at that particular time of the night was still a rarity and therefore an ominous sign. Ngozi could've given anything at the moment to have their parents and brothers back home with them as they huddled together crouched in fear.

'Mama, mama, I want my Mama.' Ifedi wailed frightfully as the sound of the successive gunshots resonated.

'Please, stop crying. Papa and Mama will soon be back I promise.' Ngozi beseeched in a whisper and continued to try to stifle his wail with her hand clad tightly across his lips. It was clearly prudent to avoid attracting unnecessary attention in the face of looming danger. She was sure it was the *'abani di egwu'* or *Night terrorists/armed robbers* at large.

'Sorry now, Ifedi. If you continue, the *abani di egwu* will come here to catch you.' Chidinma whispered threateningly echoing Ngozi's prediction that the *abani di egwu* were at large.

Ifedi amazingly ceased wailing, the threat of the *abani di egwu* coming after him was enough to get him to calm down. The three terrified kids huddled closer together but never made any connection between the shots and their absent family members.

After they woke up the next morning, Ngozi took charge. She bade her younger siblings to commence their usual chores and estimated that if they complete early enough would prepare breakfast as a surprise for their expected family members. Chidinma started to tidy their room while Ngozi set off to fetch water from the general tap a few blocks away. They were supposed to fill up their water drum daily but she decided to go solo in the meantime. She bade her younger ones to stay put until she returns or their parents arrive. She was still apprehensive of the preceding night's event so was wary. She knew the other members of their yard were bound to discuss the gunshots that morning and Ola will surely tell her all about it later. She had only dared to venture out with her bucket after overhearing bustling activity around and within the yard. She was joined by Ola as soon as she stepped out of the main exit as if she'd been lying in wait for her to appear.

'Ngo, wait for me.' Ola called after her. Ola was her best friend and resided in same yard, in addition to filling her in on the local gist and gossips.

Ngozi's parents actively discouraged them from interacting freely with those neighbourhood kids whom they considered wayward or possible bad influence. They were only allowed to interact with a select few, even then were not encouraged to stay out in the streets for any extended period.

'Did you hear the commotion last night?' Ola queried in a whisper after initial greetings.

'Yes, the whole street must have heard. We were so scared. You can imagine with my parents and brothers not coming home last night. I had to stifle Ifedi's cry by clasping over his mouth with my bare hands.' Ngozi narrated demonstrating how tightly she had clasped his mouth.

'Oh, they didn't come back? They should be home today then,' Ola stated factually. 'No one had said anything about the gunshots yet but I'm sure we'll have the full details before the day is over. I wonder which unfortunate family was robbed last night.'

'It is a great tragedy. Please tell me the details as soon as you find out.' Ngozi pleaded as they strode along making a right turn into the major street leading to the public tap.

'What's happening over there?' Ola asked aloud pointing at the crowd ahead of them. They were both surprised to find a crowd gathered at the end of the street a few meters away from the public tap as they trudged along the semi-tarred street and playfully swinging their buckets in hand.

'C'mon, let's go and investigate. I'm sure it must have to do with last night.' Ola urged, quickening her steps.

Ngozi was hesitant about joining Ola because of her parents' persistent forewarning. They had always been prohibited from ill-advised nosiness and she was more likely to walk past a crowd or concentrate on her particular errand than stopping to actively seek to find out what was happening in a crowd.

Ola skipped off without waiting for Ngozi to make up her mind to join her. She quickly slithered through the crowd and instantly recognized the corpses strewn on the street as soon as she spied on them. She was stunned and repulsed at the same time. Who would have imagined that the gunshots of the previous night were directed against her best friend's family? She was suddenly overwhelmed by a swift claustrophobia and quickly ducked out of the enclosed fold for fresh air.

She stooped, gulping and gasping for fresh air as well as retching futilely and bringing nothing up. She tried to steady her nerves while backing the crowd before it occurred to her that she had to stop her best friend from viewing the horror. She quickly sped back towards the direction where she had left Ngozi earlier. Ngozi was slowly sauntering up to the crowd as she headed back to her.

'Let's go back Ngozi. Let's go back.' Ola urged briskly as soon as she reached Ngozi's side. She grasped her arm and started to shoo her back towards the opposite direction from the crowd.

'Why? Why? What happened there?' Ngozi asked baffled at her friend's sudden change of attitude. Why Ola was trying to dissuade her from going to the crowd now, she wondered.

'I'm begging you, please don't go there.' Ola pleaded and held her tightly by the arm to stop her from advancing towards the crowd. She couldn't possibly tell her friend why, at least not presently.

'Stop Ola, you're acting really weird. I want to find out for myself.' Ngozi insisted, baffled and suspicious of Ola's strange conduct. She quickly extricated her friend's hands off of hers to advance forcefully forward to the direction of the crowd. She started to run when Ola made to grab her hand again and deftly pushed her way through the throng. Ola failed to stop or prevent her from witnessing the gruesome sight.

'Jesus Christ of Nazareth!' Ngozi screamed as she first caught sight of and recognized her father's corpse, followed by her mother's and subsequently Obinna's. Her ensuing bellowing shrill scream ricocheted through the crowd to the surrounding neighbourhood and back. The assembled throng turned to stare at Ngozi who was by then screaming hysterically with hands flailing up towards the skies.

Ola arrived winded at her side and embraced her best friend tearfully. They held each other tightly for a brief moment before Ngozi broke free from her hold and dashed back to the corpses of her family members strewn on the street. Ola unsuccessfully tried to restrain or hold her back, more so because Ngozi was suddenly empowered with a greater vigour in the manner in which she effortlessly wrenched herself out of Ola's hold to rush once more to them.

'*Chim egbum* o! My God has destroyed me oh.' Ngozi yelled powerlessly clasping her hands on the back of her head. 'Papa, Mama, Obinna! Where is Zube, where is Zube?' She wailed frantically, half screaming, half sobbing as she rushed from one family member to another.

'Over there.' A lone obliging voice replied indicating a separate corpse laying a few metres away from the rest.

'What would you have us do now, Lord?' She enquired in unbearable anguish supplicating towards the heavens.

66

The crowd needed no formal introduction as to the identity of the tragic heartbroken youngster. They compassionately tried to hold back the pathetic small figure thrashing and writhing all over the floor in pure torment before she would hurt herself. They embraced her to stop her threatened bid to break free and rush back to the bodies of her family members. They comforted and tried to calm her down. Ngozi continued to wail and batter wildly struggling to break free and reach for her parents and brothers. It was a heart wrenching spectacle.

The crowd grew steadily as the tragic news spread fast like wild fire. The assembling throng stood in stupefaction at the hideous sight before them as they contemplated and tried to piece together the pieces of the tragic incidence and what could have happened during the previous night to warrant such a ruthless bloodbath. Some of the initial passers-by to stumble unto the dead bodies had volunteered to alert the police but two hours on, none had arrived yet. A few female spectators lent their top wrappers to wrap up the bodies while the crowd waited for a responsible adult relative of the deceased to show up and assume liability for the corpses. Ngozi calmed down enough to direct the sympathetic crowd that it was best to contact her Aunty Mary or Uncle Ijem, her father's best friend. Someone in the crowd knew and immediately left to fetch Ijem.

Ijem was staggered beyond words when he heard the appalling news. 'What happened? How could such a gruesome and incomprehensible tragedy have happened?' He queried glumly, knowing no answers were forthcoming. He could barely control the tears that flew freely down his cheeks or his immense sorrow. He had only travelled with his friend and family just the previous night for Obinna's knocking ceremony. How on earth did this mammoth crime happen? 'Who is responsible for this atrocity?' He bewailed but to no avail.

He had to lay his grief aside to take charge of the situation. He organized for the bodies to be transferred to a mortuary immediately and the three devastated kids transferred to their Aunty Mary's home. He assigned a willing group of sympathizers who had willingly volunteered to travel and notify both Chief Ubaka at Ubi while another group left for Ogbani to alert the Ejike family members of the tragic news.

Four

Nkiru had retired to bed the previous night without a single care in the world, contented in the knowledge that she was absolutely in love and was loved in return. She missed Obinna every minute that they were apart and couldn't wait to converse with him and to further augment their wedding plans. They both sounded as excited as little kids left at their own device in Lego Land.

She had been very worried about his drawn out trip the previous night as a result of the traffic jam induced by the devastating vehicular accident but he had assured her it was easing off just before she had retired to bed. She had rapidly dozed off wrapped in the warmth of the affection that they shared and fantasizing about their upcoming wedding.

Her Ubaka household woke up the next morning relishing in the events of the previous day. Nkiru postponed calling Obinna immediately on waking up but decided she'll call him much later after he must have recovered from the trip. He most certainly would be exhausted from the protracted journey of the previous night and as such she wouldn't want to disturb his well earned sleep. She and her family members chatted amicably sharing a light banter at breakfast that morning after Sunday church service.

'Thanks Dad and Mum, yesterday was really lovely.' Nkiru commended her parents once again.

'Thank God. It was by His Grace.' Lolo replied modestly.

'You are our daughter so deserve the best.' Chief Ubaka added affectionately. 'I hope Obinna and his family arrived home safely yester night.'

'They must have. Obinna assured me the traffic had eased before I retired to bed last night. I'm planning to call him later than wake him up now. He must have slept pretty late judging from the traffic yester night.'

'That's thoughtful of you.' Lolo commended.

'I'm happy you didn't pay any heed to Nnanyi, dad. I think he might be growing increasingly senile by the day.' Nkiru remarked, readdressing the previous day event.

Nnanyi was the eldest member of their Ubaka kindred. He was due to have presided over her knocking ceremony but refused to show up at the last minute. He pleaded a preliminary premonition which was further reinforced by a nightmarish dream the penultimate night. The exact details of which he was unable to recount but insisted had left him shivering in cold sweat. These forewarnings were further mystified by the nuance of a black cat appearing just as he stepped out of his threshold while on his way to attending the ceremony despite his initial misgivings. Nnanyi had claimed that a big black feline creature had suddenly appeared from out of the blues and stopped momentarily staring at him with sharp piercing black eyes as if reproving him before ambling away. The creature had most significantly crossed over from the right side of his threshold to the left before disappearing into thin air. It was a categorical sign of ill luck. Nnanyi contended that he had been prepared to ignore his initial misgivings but the mysterious cat's appearance was the last straw that broke the camel's back. It was portentous enough notification to stop him. He charged that the vision was an ill-omen and as such refused to attend the ceremony. He also advocated that the ceremonies including the current knocking ceremony, impending traditional as well as church weddings be scrapped.

'We'd had enough drama as it were so I knew I had to put my foot down at some point.' Chief Ubaka explained. He had been undeniably displeased on receiving Nnanyi's message. He would have rather preferred that his daughter's knocking ceremony proceeded without any further drama after the initial hitches. He chose to disregard his elder kinsman's foreboding and declared the ceremony open as well as gave the go ahead for the formal weddings to proceed as per plan. 'We're only praying for you and Obinna to settle and provide us with many grandchildren. We don't require more, do we?' He suggested and turned to his wife, Lolo for affirmation.

'That is true, Nnam but no undue pressures on the kids. Let them wed first and nature will take its natural course.' She concurred rather cautiously, her caution born out of her private ordeal in the hands of her husband's deceased parents. They had given her much grief after they reckoned that she failed to deliver an heir apparent timely enough for her husband.

'Of course, but you know what I mean.' Her husband responded with a good perception of her concern.

'I do, Nnam and I wasn't arguing with you.' She explained.

The family engaged in light banter as they shared a leisurely breakfast, enjoying **akara** (bean cakes, *made from a mix of ground beans, salt, pepper, onions and crayfish*) and custard.

Nkiru and her younger sister, Azuka retired to their respective rooms afterwards while her soccer crazy youngest brother; Chuka opted to join his friends at the nearby track for an early game of soccer since they were on vacation. Her parents, Chief Ubaka and Lolo withdrew to the upstairs cosier family lounge. They were expecting a few close friends to drop by and laud the success of their daughter's knocking ceremony.

A rickety looking yellow cab drew up an hour or so later to their gate instead. Three rather grim looking strangers stepped out of the cab demanding to see Chief Ubaka. It was immediately evident that they were harbingers of bad news from their grim demeanour.

'We've come to see Chief Ubaka.' They announced to Mallam, the new Hausa gateman manning the gates.

'Who you be?' Mallam returned while appraising them warily. He visibly exposed his sword.

'We've got a message from Ijem. It is about Obinna.' The men replied.

Mallam wasn't too impressed by their explanation nor had they been here in the past but they insisted that their purpose was linked with Obinna so he reluctantly let them in. Obinna was the very nice gentleman that his Oga's daughter will wed. Mallam deliberated that Obinna wouldn't have been expected to keep such elderly company but if he had sent these men to see Oga so be it. He proceeded to open the gates to let them in and visibly brandishing his sword.

'Nnam, I hope all is well. Ada just said there are visitors waiting downstairs from Obinna.' Lolo reported to her husband after Ada notified her of the unexpected visitors who had arrived from Obah.

'Really?' He expressed. 'Obinna and his family were here yesterday so why emissaries today?'

'Should we go down then to learn their mission?'

'Just a minute dear,' He requested and headed first for the bathroom after which they went downstairs together to meet with the guests. Their apprehension was evident as they hadn't been expecting them. What could possibly have changed overnight to necessitate Obinna sending emissaries? Nkiru hadn't intimated of any glitch.

'Chief, **onwu egbuna dike**, *Death shall not fail the mighty.*' The men hailed him by his chieftaincy title after introducing themselves. 'We have arrived from Obah.' They informed the couple.

'**Nno nu**, welcome.' Chief Ubaka greeted. 'I hope you have come well.'

70

'Chief, **aru melu** - *An outrage has occurred.*' One of the men intoned mournfully, sighing heavily and shaking his head at the same time.

'Please come in and sit down first.' Chief Ubaka invited, ushering them in. He feared for the worst.

The visitors were initially reluctant to go in or sit until their hosts' appeared.

'Chief, **aru emego** - *An outrage has been perpetrated.*' The man repeated ominously.

'Can you tell us what the matter is then?' Chief Ubaka demanded, a tad impatiently.

'Chief, Obinna and his entire family members were found dead on the streets this morning.' The man announced gravely.

'**Gini,** *what*?' Lolo exclaimed loudly in disbelief and shock, involuntarily folding her arms across her chest concurrently.

'My young men, can you repeat your statement.' Chief Ubaka charged, hoping his ears heard right.

'It is true, Chief. That is why we have come. Ijem asked us to come and inform you immediately.' Another confirmed. 'The family were shot dead.'

'How, what happened?' Chief demanded calmly as the enormity of the news hit him. How possible was it? Obinna and his family were here; right here in the same sitting room with them the previous day. He glanced around his sitting room re-visualizing the family in the room from the previous night. Yet these strangers have arrived to announce that they were dead. Were they con men involved in some sort of scam to dupe him? If that was the case then they'll definitely discover that they had picked the wrong fellow to meddle with. He mused indignantly. 'Tell us how this happened.' He ordered in a quieter but more menacing tone.

Lolo recognized her husband's atypical tenor and immediately stopped her hysterics while they both waited for the men to supply a more detailed account of their story.

'No one knows what had happened exactly. We don't know if it was the police that shot them or armed robbers disguised as police since there was a roadblock at the site of the calamity. The family were undeniably robbed of both life and possessions. We know the police mount road blocks but armed robbery cannot be ruled out.'

'Why couldn't the robbers or whomever steal valuables and spare lives?' Chief Ubaka mused rhetorically. 'I don't think Obinna or any of his family members would have been boneheaded enough to argue with a gunman.'

'We might never find out the truth of what had happened and can only speculate at this stage. Unfortunately, there are no witnesses to help us unravel the truth. Ijem had wanted us to inform you. He had also sent people to notify the Ejike family members at Ogbani.' The strangers informed them. 'It is a very distressing tragedy.'

'*Dalu nu, thank you* for coming.' Chief Ubaka applauded. He had no reason to doubt them because they couldn't be trifling with such a grave matter. He was shattered and shocked beyond words. It was astounding to think that the Ejike family members had mingled and celebrated with them in their home the previous night, only to be reported as dead within hours. How could he break this devastating news to his daughter, Nkiru? What could he possibly say to her to make the news any easier? He mulled over and over again.

Lolo was weeping agitatedly and sniffling into a handkerchief. This was a horrendous and inconceivable piece of news.

The men insisted on leaving immediately after delivering the shock news. They declined food or drinks but broke kola nuts and drank water before departing. Chief Ubaka asked them to convey to Ijem that he'll be at Obah after breaking the news to his beloved daughter.

'Nkiru, Nkiru where are you?' Nkiru heard Ada yelling her name as she galloped up the stairs to her room. Ada was one of the house helps.

As for Nkiru, the rest of what followed was simply a blur. She couldn't recall her preoccupation when she heard Ada or the exact words or way in which the news was broken to her. All she remembers was the fall and her tumble down a cascade of endless stairs. Life was rapidly ebbed out of her leaving behind an empty hollow shell.

The unfortunate tragedy was far reaching. Obinna's father was not rich by any standard. Ijem had only managed to find a few bundles of naira notes that amounted to less than three thousand naira hidden inside Obinna's father's mattress. Mr Okechukwu Ejike owned no bank accounts or landed property that could be recovered or sold to recoup finances for the upcoming multiple burials and subsequent upkeep of the unexpectedly orphaned kids. The family had resided in a rented accommodation and he had conducted his small trade on borrowed funds. His creditor on hearing the tragic news laid claims to the goods and stock in his stall to recoup his outstanding arrears.

Only a fraction of his actual savings was recovered from Obinna's bank account. He had made a substantial withdrawal a few days prior to his tragic death but no stash was recovered on his person or found at his father's home. The outstanding fund in his account was subject to tax duties and deductions as well as kickbacks in greasing the hands of a few crooked bank officials before they would finally release the remaining funds.

The tragedy was more than a double whammy; innumerable intricate details required ironing out including the final resting place for their burials. The natural choice was their homestead at Ogbani but another startling facet erupted. The Ejike family members at Ogbani refused to have the bodies buried at the extended family homestead. The late Mr. Ejike and his family were Osus and as such the bona fide members argued that burying the bodies at their family land was tantamount to a waste of family resources since they shared no actual blood ties with them. They also feared repercussions from the gods as a result of the unnatural circumstance surrounding the deaths.

'How could a whole family meet with such tragic demise?' The elders pondered and decided there must be an underlying import behind the untimely deaths and what ever it was; they didn't want any part of it.

The alternative option was for the burial ceremony to hold at the Church cemetery. Mr. Ejike was not a dedicated Christian though. He had left the business of religion to his wife and kids while he wholly engaged on his trade and fending for them. He was neither baptized nor confirmed so the officiating priest at the Catholic Church was reluctant to have a pagan buried on their grounds. A lot or arbitration and placation went into place as well as money changing hands to overturn the decision and arrangements finally concluded for the burial to take place on there.

Various National and Local Newspapers headlined the carnage of Mr Ejike and his family as a *National Outrage*, a case too many of the rampant atrocities or crimes that had riddled the Nation. Numerous editorials unequivocally appealed for a major shake up by the federal government and police. The Police on its part pledged to bring the perpetrators to justice be it one of theirs or armed robbers but two months along the line, no single suspect has been arrested.

73

In the inner villages, the reactions were varied especially in relation to an OSU link. The vast out cry was however of a united sense of shock and outrage.

In Ubi, two women discussed the debacle and others when they accidentally ran into each other on the street. One of them was the spouse of a distant relative's of Chief Ubaka's.

'Nwakego my sister, I heard the news. This is a big disaster. Wasn't it the other day your husband's family celebrated the knocking ceremony.' The woman started, untying and retying her top wrapper.

'My sister, please help me talk. I didn't feel well so had not attend the actual ceremony but my tongue is tied. It is a shock to all of us. I haven't told anybody but I had felt a premonition for no justifiable reason throughout that day. I had woken up the same midnight when they were shot holding my chest like a bullet had hit me personally and covered in cold sweats. I couldn't fathom what the matter was until I heard the news in the morning.' Nwakego narrated. 'I had never had a similar foreboding in the past so was mystified. It is a great misfortune.

'Do you trust there is nothing behind all of these?' The woman asked in a near whisper, glancing around fugitively to ascertain there was no one in sight to overhear her.

'My sister, what do you want me to say? *Tufia Kwa*, *God forbid*. It wouldn't come from me.' She embellished by encircling her fingers around her head and snapping into her right ear to refute that condemnation of the issue should derive from her. 'I hate to say I told you so but I remember when the first family meeting was held to discuss this proposed wedding. My husband was among those vehemently protesting against the union but at the end of the day we decided to leave it alone. Our people have chosen the white man's god over ours but it's the same gods we worship at the end of the day whether it's our god or their god. Does any one kneel down and pray for bad things to happen to others?' She queried rhetorically and without expecting an answer continued. 'No, there is no unjust god. We are only required to accord them their due respect. What we all pray for is our own betterment and those of our close ones. As our people rightly say my good friend, the rat that foolishly follows the lizard out in the rain will ultimately learn that the sun that easily dries the lizard's skin will not dry his. What had happened is a big lesson for all of us.'

'What will the family do now?' The woman persisted, referring to Chief Ubaka's family.

'How can I tell, my sister? We'll just have to wait and see. I must tell you one thing though, life is life and no one deserves to die in such an awful circumstance.' Nwakego denounced and stopped to take a bite off a piece of kola nut that she had untied from the edge of her wrapper.

'Is it policemen or armed robbers that perpetrated the crime?'

'It doesn't make any difference either way.' Nwakego retorted. 'They are all one and the same. The policemen are in cahoots with armed robbers most of the time anyway. In all of this drama, have you heard of any arrests? Let it be. I tell you my sister; my philosophy these days is to become a silent observer. There is nothing these eyes of mine haven't seen but no vision is horrific enough to make them bleed. I've recently decided to keep my counsel unless it is specifically sought for. It is a different world now. No one can tell their left from right any more. Didn't they claim that the poor boy wasn't aware of his OSU legacy until lately?' She added in an undertone

'I never bought that story personally. How could he not have known? But what you say is true my sister. Our world has definitely changed. I must admit that I don't care much for the present era. You know Efuru's son is said to have married a white woman recently and I say better that than an OSU girl. I have warned my sons that if any of them dares to bring an OSU girl home for a wife that I'll have their heads first.' She announced with a definite firmness.

'I agree with you my sister. It is difficult to decide which a better choice is. I wonder what Efuru's son that is said to have married a white woman has in common with an **oyibo** (*white*) woman. I hear this *oyibo* people eat leaves like goat so ask me who would pound fufu or make delicious egusi soup for him.' She wondered aloud.

'That is a good question.' Her friend agreed.

'He doesn't really deserve any pity because our sons are basically stripped of manhood and forced to share chores with their wives when they reside overseas.' The woman gainsaid. 'I hear they cook, wash and share chores with their wives. It is said to be worse when they marry oyibo wives whom they start to serve while the women sit and give commands all day.' Nwakego shuddered. 'My sister, change is good but sometimes I wonder if it's really for the better. It is bizarre enough that men cook and wash for woman, maybe they'll soon start to bear kids too.'

The two women laughed at the ludicrous idea.

'How's your family by the way?' Nwakego politely enquired soon after they stopped laughing.

'My sister, I was overjoyed when my son travelled overseas last year.' Nwakego's friend started, using the opportunity to release her pent up anger at her son. 'We were hoping his trip would herald an end to our financial woes but my sister, look at me. Do I look like somebody whose son resides overseas?' She posed with a heavy sigh. 'This wrapper,' she said at the same time untying and holding the edges of her top wrapper from behind her waist. 'It's the same wrapper that I carried him in and it is the same one that I'm still tying almost two decades afterwards.'

Nwakego couldn't help but burst out laughing at the obvious exaggeration. '*Ewo!* Oh! Please don't make me laugh but never mind; I'm sure that your son will send money once he settles down. I hear life abroad isn't as rosy as we envisage either. Some of our children have to work like slaves, holding down two-three jobs in order to make ends meet.' Nwakego soothed her.

'No, my lot is always worse.' She insisted unappeased. 'I'm sure you heard about Anedi's son who came home last month. He had only stayed abroad for only six months. I tell you six months only.' She repeated, raising six fingers in front of her to enumerate. 'He brought cars and bought a new plot of land to start constructing a new house for his poor parents. Yet my son after a year has me living in the same dilapidated kindred home surrounded by witches.'

'Did you know how Anedi's son suddenly came into such good fortune?'

'Do I care? Let him follow others and do whatever they are doing for money. We attended our age grade's second funeral ceremony last month and Anedi's attire was the talk of the town. Her whole neck was bedecked with layers and layers of gold chains. We were amazed and watching her in envy. No one could believe it was the same woman who was begging us to lend her money for food a few moths ago. But trust my luck, what do I get?' She complained bitterly. 'We receive a letters from my son indicating that he was fine. A common letter! Eight months abroad and he doesn't enclose a single dollar. Does he think we'll chop the words of his letter?' the disgruntled woman berated her son.

'I take it that you aren't aware of Anedi's son's fate after he returned to his base. He's presently languishing in prison, my sister.' Nwakego announced triumphantly. 'He nearly died after the illicit drugs he had swallowed burst in his stomach and that was his so called job. He was basically renting out his stomach to ferry illegal drugs for some criminals in a get rich quick scheme. These are very dangerous drugs that can induce madness or kill. I hear that those medicating on them are left quivering and desiring more. Its grip is worse than when one is gripped by malaria fever and it kills instantly.' Nwakego elucidated dramatically.

'*Ewo! Oh!*' Her friend exclaimed, taken aback. 'I didn't hear that story at all. Why would anyone buy or sell such drugs then? Is Anedi's son a doctor or chemist that he is dabbling in selling drugs? Does the drug cure disease?' The ignorant woman enquired.

'I don't know why anyone buys or sells them. It is the same supposed modern world that I'm raving about. How a supposedly sane person would deliberately purchase or swallow drugs that could induce madness in them or even kill them is completely beyond me. Can you comprehend such folly?' Nwakego posed in great bewilderment before continuing. 'My policy these days is to watch and observe. All that glitters is not gold, my sister. You know you were wishing for your son to be in Anedi's son's shoes but I bet you wouldn't want your son languishing in prison, would you now? I tell you be satisfied with your lot because worse calamities happen across the board. Honesty and integrity ultimately has rewards, trust me.' Nwakego opined. However instantly retrospective, she deigned that she might have been too harsh so went on to reassure her friend kindly. 'It is said that whenever one wakes is their morning so when your son has enough money, I'm sure he'd send you some. He'll be stupid to neglect the woman that suckled him at birth.'

'You're wise my sister, I shall depart now.' Her friend stated hastily.

'Go well.'

'Go well.' The two women parted ways.

Chief Ubaka had come home after one of his numerous recently necessitated trips to and fro Obah and helping to oversee the funeral arrangements for Obinna, his brother and parents. His kinsmen had come to visit but he wasn't in the least surprised at their reaction.

'*Onwu egbuna dike*, this is a big tragedy indeed. We are in shock and you must comprehend our initial doubts regarding the knocking ceremony and why we had vehemently opposed your daughter's union with an OSU.' One of his brethren intoned with a hint of vindication. They had arrived albeit to commiserate with him and his family but could scarcely conceal their denunciation and reproach.

'This resulting calamity was always our major fear. It is an abomination for a freeborn to marry an OSU.' Another reiterated.

'I had a premonition all along that something bad would come out of it.' Another asserted.

'You know the effigy buried at the centre of our **umunna** (*kindred home*) was defiled.' Yet another reported.

'No, what had happened?' Chief Ubaka enquired curiously knowing this was bad news.

'It was defiled.' They intoned gravely.

'Yes but how?' He was keen to learn. The effigy was received after the cleansing ceremony and was implanted at the centre of their kindred home.

'It was unearthed the very night of the tragedy by mysterious design.' Nnanyi announced gloomily.

'The thunderstorm on that night debased the effigy after a bolt from the heavens struck the exact spot uprooting the effigy in the process.' One of the elders explained.

Chief Ubaka couldn't recall rain falling that night, much less a thunderstorm. 'Are you sure it was a thunderstorm because I can't recall any. We've had a dry spell lately.'

'It wasn't a thunderstorm,' Nnanyi countered. 'Ododo privately swore to me that he had seen a black cat appear furtively out of nowhere to ferociously burrow unto the spot unearthing the effigy.'

A minor argument erupted as to the actual circumstance of the defilement. Each camp insisting their version was more accurate. That the effigy was defiled either by human design or otherwise was not in contention. They also contended that the deaths of the Ejike family members were a reprisal from the gods. They also claimed that the tragedy was a manifestation of the god's wrath in view of the abomination perpetrated against them.

A few supposedly devout Christians amongst them and who had previously supported the union arguing that the whole hullabaloo about the OSU diatribe was only but a fallacy, now danced to a different tune. They were now converted to the idea that the gods' hands were at play. The timing and circumstances of the catastrophe was damning, the clan collectively postulated and as such there was no reservations regarding the fact that the unfortunate tragedy was the upshot of their folly.

The calamity was a major conversational piece, not only in the town of Ubi but beyond. "Was the calamity a result of the ire of the gods or just an unfortunate twist of fate" was the overriding query upon the lips of many. The topic was also hotly debated across the land. The issue tabled in private conversations, television shows, newspapers and public arguments. It was discussed in the privacy of homes or out in the public including on the streets, market places, village meetings or you name it.

Opinions on the matter were widely varied while rumourmongers had a field day but most were skewed in thoughts and beliefs. A majority of hardcore traditionalists, idol worshippers, a few superstitious Christians, atheist especially in Ubi town affirmed the tragedy was retribution from the gods.

Staunch Christians and a minority of others insisted the incidence was just an unfortunate misfortune. They suggested that the incident was more coincidental than consequential. They also alluded to the fact that random individuals were consistently mugged and could have been travelling in the middle of the night and met with death in the hands of nefarious armed robbers. They dismissed the growing rumours. Priests and clergymen incorporated the happenstance in their sermons and beseeched their congregation to remain steadfast and unwavering in the face of what they termed 'inane superstitions'. The unfortunate carnage was a terrible mishap, they proclaimed without equivocation. They also implored that the emphasis on the matter should be geared towards apprehending the perpetrators of the heinous crime than propagating a nonsensical concept. They concentrated on prayers for the deceased and their grieving families.

The population outside of Ubi or non OSU caste regions couldn't quite understand what the fuss was about. The public took more umbrage at the wave of countless similar senseless and heinous crimes perpetrated daily in the country. They summarily joined in the call for the government and the police to crack down on heightening crime wave.

Nnanyi, the eldest of the elders of Ubaka family revisited Chief Ubaka's home a few days after their initial visit accompanied by two other elders. He has always been the leading protagonist against the proposed nuptials between Nkiru and Obinna as well as the head of the Ubaka kindred.

'Okam,' he addressed Chief Ubaka by his first name. 'The other day we came to commiserate with your household but having said that, this tragedy affects all of us directly or indirectly. Our people say that if a human itches, he asks a fellow human to help him scratch the area but if it's an animal, it rubs himself against the bark of a tree. Whatever happens to one of our brothers affects all of us. That is why we say that blood is thicker than water and is that not why we have come?'

'True.' His cohorts agreed.

'My philosophy has always been to accord every man his due. What has happened has happened but none of us is greater than the gods. We have to move forward nevertheless. I have consulted with the priests of the oracles and took time to travel to three different oracles just to be absolutely confident. Lest it be said that old demented Nnanyi is at it again.' He couldn't resist taking a dig at his detractors. 'The priests all but confirmed what we already know. The gods are angry. They are very angry and we must act fast to appease them and circumvent a greater doom.' He urged worryingly.

'Nnanyi, **onye eji eje mba**, *our eminent ambassador,*' Chief Ubaka greeted Nnanyi. 'Thanks for your concern and efforts. I must however inform you that my immediate concern is organizing the funeral ceremony for Obinna and his family. Our overriding aim is to ensure that they receive a befitting burial ceremony before we dwell on other issues.' Chief Ubaka countered diplomatically.

'Okam, you are a good man and I know you have good intentions but first things first. Our people say that the stubborn ear goes with the head when it is beheaded so I beseech you my brother to sit back and revaluate this situation. Leave the white man and his foreign religion alone. This is our land and we have our way of handling things. Our forefathers who enacted specific rules were not foolish and neither is our gods. Please do the right thing and placate them. It is better to be safe than sorry.'

'I thank you once again for your concern, Nnanyi but as I've said earlier we'll dispense of the burial arrangements as well as certify that the unfortunately orphaned kids are well taken care of before we dwell on any other matters.' Chief Ubaka reaffirmed empathically.

Nnanyi had no option than to depart with his companions. They were very dismayed and surprised at Chief Ubaka's obstinate stance.

Chief Ubaka on his part had expected a backlash and also had braced himself in advance but was nevertheless staggered at the relentlessness and ferocity with which it came. Denunciation sprung from just about every corner including the claims by relatives' who prophesied to have foreseen the misfortune forthcoming to friends and even strangers attesting to similar claims and more. He struggled to avoid an open war of words, resolving at the same time to stay firm in his own Christian convictions. He didn't want to thread on a doubtful path again and entreated God for fortitude.

Reverend Father Joseph visited his home often to offer prayers and support for the entire family.

'I understand your predicament but I beseech you not to despair,' Reverend Joseph counselled as Chief Ubaka saw him off to his car after another prayer session. 'Our people thrive in controversy; the talks and gossips are to be expected but continue to maintain your personal counsel.'

'I know, Father. We're just trying to take everything in our stride but it is difficult.' Chief Ubaka admitted to the good Reverend Father.

'Do remain steadfast in your faith and I know the good Lord will surely see you through.'

'Those are our payers, Father. I know that we individuals are all entitled to our individual opinions but what baffles me most is how everyone else seems to neglect the fact that random muggings and massacres although an infrequent norm does occur. However they are all insisting that this tragedy is retribution from the gods.'

'This is why I urge you to maintain your wise counsel. It is a tragic calamity indeed.' Reverend Joseph reiterated. 'And a twist of fate rather than design but of course most will choose to hype up a pointless intrigue.'

'My exact thoughts precisely,' Chief Ubaka agreed enthusiastically. He was happy that the priest shared his view.

'I'll entreat that you ignore the rumours.' Father Joseph implored once again. 'None of what has happened is your fault or anybody's for that matter. We can only place our faith and trust in God. He is the alpha and the omega, the beginning and the end. He gives and he alone decides when to take so stay strong and uphold the spirit of your family. The blessings of the good Lord will be bestowed upon you all.'

'Amen. Thank you Father.'

'I'll continue to pray for you and those unfortunate kids who have been unceremoniously orphaned.' He promised.

'Thank you very much, Father.' The two men shook hands before Father Joseph departed.

Chief Ubaka returned to his home with a greater resolve to remain steadfast to his faith and desist from falling into a doubtful spiral. He had no reason to query The Almighty Father or doubt his faith. Only God gives and he also decides when to take. *Que sera, sera, whatever will be, will be.* He reasoned to himself as he beseeched his family to remain unshakeable in their conviction that the tragedy was unconnected with the OSU legacy but his only fear was his beloved daughter, Nkiru.

She was absolutely heartbroken but worse still unable to express her grief openly. There was a frightful vacancy in her seemingly spaced out stare. She appeared attentive intermittently yet detached. Please help her Lord, Chief Ubaka implored his saviour and prayed for the sanity of his beloved daughter to remain intact.

He and his wife conferred on various issues that night after they had retired to bed. 'The Reverend Father at Obah had given his final word today.' Chief Ubaka confided in his wife. 'He had confirmed the use of the church burial grounds and I have notified Ijem already.'

'Nnam, you did well to intervene or he'd never have changed his mind.' Lolo commended her husband. 'Ijem seems to have everything else in control.'

'I presume so, he is a good man. He practically put his own business on hold to organize a befitting burial for his friend and family.'

'He is a good man.' Lolo concurred.

'I've also assured Mary that we'll try to transfer the kids into Azuka's and Chuka's schools to offer her respite.'

'That is great Nnam. Aunty Mary is understandably stubborn. Those kids are her only brother's children.' Lolo stated in reference to the fact that they had offered to have the kids move into their home but Aunty Mary was reluctant to relinquish them from her care. She insists they will fare better with her since she was their closest blood relation besides there was no way she was going to relegate her personal responsibility to a second party.

Aunty Mary in reality was a rather frail old lady in her sixties. She appeared older than her age due to longstanding poorly controlled diabetes. In the last decade or so, her brother had practically sustained her after her eyesight started to fail and she was forced to give up her modest dressmaking business. The kids now shared her overly cramped one-bedroom rented lodgings.

'I'll meet with the school principals in the near future then to initiate the transfer plans.' Lolo said and jotted down a reminder in her diary. 'That's a very good plan indeed Nnam. Having them board will surely double as both respite from overcrowding and also offer some relief for Aunty Mary who irrespective of her bravado is in dire straits.'

'I know. We might persuade them to find a more spacious accommodation in the absence of nothing if she'll be agreeable.'

'She is so obstinate. Bless her because she is a kind soul.'

'We shouldn't be derailed by rumours.' Chief Ubaka projected.

'I know Nnam. My main concern is our Nkiru.'

'Yes, she is still in shock but she'll snap out of it soon.'

'I hope so, Nnam.' Lolo agreed. 'The deaths were an alarming shock for all of us and Nkiru in tow but she's hit hard.' Lolo was very concerned about her daughter's state of mind. They had assumed that Nkiru would snap out of her daze soon but she was growing less optimistic now that she seemed to be getting worse than improving. She wasn't as convinced as her husband seemed to be of Nkiru's spontaneous recovery. She was of the mind that they need to intervene but kept her private counsel in the interim hoping that Nkiru would prove her wrong. Let the funerals conclude first.

There were no tears left in the church or in the eyes of the mourners during the funeral ceremony of Obinna, his brother, Zube and their parents, Okechukwu and Ego Ejike a fortnight later. Their four identical caskets at the front of the pulpit drew gasps and sniffles from most of the mourners in attendance when they arrived to commiserate with their remaining family members and friends.

The poignant appearance of the three young kids at the front pew clad in black mourning garments and who had become concomitantly bereft of a father, mother and two brothers attracted hysterics. The sight of a gaunt looking and forlorn Nkiru in her ill fitting black dress and flat sandals however depicted a more pitiable picture. She had lost an excessive amount of weight and was haggard. Her eyes were alarming glazed and she stared into empty space, leaving the crowd shuddering and fearing for her sanity. The sizeable Cathedral hosting the service was filled to the brim; every single seat in the church was taken as sympathizers spilled into the street.

Mr. Ejike, who had always maintained only a handful of close friends in life, had many new friends attending his burial ceremony. His entire neighbourhood turned out in full show of support and empathy. His fellow traders and trade union representatives came to show respect. His Uncles Lekwa and Anele arrived from Ogbani accompanied by a few bona fide Ejike's to mourn the tragic death of their unfortunate kinsman and his family.

Ego, Mr Ejike's demure and unpretentious wife with barely any close friends or identifiable relatives attracted few sympathizers in her own right. The womenfolk of their yard and a few customers who still remembered her from her short-lived seamstress tenure arrived to show their respect. They rallied support for the very reserved and unpretentious lady with her cheerful disposition and an eagerness to please.

Obinna's firm assigned representatives and a few of his colleagues attended on their own accord. His best friend, Sanni accompanied by his affluent father and few dignitaries arrived in a motorcade escorted by armed police guides. They also donated a substantial amount of money to the bereaved family.

Zube's friends and school mates poured in from his alma mater.

Nkiru's friends, childhood mates and her Igbaje cycle of friends arrived to show respect for Obinna and support for her. Lily, her best friend stood beside her in the front pew holding her hand while her husband Okon stood a few pews away with the rest of their special clique.

A large number of Chief Ubaka's kinsmen were in attendance too, albeit a few had declined to attend vowing to have no further dealings with Osus. The Reverend Father Joseph attended with a few parishioners from Ubi.

A group of policemen patrolled the area ensuring security and order especially in view of the eminent dignitaries present. Strangers, sympathizers as well as spectators arrived from far and wide to pay respect. The officiating priest gave a stirring sermon extolling the family and their humble circumstance. He charged that the nation had lost a dynamic duo whose rising star were cut short in the form of Obinna and his younger brother, Zube. He chastised those continuing to propagate that the tragedy was anything but a plain calamity, denouncing them to hang their heads down in shame. He prayed for the departed souls and their family and loved ones left behind. His sermon was so stirring in parts that a few of the congregation were reduced to tears. Nkiru mustered a single tear which trickled down her left eye signifying that there was still something human left in her. The choir and worshippers sang the accompanying requiem with a touching heart rendering emotion. The mourners advanced to the adjoining church burial ground after the solemn church service. The bodies were laid to rest amidst hollering wails from family, friends and sympathizers alike. The ensuing reception was very sombre after which the mourners departed for their respective destinations still laden with immense grief and sorrow.

Five

Two months had transpired after the burial of her beloved Obinna and his family but Nkiru hadn't shed any more tears than the lone tear that had trickled down her cheek during the ceremony.

A vigilant onlooker could easily discern that her existential mode was as robotic as that of a seasoned artist performing a tedious scene for the umpteenth time so merely observes the motions. Her parents were very concerned about her subdued state and her mother decidedly broached the topic with her husband as they lay in bed at night.

'Nnam, I know Nkiru is inclined to recoiling into herself when despondent but her present condition is a different matter. I think we should seek proper medical assessment in case there is a more fundamental element to her condition than ordinary grief.' She suggested worriedly to her husband.

Nkiru was always prone to recoiling into herself when forlorn. They'd observed her emotional withdrawal on many occasions, most recently when her best friend, Ebere had drowned in a tragic accident. She had on the other hand wept her eyes out irrespective of the withdrawal bit. She jokingly equates her peculiar trait to that of a turtle's known to retract back into its shell when it meets with an obstacle. She hadn't however displayed the lifeless glazed stare that was primed in her eyes now and worried her parents.

'I agree,' Chief Ubaka concurred. 'The shocking demise of her fiancé, his family and the mysterious circumstance surrounding their deaths are gruesome enough to induce shock in anyone but I've been optimistic that she'll pull through sooner than later.'

'She's deteriorating with each passing day, Nnam.' Lolo restated. 'It breaks my heart to see our daughter in her present state.'

'I know, Lolom. Both of you shall accompany me to depart at dawn tomorrow for Isako. We might as well seek for the best medical care available and convey her there. I hear there is a new state of the arts private clinic run by our tribesman which we can attend.' Chief Ubaka suggested.

'Thank you Nnam, I'll be more reassured if she's reviewed by professionals.' Lolo declared and was significantly relieved by her husband's timely suggestion.

They set off early the next morning as planned with Nkiru in tow and arrived at the reputable clinic after midday.

'Dr Igwe, I'd like to present the patient in room 2B.' A junior doctor who had reviewed Nkiru initially reported back to his superior, detailing her history of presenting complaints and his findings. 'I couldn't conclusively elicit any physical problem but my diagnosis is bereavement and grief induced shock.'

'I had cast a glance at her briefly when they arrived and she does look like she is in shock. What's your management plan then?'

'I think her major problem is bereavement so we can afford to observe her for a short time interval. With the stigmatization that goes along with mental ailments, I'd err on the side of caution before seeking psychiatric review besides there is a fair chance that she might simultaneously snap out of her shock soon.'

'I agree. I'll personally review her before we talk to the family.' Dr. Igwe agreed.

Mental disorders were highly unattractive in their society. The general attitude towards such afflictions was both deprecating and reckoned tantamount to severe psychosis. Psychiatric patients are usually secreted away from public eye as if taboo and ostracized. In severe cases, they are conveyed to nonconformist churches or juju-men for spiritual healing or rituals respectively in place of appropriate psychiatric attention. Such patients are occasionally shackled and bound in chains to restrain and subdue them while undergoing supposed healing processes. They are also habitually subjected to caning and other such nonconformist measures in a hypothetical bid to dispossess them of evil spirits misguidedly indicted as responsible for their disorder. A majority of psychiatric patients are more likely to be found destitute or abandoned by immediate family members and society thus driven to deeper abyss. They are as such more likely found to be found loitering unsupervised in the streets demented and oblivious to their environment. It must be acknowledged too that there is also a fundamental dearth of appropriate mental institutions in any case. The extensive stigmatization involved makes most wary to infringe upon the premise of a psychiatric consult unless absolutely crucial.

'Chief,' Dr. Igwe greeted, initiating a discussion with Chief Ubaka and his wife after he had reviewed her. 'Nkiru has no any physical ailment but is in a mental shock which is understandable in the face of the misfortune that you had described. I admit she is very hard hit but we'll prefer to monitor her for the moment. There is a great chance that she'd recover simultaneously otherwise we'll have to explore other options.' He explained guardedly.

'When you say you want to monitor her, what time interval are we looking at?' Chief Ubaka asked.

'No longer than two-three months.' The doctor estimated.

'Are you going to admit her for that interim then?' Chief Ubaka wanted to know.

'No but we'll review her at regular intervals.'

'Are you sure that it's safe to wait, Nkiru seems to be deteriorating further with every passing day?' Lolo queried anxiously.

'I understand your concern, Lolo but there is a great chance that she'll pull through given that there is a specific trigger besides this is her first episode of a similar condition. You're sure there is no prior history of mental illness in either of your families.'

'None at all,' Both Chief Ubaka and Lolo denied vehemently. 'Which options might we explore if her condition fails to improve?' Chief Ubaka asked.

'It depends on her condition when we review her again.' The doctor replied tactfully, avoiding the mention of psychiatric consult as a very likely option for the moment. He deemed his patient was undoubtedly grief ridden. In the course of his practice he had witnessed patients in worse states recovering simultaneously so he was hoping same will be the case for this young lady in question. He would defer psychiatric consult for the time being taking into account the antecedent stigmatization. He reassured the family and scheduled another appointment optimistic that Nkiru might pull through before then.

Chief Ubaka and his family departed for home in a more optimistic state of mind, hopeful that their daughter would make an expected quick recovery. On the contrary however, they were disappointed by her continued decline in ensuing days. They tried everything from casual discussions, scolding, cajoling, comforting to beseeching her but none proved to overturn her partial amnesia or selective mutism.

Nkiru would nod or answer 'yes', 'no' or any such appropriate monosyllable in response to conversations or queries but most of the time stared blankly back offering no response whatsoever. She was mesmerized in her own world and steadily turning into a shadow of her old self.

Her anxious parents enlisted Reverend Father Joseph but his regular prayers and anointment sessions failed to alleviate their daughter's condition.

Nkiru had become reclusive, refusing to socialize and preferred to stay in bed all day long. She became voluntarily confined to her bedroom and in next to no time was refusing regular showers and declining food or drinks.

A few relatives and visitors who accidentally caught a glimpse of Nkiru as her condition steadily deteriorated, stared back at her in shock and dismay. They could hardly believe that it was the same sweet, pretty, carefree and confident Nkiru that was fast transforming into an emaciated robotic hag.

Rumourmongers went straight for the jugular. A new buzz was created aside from the suggestion that her condition was a reprisal from the gods. This new fodder of gossip postulated that Nkiru was an *ogbanje.* These propagators of this novel concept argued that was the only plausible explanation as to how Nkiru could have transformed from a carefree lively lady to a zombie the next, her OSU calamity notwithstanding.

The reality of her shock or the fact that she had never previously exhibited any of the archetypal peculiarities of an *ogbanje* did not deter them from promoting this novel theory.

In her Igbo culture, reincarnation of the departed and incarnations of evil spirits are fundamental ideologies. The general belief is that it is possible for a dead person to reincarnate, either wholesomely or in parts and manifests in successive descendants or relatives. It is also alleged that this benefit can be lost through immorality and as such those who reincarnate are the more righteous ones. An Ogbanje on another hand is basically an incarnation of evil spirit or purported *'child spirit'* who reincarnates repeatedly via the same mother. They die young, yet return or reincarnate repeatedly to their mother's womb to be born again. They are also termed evil and wicked because they wilfully decide to die early without any prior ailments but return or are reborn to torture their parents relentlessly. Anxious parents would brand these purported ogbanje kids when they die to discourage them from reincarnating back to life. If they defy the odds to return are easily recognizable from the inscription. These evil spirit reincarnated kids or *ogbanje* are also believed to maintain a link with the spirit world via a *sacred stone* or *iyi-uwa* which when located and destroyed breaks the hypothetical vicious cycle. In the present, more contemporary times, children most especially female who exhibit peculiar or odd traits are also loosely tagged as "*Ogbanje*".

Lolo wasn't aware that her beloved daughter's current physical condition was touted as typically *ogbanje* until she accidentally overheard a conversation between the house-helps in her home.

'Aunty Nkiru's condition is fast declining so I'll suggest we put her in our prayers.' Lolo had heard Ada propose to the others.

'Ada, our people say that the lizard does not break into a run in broad daylight for no just cause. Oga and Madam must find the root of Nkiru's problems. There is no smoke without fire.' One of the other maids asserted.

'Mgbeke and her propaganda again, I suppose that if Aunty Nkiru's ill luck was to befall you then you'll still have the mouth to talk rubbish.' Ada retorted, admonishing the usually superstitious Mgbeke.

'I don't know why you are attacking me for telling the truth.' The girl protested. 'I know you've lived in this household longer than most of us but that does not mean we'll all pretend to be blind. There's an underlying evil in this house.' Mgbeke insisted unruffled.

'Yes there is and that evil is you.' Ada responded contemptuously to the amusement of the rest of the helps who burst out laughing.

'You can joke all you want,' Mgbeke retorted undaunted. 'I'm not kidding and I'll tell you something else too,' she added in a near whisper. 'Without bothering to recount the OSU palaver or how this family had blatantly defied the gods by sanctioning that wedding,' Mgbeke sniffed. 'I'll tell you what else is true, Aunty Nkiru is an *ogbanje*.' She announced with much decorum.

'**Tufia Kwa gi**, *God forbid you*. How can you say that? Let me stop you before you go around poisoning other people's mind with your evil tongue. Nkiru is not an *Ogbanje*. Do you hear me?' Ada screamed angrily, confronting Mgbeke to her face. 'I've known Nkiru for more than ten years and she is the nicest person ever. She'll recover with or without your prayers. She is just grieving for her Obinna and that is the only problem that there is. I had merely suggested that we intensify our prayers on her behalf without you twisting the story around with your evil mouth.' Ada fumed.

'Don't say I didn't tell you so.' Mgbeke insisted undeterred by Ada's obvious fury.

'I'm warning you not to bad mouth anyone in this household for the last time.' Ada cautioned, bracing for a fight if that was what it would take to silence foul-mouthed Mgbeke. She readily tucked the hem of her frock into her underpants and reached for Mgbeke's shirt collar before the other servants moved in to separate them.

'I don't care if they pay you more than everybody else so that you feel compelled to be blind.' Mgbeke yelled defiantly, refusing to back off. 'I'll be gone from here if they dare to bring those OSU kids to reside in this house.' she stated publicly. 'None of you can even begin to imagine the repercussions of such a dastardly act but I won't be hanging around to find out. This family is wilfully playing with fire.'

'*Ifugo gi*, look at you.' Ada pronounced slowly and disdainfully. 'You're plain evil. It is unfortunate that bad things happen to good people. As for you, I pray no evil befalls you because your mouth will prove to be your undoing.'

Mgbeke laughed derisively in reply to Ada's suggestion.

'I think you should thank your lucky stars for now.' Ada recommended, realizing that there was no convincing Mgbeke against her conviction.

'I stand by my words; you're just letting sentiment overrule your logic.' Mgbeke insisted.

'Continue,' Ada returned resignedly, tired of arguing with the obstinate Mgbeke. 'I hope you can pray because all I was trying to suggest is that we put Nkiru in our prayers.' Ada beseeched the others wisely ignoring Mgbeke and her deluded remarks.

'I'll pray for her naturally but if her parents refuse to see the handwriting on the wall then this problem will only degenerate.' Mgbeke persisted.

Lolo could hardly restrain herself from confronting Mgbeke but managed to rein in her anger against her better judgment. She was mystified as to how Mgbeke or anyone else could allege that her daughter, Nkiru was an *ogbanje*. She tried to picture how any one could arrive at such an absurdity given that she, Lolo was neither prone to miscarriages nor lost any child at childbirth. Nkiru was her first child followed by Azuka and then Chuka. Azuka arrived nine years after Nkiru while Chuka is three years younger than Azu. She never miscarried or lost any child in-between them yet these imprudent gossips were spreading hurtful and offensive rumours as if her family didn't have more than enough on their plate to chew already. She resolved to broach the topic with her husband later.

'Nnam, what are we going to do? Nkiru's condition is not improving.'

'Lolom,' He responded, affectionately calling her his Lolo. 'My good wife, I'm very worried too. The doctors said nothing was physically wrong but shock. Our daughter is grieving for Obinna but the bane of the matter is that she's not doing so in a natural mode. If she could only let her sorrow out than bottling it up inside, she would fare better.'

'I know. The doctors also said that she would snap out of this daze rapidly but if you ask me, her condition continues to deteriorate. It tears my soul apart to see our lovely daughter like this and to complicate issues I overheard that useless girl, Mgbeke asserting that Nkiru is an *ogbanje.'*

'Where did she get that from?' Chief Ubaka was equally puzzled.

'I don't know my dear, look at my armpits there is no hair yet these gossips keep picking at them. These redundant rumour-mongers and their like are surely having a field day at the expense of our family.' She bewailed bitterly.

'It is okay, none of them is God. They can have their fun because if they don't derive their pleasure at our expense then it would be another unfortunate victim or else they'd make up stories.' He consoled his wife. 'I wouldn't worry too much about what outsiders are saying. It is human nature for detractors to dig one into a deeper hole once one is falling. On the other hand, my mother used to say that if no one talks about you then you might well be dead. Sadly enough, the dead are not spared nowadays. Don't worry my dear; today's headline is stale news by the next day. My major concern is really Nkiru's recovery. I'd be dishonest to say I'm not worried.'

'We should send her away from here.' Lolo suggested. 'A change is bound to do her some good.'

'Yes but where?'

'Abroad,' Lolo stated firmly without dithering. 'The further away we travel from Ubi, the better.'

'I understand your point but we can't just dump her abroad by herself. One of us will be required to stay with her for the duration it takes for her to get back on her feet. I've mulled similar thoughts and wouldn't have bated an eyelid to send both of you away but you're conscious of our current financial constraint. We need to be extra careful with our resources at the moment. The new directive from the Central Bank has thrown us all into a major quandary. The reality is that most of our finances are tied up with our proposed new bank venture. This new mandate released by the Central Bank or should I say Federal government has crushed everything and everyone.' He confessed. 'I was hoping we would have had the bank up and running by now only to receive the shocking new mandate that has destabilized our plans. You know I had practically invested everything with the hopes that once the project kicks off, we'll easily recoup our original capital. Right now my main concern is recovering the fiscal cash invested since our group didn't meet the set criterion for licensing a private bank. Even though the Central Bank stipulated that those of us who did not fulfil the criteria will be refunded our money but you know as well as I do how that goes. The whole bureaucracy that will be involved in trying to recover the money will prove to be yet another uphill task. Any individual that comes in contact with money demands a substantive kickback not to take into consideration the funds invested in getting us to the position we were in before the set back. I can't even dare to estimate the full extent of our expected losses because I could sincerely suffer a breakdown.'

'This is a major catastrophe, Nnam. What are we going to do now?'

'We'll just have to see how this one plays out and hope for the best possible outcome. I wouldn't even know how to strategize in this case if I were to try. Man proposes but God disposes so let's pray his disposition will ultimately be in our favour.' He intoned sounding upbeat.

'I hope so too, Nnam.' Lolo echoed.

'This mess should clear up soon so we can count our losses and start afresh. We might have to aim for Nkiru's next hospital appointment and God willing this bank dilemma would have sorted itself out by then too, otherwise we would have to explore alternative measures.' Chief Ubaka stated.

'I understand Nnam.' Lolo agreed. 'I pray we'll overcome this hitch early enough. I just don't want Nkiru to learn of this new rumours swirling around as it would only worsen her present condition.'

'We'll do whatever we have to do to protect her. Let me tell you the truth dear but I had succumbed to speculating lately. In as much as I try to deny it but I've also pondered on if our daughter's condition is retribution from the gods as everyone else seems to think.' Chief Ubaka cogitated aloud as they rehashed their ongoing family crisis. 'I know I shouldn't doubt God or our faith but I'm suddenly inclined to wondering if our recent hard luck is actually linked to this OSU debacle. I've speculated if any of these mishaps would have transpired but for our endorsement of the wedding between Obinna and our daughter?' He tendered. 'I feel guilty contriving such negative thoughts. I've always contrived that lesser men tend to apportion blame or attribute their misfortunes to others in hopes of making

93

themselves feel better but I have found myself falter.' He admitted. 'I wish I could understand why we are suddenly faced with multitude trials however I'm a true believer of destiny that ultimately runs its natural course. I could easily agree with my kinsmen for selfish reasons but then if these things were meant to happen then they would irrespective of our personal actions. I'm therefore convinced that this whole matter would resolve and our daughter would fully recover, right?' He sought affirmation from his wife.

'Nnam, you're right.' Lolo affirmed. 'It is funny that you mention your doubts because I've personally mulled similar thoughts. I've revaluated our situation numerous times and I'm convinced we acted in the best interest of our family. Like you rightly stated, everything happens for a reason. We can only keep hoping for the best. I don't know how we can justifiably state that Obinna and his family's death were a reprisal from the gods when it could have been anyone of us in that cab that night and could have inadvertently met with death in the hands of callous armed robbers or police. Our financial constraint on the other hand couldn't have been more ill-timed but we can't attribute it to the gods too. Our major concern is our daughter's recovery in addition to the welfare of those poor kids who have been unexpectedly orphaned.'

'Those are my exact thoughts too.' Chief Ubaka declared. 'Did you get in touch with the kids lately?'

'Yes. I sent Emma to deliver provisions for them a few days ago. They are fine and send their regards. I spoke with the Azuka's school head and she suggested it might be better to wait till the upcoming academic year considering this session is coming to an end soon. The kids will be better off starting afresh in a new class than joining midterm. There's also the matter of an entrance exam to assess their aptitude for appropriate class placement before they are allowed to join.'

'I'm sure the kids would have no trouble passing those entrance exams if they are anything like their brothers. We'll endeavour to make sure that they are well taken care of especially education wise. I can well imagine their predicament in losing their family at such a tender age. I can't bear to think of what could happen to our own kids if they were ever to contend with a similar situation.'

'I couldn't imagine that either but God forbid. Their situation is tragic indeed. I would have wished they could move in with us. Fending for them wouldn't be too much of a hassle.'

'Let's see what happens in the future. We might be able to sway their aunt after we've pull through our present financial rot. For now, our daughter's welfare should remain our first priority.'

'True, Nnam.' Lolo concurred.

As for Nkiru, she lived in her own realm. She couldn't understand what the furore around her was about. She knew her mother's repeated visits to her room under the guise of desiring a quick chat, in search of a misplaced object or similar flimsy excuses were actually to check on her. Her father was another culprit though he tries to be a bit more discrete. Azuka had returned to school or would have been lurking around her room like a permanent fixture. Even, Chuka her little brother tagged along their mother to visit her frequently.

Both her parents and siblings persisted in hovering around her for some reason and she could perceive the worry lines etched on their faces. None of them needed to worry about her though because she was fine, she thought. They just had to realize that it was imperative for her to wait for Obinna to return.

She was more disappointed and mystified by their reluctance to discuss Obinna or her upcoming wedding anymore. Obinna was expected to visit so they could align the rest for their wedding and impending travel plans. She was yet to pick her wedding dress too. They had a lot of outstanding plans to make and issues to deliberate on, like her bridal train and others.

She was expecting her door to open and it wouldn't be her mother, father, Azuka or Chuka but Obinna come to visit or else Ada come to announce his entrance. She needed to conserve what was left of her strength in the meantime because she was starting to feel frail.

None of her family members seemed to understand her and expected her to act as usual but she couldn't. She wanted to communicate to them how everything now depended on Obinna showing up but words failed her. She could only muster a few words occasionally like 'yes' or 'no' but the rest of her speech was stuck in her throat. She wasn't overly upset because everything will be fine once Obinna turns up. Her tied tongue will surely slacken and overflow with words pouring heavier than the rainstorm of the penultimate night.

She had surprised herself by incredulously sitting up in her bed and savouring the staccato beat of the heavy downpour as it drummed on her roof. She had marched boldly up to her bedroom window, drew the curtains back and stood calmly observing the heavy torrents pelt the earth surface. She listened to the intermittent deafening clap of thunder strike earth surface without a single flinch or fear. She had reflected bemusedly that the thunder clap was akin to heaven whip-lashing an impenitent earth. The angry rumble shattering the monotonous drone of the rainstorm failed to terrify her; rather she relived the spectacle like she and heaven were washing out their grime. In the not so distant past, she would have been petrified and hidden her head underneath her pillows to obscure the angry rumble of the thunderbolt but not anymore. She found herself relishing the blizzard instead. The thunderstorm has lost its formidable bite and she was fearless. She felt bold, empowered by her confidence in Obinna's return. The only snag was that he had been gone for too long.

What was keeping him away from her? Did he have any clues as to how tormented she was by his absence? He was simply supposed to travel home and return a few days later but hadn't as much as called her yet. She was so weak now and unable to muster up enough strength to move or she could have gone to fetch him personally. She believed that he'll come as sure as the air that she breathed in. he was her beloved Obinna and had never failed her. She was the love of his life; he had repeatedly assured her that was the case and she trusted him. Neither of them could survive without the other. They were soul mates. She knew he'd come for her as soon as he could get away from the obligations that kept him away. He'd better have a good explanation as to why he kept her waiting for so long still, she mused with a slight hint of anger. His prolonged absence and silence better be crucial or she wouldn't be able to find it in herself to forgive him for putting her through this turmoil. She loved him so much and just wanted to see him again. She cradled her phone once more to her chest and willed for it to ring and Obinna to be the caller. She wasn't going to answer any other calls but his because her words were especially reserved for him. Those thoughts encompassed her solace and hope.

Her phone failed to ring though because it was essentially dead. She had been clutching on to it for days on end refusing to let it out of her clutch or recharged the battery. Her thoughts were firmly fixated on Obinna and his expected return.

She evoked his endearing smile and ever gentle deportment once again, both traits that she adored and envied in him at the same time. However, her wholesome image of him was nearly shattered when Jude came into the picture. Obinna is always unpredictably thrown into a jealous frenzy whenever Jude's name cropped up. He seemed to consider Jude as his rival after he learnt that Jude had wooed her but Jude wasn't her only suitor. She had received quite a number then. Obinna was cynical irrespective of her continued reassurances that there was nothing but a platonic friendship existing between herself and Jude. She was partly amused by his jealous antics because it was so out of character with his usual affable nature but in an odd twist also reassured her of his immense fondness for her.

She recalled his very peculiar idiosyncrasy or when he intones, "Baby, you are right but why don't you consider this other opinion too" during an argument. It was his usual strategy to curtail an argument. Why would he agree with her and then ask that she reconsiders her stance in same breath? His underhand ploy used to irritate her to no end and she'll start to nag or tell him off for his 'fake diplomacy' or so she termed his ruse. They'd typically make up when he pulls her into his arms and kisses her to stop her protestation or nagging. He claims that she rants and raves. They'd end up clinched in a reconciliatory passionate lovemaking. She relived her excitement when he gently cups her breast and tenderly kisses her nipples or the painfully sweet sensation when he sucks at her breast. He would literally kiss her from head to toe jokingly asserting that he was leaving an indelible stamp of his love all over her body in case any other fellow tries to touch her. He claimed they'd easily recognize his stamp which would both repel and scare them off at the same time but there was never going be a case of her letting another man to touch her because Obinna was her one and only bloke. She adored him so much.

She vaguely remembered Jude had come to visit her recently but couldn't pinpoint the exact circumstance of that visit or their conversation to no avail. She realized that she no longer had any real grasp of time but none of that mattered much. She had no qualms about turning into a hermit for Obinna. Her very reality was grounded to a halt until Obinna appears to lease her back to life.

She'd wake up daily, shower, dress up and resign to waiting for Obinna. She'd convince her self in the morning that he would visit during the day, and by night fall will be reassured he'll arrive the next day until she could hardly differentiate between day and night. She was gradually weaker as the days went by and her appetite waned to the extent that she could hardly stand the sight or smell of food. Her mother started to force feed her as well as coerce her to bath by actually leading or carrying her to the bathroom for a wash when she started to decline to get out of bed or shower.

The resident house helps and visitors were barred from attending her room. Lolo took full charge and personally tended to her ailing daughter. Both of her parents initial expectation that she would simultaneously snap out of the doldrums was fading in view of her continued deterioration. Lolo didn't want any witnesses recording her daughter's present pathetic state or spread any further false rumours. She realized that between them, they had regressed to her daughter's infancy. The present was no different from her infancy when Lolo had nursed her then young newborn daughter, washing feeding, dressing and putting her into bed.

Six

The Ubaka kinsmen revisited Chief Ubaka's residence during the same intervening period. They reiterate their call for the urgent pacification of the gods. They feared that far reaching consequences will encroach on the welfare of their entire kindred and village barring a timely intervention. They were also convinced that therein lays the key to Nkiru's recuperation.

Chief Ubaka clearly visualized himself at a crossroad anew. His dilemma was so multifaceted that he was stumped as to how best to deal with the dicey situation. His beloved daughter ailed and he would do or give anything to help her get better. Hitherto, he had vowed not to relapse or be coerced back into consulting with native doctors but was he left with any options really? His mind played games on him as he mulled over a multitude of possibilities.

It was very obvious that his daughter was mentally incapacitated. While he was of the mind that this was decidedly shock induced, his kinsmen were attributing her condition to reprisal from the gods. He was indeed confused especially as her condition had continued to deteriorate.

In spite of his strong conviction that her ill health was derived from mental trauma but at his most vulnerable periods, began to harbour self doubt. What if there was a minute chance that his relatives were right? That lone uncertainty dogged persistently at him. They resolved to take Nkiru back to the doctors earlier than their scheduled appointment at his wife's behest. She was also alarmed at Nkiru's progressive decline.

The doctors were shocked at Nkiru's present state when the family arrived at the hospital at Isoka. She had definitively taken a turn for the worse. She was not only severely wasted but weak and delirious. They immediately admitted her to a private room and commenced intravenous re-hydration without any further delay.

Lolo stayed behind with her daughter in hospital while her husband returned home to the rest of the family.

'Welcome Chief,' Dr. Igwe greeted before initiating an update on his daughter's condition on Chief Ubaka's return two days later.

Chief Ubaka was glad to note some improvement in the few days that Nkiru had stayed on hospital admission. His wife had excitedly reported that Nkiru had managed to swallow a few spoonfuls of cereal that morning, although she still wasn't very verbally communicative.

'Your daughter's physical weakness obviously is a result of poor oral intake but the root cause of her illness is still the psychological shock she had endured like we had stressed earlier.' Dr. Igwe continued. 'She is exhibiting delayed expression of grief but I'm afraid also that she has developed severe depression and her selective mutism is another major cause for concern.'

'What do you suggest we do then?' Chief Ubaka asked and fixed his glance on his frail daughter. She was seemingly awake in bed but preoccupied in her private world, detached from them.

'I think we'll need to start her on antidepressants and arrange a review by a psychotherapist for possible counselling sessions. I'll have a word with one of my psychiatrist friend to make necessary arrangements but I must warn you, psychotherapists are hard to come by.'

'Please do whatever is necessary, money is no issue here. We just want our daughter to recover.' Chief Ubaka entreated. He sincerely would give anything to have his daughter to recover.

'Please help her get better.' Lolo implored with tears drifting down her cheeks. 'Are you sure she wouldn't fare better if we were to send her abroad?'

'The choice would be yours at the end of the day.' Dr Igwe responded. 'But I don't think our colleagues abroad would intervene any differently than what we are doing here. I'd suggest we see how she fares on the new medication before we think of other options. The only snag is that the benefits of antidepressants usually take weeks to manifest. We'll try to arrange and secure a psychotherapist as soon as we can. I'll go as far as suggesting that you should try not to worry too much. I have no doubts that her condition would improve.' The doctor reassured them.

'Thank you Dr. Igwe. We are relying on you otherwise I have no other explanation as to how my daughter's condition could have deteriorated so drastically in such a short interval.

'It is a disheartening situation but I have no doubts that she'll improve and recover.' The doctor reaffirmed.

'Thank you, doctor. I hope there are no long lasting or lingering effects of this problem.' Chief Ubaka enquired fearfully.

'I wouldn't think so.' Dr. Igwe replied.

'How long do you intend to admit her for?' Chief Ubaka enquired.

'If she continues to make progress then it shouldn't be for too long. If we can get her to start eating and drinking again then half the battle is won.'

'Thank you very much, Dr Igwe. Thank you.'

'Not to worry, Chief. I'll see you again soon. Take care, Madam Lolo.' The doctor bade them goodbye and departed to continue his rounds.

'Thank you doctor, Thank you very much.' Lolo greeted appreciatively.

'Lolom, thank you too.' Her husband commended her after the doctor left. 'I appreciate your sacrifices. I wanted to bring Ada along to help you but on second thoughts, the fewer people aware of our daughter's real condition, the better but I know she'll improve. We haven't knowingly wronged anyone.'

'That is true, Nnam. It will be well. Nkiru, **nwa** daddy (*Daddy's girl*), reassure your father that you would be okay.' Lolo pressed, cradling her.

Nkiru on her part was lost in her wilderness as usual. She felt her mothers embrace but was too weak to reciprocate. She found herself fleeting in an indeterminate state, drifting in and out of consciousness as she waited for Obinna to show up.

She had envisioned both of them earlier wandering hand in hand before they became lost in a maze. She had started to feel giddy so he had to lift her in his arms while they sought to find the exit route. Obinna was practically keeling under the strain of her weight before they decided it might be more convenient if she were to wait up at the centre of the maze while he left solo. He'd find an escape route quicker and then return for her. They stood a better chance of survival that way.

She lay at the centre of the maze waiting patiently for his return as hours progressively turned into days and days into nights. She sat rooted to the same exact spot where he had left her reluctant to budge lest he would come back and miss her. She didn't have the strength to get up and go searching for him after a lengthened wait. She soon heard her parents' voices in the milieu and tried to raise her voice to tell them what had happened. She wanted to ask them to find Obinna who must be entangled somewhere in the maze or lost his way. Her parents couldn't hear the words that refused to escape from her lips. She struggled to get her message across to them in vain. Her attempt to raise her hand and indicate distress failed to attract their attention.

She couldn't muster enough strength to raise a finger much less a limb. Tears also deserted her when she tried to muster a cry in frustration. She was perturbed by her inability to talk or move before she drifted back into oblivion.

Lolo had their bags packed and ready for discharge two weeks later. Her husband had arrived that morning to take them home and was taking care of the bill. Nkiru's condition had miraculously improved in her short hospital spell. Her overall intake of both food and drinks had improved, even though she was tolerating small amounts. She had woken up like on the fifth day into her admission and decidedly finished her breakfast without prompt as opposed to her usual coerced few spoonfuls.

If Lolo didn't know any better she would have contended that her daughter's sudden change was prompted by a secret agenda and she wouldn't have been off the mark. Nkiru had reflexively resolved to regain her strength to search for Obinna by herself. He was lost and probably hurt and she needed to reach him. There could be no other plausible reason for him to leave her stranded in the wilderness. He had only agreed to that arrangement after she insisted he should depart solo. They would have been together but for her insistence. She had persuaded him to believe it would make more sense for him to find the route then come back to fetch her. They could both be trapped in the maze otherwise and it had sounded like a good plan at the time but she hadn't expected him to take so long. It was her fault that she was stuck at the centre of the maze while he was lost, neither of them able to reach or rescue the other. She would therefore regain her strength so she could find him.

'Nkiru, your daddy is here. It is time to go.' Her mother's words broke into her thoughts.

'Okay.' She replied and abruptly stood up.

Lolo's right hand flew to cover her open mouth at Nkiru's unexpected response. She had responded appropriately too and those were her first proper response in weeks.

Chief Ubaka had witnessed the scene too as he waited for them and was overjoyed. He watched wit h fascination as Nkiru stood up and reached for her mother's proffered right arm. The two women linked hands to stride along side by side. Chief Ubaka linked his hand through his daughter's left arm as they shepherded her to the car.

Her parents' cheerful disposition didn't escape Nkiru. They might have a surprise for her. Obinna might have found his way home and they had come to fetch her, she decided. She was elated and began to rehearse the speech that she would deliver to Obinna. She contemplated apologizing to him first before reprimanding him over his long absence. She'd also reveal her bleakness and how she had missed him so sorely that it felt like her heart was being ripped apart. She vowed to wrench a promise from him that he'd never leave her alone for any prolonged period because she couldn't withstand it. She was lost without him. Her parents had better hurry; Nkiru reasoned and quickened her steps as they strode towards the car. She couldn't wait to meet up with her beloved Obinna and was still engrossed in her thoughts picturing their reunion as her father's car sped off towards her hometown, Ubi. She dimly sensed her mother whimpering in the car a moment later. Lolo had apparently tried to engage Nkiru further in conversation presupposing that she'd respond like she had earlier but met with silence. Nkiru was retracted back to her illusory state again. Her blank scare was back in place.

Lolo was disillusioned once again and whimpering loudly. Nkiru grew more attuned to her mother's sob as it grew louder but couldn't understand her new upset. Didn't her mother realize know that Obinna was back? She wished to allay her mother's fears and stop her from fretting because everything was going to be fine now that Obinna was home but words failed her again.

'Nnam, I know Nkiru's condition has improved but I still think we should take her abroad for proper check up. She is far from 100% right. Let's seek a second opinion because if there is a more fundamental cause of her condition then the sooner it is sorted out, the better. Let's stop trifling with our daughter's welfare.' Lolo advocated resolutely through tears.

'You're right Lolom. We should make immediate arrangements for consultation abroad. I've always anticipated that Nkiru would snap out of her shock without recourse to physical intervention but you are right, we've procrastinated enough.' He agreed.

'I understand our financial constraints but I'll sooner sell all the jewellery in my trunk than continue to see my daughter in this state. I don't think I can bear this any longer.' Lolo wept.

'Please Lolom, wipe your tears. I've heard you and we'll proceed as you suggest. I'll personally initiate plans immediately for both of you to travel. Nkiru, my dear, how are you doing?' He turned to ask his beloved daughter.

There was no reply. Nkiru was gazing steadily ahead of her oblivious to the fact that her father had addressed her. Lolo's whimpers heightened.

'Please, Lolom. Stop crying. I know our daughter will improve.' Her husband appealed and reached across Nkiru to squeeze her hand. 'Please stay optimistic. I doubt if God in his infinite mercies would deliberately set out to punish us in this manner. Our daughter is going to be well. Do you hear me? She is going to be well.' He repeated as much to convince his wife as himself.

'Nnam, I'm sorry but I want our daughter back. Please help us, Lord.' She prayed.

'She'll be fine.' Chief Ubaka repeated, embracing and stroking his daughter's hair. 'Nkiru, reassure your mother that you'll be fine.'

Nkiru momentarily turned to her father as if she understood him and nodded. Lolo could hardly contain herself after she observed that gesture and wailed more heart wrenchingly. She reached for the rosary beads in her handbag and started to recite prayers. Nkiru hurried into the house as soon as they arrived home in anticipation of seeing Obinna. Her parents were baffled at her haste because she strode off no sooner than she had alighted from the car and without waiting for them. She headed straight for the lounge downstairs before climbing upstairs. Obinna wasn't in the family lounge either. She shuffled to her bedroom with heightened expectation but met his absence. She proceeded to go from room to room, hoping to find Obinna in one but he was nowhere to be found. She finally returned to her room dejected and deflated. She had been so sure that he was going to be there and waiting for her. She sunk back into her bed wanting to burst into tears of frustration and rage but tears failed her too.

Why wasn't Obinna in her home and waiting up for her? She fumed as gazed blindly up at the ceiling. Her patience was fast running out and there was so much pain and disappointment that she could bear. She couldn't understand why Obinna was deliberately torturing her. She had trusted him to be back so that they conclude their plans for the wedding and travel, yet he had disappointed her once again.

Nkiru became more capricious afterwards, refusing to take her prescription medication and categorically declining the disguised drinks that her mother offered. Lolo had deviously laced the drinks with her prescription medication after crushing and dissolving them prior to offering it to her. It wasn't as if the medication had tainted the colour of the drink but Nkiru refused them. Her feat was even more astounding considering that she refused the drink without tasting it as if she suddenly possessed a weird sense of foresight. This was more evident when the same drink was offered to her in a similar glass but without any disguised medication and she accepts. Her parents were astounded but couldn't applaud her prescience for obvious reasons. They became more determined to expedite plans to ferry her abroad before her condition deteriorates irretrievably.

Two days after their return from hospital, Nnanyi and a few emissaries turned up to reinforce their call for an immediate consult with the oracle. They were agitated and desperate to appease the gods sooner than later.

'Okam, you must understand our foreboding by now which is why we keep revisiting this same topic over and over again.' Nnanyi started without inane preamble as soon as they sat down. 'We don't want it to seem like we are pressurizing you but we are very disturbed. An elder cannot sit and watch while things fester in his household that is why I'll not rest until you do the right thing. I might not subscribe to your supposed modern ways nor am I one to enforce you to act against their will but desperate situations ask for desperate measures.' Nnanyi declared. 'Our people say that an ear that persistently refuses to heed to good advice will ultimately die with the head when it is beheaded. One word is enough for the wise.' He warned. 'My younger brother, this matter transcends beyond the security of our immediate family. It affects not only us and our extended kindred but the entire village as a matter of fact so I plead with you to do the right thing. If you don't want to listen to us then consider your daughter's health or worse still humour the white hair on my head. I hope you don't think I'm senile or that my senses have deserted me. I might be tedious but I am not doing this for the sake of hearing the sound of my own voice. We must act now before it is too late.' He entreated ominously.

'You should pay attention to our call because an individual that consistently pretends to be deaf does not require a formal announcement to know that war has commenced. This situation has practically gone beyond a joke.' Another elder implored less diplomatically.

'I chose to hold my counsel when you proceeded with the *iku-aka* ceremony against my counsel since my words were that of a foolish old man. In as much as I'm not here to reopen old wounds, I have to ask you to reassess the events of the recent past. Something is definitely not right without being told. The lizard does not break into a run in broad daylight for nothing. An imminent calamity will ensue if we don't strive to contain it while we can. We are not your enemies nor are we contesting any dispute. What we all pray for is the betterment of ourselves and our respective families. I understand your reluctance to associate with native doctors because of your so called religion but there comes a time in a man's life when he has to ask himself questions. Are you being stubborn just for the sake of being stubborn or is there a fitting justification for you to continue to disregard the warnings that are stark there in your face?' Nnanyi queried ardently and without waiting for a reply continued. 'What has happened here is beyond the white man's medicine and religion. This is a matter between our own gods and our people. Let us deal with the situation in our own way.' He pleaded. 'I'm not a soothsayer but it is no rocket science that your daughter is expiating for this transgression.' He declared. 'The gods have tied her tongue and until the right sacrifices are made, she will remain so. I plead with you to do right by her even if you chose to discount us. Worse calamities would abound if appropriate measures are not taken to forestall them. We must act now. I beseech you, my young brother to heed to our call. If I could, I would have taken matters into my hand and dispensed of the rituals but my hands are tied. The resources aren't available.' Nnanyi lamented.

'Thank you Nnanyi,' Chief Ubaka started after his kinsman's passionate plea. 'Thank you my brothers. Our people say that when an animal itches, he scratches his back on the bark of a tree but when a human itches, he invites a fellow human to help him scratch the itchy spot. I don't have all the answers but I've heard you. Let us sleep on this until tomorrow.'

'If you've given your word then we have no choice but to return tomorrow, Okam. Time is no longer on our side. We need to act fast.' Nnanyi reiterated.

'We'll give you our word tomorrow.' Chief Ubaka promised and their visitors departed shortly. He and his wife mulled over the issue after the visitors left.

'Lolom, I'll be dishonest if I say that I'm not totally drained by this whole affair. We are now in a bind and this reminds me of the saying that if one doesn't stand for something then they'd fall for everything,' Chief Ubaka acknowledged. 'In as much as I might not necessarily subscribe to the claim that Nkiru's situation is a reprisal from the gods but I can't help my secret doubts. There is that little doubtful voice inside of me that keeps reiterating the slight possibility that kowtowing to our kinsmen will certify Nkiru's recovery. Then how could I possibly live with myself afterwards knowing or thinking that we've failed our daughter in some way?'

'Nnam, I understand your doubts because I have entertained similar worries. We are both caught up in this dilemma. I wish to remain steadfast and take no notice of the nonsense our kinsmen and others are propagating. On the other hand our daughter's welfare is at stake here. Everything is said to happen for a reason but at this point I wonder which lesson we are supposed to derive from her ill health. To tell the truth, I've just reached the end of my tether and want Nkiru to recover and by any means possible.'

'I know our kinsmen will never let us rest unless we concur to their demands. We have unwittingly played right back into their hands but if we give them the funds to dispense of the rituals then we would have indirectly covered all grounds.'

'I agree. There will be no end to their talk unless we appease them and their gods. Where I'd suggest we draw a line is if they should insist that we physically participate or suggest that Nkiru should appear before an oracle.'

'We'll provide them with the funds and nothing more. I'll depart next week to arrange for your visas and collect the loan from the bank. We must act fast; time is no longer on our side.' Chief Ubaka repeated, unwittingly echoing the elders' sense of urgency.

'Nnam thank you. That would be the best approach.' Lolo agreed and the couple settled for the night on that note.

Nnanyi and company reconvened the next day and Chief Ubaka outlined his decision. 'We will provide the necessary funds for the rituals.' He announced to his elated kinsmen.

'You have made a wise decision.' Nnanyi and the others applauded. 'We shall require that Nkiru appears before the oracles.' He further intimated the couple confirming their earlier suspicion. 'She would be required to undergo cleansing and consecrating to the gods in order to have her tongue loosened.'

'I'll beg to differ there but we wouldn't allow our daughter to attend any oracle.' Chief Ubaka categorically stated.

'You must know that this isn't the type of ritual that can be performed in absentia or delegated.' His astounded kinsmen retorted.

'I'll not have my daughter attending any oracle.' Chief Ubaka insisted unwaveringly.

'We'll dispense of the initial rituals.' The elders decided, relenting momentarily from trying to pressurize Chief Ubaka. They accepted the funds and departed the next day to consult with the Oracle of Okirikiri as well as initiate the necessary atonement sacrifices. They were also scheduled to travel to Ogbani to re-sanctify the unearthed effigy. They avowed to readdress the matter of presenting Nkiru before the oracles after concluding this initial step. They were confident that they would be able to convince Chief Ubaka to relinquish his daughter for consecration before the gods in due course.

On the same day that the Ubaka kinsmen left to consult with the Oracle of Okirikiri; Aunty Mary and Obinna's remaining siblings in tow arrived without any prior notice to Chief Ubaka's residence. They stood awkwardly waiting at the front porch for their hosts to emerge.

*   *   *   *   *   *   *   *

'I'm hungry,' Ifedi griped. He was usually prone to throwing tantrums at every opportunity of late but for once he was justified.

'Here, have this.' Ngozi, his elder sister offered, handing him a piece of coconut she had delved out of her school bag.

'But I want food.' Ifedi complained after munching the coconut and subsequently started to stump through the compact space left in Aunty Mary's crammed one bedroom, working himself up in fit of temper.

'Don't worry. Aunty Mary will be home soon with some food.' Ngozi tried to placate him.

'But you said that before,' Ifedi reminded her tearfully. Hunger was gnawing at his stomach. 'I'm hungry.' He reiterated wailing more hoarsely. He and his elder sister had only eaten breakfast for the day and it already was dinner time. There was no definite guarantee that the dinner was forthcoming in any case.

'Ifedi, please stop crying. Aunty Mary will bring food with her.'

'Ndo, sorry Ifedi. Aunty Mary will bring food.' Chidinma added to reassure him before mumbling in undertone. 'I hope she does or I'll soon be howling worse than Ifedi.'

It was a rather tough life for the trio. They had moved in to share their father's senior and only sister, Aunty Mary's humble abode since losing their parents and brothers. It wasn't really bad in the beginning but had gradually gotten worse. They've only one meal for the day and were starving, a similar situation that they've had to endure lately.

'Here, have some water.' Ngozi suggested handing him a cup of water at the same time.

Ifedi quickly gulped the water down but remained disgruntled. His sister, Ngozi cradled him to her chest to comfort him and he was soon lulled into sleep. They were all famished but none of their present predicament was Aunty Mary's fault. She'd sooner sacrifice her own life for their welfare. The hard fact was that they were cash strapped.

Aunty Mary was half-blind and had no steady source of income. She gave up her modest sewing business decades ago as a result of her failing health. Her now deceased younger brother had helped to provide her with a handy regular stipend to sustain her which had terminated with his death. His untimely demise and those of his family was a big blow besides necessitating that she takes over the upkeep of her nieces and nephew too. Life has subsequently become an even bigger struggle for all of them.

'My children, I know you must be very hungry. Forgive my delay but I hadn't anticipated I would be out for a prolonged period.' Aunty Mary apologized as she stepped into the room from her errand. She had gone in search of lenders to borrow money from in order to procure foodstuffs for them. Most of them were reluctant to lend her any more money when she hadn't repaid her outstanding debt. She shared her modest accommodation with her brother's kids but the space was far too squashed for four of them to comfortably settle in. The compacted room was the least of their problems in any case, she mused as she tried to negotiate through the space to unpack her bag. The children had been lying on a mat spread on the floor.

'Welcome Aunty.' The two older girls greeted her, groggily sitting up and rubbing their eyes after they were awakened by the noise from her entrance.

'Please forgive me,' she apologized yet again. 'I didn't envisage that I'll be gone for so long. Ngozi wake Ifedi up. I brought *"agidi"*. You should have that to hold your stomach until I finish preparing dinner.' Aunty Mary urged while laying out the food products she had bought on a small corner table.

'Welcome Aunty Mary, did you bring food.' Ifedi enquired promptly on rousing from sleep.

'Don't be angry with me, my son I know you must be very hungry. Here, take *agidi*.' Aunty Mary said while handing him a green palm frond wrapped delicacy.

Ifedi hurriedly undid the frond uncovering the cold whitish jellylike moulded delicacy made from ground maize. He hungrily stuffed half into his mouth without waiting for necessary reheating or sauce to dip into.

'I'll have mine reheated first.' Chidinma declared.

'Give it to me then, I'll warm both of ours together.' Ngozi offered accepting Chidinma's before heading for the stove at their kitchen corner in the central communal kitchen of the yard.

'Can I have some more.' Ifedi demanded with a full mouth. He was ferociously munching on his last bit.

'You're just finishing yours.' Chidinma pointed out.

'Never mind, I'll share with you.' Ngozi offered to mollify him.

Aunty Mary had started to gather the condiments that she required together to head for the kitchen to prepare a proper meal for them. 'Where's the salt?' She enquired unable to locate the jar in its usual location.

'Ifedi must have displaced it while he was ransacking the whole place for food.' Chidinma reported.

'Help me find it then.' Aunty Mary requested. It was undeniably a difficult position that they have all found themselves in, she lamented. She had always been able to hack it by placing stuff in a particular order so she could easily grope and manoeuvre her way around given her failing sight. It was harder now for her to perform minor tasks because of the difficulty in maintaining a similar precision while the kids cohabited with her. There was also the matter of financial constraint. Her meagre private savings, her deceased brother's family funds as well as the resources accruing from donations made by sympathizers and well wishers alike during the burial ceremony had fast depleted. A huge proportion of the finance had gone towards paying for the lavish burial ceremony but a substantial fraction had also mysteriously disappeared. She had at the end of it all, received much less cash than she had anticipated. She had entrusted the handling of the donations and funeral arrangements to Ijem and a few self appointed volunteers. The substantial amount missing was no fault of Ijem's, he was irreproachable. He had unsuspectingly entrusted the handling of some accounts to strangers that ended up misappropriating the funds.

The overall assets entrusted to her keep were abysmal compared to the original amount that she had initially contended. She had tried her utmost best to be frugal in expenditure, purchasing only discounted goods be it food or personal effects.

Their major expenditure was house rent; the children school fees and other such basic amenities yet amazingly the resources had quickly dwindled. Their situation was more hampered by the fact that they had no guaranteed source of incoming funds to replenish the dwindling account. It was barely seven months since her brother's tragedy occurred but they were already scrimping to keep their heads afloat.

The kids had left for school a few days later and Aunty Mary was home alone. She was seriously pondering on their predicament and wondering where or how she was going to raise their next meal or replenish their funds after they run out again.

She had unwittingly dozed off when an unfamiliar voice screaming her name roused her. She initially thought she was dreaming only for the voice to grow louder and more prominent. A stranger was truly yelling her name in a fairly distressed fashion and approaching closer to her doorway.

'Mary, Mary. Are you home?' The voice queried repeatedly.

'Yes, yes. Who is there?' She abruptly sat up and stumbled to the door to find out what the rumpus was about. She was astonished on opening the door to find the shopkeeper from the next street dragging a reluctant Ifedi by the ear.

'*Ewo-oh*, what is the matter? Ifedi what have you done? Aren't you supposed to be in school?' She queried, alarmed to see him dragged forcibly up to her doorstep.

'Mary, you are a very good woman and your brother was a very hard working fellow too. What happened was a big tragedy and that is why I have to report this young fellow to you personally. My sympathy lies with yourself and his family.' The fellow gushed. 'I know your brother's kids are usually very well behaved. They have taken a big knock lately but I'll hate to see them turn out like the rest of the goons in this neighbourhood. I caught this young man stealing from my shop. You must do something about these kids. That is all I have to say.' The shopkeeper warned anxiously.

'Thank you, thank you. It is only the people that love one that will tell us the truth. I am very grateful. Thank you for taking the trouble to bring him back to me directly. Please tell me how much do I owe you? I must pay for the goods he stole.'

'Don't worry Mary; just do right by these kids.' He repeated gravely.

'Thank you very much.' Aunty Mary couldn't express her heartfelt gratitude enough. 'And you, where did you learn to steal?' She grasped Ifedi from the shopkeeper's hold and shoved him into the room, charging after him. 'You want to out me in this neighbourhood.' She turned to thank the shopkeeper again before joining Ifedi in the room.

Ifedi staggered into the room at his aunt's shove and ran cowering under the bed, afraid of the punishment that she was bound to mete out to him. He had recently made new friends in his new neighbourhood who suggested that it was more fun to steal from the shops than attend lessons in school. This was his second time of joining them and he had relished the supply of candies and biscuits they realized from their first escapade. He had shrewdly resolved not to show or share his booty with his sisters. They would have demanded to know how he got them and probably would have reported him to his aunt. He hadn't exactly bargained on the shopkeeper apprehending him or dragging him by the ear and shamefacedly down the street to her. His exploit wasn't funny any longer in the face of Aunty Mary's wrath.

Aunty Mary gave him a really good hiding. She was determined to reinstate discipline in him or he would turn irrevocably delinquent. She had always been keen to dispense of her responsibility and caring for her brother's kids to the best of her capability but their current situation called for a drastic change. She sat down dejectedly, deliberating on possible solutions and how best to deal with the situation. She finally arrived at a firm conclusion by the end of the day.

She decided that she'll take her brother's children over to Ubi to reside with Chief Ubaka and his family. She was somehow convinced that placing them in such a stable environment with proper control and firm discipline was the only way to salvage and nip Ifedi's atypical conduct in the bud.

Chief Ubaka and his wife had come to her mind because they had remained faithful to their promise of helping cater for her brother's kids. After the initial hoopla over the deaths settled, she and the kids had practically been left on their own except for the Ubaka's. The couple continually enquired after their welfare as well as intermittently sending food and other commodities to them. She was also significantly impressed by the fact that despite the fact that their daughter, Nkiru was severely mangled by the disaster but still pulled all the stops to try and help them out. After she made her resolve, she prayed that the Ubaka's would live up to their earlier promise of fending for her brother's kids.

* * * * * * * *

'Welcome Aunty Mary, Ngozi, Chidinma and Ifedi. Welcome, please come in. I'm sorry that you were kept waiting outside' Lolo greeted ushering them into the spacious downstairs lounge. 'Ada you shouldn't have left them standing outside, they are no strangers.' Lolo chided Ada.

'I'm sorry, Ma.' Ada apologized.

'It is not her fault; we insisted to stay out here until you arrived.' Aunty Mary explained.

Lolo was surprised but happy to see them, albeit they had arrived without prior notice. The mere fact that they turned up with luggage left little to the imagination as to their purpose.

'Welcome, please sit down. I hope all is well.' Chief Ubaka added.

'Chief and Lolo, Thanks for your hospitality and forgive our effrontery for arriving without prior notice but we are helpless.'

'There's no need to apologize. You are always welcome to our home.' Lolo reassured her.

'Thank you very much. I brought the kids over because it had become extremely difficult for us to cope lately. I know you have your personal worries and I hate to think that it seems like I'm ducking from my private responsibility. The truth though is that the blind does not lead the blind so to say. It's not so much for my sake but for the superseding welfare of my brother's kids who I know will fare better in your home. I hope that your offer to cater for them still stands.'

'Of course, we'll be happy to have them. How are you doing kids?' Chief Ubaka turned to ask them again.

'Fine, thank you sir!' they replied in chorus.

'You are all welcome. Consider this your new home.' He announced. 'We always had it in mind that you'll come to live with us some day and today is as good as any other.'

'Thank you both very much and God will bless and reward your kindness a thousand fold.' Aunty Mary responded tearfully, overwhelmed by their unremitting kindness. 'How's Nkiru?'

'She's still struggling but we're praying and imploring God for a miracle.' Lolo replied gravely.

113

'She'll be well. Just remain patient with her. Bad things do not happen to good people. Do you hear me? You are good people and I know the good Lord in his infinite mercies will surely ensure her recovery.'

'Amen. Ada, please come.' Lolo called out loudly.

Ada appeared instantly. 'Yes Ma.'

'Please help the kids with their bags and show them upstairs. Or better still lets all go. Nnam let me show them to their room.' Lolo excused herself before leading the guests up the stairs to show them their new lodgings.

The children shuffled timidly behind Lolo and Aunty Mary as they went up the stairs. Ifedi tugged fearfully at his big sister's skirt. Ngozi was apprehensive too. Her aunt held a private conversation with her to explain her decision. She insisted that she and her siblings would be better off residing with Chief Ubaka and his family. They would have more stable existence, guaranteed meals if nothing else and Ifedi would be prevented from turning into a vagrant. Ngozi hadn't liked the thought of them moving in with complete strangers. Yes, life has been tough lately but they were ready to hack it out with her besides wouldn't Aunty Mary still have similar difficulties fending for herself if they left? Aunty Mary had however assured her that she would be much better off knowing they were well taken care of, she was an old woman anyway and could afford to cope with any adversity. Aunty Mary also countered that for her part, she didn't want them to construe her action as abandonment or that she was relinquishing their care into the hands of strangers'. She explained that their dire situation had necessitated her decision which was solely guided by their best interest. She was sure that they'd realize that it was for the best sometime in the future if not soon. She promised to visit frequently to ensure that they were settling in fine and insisted that if they should insist on returning to her after a fair trial of this new abode, she'll gladly have them back.

Ngozi frequently and secretly cries her eyes out since the demise of her family members but most especially last night when the move to Ubi was more imminent. She didn't let her younger ones see her cry nor did she want to unnecessarily alarm them. It was a tough call for all of them and having to contend with new and sudden changes. They were yet to fully comprehend why their parents and brothers were taken from them and to top it all, they have to relocate and move in with strangers. Yes, it was admittedly rough sharing Aunty Mary's one room accommodation and having one meal a day but they were with family. She rationalized that her younger ones were her responsibility now and she was determined to protect them. If Aunty Mary was confident that relocating to stay with this Ubaka family is their only solace then she'd have to accept it. She trusted Aunty Mary's judgement and wouldn't expect her to mislead them. She and her younger siblings were still together if that were any consolation and she would most certainly have resisted any attempts to separate them. They'll be fine for as long as they stuck together, she conceived, coming to terms with the arrangement.

She trailed after her aunt, Madam Lolo and her siblings in tow as they went upstairs, assessing her new plush environment with reservation. It wasn't like she was not impressed by the luxury or kindness of their hosts so far but was apprehensive of the unknown future that lies ahead of them. She grasped Ifedi's hand reassuringly as they ascended upstairs.

'Ngozi and Chidinma, you'll share this room. Do feel at home and don't hesitate to ask if you need anything.' Lolo announced as she ushered them into a spare guestroom. She opened the wardrobes and drawers indicating that they can store their belongings in them.

'Thank you, Ma.' Ngozi and Chidinma chorused gratefully while Ifedi abruptly burst into tears without any provocation. 'I want to go home.' He wailed.

'Why are you crying? Oh don't worry I haven't forgotten you, you'll share a room with my son, Chuka.' Lolo reassured him gently but Ifedi wasn't placated.

'What's the matter with you?' Aunty Mary asked him angrily, exasperated by his unprovoked tearful outburst.

'Please don't cry. This is your new home and we are your new family. Okay.' Lolo stooped to one knee by his side and held his hand while trying to cajole him.

'Stop the crocodile tears now.' Aunty Mary remonstrated sternly. 'They are very kind folk and you should be grateful.'

'Don't be hard on him, Aunty Mary. He's only a kid.' Lolo intervened.

Ngozi carried Ifedi away to a corner of the room to comfort him. 'I want us to go home with Aunty Mary.' He wailed to her, visibly distressed and confused. 'I don't want Aunty Mary to disappear like Mama, Papa, Brother Obinna and brother Zube. I don't want her to

115

disappear too.' He repeated, sobbing and with tears running down his cheeks.

'But she is not disappearing. She'll still be at Obah and will come to visit us and we'll go to visit her too.' Ngozi explained.

'I don't want to live here. I want us to go back to Obah.' He continued to whine.

'That's not possible. You don't have to worry though because I and Chidinma are here with you too.'

'I'll miss my friends.' He whined petulantly.

'I'm sure you can make new ones here. Now Ifedi you have to stop.' Ngozi ordered more assertively. 'You really have nothing to worry about.'

'I'm afraid.' He admitted to her.

'You shouldn't be. I and Chidinma are here with you so there is nothing to be afraid of. Now stop Ifedi. You don't want Aunty Lolo to be angry with you again, do you now?'

'No,' Ifedi finally dried his tears and ceased crying.

Ngozi was greatly reassured by all of them staying together in one household which had helped to buoy her own spirits. She led the calmed Ifedi back to the others.

Chidinma on the contrary gazed around her new environs in total awe. They had arrived to reside in a mansion, she mused silently to herself, unable to believe their luck. This place was a far cry from their original home that they had shared with their parents. They had lived in a three bedroom flat in a very noisy overcrowded yard. The three of them had shared a room although Ifedi slept mostly in their elder brothers' room when they were away or with their parents. They were more recently forced to share Aunty Mary's crammed abode and slept on mats which they laid out on the floor at night. Ifedi was luckier because he shared Aunty Mary's bed. This new place was a totally different story. She had been uneasy when Aunty Mary mentioned they were going to relocate to Ubi to stay with Chief Ubaka and his family. She recollected them clearly. The couple had been ever so kind to them since they lost their parents and brothers. Nkiru, their daughter was supposed to have married Obinna so they were family to an extent. Chief Ubaka and his wife always brought them gifts whenever they visited and had also promised to reassign them to better schools. She had conversely stopped taking any particular notice of anyone or their false promises. People were extra nice to them at the initial stage when their parents and brothers died and making lots of promises but it was just them and Aunty Mary left at their own device lately.

She admired the new plush setting. The compound in itself was larger than half of her street. There was another smaller structure at the back of the huge storied building where they were situated at the moment. There was also enough surrounding space to build five or more houses within the enclosed space. Three or four pricey cars stood in the parking lot, all of which belonged to this one family. She had noticed the huge generator and water tank, both of which should guarantee a constant supply of electricity and water respectively. In fact they wouldn't be required to venture out in the streets in search of or to fetch water. The sitting room was out of this world with its tasteful decorations and furnishing, she marvelled. It also contained the largest TV that she had ever set her eyes on in her young life. She had hesitated to sit on the lush sofa and would have preferred to take a seat on the downy deep rug that covered the expanse of the spacious sitting room but Madam Lolo had beckoned them to the settee. The bedroom that she had just indicated would be hers and Ngozi's was larger than her parent's room or Aunty Mary's one bedroom accommodation for that matter. There was an adjoining small room within the room containing a white large basin-like bowl that Ngozi whispered was for bathing and a smaller oddly shaped similar structure that looked like a small seat attached to the wall that she said must be a toilet. She didn't know how Ngozi learnt these things because she'd never seen them before. The room contained spacious wardrobes and a large mirror too, only their mother had afforded such luxury but hers was tiny compared to the one in the room. Chidinma was both excited and elated but refrained from jumping into the air to express her huge delight. Her siblings were subdued at present but she knew that they must be as excited inwardly just as she was. She didn't want to give Ngozi any reason to reproach her later if she were to act overly excited which would have been inappropriate in the circumstance. She missed her parents very much and maybe this new home was surely compensation from God. He must be making amends by bringing them to this fairy tale place, not that any thing or any one will ever replace her parents or brothers. She hoped that this couple would remain as kind and pleasant as they sounded now but for now she has to be composed lest they disappoint them in the future. It was better to act unaffected like Ngozi. They couldn't afford to trust anyone anymore.

'Ada, please go and see if the food is ready. Aunty Mary and the kids must be starving after their long trip.' Lolo ordered Ada.

'Yes Ma.' Ada concurred and left for the kitchen to ascertain if the meal was ready.

'You don't have to go into any trouble on our behalf.' Aunty Mary protested.

'You are family, not strangers' Aunty Mary.' Lolo insisted. 'You must have a meal with us before you depart. You still have a long journey ahead of you so need the food to hold your stomach. Please feel free to visit us anytime in the future or whenever you want to see the kids. Consider our home as yours.'

'Thank you very much. God will bless you and your family.' Aunty Mary pronounced gratefully, nearly moved to tears.

'Amen.' She concurred. 'Azuka and Chuka are in school but are vacating by the end of the week. We hope to arrange for Ngozi and Chidinma to attend the same school as Azuka. Ifedi would hopefully join Chuka is his. I'm sure they would all appreciate each other's company.' Lolo recapped.

'I don't know how we can be able to thank both you and Chief. You've been kind to us beyond words. God will reward you both a thousand fold.' Aunty Mary invoked again

'Thank you, Ma.' Ngozi seconded.

'Thank God, it is his hand.'

'Can I see Nkiru before I leave?' Aunty Mary requested.

'Yes of course. I'll take you over to her room now. Please don't be offended if she doesn't respond when you speak to her.' Lolo warned. 'She has her days, some are better than others but we believe in God for infinite mercies.'

'That is all we can do.' Aunty Mary agreed. 'We can only trust in God's mercy and prayers but he never fails. I know in my heart of hearts that everything shall be fine with your family. You are virtuous and will surely overcome this and any adversity.' Aunty Mary reiterated.

The group trooped down to Nkiru's room and entered after Lolo knocked loudly to denote their entrance. Nkiru was lying motionless in bed barely acknowledging their presence. She had her hands crossed perpendicularly across her chest and was staring blankly up at the ceiling.

'Hello Nkiru, guess who has come to see you.' Lolo announced cheerily as she approached her bed. She reached to pat her daughter's hair at the same time and gently aligned her head towards the direction of the guests. 'Look, Aunty Mary and the kids have come to visit.'

'Good afternoon, Aunty Nkiru.' Ngozi and Chidinma greeted in unison but there was no reply or acknowledgment whatsoever from Nkiru. The two girls stopped near the exit.

Aunty Mary advanced towards Nkiru's bed with Ifedi clutching nervously to her arm. 'Nkiru my daughter, how are you?' She asked taking in the frail unfamiliar looking figure lying forlornly in bed with slight shock.

Nkiru raised her head slowly following the direction of her voice before stopping abruptly on catching sight of Ifedi. She stared at him with an obvious fascination, a wide smile spreading through her face. What had made Obinna shrink to this small size? She thought in confusion. Hadn't she always maintained that Obinna will be back? Here he was but in a diminutive proportion of his old self. Was this some sort of a joke? She sprang up swiftly stretching out her arm to reach and touch him. Her coarse fingers brushed across Ifedi's soft cheeks ascertaining that he was for real. It was not a dream but her Obinna.

Ifedi darted away from her immediately to hide behind his aunt's back as Nkiru leaned extra forward to grab his arm.

Lolo was watching her daughter in amazement. It was the first time in ages that Nkiru had displayed any affinity to anyone. They were all confused at her action.

'Obinna, Please don't hide from me.' Nkiru implored in a small pitiful voice and made to go after him. She took a few steps diffidently and wobbly, stopped briefly to steady herself before reaching out to grab Ifedi again.

Nkiru's mix-up was evident from her statement. Lolo hadn't paid any particular attention to their likeness but Ifedi bore a striking resemblance to Obinna. He was a miniature replica of Obinna. Her eyes brimmed with tears which were fast trickling down her cheeks as she observed her daughter's anguish. She wasn't oblivious to the fact that Nkiru had also vocalized a complete sentence. Her daughter had strung together a full sentence; she repeated to herself in amazement and delight. It didn't matter that those were poignant words. Her instant elation was comparable to when Nkiru had articulated her very first words 'dada' at about five months of age. She recalled her then personal transient wave of jealousy when Nkiru had uttered "dada"

119

first than "mama" even though she had stayed home for a whole year nursing her. Nonetheless her ephemeral jealousy on that occasion didn't diminish her pride nor would the actual words that Nkiru had articulated on this occasion. Her daughter was eloquent once again

Nkiru in the meantime strode purposefully towards Ifedi who ducked away and ran, shrieking with fear behind his Aunty Mary's back.

'Why are you running from me Obinna?' Nkiru repeated, bewildered by his reaction.

Lolo rushed to her daughter's side while Aunty Mary gently coerced Ifedi to stop his hysterics, nudging the terrified boy forward to face Nkiru.

'Nkky my dear, he is not Obinna. This is his little brother, Ifedi.' Lolo explained gently.

'Then why does he look so much like Obinna?' She queried, visibly perplexed.

'They are brothers.' Lolo responded in the same gentle tone.

'Where is Obinna then?' She queried.

'My dear Obinna has left us.'

'He has left us.' Lolo and Aunty Mary repeated concurrently as if they had previously rehearsed the line.

'Are you saying Obinna is dead?' She repeated to establish that was what they were both inferring.

'Yes, Obinna has left us.' They reaffirmed.

'How is that? Why? What happened? What happened to Obinna?' She queried, shivering and shaking like a leaf bellowing in the winds as her mother held and supported her to stay upright.

'He was unfortunately murdered by criminals alongside Zube and his parents while on their way home after the *iku-aka* ceremony.' Lolo explained.

It seemed like it was the first time that Nkiru was receiving the news. 'Oh my God, what happened? Why? Why?' She crooned distressfully, collapsing into her mother's arms and raking with sobs at the same time.

Lolo held unto her daughter protectively and sobbed along.

Ifedi's appearance was clearly a long awaited breakthrough that was required to free Nkiru from the mental bondage that had encased her since the news of Obinna's death broke. The shackles that had held her captive, numbing all her senses were finally freed. Nkiru had been in denial refusing to acknowledge that Obinna was dead or never

120

going to come back until now. Her tears surged torrentially like a profound deluge and releasing the grief that she had been repressing for so long. She wept like her eyes would drop from their socket but she was also starting to grieve openly for the loss of her beloved soul mate in a more natural mode.

Lolo, on her part was engulfed by anguish, relief and gratitude at the same time. She very much understood her beloved daughter's anguish and empathized with her pain. She was also grateful that Nkiru's mental shackle was released so she could grieve naturally. The mysterious spell bounding hold on her was finally broken so that her daughter could mourn freely for her beloved fiancé like she should. It was a heart rendering sight but definitely a step in the right direction. She and her husband will be right there to support and help their daughter through it all. She enfolded Nkiru more tightly to her bosom, rocking her like she was a baby. They were inadvertently transposed to the period when she had rocked her precious bundle of joy in her arms and cooed her to sleep. Their tears mingled together as mother and daughter bashed their soul out in tears.

Aunty Mary and the kids were greatly stirred by the astounding drama that they had watched unfold.

Ngozi and Chidinma were initially amazed when they entered the room to find a scrawny looking Aunty Nkiru. Her present state was a far cry from the pretty, tall, fair and elegant lady that had visited their home a few months ago with Brother Obinna. They had been excited when their brother Obinna announced that she was his betrothed and their new aunt. She had brought presents along with her for them as well as spent a great deal of her time chatting and playing with them. She also helped them go through their homework before departing. They had seen her again during the funeral of their parents and brothers and she had looked significantly odd. They had assumed that she was riddled with a comparable grief but hadn't bargained to witness a significant transformation. She was almost dark complexioned now, lean and dazed. Aunty Mary had informed them that Nkiru was broken-hearted from Obinna's death but they hadn't anticipated that she'd look so gruesome.

Ngozi was evidently more clued in to the drama that had just emerged and marvelled at how anyone could love another so deeply. She wept silently for both her brother and his frail looking fiancé who seemed to have loved him so immensely.

Chief Ubaka heard the commotion and rushed to Nkiru's room to investigate. He was surprised to find his wife and beloved daughter on the floor and weeping.' What is the matter Lolom, Nkiru?' He queried.

'Chief, Nkiru had mistaken Ifedi for Obinna but she knows the truth now.' Aunty Mary reported before Lolo could reply and went on to narrate the rest of what had emerged. She spoke softly like she feared that she'd break the spell if she were to speak any louder.

Chief Ubaka rushed to embrace and enfold his wife and daughter in his arms after hearing the full story. Tears flowed freely down his cheeks. He was happy that the dark shadow that had hovered over his household lately was dissipating. He could glean a ray of hope shining through as he hugged them, unable to find the appropriate enough words to indicate his relief or profound joy as he held unto his wife and daughter. Nkiru was back; his daughter was resurfaced from the deep dead end where she was submerged by enormous grief. She had finally re-emerged from the cocoon that had enclosed her world since the day it was announced that Obinna and his family members were callously shot to dead by unknown assailants.

Seven

Nkiru was on the mend while Obinna's siblings were fast settling into their new household.

'Did you ever imagine we'd be as lucky as to be residing in this household with Aunty Lolo and the rest of the family?' Chidinma put across to her elder sister in a half whisper, still awestruck. 'They are actually very nice folks.' She added before Ngozi could reply.

It was Saturday afternoon. She and her siblings were alone in their room. Their recent change of fortune was surreal and she couldn't live it down without commenting. They've been in Ubi for a fortnight so far.

'There's no doubt that everyone here is nice.' Ngozi agreed before guardedly counselling. 'We must not forget where we came from or our late parents and brothers.' She was determined to ensure that her younger ones wouldn't forget their family or origins in the face of this good fortune. It wasn't like she wasn't appreciative but it was her duty to keep her siblings grounded. She constantly relived the horror of discovering the corpses of her parents and brothers on the street. She was relieved that Chidinma and Ifedi were luckily spared the gruesome sight which continuously haunted her dreams. She intermittently woke up drenched in cold sweats and reliving the horror but was reluctant to share her despair with them. She didn't want to alarm her younger ones with the gruesome details. She used to talk things over with Ola but Ola lived at Obah while they were now in Ubi. She didn't know when or if she would see Ola again. She missed her and their old home. Her deceased family members were a constant in her dreams and mind. She had heard her father evidently bidding her to take care of her siblings on one occasion. His voice was clear as he stated that their care was entrusted to her hands now. She had known it was a dream but the vision had too very vivid as to persuade her of its authenticity. She strongly believed that her father had intentionally appeared to give her the instruction and she was resolved to do him proud. She was therefore avowed to ensuring that they never lose the basic values that their deceased parents had strived to imbibe in them or forget their memory.

'How is it possible for one family to be so affluent and others so poor?' Chidinma pondered aloud and pensively. She stood up from the bed to stride over to the window to survey the surrounding pristine complex. The place was oddly calm and peaceful.

'There is abundance of everything. We can eat as much as we want and there's always plenty left over.' Ifedi chipped in rather immaturely.

'You always perk up when it comes to food.' Chidinma remarked jokingly ruffling his hair as she returned to sit on the bed with her siblings. They were sprawled on the bed while the rest of the family were having siesta. It was a habit that they were yet to adopt or grow accustomed to.

'I didn't imagine that they would actually invite us to sit at the table with them or eat with spoon and fork like oyibo people.' Chidinma continued to exalt their new circumstance.

'Uncle Chief and Madam Lolo are God fearing folk and there is no denying the fact that we are very lucky. My main joy is that we are together. We must stay united and always remember our family.' Ngozi reiterated, reinstating her big sister role.

'I like Aunty Lolo, Aunty Nkiru, Azuka and Uncle Chief but I like Chuka best.' Ifedi announced.

'There is no one here that has not gone out of their way to make us feel welcome. We must be thankful.'

'I say thank you after meals.' Ifedi reaffirmed to prove that he has been kowtowing to plans.

'And so you must,' Ngozi commended with an indulgent smile. 'You should also say please when asking for things.'

'Okay.' He agreed, subsequently heading for the adjoining toilet.

'Aunty Mary is visiting us next month after we must have sat for our entrance exams.' Ngozi informed Chidinma excitedly.

'I miss her. I wonder how she is faring without us. Is she well? Did she get our messages?'

'Of course she did. Emma said she was overjoyed to see him and bombarding him with queries about how we were coping and wishing that we could have come along with him. She was also overjoyed to receive the foodstuffs Emma delivered from Aunty Lolo for her.'

'This family are too kind and I want to be like Aunty Lolo when I grow up.' Chidinma attested. 'I would never have dreamt that we would end up living in a similar mansion like this one, and you?' She persisted in asking Ngozi, keen to know if her elder sister was as equally enchanted. Or else, it was practically impossible for any of them to have envisaged living in such a plush environment or with a kinder family than Chief Ubaka and his entire family.

'Don't get me wrong, I'm happy here too but I'm more concerned about us living up to their expectations. We must do more chores and generally help around the house. I know Aunty Lolo had only stipulated that we must keep our room tidy but we should be more proactive.'

'Do you think that they'll ever change in their attitude towards us?' Chidinma voiced an internal concern. She had often wondered if they'd wake up one morning and everything will be different or disappear just like their parents and brothers had suddenly gone without notice.

'I certainly hope not but we should never take any of these for granted.' Ngozi advised cautiously while gesticulating around the room. 'We must strive to justify this family's trust and make our own parents proud too because we are a reflection of who they were.' She suggested with a maturity ways beyond her age.

'It's not that I don't miss Papa, Mama or our brothers Obinna or Zube but would you say God is making amends for taking them from us by bringing us here?' Chidinma opined gravely.

Ngozi was touched by Chidinma's profound query and paused to contemplate an appropriate reply. She had no prior insight that her younger sister construed their new situation as such. 'I don't think God operates that way,' she finally offered. 'I doubt if God would have taken our parents' and siblings away from us simply so that we can live here. One thing I know for sure though is that God always finds ways to alleviate our pains or suffering which is why we should trust in his mercy at all times. You remember Mama always used to say that.'

'I know. I miss them so much, Mama, Papa, Brother Obinna and Zube.' She whispered tearfully.

'I miss them too.' Ngozi concurred and drew her closer for a brief hug. They were soon struck by Ifedi's long absence. 'Where is Ifedi?'

He had stepped into the toilet awhile ago but had stayed in there far too long unless he left the room without them noticing. She and Chidinma instantaneously heard the toilet flush in answer to her query.

'Ifedi!' They hollered together. He was at it again, twiddling with the toilet flush. They couldn't seem to stop him from his new irksome habit. He was besotted with the water cistern. They consistently warn him to desist from pointlessly flushing the toilet and wasting water. They, notwithstanding also had been equally taken in with the water cistern after they moved here. This was because the toilet system previously known to them was the bucket system.

This consists of a rectangular concrete sheath structure with a central hole on top and with a sizeable bucket underneath serving for collection purposes. It has an exterior outlet or small door to the outside providing access for the '**onye oburu nshi'** or '*crap disposal/night soil man'*. The night soil man usually rolls along with his wooden handcart every fortnight at midnight to empty pre-designated household toilet buckets into the huge drums preloaded on his cart. He would subsequently cart the waste away to a central incinerator. There were isolated incidents of errant kids laying in wait for him. They would subsequently goad him as he carts along his wooden foul smelling laden handcart down the street chanting,

Onye buru nshi, Kedu ihe ina eri?
Obu nshi, obu moi-moi oloko?

Translating to "*night soil carrier what are you eating, faeces and bean cakes?*" The night soil man in turn would daub at them with a broom dipped into the waste and end up littering the street with excrement. The disgusting crappy mess on the streets the next morning usually attests to their delinquency.

Ego, the kids' late mother was meticulously neat and would insist that their private toilet was cleaned no lesser than twice a week with a very potent disinfectant, **Izal** to swath the putrid smell. She would go as far as occasionally asking their elder brothers to empty their bucket if the night soil man was late in coming or their bucket was full ways before he was due to show up. They used to dig a shallow ditch at the back of their quarters opposite the exterior outlet of the toilet to empty the bucket. Their home toilet as a result was fairly decent when they had lived with their parents and brothers. It was a different story however in the short spell that they shared Aunty Mary's place. There were two toilets only to twenty or so tenants in the yard. Each household was mandated to clean the toilet on a weekly rotational basis; however it was a real ordeal to use the toilets by midweek because of the disgusting state.

Ifedi shamefacedly stepped out from their room's en suite bathroom cum toilet. 'What?' He countered rather defensively in answer to the manner in which they had yelled his name.

126

'Didn't I warn you about unnecessarily wasting water?' Ngozi demanded angrily.

'But I had used the toilet,' he protested.

'Did you wash your hands then?'

Ifedi returned to the toilet indicating he hadn't.

'Please close the door after you.' Chidinma ordered sharply, indicating her disgust at the disgusting stench emanating from the open toilet. She covered her nose to minimize the stink.

'You should really watch what you eat. There is no need to drop everything you see into your mouth simply because you have seen food.' Ngozi admonished. Ifedi had left a rather dreadful stench from using their toilet. He was justifiably turning into a glutton given the abundance of food in his new home.

'That's enough now, turn the water off.' Ngozi remonstrated because she guessed Ifedi was running the tap longer than she deemed necessary for a mere hand wash.

There were abundant perks to their new life here and she didn't want any of them to abuse the privilege. They were no longer mandated to rise early at dawn to fetch water out in the streets as was the case in Obah. Most of the rooms in their new home had taps and sinks in adjoining en suite bathrooms and constant water supply. The bore hole dug within the compound and an overhead gigantic water storage tank ensured constant water supply amongst others. The most interesting facet for them was conversely the hot and cold water faucets that actually issued hot or cold water depending on which knob was turned on. They have also been spared the regular incidence of protracted total blackouts, being thrown into pitch darkness or having to resort to utilizing dim kerosene lanterns from moribund or constant electricity power outages. This was circumvented here by the availability of a giant electricity plant housed in a detached little room at a corner of the mansion. The plant was consistently switched on once a central power outage occurs. The relative serenity of their new home and Ubi town was also surreal when they arrived. It wasn't like they missed the flurry of activity that heralded daybreak in their old homes or the normally raucous town of Obah. Ubi was a rather calm quaint little town with all the amenities of a big city and the tranquillity of suburbia.

'I think we should go down and help Ada with preparing dinner.' Ngozi suggested.

'Okay.' Chidinma agreed. 'Aunty Lolo is making a special dish and requires that we attend anyway.' Chidinma informed her sister.

'Let's go down then or we'll be late.' The two contented sisters proceeded downstairs to the kitchen while Ifedi made a detour to find his best buddy, Chuka.

Lolo was already in the kitchen when they arrived. 'Hello girls, I hope you are well rested.'

'Yes, thank you. Good evening Ma.' They both greeted.

'Good evening, Chidinma come give me a hand with this,' she directed, handing her a bowl of vegetables to Chidinma to peel, cut and wash.

'Ngo, come and clean the periwinkle with me.' Azuka invited.

Lolo explained that she was making '*edikaiko*', a *unique vegetable soup* peculiar to a different tribe but adopted by most because of its delicious flavour. It was made from assorted vegetables, seafood including fresh periwinkles and assorted meat parts. Lolo occasionally assumed kitchen duties and liked to invite her daughters and now Ngozi and Chidinma along. She used the oppourtunity to teach or update their culinary skills. In as much as she didn't advocate that a woman's place was in the kitchen, she nonetheless insists that there is no excuse for any woman that couldn't hold her own in the kitchen. Cooking was an inherent feminine attribute; she upholds and as such encouraged her girls to be versatile.

Nkiru was still recuperating in the meantime. She was excused from similar family rendezvous, especially if she were to expresses no personal inclination to join.

Ngozi was a fairly good cook but a couple of dishes were novel to her in her new home. She was therefore keen to learn as was Chidinma. They loved these nurturing sessions with Aunty Lolo as she explained the intricacies of the tasty *edikaiko s*oup.

Lolo had endeavoured to ensure the wellbeing of her new family members after they moved in. She had taken them shopping at Akwaete the previous week and purchased a complete new wardrobe for them.

The kids were also due new school uniforms once their school placement was established. Lolo had originally feared her younger children's, Azuka's and Chuka's reaction when they'd return home on vacation to find strange kids invading their home and privacy but needn't have worried. They had both been in attendance on prior numerous occasions when she and her husband had bandied the idea

128

of having the kids residing with them. Their own kids hadn't contributed much to the discussions nor voiced any disapproval. She and her husband however hadn't necessarily sought their view because their discussions had been of a tentative nature as of then.

Azuka and Ngozi after an initial guardedness were able to establish a firm friendship. The age gap between them was minimal. Chidinma was initially piqued by her sister's budding closeness to Azuka because it has always been the two of them before then. Her sister dutifully made sure that she was incorporated into the new cycle. Azuka actually thought Chidinma's bluntness and chirpy remarks were entertaining.

Chuka had quickly adopted Ifedi under his wing. Boys don't have as much hang-up as girls when it came to same sex relationships or so he liked to tease his sister. Ifedi adored football just as much as he did and had asked to accompany him to the tracks for a game of football the very evening that he returned home from boarding school. When they arrived home later, Ifedi proudly narrated how Chuka had rescued him from the hands of a bully who was picking on him at the tracks.

Lolo was reassured thereafter that her newly expanded family unit will thrive cohesively but not everyone shared their joy naturally.

Mgbeke, who had previously vowed to vacate the household if the "OSU kids" were to permanently move in, lived up to her words. No sooner had they moved in than she packed up her bags and informed Madam Lolo that she was quitting. She maintained that she wouldn't sleep under the same roof with Osus because of her superstitious convictions. She predicted a greater calamity would befall the household for harbouring them.

Lolo reckoned Mgbeke's departure was good riddance. She had always had it in mind to discharge the girl after overhearing her badmouthing her family. Somehow she had gotten sidetracked and her time overtaken by more pressing issues that she had neglected to dismiss her. She was therefore thrilled when Mgbeke voluntarily quit and happily paid her off.

The Ubaka kinsmen's reaction to the kids' arrival was another highlight. Nnanyi and the elders who had journeyed out of town to consult with the Oracle of Okirikiri returned after a successful atonement session and re-consecration of the effigy at Ogbani. Next up was the sacrifices to revoke Nkiru's tied tongue or so they thought. They reconvened at Chief Ubaka's home the same evening to report their trip and convince him to relinquish his daughter for the crucial rituals guaranteed to loosen her tongue. A few had gotten wind of the new development prior to arriving at Chief Ubaka's abode and were clearly knocked for six. They could hardly believe that Chief Ubaka had actually invited OSU kids to reside in his household in spite the tribulations that had transpired. It seemed to them that he was wilfully playing with fire or adding salt to injury so to say.

'Welcome my people,' Chief Ubaka greeted, after his guests settled in his spacious downstairs sitting room. There was an unmistakeable gloom and discomfort to their visit on this occasion.

'Thank you, Okam.' Nnanyi replied in a rather subdued voice. He was frankly exasperated with Chief Ubaka's insolence and completely clueless as to how to address the latest transgression.

'Kola nut has arrived.' Chief Ubaka announced cheerily as if nothing was amiss as he passed a platter containing kola nuts, garden eggs and ornamental small knife to his elder kinsman.

Nnanyi accepted the plate from him and wearily stood. He started to intone unenthusiastically. 'He who brings kola brings life. Let the kite perch and let the eagle perch but any of them that prevents the other from perching, should have his wings fail him. That is how we do things. True?'

'True.' The others chorused half-heartedly and equally disillusioned.

'We pray for good fortune for both ourselves and our enemies for when their minds are joyous, they have less desire to plot evil against us. True?'

'True.' They others echoed again.

'My people, I pray your lives and mine be prolonged and enriched.'

'*Ise, Amen.*' They chorused.

He broke the kola nuts into bits and passed on the platter for the others to share the kola nut and garden eggs.

'I hope your journey was fruitful.' Chief Ubaka started after they had settled into an uncomfortable silence.

'Mmh ....mmh,' Nnanyi cleared his throat. 'Our journey went well but I'll be lying if I say I'm impressed by this latest development. Okam my dear younger brother I will be failing in my duties if I neglect to point out that one is purposely asking for trouble when they start applying ear drops intended for the ears into the eyes.' His discontentment tendered plainly in the adage. 'We were in the process of controlling your prior damage but you've endangered everything by this singular act. If I didn't know any better I'll guess that evil spirits and our enemies are using you as a tool to taunt us.' Nnanyi charged, making no pretences of hiding his very obvious disenchantment.

'I'll pretend not to have heard your last remark,' Chief Ubaka stated in subtle admonition. 'Nnanyi I respect and cherish your counsel. I also appreciate your concern and efforts; however I hope you can respect my right to run my own household.' He stated, reasserting his authority and leaving no room for further discussions on the matter of his new residents.

'*Onwu egbuna dike*, I think we've both had our say. A word is enough for the wise. As for me, I'm too old for this.' Nnanyi stated resignedly indicating he had reached the end of his tether.

'My people, I must take my leave now. Okam, I wish your household well.' Nnanyi so saying struggled to his feet, picking up his two walking sticks and hobbled out of the room in a huff. Most of the elders rose in support and the group solemnly walked out of Chief Ubaka's residence.

'My dear brother,' Chief Ume, Chief Ubaka's younger brother started soon afterwards. He, along with a handful stayed behind after the majority departed with Nnanyi. 'You must understand Nnanyi's anger. I don't think that he meant any harm.'

'Of course I understand he is aggrieved but that is not to say that he can insult me in my own home.' Chief Ubaka retorted angrily.

'This is a big mess. We must find a way to broker a peaceful resolution.' His brother pleaded.

'I don't see what the problem is really. If I refuse to be drawn into his fallacy that shouldn't give him the right to insult me. I don't owe him or anyone else any explanations or apologies.'

'*Onwu egbuna dike*,' one of the remaining elders hailed Chief Ubaka. 'Our people have a peculiar way of doing things. I'm not trying to pass judgement here but certain situations call for a little more decorum than others. No one knows what tomorrow will bring and I hate to think that both of you might require each other's help in the future and this little disagreement would have ruined your bond. We can all agree to disagree without fostering bad blood.'

'I'm not sure why you are laying the blame on me. I didn't insult Nnanyi. On the contrary he was discourteous in the manner in which he had addressed me.' Chief Ubaka complained petulantly.

'I'm sure neither of you intended to insult the other but that is not the bone of contention now.' Chief Ume continued to play a good arbitrator. 'We must keep in mind that we are family and what affects one, affects the other. We should not let this minor contention escalate to such a point that it disintegrates our bond as a family or our kinship.'

'I've heard you and thanks for your words. I agree that I might have been harder on Nnanyi than I should have. I'll try to see him to make amends.' Chief Ubaka conceded ruefully.

'**Onwu egbuna dike**, you are a great man indeed. It takes a strong man to admit he has erred. Please approach Nnanyi as soon as possible.' Another elder praised his mea culpa.

'My people, I thank you again. We had neglected to discuss the full details of your trip but I hope all went well.'

'It went well but I suppose we'll leave the rest of the discussions until we can congregate as one unit again.' Another recommended.

'That is fine, Ume we shall see Nnanyi tomorrow.' Chief Ubaka told his brother. The guests departed shortly afterwards.

Chief Ubaka set off with his brother Chief Ume the next day to visit Nnanyi. They took a bottle of gin along to offer in pacification. It was rather busy at Nnanyi's household when they arrived. The elderly kinsman was supervising the renovation of his '**Owu**' masquerade in readiness for the forthcoming '**Owu**' dance festival.

Chief Ubaka and his brother by the virtue of their strong religious affiliations had renounced their right to commission Owu masquerades. They would have been preoccupied with or delegated similar duties at present. The festival was impending following the New Yam Festival.

Nnanyi took time off overseeing the adornment of his masquerade to attend to his new guests.

'**Nno nu**, Welcome, I hope you have come well.' He greeted adjusting his wrapper as he rose by tightening the end folds of his loose draping wrapper, crisscrossing the ends and folding them into a huge knot before tucking the knot firmly underneath the middle fold. He hobbled down leading them to his '**obi eze**' (throne/*central lounge)* to sit. Nnanyi's *obi eze* occupied the length of his rectangular shaped family homestead. The area was spacious and open with a separated central throne and elevated concrete cast seats on either side of it. The walls were adorned with specially preserved whole lion hide at the centre. The lion had been dissected such that its entrails were removed and subsequently nailed to the wall as if it were prostrating. The lion as the king of the forest also symbolized Nnanyi's rank of office. There were also masks; various other animal skins and decorative mats gilding the rest of the wall. They were all representative of his eminence and stature.

'We've come in peace and have also brought you a drink.' Chief Ubaka responded handing over the bottle of Gordon Gin to Nnanyi before taking a seat on the elevated concrete cast seats covered with decorative mats

'Thank you very much.' Nnanyi acknowledged his gesture and requiring no extra prompt to grasp the connotation of the peace offering.

'Nnanyi, *onye eji eje mba*,' Chief Ubaka hailed him. 'I ask you not to take offence. I should not have spoken to you in the manner that I did yesterday, please forgive me.'

'It is fine. I accept your apology. It takes a greater man to admit that he has erred so I commend you Okam. We are one family and one blood. We can fight but make up without harbouring malice. Blood is thicker than water.'

'Thank you Nnanyi. I think we'll take our leave now. We don't want to distract you from your work.' Chief Ubaka hurriedly recommended, keen to beat a hasty retreat.

'The masquerade can wait besides the children can take care of it, there is no rush. You must break kola nut with me before you leave. That is how we do things.' Nnanyi insisted and subsequently raised his voice to call out loudly. 'Oyibonanu, Oyibonanu are you there? Foolish woman,' He muttered the latter under his breath. 'Didn't you see that we have eminent visitors to bring kola nuts or must I come chasing after you?' He was addressing one of his numerous wives on duty for the day.

The referenced Oyibonanu soon appeared, hurrying and bearing a slightly damp saucer with kola nut and knife. 'Nnanyi, please don't crucify me.' She apologized to her irritated husband. '*Ndi nwem, my owners*,' she turned to address Chief Ubaka and his brother, genuflecting at the same time. 'Please forgive me. *Nno nu, welcome*. I was trying to find a decent enough plate to present the kola nut. You are no ordinary visitors.' She explained.

'Give me the kola nut before you continue with your foolish excuses.' Nnanyi chastised before grabbing the saucer impatiently from her. 'My people, kola nut have come. Kola nut signifies life and what we desire is an abundance of good health and long life.'

'*Ise*, Amen.' Chief Ubaka and his brother chorused.

Nnanyi broke the kola nut in small bits after chanting more incantations and prayers. They shared the kola nuts before Chief Ubaka and his brother rose to depart. The subject of OSU kids residing in Chief Ubaka's home was not broached but he knew it was only a matter of time before the topic would rear its ugly head up again. In the meantime he was quite happy to keep the matter under wraps.

Azuka, Ngozi, Chidinma, Chuka and Ifedi were ready to depart for the village arena to take in the Owu dance festival the following week.

Nkiru had declined to accompany them. She was on the mend and gradually making progress with regaining her full health and strength. There were evidently a lot of talks and speculations regarding her recent breakthrough in town.

Her unrepentant kinsmen and villagers attributed her revival to the appeasement rituals that they had initiated. They insisted that there was no way she could have recovered her speech if they hadn't completed those appeasement rituals, albeit she hadn't attended the special anointment before the oracles that they formerly touted was crucial. Neither Nkiru nor her parents cared much for the rumours or improbable validation. A special miracle had been bestowed upon them by the mercy of God Almighty.

It was by his Grace that she had broken through and was recuperating. Her parents regretted their lapse in parlaying to tradition once again. They planned to host a special thanksgiving mass service to offer thanks to Lord at the church once Nkiru was considerably stronger.

'You're really going to enjoy watching the Owu masquerades dance. They are very delightful.' Azuka propped up the festival to her expectant group. They were getting set to leave for the village section of their small town to take in the celebrations.

She, Chuka, Ngozi, Chidinma and Ifedi were almost ready and waiting for the driver to ferry them down there. Ngozi and her younger siblings had never attended a similar festival because the Owu ceremony was peculiar only to the town and people of Ubi.

'What does this festival denote? 'Ngozi enquired.

'I'm not sure exactly,' Azuka admitted. 'But it coincides with the new yam festival.' The New Yam festival commemorates the harvesting of new yams and heralds the end of annual farming season.

'Is there a link between the two then?'

'I suppose so. The masquerades are bespoke by titled men who had lost their father's and must also fulfil a variety of criteria including obtaining the all important "*oshi iji*" "title or "*cooking of yam*" title amongst others.'

'We know the new yam season, that's when the yam starts to taste a bit funny and Mama always said those are new yam.' Chidinma quipped.

'That is true; I don't think I care much for new yam myself. They are not particularly delicious. ' Azuka agreed.

'So does anything else go on besides the dances?' Ngozi persisted in wanting to learn more details of this new culture.

'Not that I know of but the dances are hosted annually in all the village arenas. I don't know if anything else goes on behind closed doors because we only ever watch the dance.'

'The festival holds for only a day?'

'No,' Chuka took over the narration from his sister and went on to explain further. 'It spans over four days. The masquerades dance and perform at specified arenas in all the 27 villages of Ubi for same duration. They are donned by designated young men who wear peculiar masks and head gears while the body of the masquerade is swathed in lace and 'George' materials.' He demonstrated with a sweep of hands across the length of his body. 'They also wear special beads on their feet that resonate to the beat of the drums when they dance, augmenting the dance and melody like this.' Chuka imitated the jingly dance step by standing on his toes and jiggling forward to the amusement of the others. 'I wish Dad was commissioning masquerades still so I can wear his Owu masquerade.'

'I thought it is prohibited to say masquerades are donned by humans. We say spirits.' Ngozi reproached Chuka.

'No, Owu masquerades are different. They are more like fun masquerades but we also have formidable masquerades like the **Udebube**. Those are definitely worn by 'spirits'. We wouldn't dare to venture out in the streets when he is out performing. Only those initiated to the "spirit world" are allowed anywhere close to him. The Owu masquerades in contrast belong to individual titled men. These men have lost their fathers in the first instance, been initiated into the *spirit world* or '*Ikwa mmo*' and subsequently acquired various titles including the key title of '*oshi iji*' (*cooking of yam*) 'Azuka explained.

135

'Only then are they are bestowed with the right to own or commission an *Owu* masquerade.' Chuka added.

'How come Uncle Chief doesn't commission an Owu masquerade since he fulfils the criteria?' Chidinma queried curiously.

'Dad and Uncle Ume too gave up their rights because the church frowns on fetish tradition.' Azuka explained.

'But what you just described sounds like harmless fun and shouldn't necessarily conflict with the church.' Ngozi opined.

'I don't really know if more goes on behind closed doors than we know. Dad and mummy comes along to watch sometimes but it has been a while though since either of them accompanied us to the arena.'

'I can't wait to see the masquerades.' Ifedi uttered excitedly and started to imitate the dance that Chuka had demonstrated.

'Us too,' His sisters agreed.

'Let's go, Emma is here.' Azuka suggested after she spied the car revving up at the driveway. 'I promise you won't be disappointed.' Azuka gave her word.

The group arrived at the village area with Emma, their driver and chaperone for the day. They were lucky to find any parking slot given the huge crowd and vehicles that had assembled to watch the proceedings. They headed for their particular village arena, already encircled by an animated crowd. A group of drummers sat behind distinctive sets of hefty drums within the enclosure. They were vigorously thumping the unique dance tempo while one Owu masquerade was led into the centre after another to perform their characteristic energetic dance routine.

'Do they actually compete against each other?' Ngozi whispered loudly into Azuka's ears as they watched the enthralling dance nodding their heads along with the beat.

'I doubt it. We seldom attend the full run but I haven't heard of any trophy being awarded at the end.' She shouted in reply amidst the surrounding din. 'Never mind but we can ask Mum for the full details when we return home.'

Some members of the crowd were actually identifying the masquerades by their unique family insignia that they bore on their headgear. They also discussed which was better adorned, performed most gracefully or commended the fellows behind the mask.

Azuka and Chuka had always enjoyed the performances and it was no different on this occasion. Their entourage shared their enthusiasm as they banged their heads to the beat or applauded the performances. They soon opted to stroll across to an alternative nearby village arena after noticing the few odd glances directed their way from some of the congregated village crowd.

Strange women whom Azuka could swear that she had never met in her life tucked at her sleeves to brazenly interrogate, if those were the kids?' She didn't bother to dignify their query with a reply but glared at them. She subsequently suggested that they left for a neighbouring village arena.

Her parents had recently sat all of them down for a series of chats pertaining to OSU diatribe. They had also patiently and dutifully explained their cumbersome legacy to Ngozi, Chidinma and Ifedi. They had assured them that it was only a societal tag and didn't define them or their character. They were God's children and all humans are equal in the eyes of the Lord. It was doubtful to what extent Ifedi had comprehended the explanations but the couple promised to have further talks with him as he gets older. His siblings were also urged to approach them without hesitations if they were in any doubts.

Azuka personally was no stranger to the concept because she had virtually relived the concept with her family. She had also been a direct witness to her sister's tribulation and recent events. She had been forced to acknowledge that there was really no tangible basis for the ludicrous concept and felt protective towards Ngozi and her siblings whom she considered as full fledged family members. She therefore shepherded them towards the jagged alleyway after notifying Emma of their new plans.

He was actually supposed to chaperone then but had joined his boisterous mates at a drinking joint. They were completely safe, he deemed. The people of Ubi knew and were protective of each other. They agreed to meet him back at the joint whenever they were ready to leave.

Azuka and the others proceeded through the market stalls which ordinarily served as fish market during the day or non festive periods. It was situated right opposite the lake which ran across the expanse of the twenty seven tiny villages of the town of Ubi. These villages are situated in what was known as the older and original settlement of their founding fathers. Their Ubaka family mansion was located at the new settlement district of the town but kindred home at their village site.

'Come, come, aren't you Okam's kids?' They heard a woman ask, drawing Azuka closer to her by the arm. 'How are you?'

It was Nwakego, a distant relative of theirs. Azuka could vaguely recognize her from a few times that she had visited their home.

'Good afternoon, Aunty.' Azuka greeted respectfully, unable to recollect her name. The woman was blocking their way and also staring candidly at Ngozi and her siblings.

'Those are the kids eh, Come here.' She ordered letting go of Azuka and grabbing Ngozi by the elbow instead. She peered directly into her eyes.

Nwakego had heard like the rest of the town about their arrival to Ubi. She had also spotted them on a few occasions but from afar, never in a similar close proximity as present.

She had perceived an odd empathy towards them and had gone home perturbed and unable to sleep through the night after the first time that she had caught sight of them. She couldn't fathom her unusual restlessness or why she should be perturbed by the presence of these strange kids. She had contemplated consulting the local clairvoyant but gave up the thought after much consideration. It would be entirely ill-contrived and wasteful since she had no ample reason for her anxiety. What was she going to say to the clairvoyant? That she felt disturbed by the presence of the OSU kids living with Chief Ubaka's or what? She had asked herself.

She could well understand the quandary faced by them after the multiple deaths of their parents and brothers as well as their legacy of a demeaning tag especially at such tender ages. She could also empathize with them regarding their presumed awkwardness in relocating and moving in with strangers but the fact remains that they were considerably better off than the average population. They were now residing in a rich man's house after all. Chief Ubaka and his wife were not the type to unjustifiably maltreat anyone much less kids that they had voluntarily adopted. Those are lucky kids if anything, she conceded with hindsight

Her private take on Chief Ubaka's decision to bring them into his home was guarded. She believed that he had overstepped conventional boundaries by his action. He must have foreseen the potential public outrage as well as repercussions given what had happened with their parents. She would have expected Chief Ubaka to help the kids without necessarily moving them over to Ubi. It wasn't very prudent on his part to trifle with the gods.

Nwakego also bought into the majority consensus that stipulated that the untimely demise of Obinna and his family were reprisals from the gods. Yes, armed robbers, police and the like commit heinous crimes, she had cogitated. But then, rarely would they have slaughtered an entire family in the manner in which the unfortunate lad and his family were murdered. The gods definitely had a hand in it, she was positively swayed. Whatever the case might be but what was her business in the whole drama, she countered her odd foreboding. She'd always kept her counsel unless it was explicitly sought for so decided not to get her pants twisted in a knot over something that was none of her business in the first instance. She had resolved in a bid to calm her nagging conscience.

The next occasion when she had noticed them again was also from a distance and the same feeling of disquiet had gripped her. Her anxiety was heightened further after she had a revelation of her long vanished recurrent dream on the same night. The static picture of a river and a basket of fish at the shores were re-enacted once more. She couldn't recall the last time that she seen the recurrent apparition that had haunted her from childhood until not so distant past. She remembered narrating this worryingly persistent vision to her mother. Her mother's reaction to her disclosure was even more baffling. She seemed shocked to hear the details as if the apparition denoted a particular personal significance to her but she had refused to explain the import when Nwakego insisted on knowing. Her mother assured her it wasn't important but then had heard her weeping through most nights afterwards. Nwakego had pleaded with her mother to tell her what the matter was but she refused. She subsequently promised to explain everything when Nwakego becomes more mature. That was not to be because her mother had taken ill almost immediately. She had been coughing out blood for a long time and the herbal medications she received from the native doctors weren't helping. Her husband ferried her to distant lands and to consult with the Oracles at Okirikiri but she didn't survive her illness. She was near death by the time the priests at the Oracles advised that she'd be taken home because her illness was too far gone and the gods wanted to welcome her home. It was best for her to die in the comfort of her own home. She barely lasted longer than an hour after she was brought home. She never got around to explaining the dream to Nwakego before she died, taking her secret with her to the grave. Nwakego was about ten or thereabouts at the time but the dream had persisted long after her mother's death. It only started to dwindle in frequency after she was married and vanished completely in the last ten years or so, only to be revived by the appearance of these kids.

Nwakego peered closely into Ngozi's face while Ngozi glared back at her in return, astonished by her bizarre conduct. There was an odd familiarity about her though, Ngozi reflected before swiftly freeing her arm from Nwakego's hold. The woman strangely resembled her mother; she pondered but immediately banished the thought from her mind. A very odd coincidence really and a very weird woman indeed, she decided.

It was the eyes of Oroma, Nwakego's mother that she saw staring back at her from Ngozi's face, even her deceased mothers left eye scar was replicated on Ngozi's face as was her prominent black mole reproduced at the same exact corner of Ngozi's nose just like it had been on her mother's face.

'*Ewo* oh!' My mother!' Nwakego exclaimed, staggering back in shock and folding her arms across her chest as she stared agape and in shock.

Azuka and her group gaping at her and wondering if Nwakego had suddenly gone barmy because they couldn't understand what was going on with her to warrant such her exclamation.

'Come on let's go, Aunty we are on our way.' Azuka politely told Nwakego before hurriedly steering them away from the seemingly crazy woman.

Nwakego stood rooted to the same spot as they hurriedly departed and stared at their retreating backs, confused as to the meaning of this phantom that she had just witnessed. The kids on their part were no longer inclined to attending the neighbouring village's arena as they had initially planned but turned back to return home. Their appetite for more entertainment was soured besides they've had enough excitement for one day.

As for Nwakego, she headed straight back home after recovering from her initial shock and resolving to get to the bottom of the matter. She quickly extricated a roll of cash from her savings stashed in an old canister piggy bank which she kept hidden in a hole underneath the surface beneath her cupboard. She firmly secured the cash by rolling them up at the tip of her inner wrapper before making a knot to secure the cash. She was determined to unravel this riddle by consulting with the local clairvoyant once and for all.

140

'Nwakego, Oroma's daughter, the legs that brought you here are good ones. Come in and sit down.' The clairvoyant invited as she was ushered into his shrine by possibly his grandson.

The very elderly clairvoyant was seated on a mat on the floor surrounded by different beads and cowry shells, the room smelt of incense and other fragrances that she couldn't exactly discern.

'Odimegwu Dike, It shall be well with you.' She returned as she arched her trunk to pass through the stumpy entrance into the small room crammed with an assortment of wooden carvings and paraphernalia. She stood momentarily confused as her eyes adjusted to the dim light and wondered where she was supposed to sit considering that there was scarcely enough room left in the space with all the stuff cramming the room.

'It shall be well with you too my daughter, sit down there.' He indicated, patting a little space on the mat opposite him.

Nwakego sat down on the mat as indicated before elevating her head to meet with his piercing chalk encircled raccoon like eyes. Odimegwu Dike was very old now, possibly in his nineties or hundred years as the rumours went. He was rarely seen in public nowadays. He tended to spend most of his time in this private shrine. Nwakego had last consulted him a couple of years back when her husband had unexpectedly taken ill. The herbs and concoction he had brewed for her husband was very effective.

'Your dead mother has been trying to contact you,' He stated before Nwakego could explain her mission. 'She has been agitating to impact a secret to you for ages so it is good that you've finally decided to heed to her call.'

Nwakego was startled and marvelled at how he could have read her mind but this was Odimegwu Dike. His reputation precedes him; he was a powerful soothsayer.

'*Ewu* Oh! Odimegwu Dike, I knew that if any one can help me unravel this riddle that it would be you. That is why I came.' Nwakego told him.

The clairvoyant drew three lines in the bare floor in his front, reached out to unhook a set of beads from the wall and jingled it across the lines three times. He shook his head, bit into a piece of kola nut and spat the debris unto the lines while Nwakego watched. 'Drop your fee on the plate,' He ordered without specifying any amount.

Nwakego untied her wad from her inner wrapper and placed half into the small white platter at his front. Odimegwu reached for a second set of beads and rattled them across her head before drawing another set of lines.

'It's all coming back to me. This is a long story and long overdue to be told and heard.' He stated as he reached for the smallest keg that Nwakego had ever set her eyes on and drank from it.

Nwakego could easily vouch that the potion was more potent than ordinary palm wine judging from his abrupt transformation.

The juju man became instantaneously dazed and started to sway his head back and forth. His eyes rolled back into his socket until all the black had disappeared leaving only the white. He proceeded to chant in a different voice. It was the familiar voice of her dead mother, Oroma that Nwakego heard like she was sat right opposite her.

'My daughter, thanks for coming today. I knew my soul would not find peace until I got this secret off my chest. I was not sure you were mature enough to handle the truth before my time came up. As you well know, your father married many wives. I was very young when he married me and he meant everything to me because both of my parents had died early. I was also his favourite wife. I was therefore overjoyed to conceive my first pregnancy soon afterwards. Everyone was commenting on the growth of my protruding tummy which was rapidly growing larger but I was too overjoyed to care. Let my baby grow big after all your father was a successful farmer. I was revelling wholly in the baby nestling inside my womb. Your father used to tease that I was secretly consuming all the food from the farm because of the size of my belly. I was happy and unaffected by anything anyone else had to say but my joy was short-lived when I delivered two boys at the same time. We immediately buried them without telling anyone and announced my baby had died at childbirth. How could a god that gives one womb, place two children inside it? It was a big curse and abomination. It was not something that one could openly admit in public. We buried my babies hoping that was the end of my ill luck but my subsequent pregnancy also yielded two boys at the same time. It was a big blow and I couldn't understand why the gods were singling me out to punish in such a cruel manner. Not once but on two consecutive occasions. I had to bury four infants in a similar fashion which broke my heart. Your father was also steadily becoming disillusioned with my situation.

I travelled far and wide seeking for answers. I travelled to the distant land of Ogadaga to consult with powerful Oracles. I followed all the instructions that I received to the book and made all necessary sacrifices stipulated hoping to put pay to my run of ill luck. I couldn't rid this curse however or stop whoever was bewitching me. Fingers were pointed at a number of people including your father's first wife because of her inability to produce an heir but after she finally delivered a boy before my third pregnancy, I hoped that she would have relaxed and let me be but lo and behold, I was pregnant with two again. My step wives also started to denounce and call me a witch. Your father refused to come to my bed or eat from my plate after my third set of twins, a boy and girl. His disenchantment with me elated the other wives because they always felt he gave me preferential treatment. It was a wonder that they didn't succeed in making him eject me from my matrimonial home. I was desolate and pleaded with your father to reconsider my situation after he avoided me for a whole year.

I cried and begged for another chance and he finally relented and as the gods would have it, I fell pregnant instantly. I was very happy and couldn't have imagined that there would be another chance of me bearing twins. Surely there must be a righteous god out there somewhere? I soon noticed that one quarter of the way gone, I was beginning to balloon as was the case with my previous pregnancies. I couldn't believe that the gods could be so punitive nor could I understand what crime I had committed in the past to warrant such spite from them. I was initially disconsolate but soon resolved to take matters into my own hands. I was determined to elevate my head in my husband's home, enough was enough?

I couldn't take the ribbing any longer, not the ridicule or names from my fellow step wives and strangers alike. They claimed that I was a witch which was why all my children died at childbirth. The barren Chiaku, the middle wife of your father openly declared she was better off. I was perturbed because I was no witch, nor was I barren.

I had to resort to trickery and conceived a plan before going to appeal to your father to allow me leave home. I sought his permission to stay with my good friend and customer Nwanyioma who lives across the lake to ensure a stress free delivery and he luckily agreed. Nwanyioma was the only soul that knew my secret. She was fearful that if her own people were to find out the truth about my pregnancy that they would banish both of us but she took a chance and agreed to help me. I was very ill before my delivery. I became swollen all over and couldn't keep anything down. I feared that both I and my unborn kids would die from my trickery. The gods were angry. Nwanyioma tried to convince me to go to the white people's hospital. She had a pregnant friend who was very ill but they saved her. I refused initially but after I nearly passed out, she rushed me there. I remember the two very nice oyibo women who spoke through their nose and shrouded their hair with a blue veil helped to deliver my two lovely daughters and also saved my life. The woman translating for us informed us that they were keen to keep my two babies or take one off my hands. They condemned our practice of disposing abominable twins. They alleged that we were wrong to think that delivering two babies at the same time was an abomination. Twins were a blessing from their God and an absolutely normal phenomenon, they claimed but what do they know? I couldn't understand their logic because the gods gave a woman one womb, just one so how would they then implant two babies into this one womb. I'm sure we would have more than one womb if the gods desired for us to have more than one baby at a time. That is what differentiates us from animals but these *oyibos'* have very strange philosophies. I was grateful that they had helped save my life but it was my choice to defy the gods. I didn't want any of the women who had recognised Nwanyioma when we arrived at the hospital to think that we abandoned a baby in the hospital so declined their offer to take one baby off our hands. I had to certify that word never gets back to your father that I had two instead of one girl.

We requested to be discharged from the hospital at midnight a few days later. The women were a bit suspicious but we assured them that your father and I had agreed to escape and relocate to a safer place where we could raise our children in peace. They were not entirely convinced we were telling the truth but Nwanyioma managed to convince them, I was too weak and tired to argue with them. They queried why your father hadn't shown up to visit at the hospital but I lied that he was preparing for our escape otherwise they would have threatened to take both of my babies away from me. They reluctantly discharged us but showered us with gifts and money to help us set up a supposedly new home but I left everything with Nwanyioma. She had done me a huge favour as it were. I still knew that there was no way I could return home with two daughters. Your father and our town's people will have all our heads so I was left with the difficult task of selecting one daughter over the other.

It completely broke my heart to have to choose one daughter over another but I had to make the difficult choice. I tied a scarf across my eyes and resolved that which ever baby I stumbled unto first was the one that I'll keep. As faith would have it I stumbled unto you first. I didn't have the heart to bury another live kid so I left you with Nwanyioma and carried my other daughter away. I rose early the next morning before the cock crow to trek all the way to Obana River. I was hoping to lay my baby in a safe place where a stranger was sure to stumble unto her and hopefully take her home before crocodiles devour her. I didn't have it in me to bury another live kid with my own bare hands again. I noticed a lone fisherman out in his canoe when I drew near the river. He had left a container of baiting worms and a basket full of fish very near to the shore with his clothes. I laid my baby wrapped warmly with two wrappers between his basket of fish and the container. I took one last look at my baby and she stared back at me very melancholically as if she understood that I was abandoning her but never as much as uttered a whimper. She sensed my desertion but was accepting of it at the same time. I felt like dying at that moment. I retreated behind the bushes and watched until the fisherman stepped out of the water. There was no way that I'd have left without knowing if he would rescue her.

The fisherman was relatively calm on stepping ashore and seeing the baby. He shouted for the person that had left the baby and ran into the bushes asking for the owner of the baby to appear. He continued calling out and waiting for the owner of the baby to step up for a moment. I lay crouching in the bushes watching him. At one point he had stepped so close that I could touch his feet if I had dared to stretch out my hand but he luckily didn't spot me. He waited for a period and when no one appeared, started to gather his belongings together to depart. My heart was thumping heavily as I waited and watched his every move. He fortunately acted contrary to my expectations because I had dreaded that he might drop my baby into the river to drown or leave her behind. However he amazingly turned back to pick her up from the floor after cycling a few meters. He stood gazing at her for a moment before he finally rode away in his bicycle carrying the baby along with him. It was a wonder that he didn't catch me because I had stood up to go to my baby after he rode away the first time. I knew then that my daughter would be safe. I returned to Nwanyioma's home and took you back home to show your father my new daughter.

Odimegwu Dike collapsed to the floor like a rattled doll when the eerie narration concluded. He crumbled to the floor as if the mortal possessing his body was cast out as soon as the recital ended. He was exhausted and respired heavily to recover his breath as Nwakego watched.

She was speechless after hearing the confessional narration. Her mother was virtually invoked in the soothsayer to personally narrate this uncanny tale to her. She was a twin. No wonder she always felt inexplicably incomplete like a part of her was missing. She had never actually been able to pinpoint the significance until now. Her people had long realized that giving birth to twins was certainly a natural phenomenon. It was considered an abomination in the past and twins or multiple childbirths were immediately disposed of to avoid incurring the wraths of the gods.

Okay, wait a minute; she was momentarily jolted into another reality. It means that those kids living with Chief Ubaka are her twin sister's kids. That was why she felt the odd connection to them and why the elder child was a spitting image of her mother, Oroma reincarnated with her exact scar and birth marks in place.

Nwakego's heart was racing with a multitude of thoughts and ideas as she tried to tie up all the missing links. Oh God, what a delightful coincidence and what folly? She had been castigating her own sister's kids because of a nonsensical traditional concept. Those kids were her own flesh and blood, her own sister's kids! She repeated in wonderment and was suddenly geared towards rushing to their aid. She felt like a mama bear swiftly sensing her cubs were imperil.

'That is the story.' Odimegwu Dike's voice broke into her trance. 'The Osu kids are your twin sister's children.' He confirmed her apparent deduction.

.

Eight

'Praise to the Lord!'

'Alleluia.'

'Praise to the Lord!'

'Alleluia.' Nkiru responded again with tightly shut eyes and standing upright, hands bound together in supplication.

Uche was leading the prayers and also assuming similar posture to Nkiru. 'We give you praise, Almighty Father for we stand humbled in thy sight. We offer our gratitude and praise, oh Lord. You are the alpha and the omega, the beginning and the end. Father we give you all the glory. We thank you again Lord for your daughter Nkiru who stands before thee, Father. We praise your name and uphold your might dear Lord Jesus Christ. She is a true testimony of your power.' Uche intoned, raising her right hand up in deep fervour. 'We thank you, Father for restoring her health and confirming that our faith and trust are never misplaced when we place them in your hands. Lord Jesus, the omnipotent Father who never fails, we give you thanks and praise.'

'Amen.'

'Our Father, who hath in... ... ...

They were in Nkiru's room. Uche was both a neighbour and friend but they weren't particularly close irrespective of hailing from the same town and having attended the same alma mater. She was all the same delighted to see Uche when she had visited and started to frequent her home. They always shared prayers whenever Uche turns up.

Nkiru had also been surprised by Uche's changed appearance after they met for the first time after a rather prolonged interlude. Their last meeting if she wasn't mistaken was shortly after their graduation ceremony. They hadn't maintained constant contact afterwards. It wasn't like she's been sociable in any case since Obinna's death and her consequent illness. She was especially delighted to have Uche's company while recuperating especially as she rarely entertained too many visitors lately. It wasn't however the old Uche that had turned up but a transformed beyond belief new girl.

'Welcome Uche, I'm very happy to see you again.' She remembered welcoming her initially.

'Thank you Nkiru. I had visited a couple of times but I think you didn't notice.' Uche had asserted.

'I'm sorry dear but it was never intentional on my part to have ignored you.' Nkiru had apologized.

'I understand but God is faithful. I'm happy to see you looking more like your old self again. I was praying for you all the time.' Uche admitted.

'Thank you and I'm really glad to see you too.'

'I always knew you'd recover. It was just a matter of time because God never forsakes his children. I bring good news too; I am born again. I hope we can share prayers.' Uche had intimated her excitedly.

'Certainly,' Nkiru agreed, though pondered if Uche had mentioned prayers and being "born again" in the same breath? 'You are born again?' She had repeated incredulously. Did she hear her right since Uche was a notorious party animal and self proclaimed atheist during their undergraduate days? She used to publicly denounce all things religious. Yet here she was proclaiming herself to be born again, Nkiru marvelled while trying to get around the fact that this was same lady.

Uche is very pretty and ebony black with an enviable hourglass body shape or "figure '8' as they usually likened her curvy type shape. She also tended to wear garments intended to maximally accentuate or show off her enviable curves which explained her former previous famous peculiar penchant for T-shirts or skimpy tops on tight fitting jeans. Nkiru was therefore stunned to see her not only wearing scruffy looking pairs of shoes but also dowdy ill-fitting long gown and scarf tied sternly around her hair in place of her classic long braids. This was an astounding overall makeover from the Uche that was known to her.

'Yes my sister oh, I'm born again and my life is solely dedicated to serving the good Lord.' Uche had proclaimed joyfully. 'I hope you can come to my church and witness the miracles that could be bestowed upon you.' She beseeched. 'My pastor would want to see and pray for you too, I've told him all about you.'

Nkiru was surprised to say the least and somewhat amused by Uche's words because they sounded weird coming from her, any one else but Uche. She pondered still reeling in disbelief. Uche's new attitude was a complete turnaround from her old self. Nkiru marvelled at her drastic fashion sense change but more spectacularly at her new mind-set. The makeover was even more implausible considering that Uche was an audacious, self-confessed atheist. She was always very outspoken about her religious views or rather lack of one and would

148

brashly declare non-alliance to any specific religious denomination. She snubbed religious fanatics and would continually denounce them, bragging she had no patience for religious fallacies or fantasists. That was until recently then.

'So what happened? What prompted you to become born again?' Nkiru had enquired curiously.

'I was at the right place at the right time.' Uche had answered rather mysteriously in her newly adopted mellower tone of voice. 'I have to say I was in the dark all along until my timely salvation. My sister at a point you just have to ask yourself questions and realize that the way forward is really by committing to God.'

'But what prompted your change of mind?' Nkiru had persisted, curious to discover Uche's turning point or factor. It was a real shocker to listen to the formerly self-proclaimed atheist proclaiming God and a new religion.

'I wouldn't say there was a particular reason per se.' Uche had insisted. 'What I was living was no life really. I listened up and was able to hear the voice of reason that was there all along. I had to turn my life around because pleasures of the flesh are what they are, mere evaporative thrill. I must tell you dear that I'm very happy now, very happy with my state of mind and life right now.' Uche had disclosed.

Wonders will never cease, Nkiru had surmised while pondering on Uche's words. She was impressed in spite of her doubts while listening to Uche in a newly adopted soft voice chatting earnestly about her new life in Jesus. Uche had failed to divulge the real reason behind her enormous turnaround but Nkiru could perceive that she was definitely calmer and more demure.

Nkiru on her part considered herself a committed Catholic but not 'born again" as followers of new age Pentecostal or non-denominational Churches tended to ascribe their devotion. Her mother, Lolo had lived with and served under the early missionary nuns who had settled in Ubi in her youth and fully imbibed Catholic doctrines. Lolo ensured all her family members were committed Catholics.

'I'm happy for you but I must admit that I'm still trying to take in this new you. I don't mean to sound offensive or derogatory but it's such a huge change and surprise.' She apologized.

'Never mind, I take no offence besides you're not the first to make a similar remark.' Uche assured her with a laugh. 'I have to admit though that I'm definitely happier with where I am now.'

'Good on you.' Nkiru commended with slight reservation given her private longstanding bias against supposed "*born-agains*". This actually stems from the various scandalous stories that was said to emanate from similar churches. A particular story that she'd overheard in the past did leave a lasting bad taste in her mouth. A close friend of an acquaintance of hers was allegedly brow beaten into tying the knot with an incompatible fellow in the name of so called "born again" propaganda. The concerned fellow was purported to have deliberately and specifically targeted her in the church declaring during an entrancement session to be inspired by the Holy Spirit who had revealed to him that they should wed. The gullible lady was initially wary as she hadn't received a parallel revelation nor was the fellow particularly her type. They shared little in common in terms of personalities or background. He had obtained little education, having dropped out of high school and was also from an impoverished family background. None of which should have made any difference save for the drama that unfolded shortly. This gullible lady, in contrast to the fellow held a Master's degree and hailed from a very affluent family. She also owned a car and an apartment, whereas the fellow had recently moved to the city and was sharing board with relatives until he could secure any menial job. He was alleged to have contrived to strike it rich by marrying above his rank and the poor girl was his evident prey. The girl's initial reservations about the authenticity of the revelation were immediately dispelled by fellow church members who imposed on her to wed the fellow, adamant that her wedlock was preordained so she had no choice but to see it through.

What followed after the nuptials was a catalogue of disasters. The guy showed himself up as a complete fraudster with sadistic intent. He took pleasure in humiliating his new wife. One would have thought that he'll settle down and try to improve on himself by pursing further education or obtaining a proper job but such noble intentions were far from his mind as the story went. He quickly took control of their finances which were largely her substantial pay check and supplementary funds from her parents as well as allocated her a minimal stipend. He banned her from driving claiming she shouldn't be driving when he didn't own a car. Her proposal that they should purchase another car or jointly shared hers fell unto deaf ears. He sold off her car mandating that she travelled by public transport including boarding the largely unsafe 'okada' motorcycles. He accused her of being spoilt and charged that humility was next to godliness which should be their abiding doctrine. He urged her to humble herself and relive the sufferings of the greater majority for greater spiritual enrichment. It was later discovered though that he was far from righteous and was only deliberately humiliating her to feed his injudicious ego.

The girl's parents' were distraught when they discovered the truth. They had seen through him from their first meeting but their daughter was bent on wedding him. They had initially refused to sanction the marriage but reconsidered when it was obvious that she'd forsake them for the fellow. She vowed to wed the fellow with or without their consent after she was brainwashed by conniving fellow church members into believing her union with the fellow was by divine calling. Her parents' threatened renunciation failed to dissuade her.

The fellow proceeded to alienate her from both friends and family. He continuously berated her parents and indicted her father of fraudulence in the manner in which he had amassed his wealth which he claimed was at the expense of the public. The bulk of his wealth was originally amassed while he was in public service. Her husband however failed to exhibit similar scruples while utilizing the funds derived from her said corrupt parents and incessantly coerced her into requesting for more funds from the same supposedly "fraudulent" parents.

The poor girl was totally smitten by her new husband and his fake dynamism. She hung on to his every word and lived according to his every dictate. Unbeknownst to her, he was living it up behind her back. He secretly siphoned her hard-earned cash to construct a house back in his home village without her knowledge or consent. To make matters worse he impregnated his village sweetheart while insisting they should remain chaste with his poor wife until she was spiritually mature. Neither her friends nor anxious parents could successfully make her see him for who he really was. She started to distance herself instead from anyone that insisted on castigating her husband. Her concerned relatives and friends could only stand by helplessly and watch her pitiable situation while she was hell bent on sticking by her man. They could only pray that she discovers the truth sooner than later.

Nkiru was therefore bowled over by Uche's conversion into a weighty born-again because they had been in the same company when they heard this particular tale. She could still clearly recall Uche avowing that she couldn't stand born-agains or their hypocrisy nor could she be taken in by such drivel in a million years. However here she was promulgating a new church and declaring that she was "born again". She visited frequently, urging Nkiru to attend her new church and to witness the benefits for herself.

Nkiru was steadily easing back to normality since her recent breakthrough. Her parents encouraged her to take her time in deciding her future plans, be it enrolling for further studies or securing a new job. They dealt her kid's gloves for fear of inducing a relapse, should they try to rush her right back into a hectic schedule. They had postponed the planned overseas trip in view of her recuperation. They also desired that she fully regained both her mental and physical strength before venturing out on her own again.

Nkiru had also travelled to Igbaje lately to visit her best friend Lily and also officially assumed godparent role on behalf of Lily's newborn daughter who was christened at the same time. She was thrilled to see her old friends and acquaintances again while at Igbaje. They reminisced about the good old camping and youth service program days which felt like almost a decade ago but was only a year and half. The reunion to some degree had reopened old wounds because Obinna was always an integral member of that clique. There were still many nights when she cried herself to sleep while recalling the tragic demise of her beloved Obinna but she has recently resolved to focus more on the happier memories of their time together, a more mature defence mechanism to help ease her immense sorrow. Sanni, Obinna's very close friend had come around to Lily's when he got wind of the fact that she was in town and they had a good old cry.

She was also reminded of events surrounding the burial ceremony which she vaguely recollected but most of her friends attested to their personal attendance. She couldn't help but weep while browsing through the pictures of the event from Lily's collection. Even then, she could barely sit through the two hours or so long video recording of the funeral ceremony but was amazed at the huge turnout of sympathizers. Her parents' had resourcefully concealed analogous mementos away from her at home in order not to rekindle her anguish or induce a relapse. She was however not impervious to the knowledge of having to face up to reality at some point.

She was especially glad to learn that her parents had taken in Obinna's siblings to live with them but the most incredible turn was when Nwakego announced that Obinna's mother was her twin sister.

It was the most astounding revelation that stunned the whole town of Ubi and beyond.

* * * * * * * *

Nwakego departed from the clairvoyant's shrine and headed straight for Chief Ubaka's home. It was considerably late but she wasn't dissuaded by the very late hour. This was not the kind of news that could wait another minute much less overnight. She was parched by the time that she arrived at the Ubaka residence. 'Chief Ubaka and Lolo, are you home?' She called out loudly as she was being ushered into the downstairs lounge.

'No, they are not home but expected home soon.' Ada repeated. She had explained to the woman that her bosses weren't home but Nwakego paid no heed.

'My daughter, you're sure they'll be back soon?'

'Yes, they went for evening mass and should be home soon.' Ada repeated.

'I'll wait for them for as long as it takes.' She stated decisively without ascertaining from Ada if it was okay for her to wait up for them or not. She soon settled into the sofa without invitation.

'Can I get you anything, Ma?' Ada enquired. She knew Nwakego; her husband was Chief Ubaka's kinsman.

'Fetch me a glass of water my child.' Nwakego requested.

Ada wondered what the matter was because Nwakego was visibly shaken but left her momentarily to fetch water.

'This is why I say it is good to be rich and own a proper fridge. See how cold the water taste. This is exactly what I needed.' Nwakego commented after gulping down the glass of water at a go. 'Where are the children?'

'They are upstairs.' Ada replied. What could Nwakego possibly want with them? Ada wondered while glaring at her suspiciously.

Nwakego had briefly contemplated asking to see her sister's kids but on second thoughts decided against it. It was best to wait until she speaks with Chief Ubaka and his wife first. She adjusted her wrapper and made herself more comfortable. It was late but she just had to accomplish her mission tonight. It couldn't wait.

'Madam, we have a visitor.' Ada rushed to inform Lolo as the couple alighted from their car. 'It's Aunty Nwakego. She's been waiting for almost an hour and says she has urgent news to relay.'

'*Ewo*----oh, I hope it's not bad news. She didn't tell you what it was about?' Lolo asked anxiously.

'No Ma.'

'Okay, I hope it is well. Ada, please help me fetch my bag from the boot.'

'Yes Ma.'

'Nnam, Nwakego is waiting for us.'

'So I hear, is anything the matter?'

'Ada said she has some news to relate to us.'

'Let us go and find out then.' He urged his wife without bothering to speculate on the nature of Nwakego's news. Nothing surprises him anymore; he has already seen it all.

'Welcome Chief and Lolo, *Ndi oga dili nma.*' Nwakego stood up in deference to their entrance and hailing them collectively as *'those that will meet with good fortune'*, before genuflecting and greeting, 'Chief, *Onwu egbuna dike.*

'Welcome Nwakego, welcome.' They both greeted her warmly.

'I hope we didn't keep you waiting for too long. We would have come earlier if we had been aware that you had been waiting for us.' Lolo apologized.

'No, no. I should apologize for barging in at this late hour with no warning but it was imperative that I see you tonight. I hope your outing went well.'

'It did. We had only attended the evening mass and committee meeting afterwards. How is your family?

'They are all fine but for hunger.' Nwakego joked.

'Its better hunger than ill health but I hope everything is fine?'

'It is, Chief. Thank God. It is true what you said, health is wealth.' Nwakego agreed.

'Ada, I hope you offered drinks and kola nut to Nwakego.' Lolo called to Ada.

'She did, she did.' Nwakego reassured her.

'Do you require any more drinks or kola nut?' Lolo enquired hospitably.

'No, no. Thank you very much.' Nwakego indicated with a wave. 'I was well taken care of.'

After a momentary pause, Chief Ubaka broached the purpose of Nwakego's visit by enquiring, 'I hope all is well?'

'Chief, pardon me but I have news that I couldn't wait to impart to you both.'

'Okay.' He agreed as he and his wife waited to hear the rest of her news.

'Chief and Lolo, I believe there is no easier way to break this news so I'll just go straight to the point. I know this would sound very strange but these children, Obinna's siblings are actually my twin sister's kids.' Nwakego pronounced.

Chief and Lolo simultaneously and alarmingly sprang up in their seat like Nwakego had dropped a bombshell, her information was entirely unexpected. They've had to contend with a lot of controversies lately but Nwakego's news sure took the Mickey. Nwakego was on the other hand, a sensible, astute and realistic woman as far as they knew so there was no chance that she was joking.

'How did you arrive at this conclusion?' Chief Ubaka asked calmly. He was bemused by the news. He thought he had heard and seen it all.

'I know this sound odd but I assure you that I'm not crazed. It is a long story but I'll try to give you the short version. Please I beg you to keep an open mind because I wouldn't be here if it wasn't the truth.' Nwakego implored before continuing. 'I've had a peculiar dream since childhood but it abated a few years back. However since the kids coming, my old dream was resuscitated besides a pervading strange aura any time that I as much as spied on them. I was disturbed and more flabbergasted after I noticed that the older girl, I don't remember her name...' Nwakego tailed off while trying to recall Ngozi's name.

'Ngozi,' Lolo supplied.

'Yes, that is her name. Ngozi, she looks very much like my mother, Oroma. She bears the same scars and birth marks on her faces as my mother before her and when I stared into her eyes, it was my mother's eyes staring right back at me. I was in shock and decided to consult Odimegwu Dike. As a matter of fact I came straight from his shrine to your home. He helped me unravel this whole thing.' Nwakego narrated before continuing after a pause. 'My late mother apparently had the hard luck of delivering one set of twins after another and was forced to bury all of them alive, just like they used to do in the old days. She got tired of burying her live kids and decided to take the laws into her own hands by retaining her last set of twins. She left town to stay with her friend in a distant land during her pregnancy as soon as she felt that there was a fair chance that she bore twins again. She was aware that she couldn't possibly retain both twins and would be mandated to keep only one. She subsequently laid my other twin beside the river near a basket of fish at the shores of Obana River which was the vision that had haunted my dreams for years. A fisherman rescued her baby before she could bear to return home to my father with me as her only daughter. This other twin was the kid's mother, my twin sister.' Nwakego announced. 'Don't ask me how I can be sure that this is the truth. I know it in my heart of hearts and feel it in my bones that they are my own twin sister's kids.'

Chief Ubaka and Lolo were undecided regarding Nwakego's bizarre tale. They knew she was in her right mind and was always a sensible sort. Now that she confronted them with this weird possibility of being related to Obinna and his family, they were suddenly struck by her resemblance to Obinna's mother and even the kids. How that had escaped them all along was a wonder. The two women shared more than a passing likeness except that Obinna's mother was comparable sedate to Nwakego's gregariousness.

'Well, Nwakego. I must say that this is a very extraordinary tale.' Chief Ubaka finally responded. 'I think we have to sleep over this news before we can decide how to proceed. I want to believe you but you must understand that this is all very strange and new to us.'

'I know you have to do what you have to do. I'll however like you to introduce me to the kids as their aunt.'

'Nwakego, please come back tomorrow. We'll sleep on this matter and outline the best approach to handle this delicate matter. I wouldn't tell the kids anything as of yet. They have been traumatized enough already. Let us deal with this matter in the most appropriate manner to avoid getting anybody hurt.' Chief Ubaka calmly outlined to Nwakego.

'I'll leave now. It is late but I'll return early hour's tomorrow morning. Let the day break.' Nwakego conceded.

'Let the day break and greet your family for us.' They returned.

Chief Ubaka and Lolo were still dumbfounded hours after Nwakego departed.

'Nnam, how incredible is her tale.'

'I know Lolom but Nwakego is certainly not the frivolous type. I don't think she would deliberately spread false rumours. Come to think of it, there's a resemblance between her and Obinna's mother and the kids too.'

156

'That is true; I wonder why we have failed to notice the likeness before now.' Lolo agreed.

'But who would have thought that this could ever be a possible outcome. We've been so sidetracked by other issues that we never speculated on the origins of Obinna's mother.'

'Nnam, this last year has been inconceivable to say the least.' Lolo commented pensively.

'I agree with you but I wouldn't want us to disrupt the kids' life unless we have concrete proof that this is accurate. Enough drama has gone down already.'

'I agree with you, Nnam.' Lolo concurred.

The couple discussed the issue further and outlined DNA verification of this supposed blood link prior to any other considerations.

* * * * * * * *

Most of the natives who had known Nwakego's late mother, Oroma on hearing the news confirmed Ngozi bore a striking resemblance to her late grandmother. Some members of the Ubaka kinsmen that could still vaguely recollect Obinna's mother face after meeting her at the knocking ceremony also agreed that she did look a lot like Nwakego. How they could all have missed the obvious resemblance until now was simply inconceivable. They must have, with some hindsight subconsciously refused to acknowledge the similarity because the possibility of any blood link between the two women would have been highly improbable given the pre-existing circumstance.

Nwakego on her part greatly bewailed her personal absence at the knocking ceremony because that would have been her only opportunity to meet with her twin sister. She was adamant now that she would have been able to recognize and embrace her. She proclaimed her ill heath during that period was a presentiment because she had felt utterly downcast and unwell for no unfathomable reason.

The general reactions were as varied as they come. A few Doubting Thomases went to consult the oracles on their own accord but same was confirmed to be true. The hard core traditionalists and cynics remained impervious to this new unearthing. They argued that Obinna's siblings were not totally exonerated from their OSU legacy given that their father was a confirmed OSU. The Ejike family hadn't

157

on balance taken necessary measures to retrace their lineage to Nkate or performed essential absolution rites.

A few of Chief Ubaka's kinsmen or friends who had previously castigated his household now hung their heads in shame. A majority argued that nothing had changed. Yes, even if they were to admit to the claims that Obinna's mother originated from their Ubi town but his father was a certified OSU which would therefore designate his siblings as bona fide OSU children. The kids' status was therefore unchanged as far as they were concerned. A freeborn marrying an OSU does not transform the OSU to becoming freeborn, but rather condemns the freeborn and subsequent offspring to become OSU

Nkiru reflected on her first meeting with Obinna's mother. Mama, as she recollected affectionately had looked a touch familiar but she couldn't truthfully say that Aunty Nwakego had come to her mind then. Aunty Nwakego wasn't after all a particularly close aunt of hers but was married to her distant Uncle. She also seldom visited her home. Nkiru tried to recall if the two women had met during her iku-aka ceremony but couldn't exactly remember seeing Aunty Nwakego during the occasion. She was sure that the evident resemblance between the two women would surely have been more obvious if they were both present in the same room. The whole riddle would have unravelled earlier but then who could tell with any certainty? She countered, deciding it was still better that the truth be unfurled later than never.

Her father, Chief Ubaka had insisted on DNA verification of Nwakego's claim which came back positive. He argued that he hadn't doubted Nwakego but had however required a proper authentication of the claim to avoid any future conjecture. Their family had had a lot to contend with lately as it were.

Who could have predicted or even dared to think that such an implausible outcome was possible? God does work in mysterious ways flew from many lips as they proclaimed the omnipotence of the Lord after hearing the story.

All in all, the kid's presence in Ubi town was considerably more acceptable and tolerable to most.

Ngozi, Chidinma and Ifedi's position as authentic members of Ubaka family which was never in doubt to the Ubaka's was further reinforced; the town of Ubi was their maternal home town after all.

Nwakego had agitated to take over their upkeep and also insisted on having them move in with her but relented after a series of roundtable conferences. All associated family members including the kids themselves and their new extended maternal kindred, Aunty Mary and Chief Ubaka and his wife convened for numerous discussions. The final accord was that the kids would remain with Chief Ubaka and his family. Nwakego could see them as often as she desired besides they all lived in Ubi town.

Nkiru often wondered how Obinna would have reacted to this incredible new information. His origins were fully clarified. His paternal lineage officially originated from Nkate and his maternal home was Ubi. Both Obinna and she shared a link and if care wasn't taken might even be related. It must be many generations removed which shouldn't have debarred them from wedding each other. The whole brouhaha of him being an OSU was suddenly debased as far as she was concerned. She could have given anything to see his face when the news broke out or hear his take on the matter. She was sure he would have found humour in the whole situation, which was classical Obinna. God surely works in mysterious ways. She proclaimed along with a thousand and one others. She missed her beloved Obinna, her better half and was convinced that he was too good to be true which was probably why he was yanked away in his prime. Heaven must have needed him more than she did or else there was no tangible reason for his tragic demise.

She felt lost and clueless even now because all her plans had kind of revolved completely around them being together. They had awaited his new transfer posting prior to securing a permanent job for her to ensure that they wouldn't be unduly separated. Their plans had changed after Obinna received his international posting notification. This would have necessitated that they relocate abroad to start a new and marital life in the USA. She didn't even have the chance to contemplate between further academic pursuits or securing a job over there before her world had collapsed like a pack of cards.

Obinna and his family were unfortunately yanked from the surface of the earth by immoral robbers or croaked policemen whichever the case may be.

Nkiru was infuriated at the thought that up until the present moment, not a single suspect had been apprehended with regards to Obinna's case. She rationalized that she'd soon have to take concrete steps and steer her future towards a new direction but her inherent zeal and motivation were burnt out. She realized quite alright that she could only afford to wallow in self pity and misery for so long. Obinna would have wished for her to remain strong in the face of adversity. He'd also have wished for her to be happy again because he loved to see her smile and she vowed to make him proud yet. She imagined that he was looking down on her. He and her inimitable late best friend Ebere must be clamouring for her get on with life as well as make them proud. She wouldn't want to disappoint them.

She subsequently agreed to accompany Uche to her church after she was converted to the idea of gaining a new spiritual fulfilment. At this stage she was open to any new ideas. She'd give Uche's supposedly maverick priest a trial. The church had a rather unusual name though, she mused. It was called the Sanctification of the Crucifix. The priest was Pastor Ugo Udu.

Nkiru accompanied Uche for the mass service on the following Sunday. The congregation was fairly sizeable but consisted mainly of a youthful group of men and women bustling around in readiness for the church service. The church was housed in a refurbished old warehouse. The location looked somewhat decrepit from the exterior, not given the array of expensive vehicles in the parking lot.

Uche assured Nkiru that it was temporary premises. The church was newly inaugurated but fast growing. They were hoping to relocate to a more permanent dwelling currently under construction. The interior of the church in contrast was fairly decent. A make-shift pulpit was carved out at the helm of the open hall and the congregation sat in plastic easily foldable chairs.

Nkiru noticed church wardens hovering around and certifying order and decorum. They were chiefly censoring ladies to ascertain that they were properly attired as in demurely clad. They weren't supposed to be in garments that exposed excessive skin and must also wear appropriates scarves ensuring their hair was properly covered. Nkiru was glad that she had taken the cue from Uche's current mode of attire to dress down and also wore a scarf tied sternly across her ears for the service. A few of the ladies were surprisingly ushered out of the church to rectify any impropriety or be barred from rejoining the service. The choir was clad in long flowing red and white robes. Their musical rendition was accompanied with drums and a pianist sat very close to the pulpit on an equally elevated podium. The assembly soon broke into frenzy in the name of songs and praise as soon as the warden announced the anticipated entrance of the pastor.

The congregation rose to their feet accordingly, clapping and proclaiming the name of the Lord in a sudden spiritual fervour as the anticipation heightened. Nkiru rose in accordance to the general acclamation but could not chorus the songs because those were not very familiar to her. Uche, who was sitting next to her in the third-row pew from the altar was in a right spiritual mode. Nkiru could easily discern that Uche's old love for pop music and dance was transferred to religious adulation as she gyrated and sang with extra vigour. She was also randomly interjecting with "Alleluia" or "That's true or right" in between the verses of the worship songs at the same time as was the rest of the congregation. The whole atmosphere was suddenly transformed into one of almost hysterical exuberance. A greater whirl erupted to herald the actual entrance of the priest with raucous shouts and screams of alleluia from different corners.

Pastor Ugo strode along the aisle regarding his flock indulgently. Nkiru estimated that he must be in his late thirties or early forties and relatively young to be the founding father of this rapidly expanding house of worship. He was roguishly handsome, dark, tall, well built and debonair, impeccably dressed in a greyish suit and coordinated with a matching gray shirt and tie. The handkerchief jutting from his breast pocket was also of the same colour. Quite coordinated, Nkiru mused as she appraised him striding authoritatively along the elongated aisle to the pulpit and continued to size him up. He must be very vain, she concluded. It looked to her that he had an eye for details because of his impeccable attire. He came across as well groomed and distinguished, she deduced as she watched him striding past her pew. She momentarily caught a slight whiff of his fragrance as he strode past from her seat. She watched his retreating back as he marched swiftly behind his deputies while trying to decipher his exact cologne. Another resounding ovation and banging of drums accompanied Pastor Ugo's assumption of his position behind the pulpit.

'Praise to the Lord.' He announced while holding a bible up in the air and surveying the congregation with a wide smile.

'Alleluia.' They responded.

'I can't hear you, Praise be to the Lord.' He repeated, shouting into the microphone with a slight American twang. He unhooked the microphone from the stand and proceeded to pace back and forth the breadth of his podium as he continued.

'Alleluia.' The congregation echoed loudly, accompanied by a rattling of drums and cheers.

161

'Now, that's what I'm talking about. It is right to give praise to the Almighty Father.' He stated. 'Are we happy today?'

'Yes Pastor.'

'I need to hear you say that with a little more conviction. Are we happy today?' He bellowed into the microphone.

'Yes Pastor.' The flock responded more ardently in accompaniment to another resounding beat of drums.

'Well you should be joyful. You are alive and present in the house of the Lord. I'm sure most of you think that is not a great feat but I assure you it is no mean feat. There are people like you and I wishing to be out and about but are lame or lying in hospital beds. The fact that we are all here today is a testimony of His greatness. That is one reason if none other to give Him praise and thanks. I charge any ignorant person here to proclaim that health is wealth. Alleluia.'

'Health is wealth.' They reverberated, followed by shouts of "Alleluia".

'My dear brethren, we are gathered here today to give praise and thanks to the Lord. We acknowledge the gifts and mercies both obvious and subtle which are delivered unto our lives and the lives of our beloved ones and friends and I say, alleluia!'

'Alleluia.'

'I want you to close your eyes and bring your private petitions to the Lord. Ask for His forgiveness and mercy. I encourage you to speak in any language that comes to your tongue. Proclaim His name in any words that form in your mouth, *Ajibe, ajibe okporoko tuwa tafo abracadabra* ... ...'

The rest of his words were lost in mysterious mumbo jumbo of speaking in tongue. Nkiru peered at the congregation around her through half open eyes. Most of them had followed the priest's cue and were swaying unsteadily on their feet, jumping or hopping on one foot in possessed frenzy. They looked entranced or possessed and muttering what sounded like gibberish to her in prayer. She closed her eyes but no strange words came to her tongue so she silently prayed 'Our Lord's prayer' while spying and waiting on the rest to conclude. The speaking in tongue session came to an abrupt end when the priest raised his hand again and motioned, "Stop." His flock were jolted back into reality just as rapidly as they had lapsed into speaking in tongue and entrancement like puppets drawn on a string or so, sceptical Nkiru deduced.

The priest continued his sermon. He read from the scriptures and went on to expatiate on the lesson depicted. Members of the congregation were subsequently invited to the pulpit in small batches ranging from those seeking special anointments, attesting to good fortunes and numerous other testimonials. Each testimonial group was greeted with drums and applause. Soon afterwards it was time for the church offerings. The ushers distributed envelopes to the flock and placed hampers at strategic corners of the pulpit while the choir broke into a litany of praise worshipping songs.

Pastor Ugo rose to his feet again to charge his congregation to be generous. 'Alleluia!' He raised his hand indicating quiet and attention at the same time.

'Alleluia!' A prolonged applause and shrieks followed.

'The time has come for us to make peace offerings and to indicate our appreciation for the blessings the Good Lord has bestowed upon us. Need I remind you that ten percent of whatever you earn or own belong to the Lord. That is your 'tithe' to those of you who would pretend to be ignorant. If a random individual bestows life and innumerable gifts on you and demands ten percent back, would you say that's too much to ask?'

'No Pastor.' They responded loudly.

'Are the banks that lenient with you?'

'No, Pastor.' Came the predictable deafening response.

'Do you know why the 10% is called the tithe?'

'You tell us Pastor.' They replied, clapping resoundingly in anticipation of a witty remark.

'Because some of you are tight fisted that is why.' Pastor Ugo remarked jokingly.

The congregation guffawed and clapped gleefully in appreciation of the witty response.

'I'll give you an instance to demonstrate what I'm talking about. I used to attend annual church conferences with fellow priests and I must let you into a secret, they are just as tight fisted as most of you.'

'Alleluia, God is great.' The crowd interjected with laughter.

'Well, initially I used to donate in tens, subsequently hundreds and then progressed to thousands but these days; yours truly now donate six figure sums.'

'Alleluia!' His flock responded with rampant interjections accompanied by claps and drums.

'The other priests marvel at me and what do I say to them?'

'Tell us Pastor.'

'I say God is good.'

'God is good, alleluia.'

'So I say to you, clutching a coin in your tight fist to drop into the basket. I ask you if that is what the blessings in your life are worth. Are you trying to say that you realized only a naira this week which is why you want to drop ten kobo into my basket?'

'Alleluia.' The congregation were guffawing and enjoying the ribaldry.

'Don't disappoint or make mockery of the Lord. Donate money that will hurt you, in the same way that he had suffered and was crucified on the cross for your sake and mine. I don't want anyone dropping a coin like our God is some beggar out in the street?'

'That is not right. Alleluia.'

'Come out and give him praise. Give him the praise that he deserves and more shall be bestowed unto you. Don't just come with only tithes or be tight-fisted. Come with open hands and show your appreciation and proclaim your belief. The Lord is great. He is great'

'He is the alpha and omega, he's the Lord……..'

The choir burst into song as the ushers directed the worshippers to proceed from one row to the next in an orderly fashion. They were joyously dancing up to the strategically placed collection baskets at the pulpit safeguarded by wardens.

Nkiru had actually been clutching a small bill before the pastor's reproach regarding tithes and the tight-fisted. She had to dip back into her purse to retrieve more bills. Her parents usually made substantial donations on behalf of her whole family during church services so she was rarely required to make personal donations per se. She was still cautious about the amount of money she was donating because she hadn't arrived with a load of cash and they were a long way from home. The pastor had charged them to give money that will hurt them but surely he didn't mean that she should empty her purse and become stranded. She mused. After all he had retraced his own natural progression from donating tens to hundreds, then thousands of naira which obviously translates that he was able to contribute more as his financial circumstance improved. She hoped that she read him right as she joined the rest to dance up to the pulpit and drop her offering and danced back to her seat.

New members were encouraged to stay behind and register officially after the service. Those requiring special prayers were also invited to come up to the podium for blessing and anointment from the priest before the service finally concluded.

Uche and Nkiru waited in a queue along with a majority of the congregation waiting for Pastor Ugo after the service. Nkiru opted out of registering as a regular member of the church for the time being until she had more info as to what they were about.

'I hope you enjoyed the service.' Uche enquired as they stood waiting. She wanted to personally introduce Nkiru to the priest.

'I sure did and thanks.' Nkiru replied. She hadn't been sure of what to expect from the service exactly but then she had never attended a similar service before. She didn't quite know what to make of the speaking in tongue; otherwise there were no other eventful incident. The sermon was uplifting.

Nkiru observed the Pastor approaching them. He was mingling and chatting easily with the flock lined up in the queue extending into the street. The flock genuflected as they greeted him. Nkiru sardonically imagined the ladies were quivering with a hint of sexual tension or attraction as they extended both hands to clasp his in handshake. She could garner a suspicious intimacy and familiarity between Pastor Ugo and the ladies. She thought they exchanged coquettish glances unless she was mistaken.

The Pastor rapidly drew close to them as Nkiru continued to size him up. He was slick, no doubts as he stopped for brief chats here, patted few heads there or simply shook hands as he proceeded down the line. He didn't seem hurried, yet was speedy in dispatch. In next to no time, he was standing a few paces from them and Nkiru perceived Uche's body language transforming from subdued calm to an excited fluster. The girl's face was instantly lit up and manifested such reverence that one would have thought that she was being ushered into the presence of a supernatural being. She was quavering like the rest of the ladies as she shook Pastor Ugo's hand.

'Aha Uche, how are you?' Pastor Ugo asked.

'I'm fine Pastor. The Lord is good.' She replied reverentially in her lately adopted small girl voice.

'Don't forget that the retreat is at the end of the week and you must bring your friend along.' He spared Nkiru a brief glance then, indicating he either knew or guessed her identity.

'Yes Pastor, thank you Pastor.'

He proceeded to the next person on the line. Nkiru was not formally introduced to him as she had anticipated.

'He invited you to the retreat. I can't believe it but you are so lucky he invited you.' Uche repeated excitedly hugging Nkiru as they exited the church

'Okay.' Nkiru hesitantly agreed, uncertain about why Uche was so excited. Her meeting with the priest hasn't transpired exactly like she had envisaged. She had been of the mind that they'll meet with him in a private office and he'd pray or denote scriptures for her to read to help her regain spiritual salvation and fulfilment. However, when they lined up in the queue, she had imagined Uche would formally introduce her as in, "Pastor, this is my friend Nkiru, the one I had already told you about." He on his part would welcome her formally to his church and assign prayers for her or else designate to meet her privately or for group prayer therapy sort of thing. He had however barely acknowledged her presence besides inviting her to attend a retreat she hadn't heard of until now.

'I'm so happy for you. I didn't think he'll invite you because this retreat is specifically designated for us members of the Lady's League. That was why I hadn't mentioned it to you before but you are in luck.' Uche reiterated. 'The girls wouldn't be too pleased but I'll talk them over. I'm so happy you'll be coming with us.

'Thanks then.' Nkiru muttered her appreciation still undecidedly.

'It begins next Wednesday so we can travel together.' Uche continued to strategize, already taking her attendance for granted. 'I don't know if you would like to wait up for me because I'm still going to be here for hours. We're having a meeting to finalize plans for the retreat or better still you can go and I'll definitely meet up with you before the retreat. Your presence might aggravate the group.' Uche added in afterthought.

'I should better leave then.' Nkiru concurred.

'Okay, 'Uche agreed. 'See you later. I'm so happy Pastor Ugo invited you along and I promise that you'll definitely enjoy the experience. We're planning a lot of activities including revivals, prayer sessions and private sessions with Pastor Ugo. You can't begin to imagine the benefits that could be derived.' Uche couldn't extol the benefits or her supposed good fortune enough.

'I'll be looking forward to the retreat then. Thanks once again and see you later.' Nkiru bade her friend before departing.

She pondered on the service and forthcoming retreat during her drive home. The service was entirely different from the sombre service of her accustomed Catholic Church. The exuberance and high spiritedness exhibited by the parishioners was considerably excessive to what she was used to. She reviewed her objective again or what she hoped to achieve by coming to this new church. There was certainly a hollow feeling deep inside of her but it wasn't as if she was disenchanted with her customary church or its inability to offer her same. If she truthful to herself, she knew that her curiosity about Uche's transformation was a key factor.   There was no denying the gaping void in her life right now that needed filling so she decided this forthcoming spiritual retreat might just help to provide answers to fill her void.

Lolo met her at the door when she arrived home. 'How did it go?' She was keen to learn of her new experience.

'Okay.' Nkiru replied her Mum hesitantly. 'The service was fairly invigorating and interesting. I've also been invited to attend a spiritual retreat camp.' Nkiru informed her.

'Do you really feel up to camping and what's that about?'

'I thought I might just give it a try.' Nkiru admitted. 'The retreat would involve revivals, fasting and prayer sessions.'

'I should accompany you then.' Lolo suggested.

'No mum, it's not open to the public. I'm actually privileged to be attending after my first turnout at the church as I'm made to understand.' Nkiru reported with a slight hint of cynicism. 'You don't have to worry Mum, it should be completely foolproof since it is a church event and I'll be fine.' She reassured her mother knowing her earlier offer was made out of her mother's concern for her welfare than plain companionship.

'You do have to be careful and if you were to be uncomfortable with any of their practices that you should come home immediately.'

'It's okay mum. I'm not a kid and stop worrying.'

'I know but I'm doubtful of these new mushroom churches that have recently sprung up all over the place.' Lolo echoed Nkiru's old bias. 'Most are led by dodgy priests who are only out for personal enrichment and other bogus intents so one can never be too careful.'

'I know Mum but this particular church seems to be different.' Nkiru tried to allay her fears. 'Just consider Uche and how she'd changed. Aren't you amazed at how different her attitude is now?'

'But that is Uche. I hate be judgemental but you are not Uche. You've never been a bad girl and will not start now. I'm not saying Uche is bad any how.' She expounded.' I suppose what I'm trying to say is that we are happy with you and have always been so you don't need to change.'

'Thanks Mum but let me just see what this is about and trust me, if I don't like what goes on there, I'll definitely come home.' She promised her mother.

'I trust you but be careful, my dear.' Lolo cautioned, reluctant to pressurize her into not attending. 'I'm not sure why you want to explore this new church because Father Joseph can easily arrange a prayer session for you if that is what you require at this stage.' She added.

'I'm not deserting the Catholic faith, Mum.' Nkiru affirmed. 'Just experimenting really, more so from curiosity but trust me. I wouldn't do anything that would disappoint you.' She assured Lolo.

'I believe you. When are you going?'

'Wednesday,' Nkiru replied.

'I'm not sure that your dad will be happy to hear any of this.' Lolo enunciated another major worry.

'You can take care of him for me, Mum.'

'Just be careful though' Lolo implored.

'I would.' She promised.

Nkiru had left her mother to go upstairs to her room when she overheard the laughter drifting from Azuka's room so decided to stop there first.

Azuka, Ngozi and Chidinma had bonded well. They were very firm friends now and attended the same boarding school too. Azuka had stopped sticking to her side like glue as she used to in the past. They remain close and hang out occasionally but these days Azuka will sooner be found with Ngozi and Chidinma rehashing school events or gossips than tagging along her elder sister's side.

Nkiru was glad that Obinna's siblings had settled in nicely and were now fully accustomed to their new home. They were family and nothing was ever going to change that. She was greatly touched by her parents amazing gesture when she first came to realize that they had agreed to have Obinna's siblings reside in their home. She was also immensely proud of her parents because she wouldn't have ordinarily expected them to be that magnanimous in the face of recent tribulations.

Their townsfolk and kinsmen surely had a field day making up gossips about their situation and she knew her parents must have had a very rough ride dealing with the tragic deaths, her subsequent illness

168

and then the uproar that accompanied Obinna's siblings' arrival at Ubi. As if that was not enough problems to contend with, her father's business ventures encountered a major drawback and huge financial loss. None of which had deterred either of her parents from demonstrating an unparalleled compassion for Obinna's siblings. She loved and was so proud of them too.

'Hello girls.' Nkiru greeted on entering Azuka's room. She found Azuka, Ngozi and Chidinma angled at different sides of the bed browsing through a magazine.

'Welcome, Sister Nkiru.' They chorused.

'What was the joke?' She asked interestedly.

'It's the outrageous attires on this page, look at her scarf.' Chidinma pointed at the picture of a lady in the magazine in a towering headgear.'

'Whoa! That sure looks like she is practically carrying a house at the top of her head.' Nkiru agreed. 'But you shouldn't be perusing magazines when your exam is a few weeks away.' She reprimanded Azuka. 'You should be concentrating on your upcoming JAMB exam.'

'Sorry, Sister.' Ngozi and Chidinma apologized and quickly handed the magazine over to her.

Azuka groaned disenchanted. 'We're also on vacation, Sis.'

'You do have an exam to contend with and require high scores to gain admission into my old alma mater unless you've changed your mind about my school.'

'No, I haven't.'

'That's the more reason why you need to study really hard.' She insisted. 'Where are the boys?'

'Out playing football,' Chidinma replied.

'I should have known better! So what is new with you girls otherwise, you'll be sitting for same exams in two years time, Ngozi. Right?'

'Yes Sister but I study with Azuka.'

'Good strategy.' Nkiru commended her.

'The bazaar is next Sunday.' Azuka informed her.

'Oh that's true. I almost forgot but I wouldn't be attending in any case.'

'Why? Dad would not be amused by your absence. Our special thanksgiving service is at same time too.' Azuka reminded her.

'I know but it's been postponed to the Sunday after the Bazaar. Father Joseph wouldn't appreciate any other event interfering with the church's fund raising event. You know the church raises a lot of funds from the Bazaar.'

'Why aren't you coming then?'

'I'm attending a week long spiritual retreat with Uche. It's starting from Wednesday.'

'Can we come along?' Azuka requested eagerly.

'What's with everyone asking if they can come along with me?' Nkiru laughed. 'Sorry you can't. Apparently it's for the inner echelon of the church.' She mimicked Uche's voice.

'Are you converted to her church then?' Ngozi enquired.

'No. I was invited along all the same, lucky me.'

'I wish we could go with you. This summer break is so boring that a religious retreat sounds like fun.' Azuka complained. 'We've run out of movies to watch or borrow.' She moaned.

'Don't let Mum hear you complaining. What happened to your new textbooks?'

'Oh those....'

'You'd better be more dedicated and studious. I'll let you into another secret,' Nkiru disclosed. 'You achieve really good scores and we can convince dad to sponsor you on an overseas trip. I'll help you convince him.'

'I'm really working hard but it gets boring at times.' Azuka complained.

'I'll help motivate you then. How about if I give you an assignment? I'll conduct a mock exam when I return.' Nkiru suggested.

'You're a complete killjoy Sis.'

'I know.' Nkiru concurred jovially, giggling as she left them to their own device and hobbled up to her room merrily.

Nine

Nkiru was driving as she and Uche set off early on the due day en route to the week-long retreat. She had been extra careful in choosing her garments for the trip. She made sure to pick her more modest and conservative looking garments knowing Uche as well as the other ladies in the church sported a similar look. She wasn't particularly into body baring or hugging outfits anyway but was cautious all the same.

She had also enclosed a bible, religious fliers that she found lying about the house and a novel in her travel bag on forethought, should they be allowed free time or if she were to be bored. She had relived her previous camping experience during the mandatory one year Youth Service Corps program while preparing. She had relished the then tremendous experience besides making new friends. Whereas that camp had been a physical fitness training scheme, this latest camp was for spiritual revival. She had somehow convinced herself of her desperate need for spiritual fulfilment and rehabilitation. More so for the unrelenting hollowness and apathy that had continued to engulf her since Obinna's tragedy. Her usual pep was lost and she was hoping that this retreat would help revive and reignite her usual joie de vivre. She was currently psyched to try out anything including dabbling in worship with a group that she would ordinarily have considered nonconformist if that was what it would take to regain her usual vitality.

'We'll soon be there.' Uche reassured her after they've had to reverse for the umpteenth time while negotiating for the accurate route to their destination.

'I wish I could believe you.' Nkiru retorted candidly. She hadn't anticipated that the journey would be so prolonged after Uche estimated that it would take them two or thereabouts to arrive there. They had set off that morning when Uche turned up. Nkiru had assumed that they'd meet up prior to the retreat date but Uche had called her the next day after the services to say she was tied up. She promised to try to see her the evening before otherwise early that morning. She only turned up 30 minutes before they set off. They have been on the road for almost three hours but were supposedly only half way gone. They had fortunately started off in good time and Nkiru was fervently hoping that they'd arrive at their destination before nightfall. She abhorred darkness and travelling in pitch darkness. The fact that the roads were in such poor condition besides Uche's recurring misdirection was fast getting on her nerves. Uche would ask her to take a particular turn, only to change her mind and imply that they should have been travelling in the opposite direction after a considerable distance was irritating. Nkiru was fast growing exasperated by the rigmarole and plying through an unfamiliar rough route. Uche soon assured her that they had finally hit the right course after innumerable wrong turns. She should have known they were in trouble after they veered off the familiar major highway route linking most of the major cities to Ubi.

They, on the contrary had exited via an un-tarred road path heading for their destination, Obirima village. Uche had travelled down there once before and had been confident that she could easily navigate them to the place. Nkiru nearly regretted trusting her now. She hoped that they had finally hit the right route according to Uche. She was nonetheless entranced by the region and surrounding sights.

The unfamiliar course led into a sparsely populated rural area emerging almost as a virgin land. She hadn't been previously aware that such a rustic region existed since she had never had the opportunity to explore the more rural areas of her Eastern Region or the rest of the country for that matter. She was more acquainted with major cities. Her moderately sized car jostled along the sloppy uneven path rustling up a transient sandy squall after them as she wrestled to control the wheels as well as negotiating numerous potholes on the un-tarred road path. They also swerved erratically from side to side to avoid ramming into pedestrians sharing the same narrow pathway.

'I hope you're right about us reaching Obirima in daylight because this road is really treacherous and route protracted.' Nkiru garbled, her apprehension growing as they travelled further into a seemingly end of the world territory. She interestingly didn't miss the architectural retrogression. A few clusters of corrugated iron roof dwellings soon gave way to dotted mud huts with raffia thatched roofs as they advanced further into the dense wooded land. They took in abject looking kids with unnatural tans standing outside small clearings surrounding tiny mud hut homes. Some of them were half naked or wearing small tattered loin clothes. The kids stared at them as Nkiru cautiously manoeuvred her car at snail-slow pace through the narrow clustered pathway surrounded by bushes.

They watched the car with languid fascination while some similarly clad women who could only be their mothers stooped with peculiar crooked hoes while toiling in small cleared garden spaces a few metres away from the huts. The women stopped briefly to spare them a quick indifferent glance before continuing in their toil.

The two friends drove past a dwindling number of pedestrians as they penetrated inwards including men sporting double wrappers, one tied across their loin and the other strewn across their shoulder and bearing hoes and machetes. Uche guessed they were farmers returning home from main farmlands. Nkiru on her part was entirely transfixed by the medieval scenario. Those folks looked like they were ostensibly stuck in the yester-years. She dubbed the scene, land of the forgotten and marvelled at how untouched and unaffected they seemed from modern technology or technological advancement. She was both awe struck and saddened at the same time by the correlated abject poverty and squalor. 'I can't believe this place is for real.' She mused aloud again.

'I was probably more surprised than you are now when we first drove down this way a few days ago. This area could easily be termed a hinterland.'

'Does it mean none of our present or past government has taken the responsibility to develop or modernize these areas?' She queried for the fact that the region looked to be in its innate habitat and the kids virtually lived in abject poverty.

'I can't say for sure but I think the modernization of these areas is a work in progress. Our fast expanding population is forcing the populace further afield and deeper into these woodlands and subsequently reclaiming land for new homes thereby rejuvenating the area, the further they penetrate.' Uche hazarded a guess.

'Do your retreats always hold in similar venues as Obirima?'

'Not at all,' Uche refuted with a throaty laugh. 'We relocate all the time. Pastor Ugo abhors monotony but we are forever seeking tranquillity. Pastor Ugo was really excited when we were offered the option of coming to Obirima. He had a different venue in mind but changed his mind after he saw this place. He says the untouched nature of these lands and the serenity will help to bring us closer to God. None of us could believe our eyes when we came this way to see the venue for the first time.'

'You must have a relatively good head for roads if you've only plied this route once. I don't think that I could have been able to grasp the directions so easily.' Nkiru disclosed while recognizing that she mightn't be able to retrace her way back if left on her own. She also realized that it would have been practically impossible for her to have discovered or plied this particular route to Obirima or its neighbouring environs in her whole lifetime were it not for this retreat. She couldn't wait to tell her mother all about this virgin land.

'I've always had a fairly good head for road.' Uche affirmed. 'But I was a bit muddled at the start and had misdirected you.' She acknowledged alluding to the earlier detours. Uche paused before adding more confidently. 'We're definitely on the right course now and it shouldn't be too long before we arrive at the camp site.'

'I hope you're right.' Nkiru agreed, more disposed to believing Uche now that she sounded more confident about the route. They sped through a new conduit leading into an almost impenetrable jungle with just about enough space for Nkiru's small sized car to penetrate. They were unexpectedly surrounded by loud chirping bird reverberations and various other animal sounds. The drone of croaking frogs grew distinctively louder as they advanced further into the fortress. 'I bet there is a river or pond nearby.' Nkiru speculated accurately since those amphibians required natural water habitat for survival. 'Do you know why they croak so loudly?' She put to Uche.

'I'm not exactly sure but I think it's linked to their mating season or something.' Uche guessed.

'Partly yes but frogs are generally territorial creatures. The male species croak to attract the females as well as warn off other male frogs from their territory.' Nkiru explained. 'This is quite a croaking din, I must say.' She announced as they both chuckled at the heightened squeaky reverberating racket.

'I agree. Well that sure defines them because these female frogs must be crazy to find such an unmelodious racket attractive.'

'Different strokes for different creatures.' Nkiru cited, giggling hilariously.

They evaluated other existent diversity between humans and other creatures and were also enchanted at the sight of a gang of monkeys swinging with reckless abandon from one banana tree to another following their course.

'This is a mini safari, except that I'm petrified at the thought of a giant creature suddenly springing out of nowhere to attack us.' Nkiru announced dramatically and apprehensively.

'You should see the fright depicted on your face when you said that,' Uche laughed hysterically at her unfounded fears. 'I don't think any strange creatures will be pursuing us.' She reassured her friend.

'How can you be sure? Any mysterious random creature can inhabit this forest. It's a jungle for crying out loud.' Nkiru insisted a little peeved at Uche's apathy.

'I assure you none would appear.' Uche restated confidently.

Nkiru wasn't persuaded by Uche's unfounded confidence. She peered nervously around her expecting a giant creature to appear at any moment as she manoeuvred her car through the thicket. They were practically in a no man's land as far as she was concerned. They had drove past homes, locals and pedestrians in tow to find themselves within an enclosure of trees casting a sinister shadow in addition to the resonance of noises from various known and unfamiliar creatures.

'Are you sure we're nearly there?' Nkiru enquired again; growing dubious about their actual destination. Did they really require extreme seclusion in the name of a retreat?

'We're certainly close to it,' Uche validated. 'And don't look so worried.'

'This place is far too isolated.' She voiced aloud after it had reoccurred to her again that she'd find it extremely difficult to navigate her way out if she were to opt to depart earlier on her own.

'Yes, I know but Pastor Ugo restates that solitude is next to godliness. We, as a rule seek venues that would fulfil our desire for seclusion and privacy so we can meditate and pray without undue intrusion.'

How much space or solitude does one require for prayers anyway? Nkiru mused sceptically as her suspicious antenna swung to alert. She began to mull second thoughts about embarking on this trip in the first place. A slight feeling of unease began to settle upon her but she quickly quelled the potential apprehension before it could get the better of her. She reminded herself that this journey was in a quest for spiritual rehabilitation so she wouldn't let a meaningless paranoia distract her from a worthy cause.

The dim trail soon led into a freeway and she was relieved to depart the woodland for a standard road path. Nkiru observed a few shabbily assembled tents as they drove through the open high gates and spotted a free space to park.

There was an array of pricey vehicles ranging from Mercedes Benz, Porsche to various 4-wheel drives as well as the more popular cheaper variations of vehicles gleaming in the parking lot. Nkiru couldn't help but wonder how the more hefty vehicles could have managed to negotiate through the grove at the latter course of the woodland unless there was an alternative route leading to the site. Those jeeps might be better equipped to handle road hurdles but the path they drove through was far too narrow for them to penetrate, she contrived.

'Look, a proper house after all!' She exclaimed excitedly pointing to the sturdy one-storied concrete building behind the tents.

'What did you expect to find, huts?' Uche retorted. 'But I told you we're staying at Pastor Ugo's friend's place and this is his village villa. He originally resides abroad.'

'That sure looks like a helicopter strip.' Nkiru guessed pointing at a probable airstrip as she took in the rest of the compound. 'This guy must be really loaded.' She reckoned.

'Yes he is.' Uche confirmed as they lugged their bags and proceeded into the house to meet the other members of the Lady's League Fellowship.

'Hello Sister Ijeoma, Nkechi, Ngozi, Charity Susan …etc, this is Nkiru. Nkiru, meet Ijeoma, Nkechi… …etc,' Uche greeted, introducing the noisy bunch to Nkiru and vice versa.

'Hello Tom, Dick and Harry ……,' Nkiru rattled off lamely, hardly able to take in all the names concurrently. She maintained a fixed smile as she was introduced to them but didn't miss their mixture of curiosity and suspicion as they sized her up too. She was neither a member of the coveted Lady's League nor a full-fledged member of the church. Most justifiably didn't know her nor could comprehend her mission there. Nkiru overheard   one pinch her neighbour to ascertain who she was in an overt loud whisper.

'Now ladies, put those claws back,' Uche admonished jovially, noticing the slight antagonism in the air. 'This is my very good friend, Nkiru. She has recently undergone a heart rendering experience which I'm not going to relate presently but Pastor Ugo gave permission for her to be here with us. Please be nice because she is fragile.' She added half jokingly.

'Welcome Sister Nkiru.' They responded more genially after Uche's announcement.

'Thank you very much.' Nkiru returned with evident relief. She didn't wish to start off on the wrong footing with them. This must be a very exclusive gathering judging from their reaction to her presence, she pondered dryly. I must be truly privileged indeed.

She and Uche went to drop off their baggage in their pre-assigned room which they learnt that they would have to share with two others.

There was a lone sizeable bed in the room but a stretch mattress lay underneath to supplement additional sleeping slots.

Nkiru was significantly relieved after harbouring secret fears regarding their boarding arrangements. She had momentarily imagined as they drove through the jungle that the entire retreat process might hold outdoors or else in some nondescript dormitory type edifice. 'Thank God for a proper room and bed.' She expressed her relief.

'You're funny.' Uche laughed wryly. 'I did mention that were camping in a home so why the surprise?'

'I know but what was I supposed to think after driving through that jungle. Who would've imagined there was civilisation in this neck of woods?'

'You know what your problem is?' Uche asked acerbically. 'You're too cynical.' She replied to her own query without waiting for Nkiru's answer.

'Whatever but I'm absolutely relieved. I was really dreading the prospects of camping in the open. I detest snakes and God knows what other creatures lurking in this dense woodland.' She insisted.

They left unpacking for later and returned to the spacious sitting room, temporarily serving as the central meeting point and rejoined the rest of the group again.

'Okay girls. Welcome once again.' Sister Eucharia, the leader of the Lady's League greeted them after the last of the expected bunch had arrived. She clapped her hands to demand silence before rising to continue her speech. 'We've all arrived now and I thank God for journey mercies. I hope you enjoyed the wonderful and adventurous commute through nature. It was a priceless experience for me personally; I hope it was same for you.' Her remark drew laughs from them. 'Well, none of us needs reminding of our ultimate mission or purpose here.' She continued more seriously. 'Pastor Ugo sends his regards but will be down shortly to welcome you personally. I must repeat that it is a huge privilege for any one of us to be here so we must utilize our time effectively. We're being afforded the invaluable opportunity to commune with God and nature. Those of us with private petitions must keep them short and sweet; there are many of us here in case you haven't noticed. Each and every one of us would be granted a private session with Pastor Ugo ultimately but we don't want to overburden him in the process though, do we?' she asked knowingly.

'Oh no,' the girls chorused in exaggerated denial before interpolating with outburst of 'Alleluia' and 'The Lord is good.'

'The Lord is good indeed.' Eucharia concurred and subsequently broke into their signature praise song. "*He is the alpha and omega, he is the Lord... ... .*

The rest of the ladies joined in and started to dance, raising their arms up into the sky as well as supplicating and randomly interjecting with shouts of "Christ is Lord", "The Lord is good" or Alleluia".

Sister Eucharia went on to outline their living arrangements after the sing song was over. 'There's a rota for meal preparations and cleaning duties.' She announced pointing to the list attached to the kitchen wall. 'I beseech all of you to study the full details and adhere strictly to them. The living and kitchen areas must be kept tidy at all times. Anyone that fails to adhere to these rules will face immediate eviction both from here and membership of our honourable fold.'

'Hear, hear.' The girls hailed her.

'Well you know I'm not kidding.' Sister Eucharia restated emphatically. 'I should also warn you that the upstairs area is strictly out of bounds. Pastor Ugo and Brother David will take up residence there. Our host wishes that the rest of our activities be restricted to this ground floor. We should respect and honour his wishes besides we have more than enough room here.' She indicated before continuing. 'We're also prohibited from utilizing the entertainment fixtures in the whole house including the television, radio stereo, Nintendo games and others. We haven't come here for a social congregation or for partying. We're here to seek spiritual rehabilitation and anyone who claims to be ignorant of our mission should indicate now... ....'

'Or keep their silence for eternity!' The rest echoed in a resounding chorus.

'Alleluia!' Sister Eucharia proclaimed.

'Alleluia!'

'We'll commence our mission in earnest from tomorrow morning. We would break fast at 6 pm daily, however a short midday break for drinks and snacks will help evade dehydration and to stop the feeble in our midst from collapsing.' That drew laughs from them.

Sister Eucharia went on to outline other details and in conclusion, stated. 'Well the last but not the least detail,' she stated, pausing dramatically. 'And I can't reiterate it enough. All areas including private sleeping areas must remain clean and orderly at all times. I'll be conducting impromptu inspections and woe betides any group or person that fails the test.'

Nkiru was slightly bemused because the whole atmosphere was reminiscent of High School. She recollected them as students congregated in a similar fold to hear the head girl outline rule and regulation at the beginning of the school year. She learnt later that the downstairs area consisted of seven or more bedrooms besides the huge sitting room cum dining and adjoining sizeable kitchen. It was a large tastefully furnished house overall and the bedrooms were allocated in groups of 3 or 4. She also noted one bathroom and toilet between adjoining rooms' denoting that 6-8 of them would obviously share one. Not such a bad deal, she conceded. She had feared the arrangements could be worse. She spied a huge generator and even more gigantic bore-hole overhead tank, five times the size of the tank in her home. She was reassured that a steady supply of light and water would be guaranteed. She was therefore significantly relieved and more relaxed since basic amenities were in place. Only then could she truly begin to look forward to what the rest of the retreat has to offer.

Nkiru and Uche learnt their roommates were Kelechi and Charity. The two were naturally complete strangers to Nkiru and she couldn't instantly tally the names up with any of the faces that she had met earlier. She couldn't possibly have taken in all the names at such short notice.

'I knew Kelechi and Charity ways before we joined the church.' Uche explained. 'We served in same state and attended the same camp for the Youth Service Corps. As a matter of fact, Kelechi for some reason resents me.' She confessed.

'Why is that?' Nkiru enquired.

'Long story but short version is that her boyfriend had ditched her for me. I swear that he had told me he was free when we started dating but Kelechi insists they were still together.'

'She should really blame him then.'

'I know. It wasn't as if I knew that they were together previously. They were both strangers to me before the camp and I believed Steve when he said he as free.'

'I take it that you and Steve are not together any longer since I haven't heard you mention him.'

'Our relationship barely lasted. He was a pure Casanova but Kelechi to this day insist that I had snatched her boyfriend.'

'Did they get back together after you broke up with him?'

'I don't know for sure but I doubt it.'

'Poor girl,' she sympathized with Kelechi.

'I know.'

'And Charity?'

'She's a nice girl but I'm afraid I don't know much about her. She and Kelechi are tight since joining the church. I'm not very close to her.' Uche confessed.

* * * * * * * *

Charity's background was rather grim. She was a very pretty, slim, petite and reserved lady. She was forcefully ejected from her matrimonial home a few months ago. Her husband was much older than her but wealthy fellow and abusive. He had handpicked her from an early age and specifically nurtured her. He sponsored her through school and University before deciding that she should stay home as a full housewife. A wife doesn't need to work if her husband can cater for her fully. She hadn't minded much because he was kind to her and her family too. He was however very abusive and controlling and would beat her up mercilessly, sometimes for no justifiable reason at all.

He was smart in the sense that he had ensured to secure the support of her parents from the start and they consecutively turned a blind eye to his abusive nature. Her husband built them a modest concrete bungalow as well as providing them with a car. He also helped her father take a prestigious chieftaincy title and sponsors her younger siblings in school. She and her entire family were entirely indebted to him. He constantly reminded her that of the fact that he had basically raised them from abject poverty.

Her parents felt so beholden to her husband that they forced her to condone his violence. They invariably blamed her, claiming it was her stubbornness that made him beat her up. They urged her to remain submissive and obedient to her husband.

Charity tried her utmost best to stay the submissive bride but even so, her husband would find the least of excuses to slap her around. His excuses could range from the vegetable in the soup not being fresh enough, the meat in his soup didn't commiserate with his stature, she had not dusted the living room properly, and it didn't matter what. He also constantly threatened to withdraw his gifts or discontinue his financing of her younger siblings' education especially if she absconds for her parent's home after suffering another bout of brutal trouncing in his hands.

Her parents would regardless of her misery or protestations bundle her back to him, pleading with him to forgive and accept her back like she had erred. She knew that her parents were driven by the fear of losing their comfy home and the other perks that her husband provided at the expense of her personal wellbeing.

The last straw that broke the camels back so to say was her latest brutal battering in his hands. He had struck her so ruthlessly as to induce her to suffer a miscarriage. She lost her unborn first child in a gush of blood as he deliberately stumped on her pregnant belly for chatting with their neighbour's driver in what seemed to him like in a provocative manner. He beat her black and blue in addition to callously kicking her out into the streets, unmindful of her bleed. He locked his gates after her and forbade anyone in the household from reaching out to help her.

Charity had ran down the street screaming for help and sodden in blood until a random Good Samaritan rescued and ferried her to the nearest clinic for required immediate medical attention. She had haemorrhaged so severely that the medics resorted to performing an urgent hysterectomy in order to save her life.

She was eventually entreated to return back to her matrimonial home after her gruelling ordeal by her grovelling parents. They went to plead with her husband as usual for pardon and to accept her back in spite of her latest horrendous experiences. They ignored that he had failed to visit her while she was in hospital or as much as enquired after her wellbeing, much less tender an apology. Her parents argued that his remorse was by way of footing her hospital bills. The clinic where she was treated had refused to discharge her until she paid the hospital bill in full and her folks had no other option than approach her husband for the cash.

Charity, in spite of her distress, was handicapped and doomed to return to her matrimonial home. She was helpless in the face of her own parents' indifference. She became resigned to contending and continuing with her miserable existence until her mother-in-law's arrival from the village, a week after she moved back.

The elderly lady had come purposefully to effectively eject Charity from her son's home unbeknownst to Charity who had welcomed her heartily as usual. Her mother-in law had heard of Charity's misfortune of losing her womb so her hopes for an imminent heir and grandson were in great jeopardy. She launched into a scathing tirade as soon as she settled in, calling Charity all sorts of names from useless to barren. She proceeded to throw her belongings out and sent her away same night after warning her not to bother to return since she was personally going to find her son a more appropriate bride.

Charity arrived back at her father's home distressed and weeping bitterly but her family were unsympathetic to her plight. Both her parents and two younger siblings failed to disguise their disappointment and openly voiced their dismayed at the prospects of being ejected from their concrete home or associated perks than consoling her or confronting her husband's mother. Her husband on his part also never turned up to see her or apologize for his mother's highhandedness in the manner in which she had unceremoniously ejected her from her matrimonial home. He made absolutely made no contact or tried to reclaim the house or car that he had purchased for her family.

Her parents' relentless bemoaning of their anticipated loss, persistent nagging and complaints initially left Charity feeling guilty. She was convinced that she had failed them somehow and wished there was some way that she could make amends. She ultimately grew tired and angry after realizing that they weren't being fair on her. She couldn't believe their insensitivity because none of them bothered to commiserate with her throughout her ordeal or tried to put her private feelings into consideration.

She lamentably mulled how she had always sacrificed her comfort for their wellbeing and in the process repeatedly jeopardized her own security and sanity. She had put up with her husband's abuse, mainly to ensure that her family members remained secure. Yet, they wouldn't support her now. They obsessed about minor trivialities in her deepest hour of need. She required their support dearly as she found herself fast sinking into an overriding feeling of worthlessness but none was forthcoming.

She finally decided to escape or else rejection from both her in-laws and her immediate family would drive her into the deep abyss. She felt more betrayed by her family members than her husband or his mother. Pastor Ugo's Sanctification of the Crucifix proved to be her major solace. They took her in as a ward of the church after a chance meeting with Kelechi led to her joining the church.

None of her relatives bothered to come looking for her nor did they bother about her new whereabouts. She was no longer the goose that laid the golden eggs; Charity cogitated bitterly so her disappearance was a good riddance as far as they were concerned. She therefore avowed her dedication to serving God.

* * * * * * * * *

Nkiru instantly perceived the frostiness between Uche and Kelechi as soon as they re-entered their allotted room later that evening. The other two were sat on the lone bed in the room when the entered. Kelechi confirmed her unforgiving nature by refusing to acknowledge their entrance or greetings.

'Sister Kelechi, I see you're still angry with me.' Uche affirmed. 'Please let bygone be bygone. We are different people now and at a different place. Forgive me if I had offended you in the past.' She apologized.

'I'm not angry with you, Sister Uche. I think your guilty conscience is haunting you.' Kelechi replied implacably.

Nkiru was forced to observe Kelechi somewhat critically after witnessing her rigid attitude. She noticed the weird patchy irregular colourings on her face. This meant that Kelechi must have applied specific bleaching creams to artificially lighten her skin but with disastrous effects, Nkiru apprehended. She knew that from one of her roommates in her alma mater but could never fully grasp why anyone would want to change their natural colour. It was not only the unsightly patches on Kelechi's face that looked out of place but the rest of her facial features too. Her huge flat nose contrasted with a rather small mouth, both disproportionate to her midsized catty eyes. Kelechi's disastrous skin bleaching attempt seemed to heighten the disparity. There was definitely something disconcerting about her features but most especially her unpleasant attitude. Nkiru was sure that she wouldn't have had to analyze her critically or closely if her attitude didn't suck. Kelechi would most certainly have fared better under her natural skin. She was certainly the type that Ebere, her late best friend would have designated as gratuitously trying to look whiter than the white. As the thought occurred to her, Nkiru was again reminded of Ebere's innumerable innuendos and hilarious analogies which never failed to bring a smile to her lips.

'I've already asked the two of you to cool it. You should both be ashamed of yourselves,' Charity reprimanded them.

Charity was definitely calm, cute and mature, Nkiru resolved, watching and analyzing them. She wasn't aware of Charity's pitiable history yet but her gut instinct predicted the fair chance that she and Charity could make good friends. Charity was more of her kind of person than curt Kelechi.

'We've assembled here to seek God's mercy and absolution but here are both of you, still squabbling like two silly kids.' Charity continued. 'Let it alone already.'

'I'm sorry, K.K.,' Uche apologized again, affectionately referring to Kelechi as K.K. 'I really don't want us to be carrying old grievances along and for so long too. Please forgive me.'

'I'm sorry.' Kelechi finally conceded.

'Thank you.' Uche was relieved and grateful. She went over to give Kelechi a hug after which she reintroduced the girls again. 'Nkiru is my very good friend and we hail from the same town, Kelechi and Charity.'

'Welcome Nkiru.' They both greeted Nkiru again.

'Thank you very much.' Nkiru responded, she couldn't remember either from the general group earlier. They must have only arrived.

'Now that we are settled, I think we should better go back and join the girls. We don't want to be late for Pastor Ugo's prayer session.' Charity hurried them.

They helped to set the table before sitting for dinner. The designated ladies on duty for the evening had managed to rustle up jollof rice and fried plantain at such short notice. The kitchen was well stocked up and they set plastic disposable plates, cups or cutleries on the table for dinner. They sat round the long rectangular dining table in the dinning hall. There was enough food and soda to go round.

The ladies were more considerably accepting of Nkiru's presence and engaged her in the round table discussions.

'So which route did you guys ply?' Ndidi, the lady sat next to Nkiru asked her.

'I didn't know that there were alternative routes but we came via the wooded area.' Nkiru replied.

'Same as we did. Were you enthralled by the sights?' she enquired curiously.

'Enthralled and more.' Nkiru responded eagerly. 'It's your first time around these parts too?'

'What are you discussing?' Uche sat on Nkiru's left side, broke into their conversation.

'The trip to Obirima,' Nkiru replied.

'You guys need to have seen Nkiru's face.' Uche announced dramatically but good-naturedly. 'She was completely freaked out by the jungle.'

'*Aje butter*!' one of the girls at the far end called out indulgently, insinuating Nkiru was spoilt or privileged.

'I wouldn't blame her. I was personally petrified.' Ndidi added in her defence.

The rest of the ladies soon joined in the general conversation detailing their respective experiences. Most of them had never travelled to the inner cities just like Nkiru and had shared her peculiar apprehension throughout the journey. Nkiru was gradually getting acquainted with all the ladies as they exchanged their journey experiences and other stories and experiences. She wasn't the only one relieved at the sight of the house when they arrived. Some had also contemplated that they would be camping outdoors. They informed her that the Soldiers of the Lord group which was their male counterparts had held a weekend-long rugged outdoors retreat the penultimate month.

Pastor Ugo soon made his expected entrance as they were washing up after dinner. He was casually dressed in jeans and short sleeve shirt but looking ever so dapper. Nkiru was quick to note on her second time of seeing him. The ladies cheered his entrance with a prolonged round of applause and clapping.

He delivered a speech after the ovation had died down. 'Welcome my dear special Ladies of the League. This is a special moment for all of us and The Lord is great indeed. We are gathered here in His name and by His Grace. I hope you all had a safe trip and are properly fed now, Right?'

'Yes, thank you, Pastor.' They chorused happily in reply.

'Well, tomorrow we shall resume our retreat in earnest. Some of you might wonder why we chose this location or why so far from civilization but I'll tell you why.' He proceeded to clarify. 'Our ultimate aim is to withdraw from earthly life for this short spell and commune with nature. We'll hopefully find and experience peace and serenity in this atmosphere without unwarranted distractions. We can also fully and freely meditate in addition to purifying our souls while immersed in the tranquillity of this virgin land. We shall sanctify our souls on the crucifix and find absolution of our sins so that we can move forward in the Lord and with the Lord. We'll seek spiritual nourishment and if we can't find it in this serene environment then I doubt if we can find it anywhere else. I charge you to strive to nurture and inspire your minds, bodies and spirits. Does any one have any reservations about our mission here?'

'No.' Came the resounding rebuttal.

'This is our mission.' He reiterated. 'We shall rest and recover from our trips for the rest of the day but we commence our fast and meditation in earnest from the morning. Most of our activities will take place in the open. I want us to assimilate the clean air and nature around us while we pray and meditate.

The basic arrangements are in the capable hands of Sister Eucharia and I command that you follow her instructions. I promise to make out time to address your individual petitions in the evenings after we break fast. Does any one have any questions?' He paused.

None of them raised any so he continued. 'I leave you in peace and in the name of the Almighty Christ, the Father, the Son and the Holy Spirit,'

'Amen.'

'Alleluia.'

'Alleluia.' Thirty strong female voices resounded.

'*He is the alpha and omega; He is the Lord... ...* They broke into song before retiring to their rooms later that night.

Charity and Ijeoma took to sharing the bed while Nkiru and Uche shared the mattress when they retired for the night. Uche had fortunately packed a blanket with hindsight and it came in handy because it was uncannily chilly that night.

The next morning the ladies reconvened at the large sitting room before they were led to the outdoor grounds for the beginning of the revival, prayers and meditation. Pastor Ugo was in his full element and very charismatic in his delivery of an extended sermon. He bade his congregation to speak in tongues, same as Nkiru had already witnessed during the church service. She watched mesmerized as the rest trampled around the grounds entranced and wondered why the spirit wouldn't captivate and make her speak in a different tongue too. She actually began to yearn to imbibe the art of speaking in tongue or drifting into an illusory state like the rest of them and share the experience. She once again improvised by praying Our Lords prayer, Hail Mary and other simpler prayers known to her while the others were engrossed in their transitory daze.

The group was allowed a midday break for light refreshments consisting of water and snacks. They reassembled later for more of same including meditations, prayers, testimonials and another transfixing sermon by Pastor Ugo.

They were assigned scriptures which will serve as a template for the next day's discussion. The proceedings were pretty as standard as Nkiru had envisaged until the third day when Pastor Ugo deigned that a few were set for sanctification. He asked for those with the same conviction to indicate by raising hands. He chose five ladies from the lot. Nkiru hadn't raised her hand as she was clueless as to what "sanctification" actually entailed.

Uche, Charity and Kelechi, her three roommates and others in tow had their hands up in the air as soon as the priest had asked them to indicate their keenness or readiness. Nkiru noticed that only she and two others from the lot had failed to do same. Of her roommates however, only Charity and Uche were selected but not Kelechi.

Uche bustled with her usual enthusiasm at her luck. She was amongst the chosen five when they returned to their room later. 'I can't believe I was finally chosen. I'm ready, I am so ready.' She marvelled.

'What does sanctification entail?' Nkiru enquired from Uche when they had a brief moment together.

'You'll find out at the right time.' Uche replied rather mysteriously.

'Aha, it's a secret then,' She kidded, thinking Uche was just pulling her legs but Uche was adamant and refused to divulge the secret when Nkiru probed her further. Nkiru was very surprised because she would have expected that Uche would simply enlighten her so she could indicate her willingness next time the oppourtunity arises. She had no clue the process was so exclusive because Uche refused to explain.

'So is it because I'm not a bona fide member of the church or lady's league proper that you refuse to tell me?' She suggested.

'Maybe,' Uche answered. 'Never mind though because you'll learn everything in good time.'

Nkiru was too curious to let it go and was determined to find out from anybody else if Uche was insisting on being difficult. She was truly disappointed that Uche couldn't tell her the secret and therefore approached Charity to explain the process to her instead.

'Don't worry,' Charity reassured her and repeated the same cryptic reassurance as Nkiru had received from Uche. 'Everything will be revealed to you in good time.'

Nkiru and Charity hadn't exactly become the good friends that she had originally predicted but at least they were cordial with each other. The evasiveness of the two ladies made Nkiru more curious and suspicious. She returned to harass Uche a bit more with several queries. 'What does the process entail; does she have to fulfil any criterion to learn this secret? But all to no avail. Uche was amused instead and continued to assure her that all that was required of her was patience. Nkiru doubted if any of the other girls would enlighten her if Uche was this cagey. She insisted that she had to be patient and continue in her spiritual growth after which she would eventually learn the secret. Fortitude as supposedly required in this case was easier said than done because she preferred to be acquainted with the details here and now. She had to relent though after both Uche and Charity refused to oblige her curiosity.

The pre-selected ladies were due to meet upstairs for the sanctification process later that night. The upper floor was previously deigned a prohibited area. The general group broke fast as usual but didn't linger too long for minor chatter in the sitting room before retiring for the night. They had group prayer linking hands to form a circle before turning in. As her two lucky roommates prepared to leave, Nkiru construed that the normally bubbly Uche was rather downcast. She heard her constantly muttering 'I'm ready' as if she was trying to bolster up her own confidence than for the benefit of the others. Charity, in contrast was decidedly calm and stoic. Nkiru admired her to a great extent. She came across as a naturally acquiescent individual who would sop up whatever fate throws her way whether good or bad with equal candour.

Nkiru easily gauged their disparate perspectives and continued to dwell on the process behind this sanctification. She would have imagined it might be similar to baptismal or confirmation rites as obtained in her own Catholic church but none of those were shrouded in an analogous secrecy. And why was Uche so nervous? She pondered. There must be more to the rite than meets with the eye. She might just be forced to quiz Kelechi later, the inquisitive in her contrived.

'Can we all hold hands to pray again before we depart?' Uche requested tensely.

'I've got nothing against prayers but you really need to pull yourself together,' Charity reproved, exasperated at Uche's evident jitteriness. 'If you weren't ready then there was absolutely no need for you to have indicated otherwise. Do you possibly believe that any of your sacrifices could remotely compare with those of The Almighty Father's? He died and was consecrated on the cross for your sins and mine so please get a grip on yourself.' She ordered impatiently.

'I'm ready.' Uche insisted.

'Then act it.' Charity snapped sharply.

Nkiru was bemused at the tetchy exchange between the two but couldn't fathom why Uche was so edgy as to infuriate a usually forbearing Charity. The two ladies left soon afterwards when Sister Eucharia's knock denoted it was time.

Nkiru lay on the mattress without daring to ask if she could share the bed with Kelechi. She pined for slumber in a proper bed than mattress on a cold floor. Kelechi didn't invite her up either.

The lady was ever so surly and typically ignored her. Nkiru on her part reckoned that she was better off steering clear of Kelechi's way in any case. Kelechi surprisingly and in spite of her aloofness does intermittently engage her in a dialogue when she least expects it. She was quite temperamental; Nkiru had already decided and attributed those civil interludes to periods when Kelechi must have woken up on her right side. Tonight was the first time that only the two of them had been left alone for any significant period interval.

'Are you asleep yet, K.K.?' Nkiru asked in a half whisper in hopes of initiating a conversation with Kelechi a moment after the other two had departed. There was no response from her. Nkiru sat up from the floor to see if Kelechi had already drifted off to sleep but found her awake. She was holding the bible in her face, presumably studying or praying. Nkiru was however convinced that she was deliberately ignoring her. 'I'm sorry but I didn't mean to disturb you.' She apologized, settling back on the floor again.

Kelechi absolutely gave no indication that she heard her or bothered to acknowledge her apology. Nkiru gave up on initiating a conversation with her. Kelechi had always been plain difficult and insolent. I should have really known better to leave her alone in the first instance, Nkiru remonstrated herself. She soon dozed off leaving Kelechi to her usual antics.

When she woke up the next morning, Uche was curled up beside her. She hadn't heard her roommates return during the previous night nor had she sensed Uche joining her on the mattress. She glanced at table clock and it was a few minutes to 7 0'clock. They were expected to report at the lounge in roughly three quarters of an hour. 'Wake up, wake up Uche,' she shook Uche by the shoulder to wake her before hurriedly rising to her feet.

'Please don't do that, it hurts.' Uche protested angrily on opening her eyes and quickly rolled away from her reach.

Nkiru was surprised at her friend's outburst; all she did was touch her gently on the shoulder. 'I'm sorry but you better rise or we'll be late.' Nkiru apologized. 'How did it go?' She enquired, quickly picking up her toilet bag and towel. Ijeoma and Charity were noticeably absent from the empty made bed. Nkiru realized they must have risen earlier since they were both scheduled for duties that morning.

'It went well,' Uche replied, struggling to rise simultaneously.

Nkiru noticed her wincing at every turn. 'What's the matter with you?' She enquired, alarmed at Uche's odd sluggishness.

'Aha! Nothing,' Uche grated through clenched teeth as she made one last bid to stand in a swoop. It was obvious that she was hurting terribly because she had grabbed unto the bed post for support, yet she claimed nothing was amiss.

Nkiru watched her for a moment before stepping into the bathroom to brush her teeth and a quick shower. She was happy that there was no queue because they were running late. She had the quickest of showers so that Uche could have one too before they rejoin the others. She just couldn't fathom Uche's strange mood this morning. Something must have upset her because she was usually cheery and easy-going.

It was only when Uche untied the towel around her trunk to dress up shortly afterwards that Nkiru noticed the welts on her back. The poor lady bore multiple fresh welts and bruises all over her back and shoulders for crying out loud. 'Whatever happened to your back?' Nkiru asked, horrified and unable to believe her eyes. No wonder the poor girl was in agony but how did she receive these injuries overnight?

'It's nothing.' Uche replied and diffidently turned away, shielding her back away from Nkiru. She quickly retied her towel and started to pull up her skirt.

'I saw your back so you can't say that is nothing. Uche, you must tell me what is going on.' Nkiru insisted and refused to be sidetracked by Uche's pretended indifference. Her friend was in pain and possible danger.

'It's nothing.' Uche restated more meekly.

'Uche, you know the only reason why I'm here is because I trust you and that has to be reciprocal.' Nkiru insisted calmly. 'If you can't trust me enough to tell me what is going on then I would have no reason to remain here. You'll be giving me no other alternative than to depart immediately.' Nkiru intimidated and made to fetch her bag.

'Oh no Nkiru, please you can't leave.' Uche pleaded frightfully, grabbing her by her arm to retrain her from walking away. 'I'll be in deep trouble if you were to leave. I'll lose everything. Please my dear, don't do this to me.'

'What do you mean by that?' Nkiru enquired, alarmed at Uche's rambling statement. What was going on? She asked herself before confronting Uche. 'You have to tell me the truth or I swear I'm out of here.' She threatened in escalating panic.

'No, you have nothing to be alarmed over. I guess I've been mumbling inanely but this is nothing to do with you. It is my fault and I promise that you have nothing to be afraid of.' Uche pleaded in hasty panic. 'I swear on my mother's life that no harm is intended to come your way. I beg you to stay. You must stay. Please you have to stay for my sake.' Uche pleaded more ardently.

'Why? What's going on? Why is my staying important to you personally?'

'You have to help me. I'll be in trouble if you should leave.' Uche pleaded frantically.

'What are you talking about?' Nkiru demanded furiously because Uche wasn't making much sense. 'Can you try to be a little more specific and clear? I want to know why my departure would get you into trouble.' She demanded angrily.

'Sorry, that came out wrongly. I was just trying to say that I'd be blamed if you're to depart. The ladies would blame me.' Uche stuttered lamely but more soberly.

'And even if they do so what, how would that get you into trouble?' Nkiru countered, determined to get to the bottom of the matter. Uche's caginess wouldn't cut it this time. If there was a secret agenda behind her presence here then Uche must explain to her in full before she leaves. She was not going to condone her dithering any longer.

'Look Nkiru, I'm sorry if I came out sounding a bit muddled.' Uche apologized. 'I didn't mean to alarm you. I or rather we have no secret agendas here, believe me.' She stated firmly as if she had read Nkiru's mind. 'The only reason why I am insisting that you stay is simply because I'm responsible for bringing you here and it would tell badly on me if you were to depart acrimoniously. I sincerely wish that you stay and gain spiritual enrichment and blessings through prayers and devotion.'

'That's not the impression that I got from your words. Why don't we try the plain truth for a change?' Nkiru suggested.

'I'm telling you the truth, I swear. I promise you that there are no hidden agendas and I swear this on my own dear mother's life. I wouldn't deceive you, trust me.'

'You still haven't clarified your earlier statement.' Nkiru maintained, unimpressed by Uche's vigorous denial.

'I'm sorry if I had unintentionally alarmed you,' Uche apologised again. 'You are completely safe and no one here has any wishes to harm you, least of all, me. We are not only friends but family too besides you've been here for days so can come to an educated conclusion. We are not a cult and no one is forcing into anything against their will. I guess I had come off a bit dramatic but I wish you no harm. I really wish you would stay and gain the full benefits of this retreat.' Uche pleaded.

'I wish I could believe you but you had me scared by your words. I still feel you are hiding something from me.' Nkiru insisted.

'Seriously there's nothing to this and it was never deliberate on my part. I'm sorry if I had upset you. It would be entirely up to you now to stay or leave but if you should ask me, I'd say stay.'

'Why were you then insinuating that my leaving will get you into trouble?'

'Did I do that?' Uche asked as if she was surprised to hear that. 'No wonder you're alarmed.' She added with nervous laughter. 'I'm sorry because my intention was far from distressing you. I'm hoping to gun for Sister Eugenia's position in the future and must show strong leadership qualities as well as ability to win over converts so your untimely departure will most certainly mediate against my ambition. I've really worked hard to get to this stage and wouldn't want my efforts to have been in vain.' Uche explained.

'I hope that is all there is to it.' Nkiru stated, reluctant to accept Uche's rather pathetic explanation. She didn't exactly like the idea of playing pawn to Uche's supposed recruitment of new souls besides how did Uche receive those welts on her back. 'Now, whatever happened to you?' She asked.

'You really don't have to worry about me.' Uche assured her and subsequently turned to pick up her top to don. She however burst into tears as the surface of her cotton top chafed against her fresh wounds. 'Nkiru please help me because I'm just a weak vessel.' She wailed and reached for Nkiru's hands. 'I'm so ashamed of my whining when the good Lord himself underwent a worse treatment and never complained. It is true that the mind is willing but my body is weak. I pray to the Lord to forgive me.' And so plaintive, Uche quickly sank to her knees to pray oblivious to the consternation on Nkiru's face.

Nkiru in her earlier fury had almost ignored what had precipitated the argument in the first place. Well, was Uche actually insinuating what she was thinking that she meant? Did she procure her wounds from being flogged? The Sanctification of the Crucifix indeed, she enunciated as the realization hit her. Uche and the other ladies were sanctified in other words had emulated the thrashing that Christ had received while bearing the cross. This must be the crux of their worship and belief. Who in their right minds would have thought same to be the case?

To what intent were they emulating the feat? She mused, growing more perplexed by the minute. This lot must believe that undergoing a similar process will absolve them of sins and other iniquities or else why else would they partake in such an atrocious act? She couldn't quite get the thought around her head as she contemplated this new unearthing. Hell no and to what end? She marvelled, unable to believe that Uche, Charity, Kelechi or the others could be so gullible. Does it mean every one here will be mandated to undergo this so called sanctification thing because she would be damned first. Nkiru was petrified of whips. She didn't completely buy Uche's half baked explanations in any case because it was beginning to seem like the whole retreat was a sham. She spontaneously yanked Uche to her feet, disregarding that she was on her feet praying. 'Look Uche you have to tell me the truth or I swear I'll be out of here in the twinkling of an eye. The truth, do you understand me.' Nkiru ordered. 'What is going on here? What does the Sanctification mean exactly?'

'The sanctification is … is….,' Uche stammered and stopped mid-sentence.

'They walloped you.' Nkiru supplied.

'Yes but its nothing major.' Uche replied.

'How can you trivialize the fact that your back is utterly brutalized?' She queried.

'I promise you it's nothing. Remember Christ underwent worse and was crucified on the cross too.'

'So what are you now, Christ?'

'Please Nkiru, keep your voice down. You're not supposed to know. We have to reach a certain level of spirituality before we can be sanctified.'

'I thought you were claiming that there are no secrets here. So what is this other thing about my departure? How is that supposed to affect you?' Nkiru demanded more forcefully than was in her nature. She couldn't take Uche' word at face value now, especially if there was a chance that she could be personally in some danger here.

'I've told you the truth. I swear to God that I'm not hiding anything. You know that the other ladies were not pleased about your presence here and I had convinced them to let you stay. If you were to leave then I might never get another chance to invite someone. I'm not hiding anything and you know no one here is forced into anything against their will. You really have nothing to worry about. I'm the only weak link. I should undergo my first sanctification with more dignity and courage.' Uche so contrite sank back to her knees to beseech the Lord for forgiveness.

Nkiru was baffled on many counts. Should she really afford to believe and accept Uche's offhand explanations? She cogitated over and over again. What about this sanctification thing? She couldn't for one recollect the last occasion when she was walloped if ever. Some of her tutors during her earlier school days usually resorted to caning pupils in the name of disciplining them. However she personally rarely incurred a similar punishment because she always conscientiously tried to avoid situations that will warrant same. Her parents' affluence and clout had helped to protect her too if the truth were to be told. Oh God! She shuddered vigorously at the thought of being walloped at this mature stage of her life like she was some recalcitrant kid. That would certainly be the most absurd situation, she imagined with another shudder.

She subsequently helped Uche clean her welts and apply Vaseline before they hurriedly ran to the grounds just in time to join the opening prayers for the day. Nkiru resolved to think her decision through the rest of the morning. She was shaken and confused at what she had just uncovered but was keen not to rush into making any rash decisions. She wanted to make up her mind either to stay or leave, albeit Uche had made her promise not to divulge her uncovering of the truth of the Sanctification or witnessing her breakdown to the rest of the ladies. Uche also unexpectedly averred that the sanctification rite was the church's secret weapon against the iniquities of this wicked world. It was an honour bestowed on only true believers, a supreme accolade and proclamation of their bond and faith to the church and God. Her exact proclamation was that "it was a privileged rank to attain and an honour to be bestowed the concession."

The rest of the morning session was as such lost on Nkiru as she contemplated what to do. In fairness to the group, none of the ladies were under any duress to partake in this "sanctification" thing, she mulled. They were clearly asked to indicate their readiness by a show of hands and even then, only a select few were picked.

Nkiru was still lost in her private thoughts while the rest of the group concentrated on meditation and entrancement. Was this whole retreat and worship a sham? She railed privately because she had never heard of any such practice elsewhere. Did more go on besides the whipping? That sure explains the secrecy then. It must be shameful for them to admit the act even if they try to deny the fact or why else would they make out it was such a big secret? Maybe shrouding the practice in secrecy renders it more enticing to partake in, just like the forbidden fruit, Nkiru tried to infer their logic. It was obvious that this lot have been brainwashed into buying into a baseless fallacy.

She was actually starting to enjoy the process and solitude. They had been advised to hand in their cell phones and car keys on arrival for presumed safe keeping and to commit wholly to the retreat. Sister Eucharia had charged that attaining the full benefits of this mission entailed total withdrawal from earthly life, extra-curricular activities or communication with relatives and outsiders alike. Their ultimate goal was to seek and receive spiritual refuge.

Nkiru had believed them but now she was of the mind that it hadn't been such an innocent request after all. They knew what they were doing from the beginning. What could be the possible ramifications if she were to demand to leave? How would her decision really impact on Uche or her standing in the church since she had fought for her corner and now begged her to return the favour? And what would her parents say or think if they should learn of this unusual practice by this church? She knew they'll definitely be worried but what if divulging this little piece of information will provoke them to distrust her? Worse still, if they should subsequently forbid her from embarking on any future trips on her own?

She had so wanted to rebuild their trust and belief in her again and prove that she was a capable adult. She knew they didn't blame her for Obinna's calamity but nonetheless longed to rebuild their love and trust again. What would she do now? How could she retrieve her keys and leave without ruffling any feathers? It was not as if she was in communication with anyone or she could suggest a family emergency necessitates her immediate return home. This group was actually a cult and not a religion. She gradually discerned and became convinced that they'll definitely turn hostile if she were to insist on leaving. She finally resolved to stick the remaining days out. They had barely 3 more days remaining to the end of the session. She'll afford Uche the benefit of a doubt and if it was any consolation; they were required to indicate their willingness to partake in sanctification. As such, there was absolutely no chance in a million years that she'd be raising her hand to indicate consent and be walloped mercilessly in the process as her friend bore witness.

The rest of the day was mundane but Nkiru could barely concentrate on any of the activities. She promised herself to brave the bushes should she sense any form of personal danger.

A number of ladies naturally indicated their willingness to be sanctified that evening. Nkiru's arms never went up. She reaffirmed her earlier vow to escape if anyone was too try to force her into participating in any activities against her will; otherwise she'll plod along for what it was worth. She suddenly became uncannily inspired to spy on the sanctification process later that night in order to decode the motivating factor behind the ritual. She planned to eavesdrop on the whip smacking rite and hear screams of anguish or protest in order to believe the sanctification was for real. Could the ladies indicate when they've had enough or were they mandated to receive a specific number of whips? Who predetermined this figures and based on which principle? Who wielded the whip, Pastor Ugo or his assistants? Were they all summarily whipped or in separate rooms? She was burning with a lot of questions but Uche refused to discuss the issue any further. Charity was equally inflexible besides none of the others were supposed to know that she knew the secret since she hadn't attained the required status, whatever that was. She schemed to sneak out of the room after the other ladies must have dozed off to investigate privately.

So what would you be hoping to achieve exactly? Her more conscientious psyche queried. She realized that she didn't know exactly but the whole situation might become more conceivable to her after she uncovers this secret. Curiosity killed the cat, her conservative conscience incriminated again. But satisfaction revived his life, she countered back rather humorously and laughing at herself.

She did defy her better logic to exit at midnight only to be confronted by Sister Eucharia keeping watch and standing at the foot of the stairs. 'Where are you off to?' She queried in a no compromising tone.

Nkiru quickly retreated back to the room without offering her an explanation. She subsequently strained her ears to try to eavesdrop on distressed screams from upstairs but no peculiar noises were forthcoming. Their room was at the far end of the corridor so was a tad too isolated for deciphering noises sifting from a similar distance. She soon gave up and went back to sleep.

Neither she nor Sister Eucharia readdressed her attempted exploit in the following days. Uche, who had lost her usual bubble following the sanctification, was gradually recovering her jollity in ensuing days. Kelechi in same interim grew surlier than ever after persistently raising her hands but wasn't selected while Charity remained her usual stoic self.

Nkiru had spied Charity's multiple welts but was unsurprised that the lady never bemoaned her situation. Charity had also opted for a second bout of sanctification and remained unflappable. Nkiru had gradually learnt of her poignant background as well as those of the other ladies during testimonials. They were all bonded by singular tragedies. She came to appreciate the truth in the axiom that stipulated that, "the pasture is always greener on the other side". She reconsidered how one would always think their lot was worse until confronted by others with worse tribulations. She secretly admired their resilience and had started to admire their avid devotion to the word of God. She had never been one to take anything for granted in any case but grew more appreciative of her own personal circumstance. She was nevertheless irked in spite of assimilating these palpable lessons because on the one hand, it seemed like these ladies vulnerability was clearly being exploited. She wished that there was a way she could sway them to realize that the sanctification concept in itself was a mere fallacy. She was tempted to raise the topic over dinner but found herself wavering at facing off thirty or more ladies. She had certainly lost her valour to change the world.

Uche suddenly informed her on their last night that Pastor Ugo would grant her a private audience. Nkiru was stunned because she had given up all hopes or desire of meeting him on a one on one basis. The revelation of the secret of this cult which was her impression of them now had strengthened her resolution to avoid the group like a plague from the minute that she departs the retreat grounds. She desired no part of their supposed worship or belief system if it includes this sanctification rite. She didn't want to meet with Pastor either her continued stay was for Uche's sake or she would have long been gone. Uche understood that so should have known better than ask her to meet with Pastor Ugo, she fumed. 'I don't want to meet him nor am I interested in the sanctification or whatever.' Nkiru protested.

'Pastor Ugo knows you are not ready. He had promised to have private prayer sessions with every one of us in the camp so wishes to meet you too.'

'You can relay to him that I'm really fine now and enjoyed all the group activities. I really don't need to meet with him in private.' She restated.

'C'mon Nkiru, you are acting like Pastor Ugo is an ogre. I promise you no harm will come your way. No one will force you into anything without your prior consent. He is fully aware that you're not ready for sanctification and in case you haven't noticed, none of us is forced to participate.' Uche reassured.

'I know but seriously I have no desire to meet him personally.' She continued to protest.

'He'll see you.' Uche stated decisively. 'Sister Eucharia will fetch you later tonight.'

Nkiru remained of a double mind about the session but the matter has been taken out of her hands at this juncture. She was mandated to keep the scheduled rendezvous with Pastor Ugo. She felt slightly uncomfortable at the prospect of confronting Sister Eucharia again after deliberately avoiding her since their meeting at the stairwell.

She and her fellow roommates retired to their room later while she waited anxiously for Eucharia's knock to indicate it was time.

Surly Kelechi was however uncharacteristically good spirited and surprisingly launched into a conversation with them. 'What do you guys think of Jonathan?' She posed a general query.

'Jonathan? Who's Jonathan? Uche repeated, mulling over the rather familiar name.

'Tall lanky Jonathan, he is in the choir and usually sits at the right end of the front row.' Kelechi supplied.

Nkiru was lost to whom they were referring to, she was not a regular member of their church and barely knew the rest of the congregation except for the ladies in the camp.

'Oh, he's called Jonathan then.' Uche announced on recognising whom she meant, her memory jogged alright. 'I think he's lovely.'

'I hope you haven't slept with him too,' Kelechi indicted, glowering suspiciously at her at the same time.

'Please, come off it K.K. I don't know who or what you think I am.' Uche griped angrily.

'You two should stop this juvenile attitude. Kelechi, it's about time that you let the matter rest, *ozugo kwa nu. Enough is enough.* I'm sure you've both learnt your lessons already.' Charity chided, now exasperated at Kelechi's regular inference to her prior fall-out with Uche. 'So what's with Jonathan anyway?'

'Pastor Ugo suggested that I let him know if I fancy any of the fellows in church so he'll fix us up. I'm setting my sights on Jonathan.' Kelechi declared.

Nkiru was flabbergasted but more stunned by the reaction or rather lack of one on the part of her roommates, neither of whom had indicated any surprise or affront.

'Jonathan is a good choice.' Charity endorsed him.

'I agree.' Uche seconded.

Whoa! Nkiru exclaimed wordlessly. Should she be anymore astonished? Her earlier cynicism at New Age Churches, initially born out of the story of the girl, set up for marriage by a dubious lad in a similar setting was played out. This treachery goes both ways i.e. fellows fixed for ladies and vice versa. She couldn't wait to get away from all the sneaky activities of this so called church, cult or whatever. God have mercy. She supplicated.

Knock, knock... ... Eucharia had come for her.

Nkiru stood up to go and for a moment felt literarily like a lamb being led to the slaughter. Why am I going? She pondered even as she walked to the door. She wore a long jeans skirt, long sleeve T-shirt and a scarf tightly wound sternly across her ears for the rendezvous. She purposefully designed to look sufficiently demure and credibly devout.

'Hello Sister Eucharia.' Nkiru greeted.

'Hello Nkiru,' Sister Eucharia responded, without any obvious inference to their previous encounter. She silently accompanied Nkiru to the foot of the spiral staircase before intoning. 'The Pastor is waiting for you. Enter the second room on the right, the second room on the right.' She articulated twice to make sure Nkiru understands her precise instruction.

Nkiru didn't miss the hint of a warning. She must not stray away from the specified location. 'Thank you.' She responded politely.

The upstairs area had remained strictly out of bounds since their arrival save for when Sister Eucharia escorts the ladies up for sanctification or private prayer sessions. Muted conversational voices drifted down occasionally otherwise there was no in other indication of the going-on there.

First time up; Nkiru mused as she went up. Her inquisitive mind veered to their host. She hadn't met or run into him yet, nor have any of the other girls for that matter, at least not as far as she knew. He was rumoured to be in residence but surprisingly fails to join the prayer sessions irrespective of his largesse at hosting them. Nkiru construed from the start that he must be both very generous and affluent given his immense hospitality. A huge generator specifically powered the house round the clock besides constant water supply. Provisions were also abundant irrespective of the thirty or more mouths fed simultaneously twice daily. She again contrived that the church might well be footing the bill.

She turned halfway through the uncarpeted staircase to mischievously spy on Sister Eucharia and to see if she had disappeared. Lo and behold, there she was regarding her expectantly. Nkiru chuckled before continuing. She noticed an array of doors in a semicircle bordering a wide balcony on arriving at the top of the stairs. She considered if she were to count from left or right as either would denote a different second room. She made to go towards her left, only for Sister Eucharia's voice to holler, 'Second door from the right!' Nkiru was startled on hearing her voice because she hadn't heard her come up behind her so had spun abruptly around, almost tripping in the process. She turned towards the right door. She also knocked and stood waiting for affirmation to enter. The room was dimly lit and reeking heavily of incense as she entered. She retraced the direction of the fume with her eyes and spotted the faintly glowing stick burning at a corner of the room.

'Good evening Pastor.' She greeted Pastor Ugo who was standing behind the small table and two opposite side chairs stationed at the centre of the room. There was a small flask and two glasses in a tray on the table as well as bible and leaflets. The room was empty otherwise. Nkiru hadn't known what to expect but the room was pretty mundane.

'Good evening, Nkiru right?'

'Yes Pastor.' She confirmed, catching a whiff of his memorable perfume as she approached the table.

'I apologize for ignoring you; I didn't forget my promise to your friend, Uche to meet with you personally. I've been very busy as you can well imagine. That's the nature of our calling. I hope you have had an enriching experience so far.'

'Yes of course, Pastor. I've enjoyed every minute.' Nkiru half lied.

'I'm glad to hear that. Well, tell me more about yourself.' He requested after Nkiru took the seat opposite him.

She could see his features more prominently after she sat opposite him. He was clearly very handsome and exuded a distinctive air of authority around him. There was also an aura about him that commanded trust. He was genial and she surprisingly found her distrust waning as they chatted amicably.

'There's not much to tell, Pastor from what I'm sure Uche must have told you about me already. I've been somewhat lost since losing my fiancé.'

'You must have loved him dearly.' He stated the obvious.

'Yes, dearly and very deeply.' She replied simply and was instantly tearful.

'That's understandable but you must remember that the Good Lord giveth and taketh so there must be a heavenly cause for why he was taken so early.'

'So I've been told.' Nkiru made a crack at a joke, surprisingly finding herself relaxing in Pastor Ugo's company. It was starting to feel like she was chattering with an old dear friend.

'Do you doubt God?' He queried sardonically, arching his eyebrows and with a backward tilt of his head as he observed her indulgently.

'No I don't,' Nkiru refuted immediately. 'I just miss Obinna too much that for my own selfish reasons would have preferred that he was here with me than in heaven.'

'The foundation of incidents in our lives is revealed in good time and someday you'll comprehend why he was taken so early.'

'I hope so.' Nkiru expressed hesitantly.

'I know so.' Pastor Ugo stated more decisively. 'I suggest that you work on your commitment to God and your faith.' He urged her passionately. 'You've got to believe that Lord is unquestionably the alpha and the omega. He alone gives and disposes but never fails those that put their trust in him. I'm sure that you'll be able to testify to that in the nearest future. I charge you to build your faith. Let us pray.' He ordered and stood up at the same time. He proceeded over to her side of the table towering over her medium sized frame. He placed his palm on her forehead and Nkiru could clearly discern his fragrance. Ralph Lauren? She countered uncertainly to herself. That pungent musky smell was unmistakable and stirring. She loved it because it was Obinna's favourite fragrance and was suddenly aroused by the aroma.

Pastor Ugo started to chant prayers while she stood with closed eyes and palms supplicating to the heavens. She tried hard to concentrate on what he was saying as her thoughts continued to wander. She was inexplicably drawn to him.

He anointed her forehead with water from a small plastic tube that he took out from his pocket before pouring some liquid from the flask into a cup and offering her to drink. He continued to pray and mediate for her lost soul.

The fluid tasted bland, Nkiru realized as she gulped it down. It must be holy water. She subsequently began to feel unsteady and felt herself drifting away as Pastor Ugo's voice gradually faded into the distance. She vaguely felt a rather strange sensation of being lifted off the ground and imagined floating across a cascade of snow covered stairs across the gateway of heaven on her way to join Obinna. That was her last memory before she woke up the next morning on her mattress bed on the floor of their allotted room. She squinted at the ray of sunlight slithering into the room and directly unto her which was making her headache worse too. She noticed that she was alone in the room at the same time. The other ladies must have left. She struggled to sit up as her head pounded and couldn't recollect how she had got back there from the previous night or was it early hours of this morning? She was strangely out of sorts and groggy. If she didn't know any better then she could have imagined that she was recovering from a heavy hangover. Except that she barely touched alcoholic beverages, much less on a spiritual retreat. She was still trying to gather her wits together when she heard Uche's cheerful son as she entered the room from the shower.

'Good morning,' she greeted Nkiru and continued humming her praise song as she dried her wet hair with a towel. 'How did it go?'

'Good morning.' Nkiru responded and instead of replying to Uche's query, enquired. 'How did I get back to the room?'

'Why?' Uche countered, unsure of why Nkiru had poised such a strange query. 'I didn't hear you come back but you were asleep when I rose. I had meant to wake you after my shower. Why do you ask?' Uche repeated.

'Never mind,' Nkiru replied. What would she tell Uche anyway? Last thing she remembered was Pastor Ugo praying for her then offering her holy water to drink, followed by a hazy sensation of being elevated and then waking up back in her bed. None of it made any sense. Was she drugged? Did Pastor Ugo desecrate her body, did he rape her? Nkiru sat up abruptly and startled at the improbable connotation. She headed straight for the bathroom to investigate.

She drew her white underpants down to her knees and couldn't see any signs suggestive of forceful entrant or rip. She proceeded to examine the slight stains on them, staring at a slight clear discharge and streak of blood but nothing unusual to indicate rape or forceful penetration. She was predisposed to spotting blood infrequently due to her recent irregular menstrual periods. She dipped a finger into her sensing an odd warmth and easy receptiveness before grasping at her with both hands and perceived slight tenderness. What had happened in that prayer room or was she letting her vivid imagination and suspicion run away with her? Nkiru pondered before disconsolately sinking unto the wet floor of the bathroom to bawl her eyes out at her confusion. She was doubtful about what had happened to her the previous night. She blamed herself for going against her better judgement or consenting to the private meeting with the priest. She was paying the price now, she recriminated against herself. If she had only held her grounds and refused to meet him then she wouldn't be in this lamentable predicament now. Maybe she had indirectly asked this upon herself or why else would she have been focussing on Pastor Ugo's good looks and fragrance instead of the spiritual fulfilment that she originally sought.

Uche rushed to the bathroom on overhearing Nkiru's sobs. 'What is wrong Nkiru, what is the matter?' she queried with great concern.

'Nothing, nothing,' Nkiru replied hastily, deciding on that spur of the moment not to confide in her. She couldn't possibly substantiate her possibly irrational suspicions. Uche wouldn't believe her anyhow, knowing her sustained prejudice against her church. Nkiru countered furthermore to herself that since she possessed no tangible proofs to substantiate such a serious charge then it was best that she kept quiet for now. Her womanhood felt oddly warm and easily accessible and her breasts hurt but surely if she were raped, she would be more sentient of it than just those vague intuitions. She didn't and couldn't remember any substantive details to augment her fears nor could she successfully re-enact the events of preceding night.

She mulled over telling her parents after her initial sobs had subsided. She was still sitting on the floor with hands underneath her chin while pondering her situation and options. Uche had left her alone after she refused to offer any explanations as to why she was so upset. Nay, not a good plan, she surmised rationally with regards to telling her parents. They'd insist on appropriate investigations and if those would prove to be futile then she would only have herself to blame. She would not only have further tarnished her personal reputation but also succeeded in dragging her parents through the mud with her. She could well imagine the furore that would follow if the news was to become open knowledge. The public will brand her a liar besides the various tags that they had already dubbed her, Nkiru mused while contemplating her dilemma. There would also be the matter of her parents losing confidence and faith in her. She was sure they'll become wary of trusting her again or consider her incapable of taking care of herself when she knows that was not the case. She'll never want to lose or betray her parents' trust. As she mulled her situation and possible outcomes, Nkiru became convinced of the greater likelihood that nothing had happened and this whole charade was just her overactive imagination getting the better of her. Yet major doubts nagged at her.

Nkiru evoked her avowal to stay mentally strong and avoid a relapse to her prior debilitating depressive state. She vowed therefore to surmount this latest adversity than let another catastrophe break her. Her worst possible torment was over as it were. This incident or non incident as the case might be wasn't going to send her askew, after all which calamity could supplant losing Obinna? She braced up and rose to her feet and resolutely stepped into the shower to turn on the tap. She didn't bother to remove her clothes. She felt that the grim was washing away as the tepid water drenched to her clothes which clung to her skin like second skin. She wept along silently, her tears mingling with the shower jets. She prayed her suspicions were only but her fertile imagination conjuring an imaginary trick on her. She couldn't possibly have been defiled.

Nkiru relived the events of the previous night again but couldn't arrive at any concrete conclusion. She contested that Pastor Ugo was too dignified to perpetrate a rape assault on her as her suspicions contrived. On the other hand, which grown man whip lashes ladies or adults for that matter? What was his justification for the sanctification? Was it to feed his pseudo machismo, satisfy a warped personal sexual fantasy or because he actually believed that his congregation would be exonerated from sins through the same process? The million dollars question was who whiplashes Pastor Ugo to absolve him of his personal transgression or did he deem himself as beyond reproach? Does he bear similar welts and scars on his back same as the Ladies of the league and possibly his other flock? What about the men folk? Did they undergo a similar process? Did husbands, fathers, or lovers see the welts on their respective spouses', daughters' or lovers' backs and remain unaffected? Did the ever try to denounce or stop the practice or else where they just taken in same as the ladies? How could they passively watch another fellow whip or assault their female folk without reacting? It was an inconceivable concept. How full blooded, grown adults would willingly consent to sanctification was beyond her. What would her parents think or say if she were to intimate them of this group's shock belief system whereby parishioners are physically assaulted in the name of consecration and absolution? She fervently hoped her suspicions were tenuous because if she had actually been raped then Pastor Ugo was a total fraud and a coward as well as grossly sadistic. She had no wish to cross paths with him again in her life. She knew enough now to confirm that her earlier misgivings about so called Pentecostal churches and the rest of them were not misconstrued. She stripped off her sodden clothes for a proper shower and subsequently changed into dry clothes before packing up her belongings.

A sudden and intense desire to quit the godforsaken retreat grounds prevailed upon her after her shower. Nkiru couldn't wait to escape the grounds fast enough.

Uche was mystified by her friend's strange conduct but consented to her urgent request for them to depart sooner than later. She was done with her own packing; retracting their phones and Nkiru's car key as well as dispensing with her goodbyes before Nkiru was set and ready to go.

They hit the road for home without further ado. Nkiru longed to return to the safety confines of her bedroom in her parents' home at the soonest possible interval.

Conversely, whatever happens in Obirima, will remain at Obirima.

Ten

'Hello Nkiru, how are you?' A voice emerged from behind her as she inserted her key into the lock.

It was Deji.

'I'm fine, thank you and how's work?' She returned, veering back simultaneously to face Deji and exchange pleasantries.

'I'm not complaining.' He replied complacently but with a cheerful grin. He looked to be on his way out. He was her new neighbour and his flat was directly opposite hers. He had introduced himself on the same day that she moved into the complex, voluntarily offering and helping her lug her baggage up to the flat. 'I hope you had a good day at work today?'

'I did, thank you.' She answered.

'I'm off now, see you later.' He bade her before skipping off on his merry way.

'Bye.' She returned and subsequently let herself into her flat.

It was her second week since moving in after securing a post with her former employers or National Electricity Board. She had coincidentally intimated Sanni of her desire to actively seek employment upon her arrival home from Obirima and he had immediately promised to help her out.

Sanni was a newly inaugurated Minister of Mines and Power and as such wielded even more clout than before. That is besides the fact that his father was a very influential business tycoon. Nkiru could hardly believe her luck when Sanni called her back a few days later to say she could have her old job back. He didn't just stop at that but arranged her accommodation too. He had contracted one of the new flats in his father's estate complex for her and essentially offered her the place rent free for a whole year to afford her time to settle down properly or so he claimed. The major icing on the cake for her was really when he indicated that she could resume work as soon as in the following week.

Nkiru was still utterly amazed and thrilled at the swiftness at which her situation was sorted out such that before her parents could protest or urge her to take her time in deciding her future plans; she was already moving into a new flat and resuming work. She was delighted to return to Igbaje where she had undergone her National Youth Service Corps program a year and more ago. The firm had originally offered her a permanent post after she concluded the scheme but she had declined. Her decision linked to her standing arrangement with Obinna. They had resolved then that she should only secure a permanent post wherever his transfer posting took them. They hadn't wanted anything to hamper their future plans of being together. The rest of their saga was however history.

Who'd have otherwise foreseen that she'll be back in Igbaje and reemployed by same firm? She marvelled incredulously as she stepped into her fresh smelling flat. She had resettled without much difficulty and got right back into the swing of things again. Some of her old friends still lived in Igbaje including her best friend Lily, her husband Okon and their lovely daughter or her goddaughter, Amaka who comprised her major solace. A handful of her co-worker friends from her previous tenure were still at the job so on the whole, she was glad to resettle back at Igbaje surrounded by a few familiar faces. Her mind wandered back to Ubi after she arrived back from Obirima.

* * * * * * * *

The dust had apparently barely settled beneath her feet from the retreat before Nkiru was going to embark on another jaunt to Igbaje. Her parents weren't exactly too pleased and charged that she was being unnecessarily hasty. Nkiru also stuck to her private counsel of not confiding her suspicions to them. She construed her fears might be unjustifiable besides she couldn't convince herself that Pastor Ugo could possibly be that crass. She therefore failed to disclose her fears of defilement to her parents or most especially to her oddly inquisitive and persistent mother. She smiled now remembering how her mother, Lolo had badgered her with multiple queries on her return.

Lolo had been very keen to hear the full details of her experience at the retreat, more so since they had been totally cut off from communicating with the outside world throughout the period. She would have called her daughter for daily updates if not for that. 'So let's hear all about your experience at the camp.' She had urged Nkiru excitedly.

'It was okay, Mummy. The activities ranged from worship, prayer sessions, and testimonials to meditations. We also fasted throughout the period and held private prayer sessions with the priest.' She had reported.

'I see, you look well rested.' Lolo commented and waited for more details but Nkiru wasn't more forthcoming. Lolo was disappointed by her offhand account and suspected there was more to it than Nkiru was letting on. 'That is all?'

'Of course Mum, it was a religious gathering not a social one.' Nkiru reprimanded Lolo light-heartedly, knowing her mother required more elaborate details but she wasn't keen on divulging her secret fears which was all it was going to lead to.

Lolo's gut instinct certainly indicated to her that her daughter was guarded, especially given her unusual flippancy. 'So what did you make of the church generally or the Ladies of the League?' Lolo persisted.

'They were fine, nice girls. I forgot to mention that the actual journey to Obirima was a total eye opener.' She had announced more enthusiastically. 'The retreat ground was in the middle of a jungle so I was quite relieved to see a proper house having feared we might be camping outdoors given the rustic set-up.'

'I can relate to your fears.' Lolo empathized. 'I've never been to Obirima specifically but I know its neighbouring areas are quite underdeveloped. I thought your accommodation was secure before you left.'

'Oh yes but I was a bit thrown off and apprehensive after driving through the jungle-like area and viewing the stark evidence of poverty littered along the way. We did end up staying in a stately home owned by Pastor Ugo's friend.'

'Obirima and its surrounding areas are in dire straits. It's a really sad situation.' Lolo agreed.' I hope our government would do something about the area some day. Did you make any new friends?' she continued; keen to steer the conversation back to the actual retreat.

'Yes, I shared a room with Uche, as well as Charity and Kelechi. I also met a couple of other girls, Ijeoma, Ndidi and others. I'll tell you all about their personal stories later.' She had promised.

'You're sure that nothing else went down there?' Lolo enquired more directly. Nkiru would have usually launched into a detailed account of her trip without prompt than letting her ask for every specific minor detail. Her enforced cheeriness wasn't fooling Lolo either.

'Yes, I'm certain Mum. Let it rest. I promise to tell you all about the girls later.' She had reiterated after a momentary pause, reaffirming to herself that there was no need to alarm her mother with false rumours. 'I enjoyed the spiritual rehabilitation side of things but doubt if I'll be converting to a full-fledged member of the Church.' She admitted candidly to her mother.

'They bear an unusual name, the sanctification of the crucifix.' Lolo enunciated the church's name slowly. She was very glad that Nkiru wasn't converting to the new church. She didn't want any of her children to ever desert the Catholic faith. She did abhor or rather distrusted the so called trendy New Age Churches sprouting all over the place. It was like a fast growing fad and a majority were led by rampant unscrupulous priests. It wasn't like the Catholic Church didn't have its shortcomings but she believed that there were more checks and control in place. 'So what prompted your decision?' She queried Nkiru to be sure that she just wasn't claiming not to convert for her benefit.

'I think that I really prefer a more solemn mode of worship than the screeching, screaming and talking in tongues that went on there.' She had explained.

Lolo could personally attest to that. It was true that these churches were seemingly more evangelical and exuberant in their mode of worship. She however relented on grilling Nkiru, deciding that she mightn't be hiding any secrets after all or else would have voluntarily confided in her.

Nkiru was long convinced that her father would react vigorously if she were to indicate her suspicions. There was no way he'd take such a serious accusation lying low and since she wasn't entirely positive that she was raped, the matter was best left alone. She therefore refused to divulge her secret to her mother.

She had been more surprised that Uche hadn't tried to query her more extensively about her private session with Pastor Ugo. Uche had simply accepted her explanation that nothing was the matter after she saw her crying on the floor of the bathroom. She had personally toyed with the idea of confiding her secret fears in Uche during their homeward journey until she indirectly tested Uche's reaction.

She had artfully started off by asking Uche, 'How would you describe your relationship with Pastor Ugo?'

'You want to know my personal relationship with Pastor Ugo?' Uche repeated, baffled at her line of questioning.

'I mean yours and the other ladies'.' Nkiru clarified.

'I still don't get your point.' Uche had replied cautiously, peering at her rather suspiciously.

'Seeing that he is a handsome fellow and you are all beautiful ladies.' She had replied tellingly.

'I don't know if that is supposed to be a joke because I don't appreciate it anyhow.' Uche had replied curtly and seemingly aghast. 'I'm surprised that you could pose a similar query after attending the retreat.' She chastised. 'I'm sure you would have been the first to notice any hanky panky since you are so suspicious.'

'I was just kidding.' Nkiru hastily apologized, retracting from her line of questioning.

'Pastor Ugo is a righteous man and a mentor for most of us whom he had practically rescued from the abyss.' Uche stated bluntly. 'Why do you think no one protested against a group of females camping out with him? We trust him.' Uche proceeded to answer her own query.

Nkiru there and then had made up her mind to leave Uche alone without confiding her suspicions. She knew Uche wouldn't believe her in any case. She reeled from Uche's attack anyhow because even if she relented on her suspicions in the interim but the fold still had questionable practices. She proceeded to grill Uche on those. 'Well your Pastor Ugo might be righteous and all but what about this sanctification thing? Do you really think that could be considered as a standard practice?' She had counteracted back at Uche.

'Why the sudden attack of Pastor Ugo?' Uche demanded angrily.

'I'm not attacking his person; I'm only querying the morale behind the sanctification.'

'Let me theorize on this then. What does religion mean to you?' Uche offset as they both geared up for a possible heated argument.

'You tell me.' Nkiru had retorted.

'I'll take a broad categorization i.e. Christians and non Christians. Christians as a whole have the same general core belief which is their belief in God or a higher being, however we choose to denote him, right?'

'And your point is…?'

'The bible, Koran etc is guidebooks so to say,' she continued, undaunted by Nkiru's irritated retort. 'Our fundamental differences lie in our interpretation of these guides but having said that, our ultimate aim is to emulate God's life or words.' Uche rationalized like she was talking to a kid.

'Could you just hit the nail on the head without the unnecessary rigmarole?' Nkiru had been angry at Uche's nearly patronizing attitude.

'Nearer home, the fundamentals of our belief lie in Jesus as the son of God. He was beaten and crucified on the cross to absolve our sins,' Uche continued unhurriedly. 'So why can't we emulate his sacrifice? Wouldn't that construe an ultimate tribute to our devotion?'

'First of all, none of you are Christ or specially anointed and what next? You're going to ask to be crucified too?' Nkiru had opined sarcastically.

'If that is what it would take.' Uche muttered solemnly.

'I really hope you're kidding.' Nkiru laughed nervously, unable to believe that Uche believed that. 'I think you and the rest of the girls have been unwittingly brainwashed and transformed into puppets in the hands of your so called Pastor.' She charged passionately. 'The Bible stipulates that Jesus Christ is specially anointed, his birth pre-ordained for a particular purpose. Our religion encourages us to follow his teachings which are not the same as emulating his life verbatim. In case you haven't noticed but you and I are ordinary humans whereas He is the anointed one. I hope you understand the difference.'

'We are all children of God and special in His sight so there is nothing wrong in emulating the life of His begotten son Jesus Christ. God isn't a separate entity from his teachings.' Uche stated.

'I don't think you're objective enough in your arguments. There are so many loopholes in this your new belief system. You may think that you are righteous by virtue of a few whiplashes but you are no Christ. Christ suffered for his faith and to absolve our sins and you can't say the same for yourselves. You're all of the same faith, yet your leader arrogates the power to whiplash the rest of you unto him. Come to think of it, who whips Pastor Ugo; on what criteria does he base the number of strokes that he delivers? Can't you see that the whole idea is both warped and preposterous? C'mon be realistic.' Nkiru pleaded. She was frustrated by Uche's parallel thinking.

'That is why Pastor Ugo insists that one must attain a certain level of spirituality to merit sanctification. It takes superior faith and belief to achieve this because only then can you begin to value the full strength of devotion and sacrifice.'

'Bull crap.' Nkiru had denounced, unimpressed.

'You can say what you like but I'm a better person for my life presently.' Uche had insisted.

'That might be true but I don't think it has anything to do with sanctification. That notion is nothing short of delusion. Look at your

212

back, the scars you have incurred or the unbearable pain and tell me how any of that has helped change your life?'

'Let's leave it at that then.' Uche had suggested disenchanted by a reminder to her earlier breakdown.

They subsequently agreed to let their differences be. Uche visited her later but never tried to coerce her back to her Church again.

* * * * * * * *

Nkiru presently considered the minor adjustments that she had had to contend with since resettling at Igbaje irrespective of ease with which she had resettled as her reverie continued to unfold. She had returned as a full-fledged civil servant, not Corper as was the case during her previous turn. She also stood to earn a more substantial salary. There was the absence of the fortnightly coveted conventions too. They had used to converge periodically then to perform community service duties. It was a fun gathering really because the period offered them respite from work and an opportunity to meet up with old friends. They invariably ended up going out for drinks or parties after completing the minor tasks. Her worse adjustment yet was contending with the absence of alternate weekend trips to Mekede to visit Obinna or hosting him at her joint. She could have easily burst into tears reminiscing about Obinna but she was mentally stronger now. She endeavoured not to wallow in self pity these days but conscientiously tried to concentrate on the happier memories of their time together.

She thus kicked off her moderately high heels shoes on entering her roomy bedroom and slipped into flip-flops. She subsequently undressed and stepped into the shower, after which she changed into shorts and T-shirt before proceeding to her kitchen to concoct a meal. She really admired her airy new flat; it was in a new complex and she was actually the first occupant of her particular flat. The complex was located at the outskirts of Igbaje; far from the hustle and bustle of the city centre and her former three-bedroom official lodgings which she had shared with two others.

Her present abode was smaller in comparison but more luxurious as well as situated in an elite and secured gated community. It consisted of one bedroom, a moderately large sitting room and adjoining dining section in addition to a relatively compact kitchen. She was nonetheless content with the tiny kitchen because she wasn't overly keen on cooking, especially when she was alone. Their house helps back home usually took care of preparing most meals but she prided herself on making special fried rice which was her main specialty. The Igbaje weather as in most of the Northern states was more conducive for growing carrots, large green or red chilli peppers and other vegetables so there was always a ready supply of condiments for her to make her favourite dish whenever she was so inclined.

Sanni had furnished her flat for her too, providing a brand new 34 inch television set, a three-sitter brown leather sofa as well as matching bedroom and kitchen furniture sets. He had also delivered a decorative flower pot of long dried reeds personally when he arrived to formally welcome her. She had placed a few pictures of herself, Obinna and her family to make the place more homely. She was really impressed by the manner in which Sanni had strove to cater for every detail to make sure that she settles in comfortably. She was indebted to him and deeply touched by his kind gestures. She shouldn't have been surprised since he had always proven to be a good and reliable friend to her even after his friend, Obinna's demise and hoped that some day she'll be able to reciprocate in kind.

Nkiru carefully measured a small portion of rice into a medium sized pot and placed on the gas cooker to boil. She also retrieved a frozen plastic bowl of chilli stew from her deep freezer and placed into the microwave on defrost. She then poured herself a glass of juice and walked down to the sitting room to ensconce on the sofa opposite the television. She picked up the remote control and started to flip through the channels in search of any interesting program to watch.

It was Friday but she had nothing special planned for the night. She intended to visit Lily and her family the next day. She was on her way to the kitchen to check on the rice that she had on fire when she heard a knock on the door. Who could it be? She speculated as she wasn't expecting anyone.

'Coming,' she called out loudly, quickly rushing into the kitchen and turning off the stove lest the rice would burn while she is attending to the stranger at her door. She'll need to 'wash' or rinse out the starch from the rice before adding fresh water, salt and boiling the rice to cook.

'Hello, Deji, I wasn't expecting anyone.' She said surprised to see him at her door.

'I hope I 'm not intruding but its Friday and I was wondering if you were up to anything.'

'Oh no, I'm sorry but I'm not that much of a socialite.' Nkiru replied apologetically. 'I'm having a quiet day really.' She added but before she could finish, he was already sat on the sofa, without prior invitation, so much for her wish of desiring a quiet Friday.

'That makes the two of us then.' He announced. 'I don't have anything planned either so we could hang out together if that's okay with you.' He suggested.

'Okay.' Nkiru agreed half-heartedly. She had really been looking forward to her own company besides she didn't consider Deji to be a close acquaintance to spend her Friday with. She barely knew him besides she wouldn't want to encourage him by becoming close. The last thing on her mind was another relationship at this stage, she deliberated. She didn't really relish Deji sneaking in on her or the prospects of making a new close friend.

On second thoughts though, there was effeminacy to Deji. He gesticulated while he chattered like a woman and his voice was rather odd too. She had already discerned a suspiciously feminine timbre or rather high pitched squawk to his voice and his suggestion of wanting to hang out with her resonated more like coming from a girlfriend.

'Aha, I see you have *"Ovation"* and *"Hello"* magazines.' Deji exclaimed excitedly, oblivious to her scrutiny. He reached across the sofa without permission to select a few magazines from the rack at the other side of the sofa.

Mmh...mmh... mmh, Nkiru pondered. That was an entirely effeminate gesture as if proving her point, which male gets excited over tabloid gossips and female fashion both of which were actively portrayed in those magazines?

'Please help your self.' She grudgingly invited but he wasn't exactly waiting for her permission either.

He had already fished out a few magazines which he placed on his lap. He started to leaf through the pages stopping to ogle at fascinating pictures or captivating headlines. He was *oh-ing* and *ah-ing* excitedly as he pored over them.

'Excuse me but I have to go to the kitchen. I was making dinner.' Nkiru explained after an awkward silence. 'You'll share with me.' She invited, now inclined to offer out of politeness.

'Of course,' He agreed readily, without hesitation or looking up from the magazine on his lap.

Nkiru continued to ponder his impromptu visit as she rinsed off the starchy water from her half boiled rice in the kitchen. She was not entirely convinced that it was a good idea to develop a closer rapport with a neighbour; Deji lived too nearby for comfort. She had originally envisaged days when she can walk around naked in her small flat if she so desired without pointless interruptions or unsolicited visitors. There might well be times when she might be lonesome or hanker for company but not from a next door neighbour who might feel at liberty to drop in at her place on a whim. She wasn't enchanted by this new development.

Deji hung about long after they finished dinner and proceeded to give her a load down of gist relating to the other tenants sharing the same complex and the neighbourhood in general. Nkiru considered his company somewhat surreal because he was a man yet it felt like she was hanging out with a girlfriend instead.

He was chatty and hilariously witty. She decided she'd collapse in laughter if he were to make any overtures at her. She gradually began to warm up to him after realizing she was safe on the score of an intimate relationship with him. She was so far from ready for any sort of intimate relationships with the opposite sex for the moment.

Their two respective flats formed the only flats in their particular section and were situated on the second floor. Deji narrated that he shared his flat with his fraternal twin brother, Tunde who evidently looked nothing like him. Both of them had moved to Igbaje six months prior to her arrival and were half–way through the one year National Youth Service Corps program. Deji and his twin obviously attended Nkiru's old camp and were apparently under same army chief so she and Deji recounted their similar experiences. Deji disclosed his twin brother was agitating to relocate back to Isako. He detested the slow paced life style of Igbaje, preferring the more hectic Capital city and related busy night life. Deji on the other hand confessed he was completely besotted by the place.

Nkiru wondered momentarily how the twin brothers were able to afford such plush digs given that they were Corpers. As far as she knew Corpers were paid a very moderate stipend so she pondered if Deji would be forced to vacate his present lodging if his brother was on the verge of leaving for good. She considered she would miss him already if that was the case. He described his upbringing to a small extent and she could garner that his parents weren't affluent. How then were he and his twin able to afford 500,000 naira deposit required to rent their flat? Nkiru momentarily pondered. She didn't ask him to expatiate as it was none of her business anyway. Their new friendship warmed up as Deji engaged her with hilarious tales and escapades.

She clearly recalled Deji's twin, Tunde whom she had met a few times exchanging only basic pleasantries. She knew that they were brothers but could never have guessed they were twins. Tunde was nothing like Deji or half as chatty from the little that she had garnered. The two shared an unmistakeable resemblance peculiar to siblings but that was as far as their likeness went.

Deji was darker in complexion and with a distinctive fashion sense. He seemed to have a penchant for fitted rolled up long sleeve, short sleeve shirts or hugging T-shirts on equally tight fitting slightly jump-up or ankle length trousers reminiscent of Michael Jackson's and revealing red or white socks on black slacks. Tunde on the other hand was slightly rotund and shorter than Deji. He also came across as more mature, more like his elder sibling than twin. He loved traditional long flowing agbada robes which he always donned on the few occasions that she had met him. He wasn't as friendly as Deji either. Deji coincidentally worked in the same firm as Okon, Nkiru's best friend, Lily's husband. His brother, Tunde was employed elsewhere.

Deji regaled her with details of mutual neighbours, current neighbourhood news and gossips. Nkiru had only met with a few of the neighbours, much less knowing their private details. Deji however furnished her with ample information including on other strangers living in the neighbourhood.

'You've got to be wary of Dr Babalola.' Deji specifically warned her. 'I'm surprised he hasn't made move on you yet.'

'Who is he, I don't know him.' Nkiru laughed.

'I bet you'd recognise him once you see him. I've never met a more arrogant fellow.' Deji spurted maliciously.

'What has he done to you and why do I have to be wary of him?'

'Oh, he didn't do anything to me per se except ignore my greetings,' Deji motioned with a disdainful flip of hands. 'He thinks he is glib, newly wed but constantly parades around town with numerous women.' He narrated. 'He has a private clinic in town and carries on like he was the best thing that had happened since sliced bread.'

'Oh my God, why are you so aggrieved at this fellow?' Nkiru asked.

217

'I hate his attitude. He should have respect for his wife even if he has none for himself.'

'That's true.'

'I still can't believe you haven't met him yet. He's quickly on the trot after any fine looking lady.'

'And where does this fellow live?'

'Directly above us,' Deji replied. 'He might be loosing his knack then if he hasn't made a play for you yet.'

'Oh dear,' Nkiru was greatly amused at Deji's obvious antipathy towards the fellow. 'I'm glad that he has better things to occupy him than chasing after me. I wouldn't give him the time of the day, trust Me.' she assured Deji.

'There's another creepy fellow living upstairs.' Deji continued his rant. 'I think he's called Oleg and he's European. I don't know his exact origins. The fellow is so scruffy looking that you'd wonder if he was really white.' Deji reported in his dramatic effeminate fashion.

'Please stop Deji,' Nkiru laughed at his hilarious analogy. 'So white people aren't supposed to look scruffy?'

'C'mon Nkiru, I'm not joking.' He sat up gesticulating wildly in protest. 'If he looks this scruffy with all his money then God knows what would happen if he were poor.'

'You have a point there but not all white people are rich just by virtue of their colour.'

'I know that but he must earn loads for living here and earning an expatriate's salary. C'mon you've got to be kidding me if you don't agree with me.'

'You do have a point.' She concurred.

'The key gist on him is his sallow skin tone and horrid body odour. Could you believe that even local prostitutes refuse to share his bed?' Deji announced spectacularly.

'Is that good or bad?' Nkiru asked unable to decipher the angle he was spinning this time.

'Don't tell me you are that naïve. Those women are usually eager to sleep with foreigners in exchange for foreign currency so for them to decline sharing his bed must be a first. It was no surprise that he works in the mines then.' Deji concluded.

By the end of the night, Nkiru was privy to the private details of neighbours, living both within her block and beyond. Most of them were strangers to her but that didn't deter Deji from regaling her with their stories or any secrets they might have been concealing. She couldn't remember the last time that she had laughed so much because Deji had a theatrical way of telling stories. He succeeded in keeping her in stitches through out the night. She was also amazed at his scope of knowledge; more so since he seemed to have amassed such extensive font in only six months. He sure was a good girly … sorry… boyish company, she corrected herself. It was easy to forget sometimes that Deji was male because of his effeminate mannerisms.

Nkiru went to visit over at Lily's home as she had originally planned the next day. Lily and her husband, Okon had relocated to a more sizeable flat than their residency during the "Corper" days. She had no difficulties locating the place since she had already visited them there during Amaka's christening a few months ago.

'Welcome Nne, you must have tripped on your good foot because we're almost set for lunch. How are you?' Lily asked delightfully as she stepped back from the table to hug her best friend.

'I'm fine and you? Where is our pride and joy, Amaka?' Nkiru enquired, glancing around for any sight of her energetic goddaughter who was noticeably absent given the calm.

'She fell into an exhausted sleep a few minutes ago. We'll let her to nap for a bit. She's been busy wrecking the place and her father just laid her into bed a few minutes ago.'

'I better not wake her up then.' Nkiru surmised, adopting a more muted tone.

'Oh you needn't worry, she can sleep through an earthquake but her naps are short. She'll soon be up and about again.' Okon allayed her fears.

'Who does she get her restlessness from then?' Lily knowingly directed at her husband.

'You, of course,' He replied defiantly with a laugh.

'Mmh …mmh, no.' Lily disagreed with a shake of head. 'Amaka is entirely her father's daughter in looks as well as character that I sometimes wonder if there's any part of me in her at all. I sure served as a mere incubator.' She lamented cheerfully.

'That's why I say we should have a second one so he or she could take after you.'

'Could you glean his hint?' Lily complained blithely to Nkiru as they both laughed.

'I'm sorry but I support him on that one.' Nkiru declared to Lily's mock chagrin.

'And I thought you were my friend.' Lily derided good-humouredly before explaining. 'Amaka alone is a handful, **Nne**. Two Amakas' or an additional child will undoubtedly prove to be my undoing.'

'We'll employ maids if that is what it would take. The trouble is your friend is too independent and insists on doing everything herself.' Okon complained candidly to Nkiru.

'I'm sure two of you can work something out.' Nkiru suggested diplomatically, reluctant to take sides on that one.

'**Nne**, please come with me. Let's fetch the food.' Lily invited and Nkiru accompanied her to the kitchen to fetch large bowls of jollof rice, chicken stew, fried plantains and salad after which they settled down to eat.

'So how's your new place? I hope it's not too lonesome for you. We must come and see the place soon' Lily suggested.

'You must come, of course.' Nkiru agreed. 'I like it and I don't mind the solitude at all. Actually I was beginning to enjoy my own company but for my new frequent visitor.' Nkiru admitted.

'And who could that be?' Lily queried with a glint and expected to hear she had hooked up with a new fellow.

'No, no. It's only Deji,' Nkiru announced, to Lily's disappointment. 'My friendly neighbour from the opposite flat, he sure is a real good laugh. It appears that he works in your firm, Okon.' Nkiru turned to inform Okon.

'You mean effeminate Deji?' Okon validated.

'Thank God you said that. I was beginning to think my suspicions were getting the better of me once again.' Nkiru sighed; relieved to hear Okon shared same opinion.

'Oh no, his effeminate mannerism is quite evident. The people at the office talk about him incessantly and occasionally make derogatory comments directly to him. I'll declare that he is a really strong character. He somehow manages to deflect the talks, gossips, snipes or even derisive attitude meted to him by acting indifferent. He is ever so cheery and obliging that I feel guilty on behalf of the others.'

'Is he same guy that is said to be a "**yan daudu**"?' Lily wanted to ascertain.

'Yes, same one.' Okon confirmed.

'What is "**yan daudu**" please? Nkiru enquired curiously. It was the first time that she had heard the expression in use.

'It is a Hausa expression for homosexual, transvestite or deviants. It shouldn't realistically be applied to Deji who is Yoruba but also no transvestite. He is however rumoured to be in a secret relationship with a wealthy married Hausa fellow who is keeping him in the fashion that he is presently living in.' Okon explained.

'Why is the expression strictly in reference to Hausas if depicts homosexuality?' Nkiru asked.

'*Yan Daudu* actually refers to a unique social category of males in Hausa land originating a few centuries ago. They are known to adopt feminine mannerism including speech and dress, in addition to earning their keep through selling food on the streets, prostitution, or procuring sex.'

'Really?' Nkiru was stunned to hear this new piece of information. 'I had always assumed that homosexuality is a foreign concept which has only recently started to percolate into our own society.'

'So did we too until Deji surfaced in Okon's office and kind of opened up a can of worms.' Lily admitted.

'Garuba, a friend at the office said *yan daudu* had been in existence ways before the inception of Islam but managed to thrive alongside the stringent religion. The group have since been categorized as pagans or *Magazuwa's* and are said to belong to the sacred *Bori* cults. They are said to worship various nature spirits and perform possession ceremonies with women and *Yan Daudu* officiating.' Okon enlightened them on the topic.

'How did you learn such obscure details?' Nkiru asked, awestruck and impressed by his eloquence and scope of knowledge.

'I was curious so did a little research and reading besides the info that I garnered from the office.' Okon admitted modestly.

'Why then do the majority of us Africans declare that homosexuality is a foreign concept?' Nkiru wondered aloud.

'There are abundant extant historical records indicating that homosexuality existed in different parts of Africa, Asia and the rest of the world from time immemorial. I'll tentatively propose that our present denunciation of the concept is more of a defence mechanism to undermine the spread of homosexuality than anything else.'

'I don't know if I would ever have believed that homosexuality was long-existent in our society from anyone else but you. I had assumed that homosexuality and the like were foreign concepts.' Nkiru fazed up.

'We believed same until recently. In as much as I stand liberal and openly sympathetic to homosexuals but I must admit that I secretly think it is a curse or disease of sorts.' Okon confided.

'I agree. It's certainly not a natural phenomenon. I don't think anyone of us here could honestly state that they could pray to beget a homosexual kid.' Lily stated. 'Another aspect of the whole phenomenon that perplexes me is that when you see two males in a so-called homosexual relationship, one of them would assume a proper male or dominant role while his partner will act like a female counterpart or assume the submissive role and vice versa for so called lesbians. So if you ask me why don't they just go for the real thing?' Lily opined.

'I guess it's a phenomenon that none of us will ever fully understand.' Okon stated resignedly.

'True, I've always been puzzled by the whole concept of homosexuality too.' Nkiru added. 'It must be bothersome for the afflicted if I may borrow your phrase, worst still that they have to contend with our very prejudiced society. Take Deji for example; I entirely sympathize with his situation. I know he is naturally effeminate because it's certainly not an act that he puts on at will but I admire his strength of character. You get taken by him once you can overlook his veneer. He seems unaffected by the fact that he is different which goes to prove his strength of character. I must admit that I occasionally forget that I'm interacting with the opposite sex when I'm with him but he is who he is.' Nkiru recounted.

'Really?' Lily wanted to affirm.

'Yes,' Nkiru replied. 'I don't know if being effeminate makes him homosexual too but I'm growing to accept Deji for a close friend.' She informed them. 'I had not previously been in close contact with homosexuals or effeminate looking fellow for that matter. I can easily afford to accept Deji for who he is; unfortunately the rest of our society isn't that tolerant. Deji hasn't confided in me regarding his sexual orientation. I'm only guessing he must have psychological tortures given the prejudice and denigration towards his kind. I know I would if I were in his shoes. With regards to your statement,' Nkiru turned towards Lily. 'I admit that I couldn't honestly pray to beget a homosexual kid in the same vein as imploring for a healthy child. I hope that doesn't make me a hypocrite but I wouldn't want to thrust any kid into similar hostility, our society is too prejudiced and cruel.'

'I agree,' Okon concurred. 'Deji is very brave but I'd never wish to be in his shoes. I don't think I could possibly cope with the open hostility, snide remarks or clear disdain depicted on people's faces as easily as he does. I've personally witnessed colleagues refusing to interact with him outright like he was afflicted with a contagious disease. I can't say it enough but I admire his conduct and courage. He comes off as impervious to prejudice but I bet he must still hurt inside. I can't begin to imagine his inner demons.'

'He really does come off as impervious.' Nkiru agreed. 'He is definitely beginning to grow on me. I have to confess that I wasn't exactly thrilled at the thought of making friends with him,' she admitted. 'However my aversion wasn't related to his personality per se. I just wasn't keen on befriending a next door neighbour which could prove to be too close for comfort really. I like Deji, he is hilarious. Did you say something about him having a lover by the way?' She tried to reconfirm from Okon.

'Yes, a male lover but no one seems to know his identity yet.' Okon supplied.

'Mmh... ... okay, he didn't mention one to me yet. You know he has a twin brother, Tunde who is his complete opposite both in looks and character, I suppose.' Nkiru informed them.

'A normal twin brother?' Lily intoned sceptically.

'Oh yes, they rarely socialize together but share a flat. Deji mentioned his brother is departing from Igbaje soon. He wants to move back to Isako because he prefers the social scene out there; Igbaje is too stagnant for his liking.'

'I wouldn't be surprised if it's not all the gossip about his twin that's driving him away from Igbaje.' Lily attested disdainfully.

'Maybe not, Deji must have been the same person all his life so I suppose his brother should be used to his personality by now.' Okon disagreed.

'You're right; I didn't exactly consider the situation from that perceptive.' Lily was a little mortified at her unprovoked rant. 'With no offence to you, Nkiru, I wonder who you think has a better deal between an OSU and homosexual.' She put to Nkiru after a pause.

'No offence taken, dear.' Nkiru reassured her before responding. 'It's not something that I've previously contemplated in depth but now that you mention it. I'd say none of them is any more a desirable tag than the other. OSU is an insular, inane injustice given that our culture imposes the tag on individuals based on seemingly nonsensical grounds while homosexuality is an inherent designation so to say and a more widespread concept.'

'I agree,' Okon concurred before expatiating. 'Both constitute a sad state of human affairs. Yes, OSU is a societal tag transcending only a particular culture and group of people whereas homosexuality is a much more innate characteristic, affliction or what have you. If you asked me to choose between them, I'll pass on both because they are both gratuitous handicaps.' Okon opined.

'I sometimes wonder why we can't just accept each other for whom or what we are instead of all the prejudices and segregations that abound.' Nkiru idealized.

'Our world is in a sorry state, discrimination abounds everywhere. I'm not a philosopher but from my personal observation, I'd say that our human ego is a tricky driving factor. There is an instinctive human desire for dominance which is why we undermine one another in order to attain a superior utopia. The resulting effect creates palpable differences between our human entities in general i.e. the superior verses the inferior. This parlays to some and is a handicap for others but in the long run manages to ensure a partition.' Okon philosophized.

'True.' Nkiru and Lily agreed.

'If I may be allowed to add to your theory, this division is not always in a broader context. We intermittently create them right in our homes from where it transcends to tribes, nationals, races, and so on and so forth.' Nkiru supplemented.

'Very true too,' Okon agreed.

'I hear someone crying. Amaka must be awake.' Nkiru inferred from eavesdropping a weak whimper from Amaka while they were briefly engrossed in private thoughts.

'Yes, it is my madam.' Lily confirmed indulgently. Amaka's whimper was fast turning into a howl. 'She is awake and I should better get her before she yells the whole place down.' She hurried off to fetch Amaka as her cry grew increasingly louder.

The three friends lounged and continued their chatter late into the evening. Nkiru also devoted some time to playing with her god daughter before reluctantly taking her leave. She thoroughly enjoyed the company.

Nkiru travelled back home to Ubi to spend the following weekend. It was her initial trip home since returning to Igbaje. Her romance with her new life in Igbaje was thriving and she was relishing every second of it while it lasted.

It wasn't difficult for Lolo to garner that her daughter was blooming once again when Nkiru arrived home. They had been in constant contact by phone and Nkiru had sounded distinctly cheery. It was however more enriching for her to see her daughter physically and confirm that she was looking as hearty as she sounded on phone. Her other siblings and Obinna's younger ones had returned to their respective boarding schools. Her father was also away on business so it was only the two of them home besides the helps. Mother and daughter therefore had plenty of time on their hands to reconnect and catch up on their personal news.

'I'm glad to see you looking like your old self. Igbaje suits you.' Lolo complimented her once more after they settled in the family lounge after sharing a light dinner.

'Thanks Mum. I like Igbaje. I've always said it was a cross between a city and suburbia so suits me just fine. In some way Igbaje is a modified version of Ubi and the fact that Lily and a few old friends there have helped me settle right back in.'

'I'm happy for you and Sanni is godsend too. We must invite him over to Ubi some day.'

'Yes but I think making out the time might be a bit tricky for him with his new portfolio. I'll most certainly extend the invitation to him in any case when I see him.'

'Uche came around asking after you the other day.' Lolo told her.

'Oh, did she? I hope she is fine.'

'She looked well. You didn't actually give me a full account of that retreat.' Lolo readdressed her old haunch.

'Really Mum, leave it alone. I promise you nothing else happened at Obirima than I already told you.' Nkiru reasserted with a laugh.

'If you insist,' Lolo reluctantly gave up. Her gut instincts still indicated there was something but Nkiru insists nothing was amiss. 'We can go to the shops at Akwaete tomorrow.' She suggested instead.

'Okay but you are treating us Mum.' Nkiru warned.

'No problem.' She agreed. 'We can also stop by Ebere's mother place later. She's been asking after you for ages.' Lolo planned.

'That's a really good idea, Mum. I'd like to see her again. It' ages since I saw her. I hope she can forgive me for neglecting my promise to stay in touch.'

'She understands. I'm just glad that everything has normalized now.'

'True.' Nkiru agreed and tactfully changed the topic. She had no wish to relapse into her old melancholy 'Dad's due back tomorrow morning?'

225

'More likely night, he's still trying to recoup the funds from the failed bank venture which is proving to be a Herculean task. It's a struggle trying to recover your money once it gets into other peoples hands. It's been a pretty tough year but somehow God helped us cope and survive. I hope we never revisit the same deep hole again.' Lolo pray.

'Amen.' Nkiru seconded. 'I'm so proud of both you and dad.' She commended both of her parents.

'It was only by God's grace, dear.' Lolo admitted modestly after which they both momentarily lapsed into silence.

'It's very calm without Azuka and co. home.' Nkiru noted.

'You noticed too. I'm glad you're here this weekend because with your dad away too, the house was beginning to feel like a graveyard.'

'You should come and spend some weekends over at Igbaje with me, Mum. I've got a plush little flat now, you know.' Nkiru jokingly bragged.

'So you say and I will. I can't commend Sanni enough but he has always been a true friend to both yourself and Obinna.'

'He truly is a good man.' Nkiru seconded.

They continued to chatter into the night before retiring. They travelled to Akwaete the next day and stopped over to see Ebere's mother as planned. Ebere's mother was very pleased to see them; especially Nkiru who she commented was looking more like her old self again.

Chief Ubaka returned from his business trip home later that night and spent time with his wife and beloved daughter. He was overjoyed to see Nkiru looking like her old self again.

Nkiru left home to return to her base after midday on Sunday and arrived back at Igbaje around sunset. She struggled up the stairs lugging her heavy weekend bag, laden with canisters of cooked food that she had packed from home. She had to make constant stops every other two steps to recover her breath from the excessive load. She had stopped for yet another brief rest when Sanni and Deji ran into her on their way down the stairs. Sanni's usual police escorts who accompanied him everywhere these days because of his new political post were noticeable absent.

'Hello Sanni,' she greeted cheerfully. She was as delighted as ever to see him. 'Hello Deji.' She greeted the uncharacteristically silent Deji lurking behind Sanni.

'Hello Nkiru, you must be coming from home.' He guessed noticing her heavy luggage. 'I hope your trip went well and how are your parents?'

'Hello.' Deji responded softly.

'They are fine.' Nkiru replied to Sanni's query. 'Actually my mum said to extend an open invitation to you to visit us at Ubi.' Nkiru told him. 'She can't wait to host you.'

'That would be a great pleasure. I'll let you know when I am chanced because I'll really like to go.' He agreed. 'I hope you've settled in nicely, any problems?'

'None at all, I couldn't thank you enough. Everything is just fine and I'll let my mum know that you'll visit. She'll definitely hold you up to that promise. And how are you Deji?' Nkiru leaned across to address Deji again.

'Fine Nkiru,' he responded rather absentmindedly as if he was suddenly jolted out of private thoughts. 'I'll help you with the bag.' He offered and immediately stooped down to take the heavy bag from her.

'Thank you very much but I can manage if you are on your way out.' Nkiru suggested.

'Its okay, I wasn't going out exactly. Bye Sanni.' Deji bade Sanni before taking off with Nkiru's baggage.

Nkiru was baffled at Deji's strange attitude. There must be something bothering him. If she didn't know any better, she'd have thought that he had departed in a huff. It had seemed like he and Sanni were lovers in a tiff but that was a completely preposterous idea. She bade Sanni a hearty goodbye before following sullen Deji up the rest of the stairs and into her flat. He stopped by but was noticeably not his usual jolly self.

'Is there a problem?' Nkiru enquired with some concern.

'N...o,' Deji replied hesitantly. 'Not really but never mind it's nothing you can help me with anyway.'

'Why don't you try me first?' Nkiru suggested keen to help him in anyway. They were firm friends now and she looked upon him like a close girl friend or younger sibling.

'Seriously, nothing you can help me with.' Deji insisted.

'A problem shared is a problem... ...' Nkiru started to remind him.

'Okay, okay if you insist. I suppose I can trust you. Sanni just broke up with me.' Deji announced blatantly.

'O...k...a...y,' spluttered Nkiru, hardly able to conceal her surprise. She couldn't have guessed that Sanni was Deji's secret lover in a million years. She had known him personally for some time now besides Sanni was married to his cousin who was betrothed to him from childhood. In all the time that she had known him, there had been no suggestions to suggest that he swung both ways. She had actually met his wife during Amaka's christening. Her name was Fatima and she came across as pleasant though expectedly timid. She barely contributed to any of the general chatter and wore traditional Moslem garb. Deji was suggesting therefore that Sanni was bisexual! 'I'm sorry.' Nkiru offered sympathetically while recovering from her initial jolt. 'Is there anything I can do to help? Did he explain why he is breaking up with you?'

Deji started to weep. 'He said that we should cool it off for the time being.'

'So in reality he's suggested a cool off period not a total break up.' Nkiru pointed out in case Deji had missed the point. She felt caught in the middle of an uncomfortable situation and wasn't sure how to handle it. She did have a sisterly protective predisposition towards Deji but he was a grown ass man, yet here he was openly weeping like a broken-hearted lady. Well maybe, he does feel heartbroken, she conceded, contrite. The situation was certainly weird though. She mused as she offered him tissues for his tears.

'I knew it. I always knew Sanni was too good to be true.' Deji claimed while still in tears and repeating. 'I knew he was too good to be true. I was hoping he'll be my soul mate for life. He was the first man to truly show me affection and respect. I trusted him.' Deji continued to whine.

'I'm sure the two of you will be able to work things out in the near future. Like you said he had only suggested a cool off period.' Nkiru consoled.

'What am I supposed to do now?' He wailed brokenheartedly.

'Did he say you should vacate the flat too?' Nkiru asked, for a moment worried that Sanni had asked him to vacate the accommodation.

'No, no,' Deji disproved. 'He is not withdrawing any previous financial support but that is not my main worry. I love him. I always knew his politics will come between us.' He wept, collapsing into deep sobs again.

Nkiru offered Deji more tissues which was the only thing she could do. She was tempted to draw Deji into her arms and hold him till his sobs subside. He looked so vulnerable now that she had to overcome her initial aversion at seeing him bawling like a girl to sympathize with him. How would he react if she were to physically embrace and comfort him?

'Would you want me to talk to Sanni? He is a pretty good friend of mine, you know.' She offered instead but simultaneously hoped that Deji wouldn't take her up on that offer. That will surely be one awkward conversation between her and Sanni if she were to try to mediate on Deji's behalf. She hadn't even known that Sanni swung both ways. Wonders shall never cease, she reflected inwardly.

'No, I don't think that will change anything.' Deji declined to her relief.

'Please stop crying. I'm sure both of you will surely work something out soon and if there is anything you want me to do to help then you must let me know.' Nkiru assured him.

'It's fine and I'm sorry,' Deji stopped to sniff into a tissue and perked up a bit soon afterwards. 'I shouldn't really have broken down like this, it was the shock.'

He went on to narrate his beginnings and initial meeting with Sanni to Nkiru. 'I realized I was different from an early age.' Deji recounted. 'My twin brother Tunde and my childhood playmates loved to tussle and rumble involved but I never liked any rough games.' He started. 'I hated the tumbles or fights. I also disliked soccer, wrestling, climbing trees or hunting for birds and most of the supposed masculine games that they chose to partake in. Baba, my father is a bricklayer and what I would call a total man's man. He intensely detested my mannerisms which he likened to that of a female's.' Deji regaled Nkiru who was listening absorbedly. 'Baba warned that he would rather kill me than have a sissy for a son. He was regularly whacking me ruthlessly to "beat a man out of him".' Deji mimicked his father's voice.

'That must have been very difficult times for you.' Nkiru pointed out sympathetically.

'Yes.' He agreed. 'And instead of partaking in these supposed rugged manly sports, I preferred to sit in the company of my mother, sisters and the other women in our compound. I liked to listen to them chatting, gossiping or just discussing issues with a peculiar feminine perceptive. I couldn't hang around them too long for fear of Baba. I tried very hard to conform to the behaviour that he desired of me but failed woefully.' Deji added with a nervous laugh recalling those days. 'I consistently rushed home to my mother crying, bruised as well as brutalized almost after participating and failing woefully. It didn't matter what game my brother and friends devised but I was always the last or at the receiving end. I just couldn't handle their forceful jostling, constant bullying or the fact that every one of them managed to wrestle me to the ground. I didn't derive any joy from the games either. If Baba were ever to catch me running back to the comfort of my mother's bosom, he forcibly enforces my return to those macho games or else would untie his belt and wallop me mercilessly for acting like a sissy.' Deji recounted. 'I endlessly queried why I was different from the other boys but Mama assured me that it was only a growth phase that I'll ultimately outgrow. I wondered if that was the case then why was Baba so disenchanted with me? It was not like I didn't try hard to be conventional but I just couldn't stand the heat of those rough games. Mama finally sent me away to live with my uncle or her brother at Isako after I collapsed in the hands of Baba's brutal trouncing.' Deji stopped to show her some of his old scars. 'Baba gave me those. He broke my arm once and they had to open it up to fix the broken bone. Mama feared for my life and hoped that I'll fare better living with Uncle Gbenga in a bigger city and away from Baba who had vowed to make a man out of him even if he has to kill me doing so.' He paused before continuing. 'I loved Isako. It was a much bigger and more modern city than my home village, Isalo. You couldn't imagine the disparity between the growths of the two towns, given that they were just an hour away from each other.'

'Same obtains everywhere. That reminds me of Obirima, which is not very distant from my hometown; Ubi yet is so underdeveloped that their disparity is startling.'

'That is true. Anyway, I absolutely adored living with Uncle Gbenga. He didn't bully me like Baba and the other kids were also less cruel than my childhood mates. Don't get me wrong because I still received jabs and was intermittently bullied at school but it was significantly reduced if compared to when I had lived at our small hamlet. I contrived personal survival skills by undertaking assignments and running errands for the major kingpins of bully groups in school in exchange for protection.' Deji laughed, recalling his old antics. 'I only started to recognize that my effeminate ways was more than skin deep when my brother and friends started to obsess about sex and girls in our teens. I didn't share their similar obsession. I had made a few close female friends but was never sexually attracted to them; my male geography teacher was certainly more appealing to me than girls. I couldn't dare to admit my secret longings to anyone for fear of judgement or incurring a beating. I was strangely lonesome in the midst of family and friends as well as misunderstood at the best of times. I had to develop a thick skin and try to ignore the varied horrid attitudes meted to me ranging from disdain which was more often than not, fabricated tolerance from those who pretended to be unprejudiced to overt hostility from those who couldn't stand my kind.' Deji enumerated less humorously. 'I tried to ignore it all and concentrated fully on my studies. I met a few fellows along the line that I was romantically inclined to learnt to mute my desires. I desisted from expressing my feelings or making overtures for fear of rebuff and enormous repercussions. I knew Baba would personally skin him alive if I were to embark on any relationship with the same sex. I don't even know anyone that is brazen enough to have an open relationship at any rate.' Deji stopped shortly to fetch himself a glass of water from the kitchen. 'Do you want one?'

'No thanks. You can have some food, I brought loads from home.' Nkiru offered.

'Thanks but I only need water.' Deji declined.

'Did any one in your family know that you preferred men?' Nkiru asked him after he returned from the kitchen with a glass of water.

'They must have known deep down but it wasn't a topic that we discussed openly. I purposefully chose to attend university up in the North because of the rampant stories I had heard of Alhaji's soliciting for male lovers. Their culture must be more tolerant if that was case, I had decided. I was periodically courted by these wealthy Alhaji's who discretely dispatched scouts to the campus with enticing gifts but I had no desire to be involved in such nefarious activities. I had always hoped for a proper loving relationship if that will ever be happen some day in view of the narrow-mindedness of our society in general.'

'So how did you get to meet with Sanni?' Nkiru enquired excitedly.

'I'm coming to that. In my second year, a group of cult fraternity boys picked on me for growing too attached to their leader's girlfriend. My relationship with the girl was purely platonic for obvious reasons besides I was only helping her with course work. That didn't deter the group from beating me up viciously and landing

231

me in hospital with several severe injuries.' Deji recounted and stopped to show Nkiru more of his scars including a sizeable open gash on his skull.

'I hope the police were able to apprehend them since you knew their exact identities.'

'Of course not, you must be naïve. I couldn't tell the police or the group would come back to skin me alive. No one tells on fraternity gangs.'

'It's sad how we had allowed these cults or fraternity gangs to perpetuate atrocities in our campuses.'

'Unfortunate and sad, their activities are impossible to curb Anyway I met Sanni Mumba while on hospital admission. He had been on an official visit to commission a new ward and also took time to chat with patients at the same time as I was in hospital. I think a sympathetic nurse briefed him on my case and he was especially concerned. He met me briefly and dropped his business card. He insisted that I should call him if I should ever need help. I didn't think anything of it but saved his card, knowing that having such an influential contact could come in handy someday.' He narrated.

'Whoa, so how did you finally link up?'

'My condition took a turn for the worse soon afterwards after it was discovered that I had developed a blood clot in the brain requiring immediate evacuation. There was no way I or any members of my family could afford the estimated steep hospital fees. There was only one neurological hospital equipped to offer the treatment and wouldn't undertake my treatment unless the fees were paid upfront. After much consideration, I contacted Sanni who rose to the occasion. We subsequently became friends and Sanni practically took me under his wing.' Deji told her.

'Did you immediately think he was homosexual or rather bisexual then?'

'No, I absolutely had no clue. I was overwhelmed by his kindness especially as it was obvious there was nothing I could offer him in return. What could I possibly offer this man that had everything anyway?'

'I agree. Sanni is a naturally kind soul.' Nkiru concurred.

'He became my mentor too. I could phone him up with or for just about anything and he never failed to listen to me. He always and unfailingly chatted, counselled or offered me financial support, whatever my need was at the time. For the first time in my life, I had met someone humane and genuinely interested in me. I revelled in our chats. I never discerned disdain, subversive covetousness or antipathy that was the norm with most men I had close contact with in the past. We could stay up for hours chatting and discussing politics, current affairs and life in general but rarely met up in person. I had no tangible hint that Sanni was remotely homosexual or rather bisexual but that didn't deter me from falling hopelessly and deeply falling in love with him. I didn't dare mention or discuss my growing affection and love to him for fear of destroying the friendship that we've built. We were in contact for almost a year before he offered me a ticket to join him while he was abroad and the rest as they say is history. Sanni wed his bride last year but promised that wouldn't change anything between us. He only insisted on absolute discreteness. We avoided being seen together in the streets even when we were abroad to protect him and his political image.' Deji paused before emphasizing again. 'I always knew his politics will ultimately poise a greater threat to our liaison than his bride.' Deji wailed, his hysteria resuscitated once more. In that short spell he had relished and recaptured the magic that was once his and Sanni. Deji erupted into sobs again.

Nkiru tried to console him as best as she could and he was more composed by the time he was retiring to his flat. Nkiru pondered on his situation after he left. She was still reeling from the surprise of discovering Sanni was living a double life. She would never have guessed he was bisexual in a million years. No one was perfect, except for her Obinna of course, she contended reflectively. It was rather unfortunate that she couldn't share this new titbit with Lily and Okon. She couldn't possibly betray Deji's confidence. What a life, so many secrets and lies! She recalled her invariable summation of life as a continuously churning wheel rounding full cycles that orbited from one pivot to another, each pivot a reference point to the next. She would also cast herself in the role of a passenger, cavorting these endless cycles and gathering mosses of experiences that would ultimately translate to wisdom but was she for now, the wiser at this particular pivot in time? She reflected on her transited pivots but couldn't vouch that the concurrent lessons were clear or fully assimilated. As for the present situation, some of the happenstances defy rationale. What else lies in that bag of tricks juggled by life? Bring it on; she challenged rebelliously as she settled into bed entrapped between laughter and incredulity.

Eleven

'Nkiru, Nkiru, are you home?' Nkiru heard Deji's frantic yell ways before he arrived at her door a few days later and started to rap persistently and impatiently for her to open the door.

'Hold on, I'm coming.' Nkiru replied and hurried to get the door. She had been lounging in her sitting room in shorts and watching television before the unexpected thump. Deji must have urgent news judging from his impatience, she decided as she quickly unhooked the latch to let him in.

'Hello Nkiru.' Deji managed to greet her. He was struggling to regain his breath from galloping up the flights of stairs or his bursting news.

'Hello Deji, I hope all is well.'

'My dear I've got terrible news.' He announced sinking resignedly into the sofa and disconsolately stretched his feet out dramatically.

'What is the matter?' She enquired with concern, observing his forlorn looks.

'It's Sanni. I heard someone is trying to blackmail him.' He announced between pants, still winded.

'How is that and why?'

'Apparently, a political opponent is threatening to expose his secret if he doesn't step down from running for the party's presidential candidate nominations.'

'Secret?' She repeated, momentarily baffled but then rapidly grasped Deji's inference as he made to enlighten her. 'Oh yes your relationship.'

'Yes, it's a big mess.' Deji admitted forlornly.

'So how did you learn of this new development?'

'Abbas, he is Sanni's driver. He is about the only soul that knows our secret besides you or so I had assumed.'

'Then how did it leak and what will happen now?'

'I have no clues yet. Abbas suggested that this fellow was just making random accusations but Sanni's only major secret is our relationships so your guess is as good as mine. The possibility of our secret leaking has always constituted his major fear which was why he suggested we break up. I don't know what to do because I can't even call him. It is just too risky now.'

'Oh my God,' Nkiru exclaimed, momentarily lost for words. 'I'm so sorry.' She offered in the absence of something better to say.

'I might just have to disappear for a bit until this whole thing dies down. This could prove to be a dangerous situation for both of Sanni and me if any links are established between us. It would destroy Sanni and I couldn't let that happen.'

'But what would you do, where would you go.' Nkiru queried, nervously buying into Deji's panic.

'I don't know yet but I need to find a way to meet or talk with Sanni first before making any concrete decision.'

'Look Deji, if there is anything I can do to help, I mean anything, please don't hesitate to ask me.' She pleaded with him. 'Do you have enough cash?'

'I suppose so. I'll leave now but I'll keep you informed.' Deji promised and stood up to leave.

'You are departing tonight but to where?' Nkiru asked worriedly. It was 9pm already; it was risky to travel out of town at that hour.

'Abbas promised to get back to me with a message from Sanni so I'll meet up with him first and decide from there.'

'Please be careful and take care. Don't forget to keep me informed whatever happens. I'd feel better for knowing you are safe.' Nkiru pleaded, almost tearful and afraid for his safety.

'I will.' Deji promised.

'Bye and be careful.' Nkiru begged while standing at her door and watching his dejected figure disappearing rapidly down the stairs. She wished that she could have been more helpful; she lamented and watched helplessly as his figure completely faded into the night. She mused over her not so distant conversation with Okon and Lily pertaining to homosexuality and the like. Those concepts were very much abhorred and generally labelled foreign, sinful and taboo amongst her people. It was also astounding that a general consensus of censure amazingly exists amongst all of the multicultural, diverse ethnicities and religious faiths.

Sanni's political aspirations will most certainly be in peril if there were any suggestions that he was homosexual or bisexual as the case might be. There was zero tolerance on counts of homosexuality et al, much less if a prominent political figure was exposed as bisexual. She understood Deji's trepidation. She could well imagine the furore that will erupt if Sanni's homosexual dalliance was to become public knowledge. The damage will most certainly impact on his political standing. Deji's life could be in possible danger and she feared for his safety. Political aficionados will assassinate him at the drop of the hat if he posed any threats to their patron's political ambition. She also empathized with Deji's obvious heartbreak but that was just a chip off the iceberg considering his imminent danger is Sanni's secret were to become public-knowledge. She would've wished that Deji was with a single fellow than a married man who was secretly living a double life but you can't choose who you fall in love with. Deji's present predicament reminded her of her beloved Obinna's OSU situation and the whole obnoxious realm of segregation or designated societal pariah. It was a cruel sad world; she sighed and prayed for her friend's safety as she shut her door. Our universe is imperilled by redundant prejudices, she sighed before retiring back into her flat.

Deji was crestfallen as he made his way downstairs, hands in pocket and lost in thought. He was headed towards the manned exit gates hoping to find a cab to keep his rendezvous with Abbas. He was in luck because he had barely waited for 5 minutes before one drew up to drop off a passenger at the gates.

'*Sannu* Mallam.' He greeted the affable driver behind the wheels. 'I'll take a lone drop.' He specified before settling at the back seat adjacent to him. He was preoccupied by his worries and was also keenly awaiting news from Sanni. He was meeting Abbas midtown or more specifically beside a deserted primary school block. He missed his personal ride which he had re-gifted to his twin brother Tunde. It was a gift from Sanni but Tunde had begged to have it continually while relocating back to Isako that he finally relented. He now has to contend with boarding taxis to get around Igbaje.

The taxi driver conveying Deji immediately discerned his preoccupation and anxious body language. He glared at him suspiciously through the central mirror.

'You wan commot for near Ama Hausa?' The driver tried to confirm his exact destination from Deji.

'Yes, just after Babariga junction and near the old primary school.' He explained.

The driver was unimpressed by Deji's high pitch squawk of a voice or effeminate gesturing. He was personally very religiously devout and intensely homophobic. Deji ingenuously compounded matters by asking to be dropped off at the middle of nowhere but a deserted school block.

It was pitch dark when the driver drew up at Deji's proposed destination and the taxi driver could only infer that Deji was embarking on an illicit and homosexual sexual tryst. Or else why

236

would he be attending such a deserted location at such an ungodly hour? His intense hatred for Deji's kind was at a boiling point, more so at the thought that he appeared to have indirectly abetted Deji's travesty from dropping him off there. His sensitivities were seriously aggrieved and he seethed angrily.

Deji paid him off and approached the school block oblivious to the cab driver's growing hostility. He quickly skirted through the narrow bushy pathway to the nearest classroom block and sat on an open window ledge to wait for Abbas. He intuitively reached out to switch on the light and it surprisingly lit up. It wasn't too long before Abbas drew up with Sanni in tow unexpectedly. They arrived in an unmarked car to avoid unnecessary attention.

Deji nearly collapsed with shock and joy when Sanni alighted from the back of the darkened car in place of Abbas. He hadn't been expecting to see him show up. 'Sanni, Sanni you came. Thank you, thank you.' he screamed joyfully running straight into his lover's arms.

They embraced lovingly and there was no mention or signs of their earlier separation as they clung to each other.

'How are you?' Sanni enquired and held him back to observe his face again as well as look him over affectionately.

'Marvellous for seeing you,' Deji gushed. 'Abbas told me about the new development.'

'Yes, never mind disgruntled Suleiman. He has no concrete proofs but was making random charges on the premise that you lived at my estate. We don't want to provide him with any ammunition though.'

'I understand. What are you going to do now?'

'We just have to remain careful. I won't be able to see or speak to you until this whole thing boils down even then we can't afford to be seen together at all.' Sanni outlined while adjusting his long flowing *agbada* at the same time.

'I'm so happy to see you.' Deji declared joyfully.

'Same here,' Sanni echoed.

'Should I have to move out of the complex then? Tell me what I have to do. I'll readily comply with any measures to make the threat go away.' Deji promised ardently.

'There's no need for that now, stay put. Abbas would let you know if anything changes. We'll only be fuelling more rumours if you were to move out in a rush. The situation is under control presently.' Sanni informed him.

'Thank God. I was so worried for you.' Deji stated with great relief.

'I've got to go now. Take care of yourself and let Abbas know if you need anything.' Sanni said and passed him a wad of notes.

'No, I don't need it.' Deji protested, refusing the money.

'Please have it. Take it.' He insisted.

'Thank you. I love you so much.' Deji whispered, holding him tightly and was reluctant to let him out of his embrace.

'I have to go now.' Sanni informed him.

'Okay.' Deji agreed, reluctantly let him go.

'We'll drop you off on the way to catch a cab.'

'Okay,' Deji agreed in a small dejected voice. He wished that Sanni didn't have to go. The thought that this was their last meeting until further notice deflated him.

'*Sannu hello* Abbas,' Deji greeted as he took the front seat beside Abbas at the front of the car.

'*Sannu, ya ya dai? Hello how is it?*' Abbas returned in his ever impassive deportment.

'I'm fine, thank you.' Deji replied.

All three of them were rather silent for the short ride before Abbas stopped to let Deji off. He waved them goodbye and walked across to the opposite side of the road with hopes of catching a cab going in the opposite direction. Sanni and Abbas continued on their way.

Deji's heart was practically wrenching with sorrow while watching Sanni's car disappear in the distance. He didn't know how long their separation would last but put his worries aside when he saw a car approaching. He proceeded to wave it down in hopes that it was an available cab.

The vehicle gradually drew to a halt near him at the sidewalk stopping a few inches away. Deji was surprised on approaching the car to find it was the same Mallam who had dropped him off earlier at the wheels but unfortunately had two passengers at the back of the taxi.

'Hello Mallam,' Deji greeted delightfully. 'Sorry but I didn't realize you had passengers.' He apologized before stepping back for the car to proceed on its way. He preferred a lone drop besides the passengers he glimpsed briefly at the back in traditional Hausa attires didn't look exactly friendly; they were regarding him rather malevolently.

The cab however didn't depart immediately. The rear door of the car on his side opened and one of the passengers stepped out. He gesticulated at Deji while speaking in his native Hausa tongue. Deji drew nearer to hear but was forcibly grasped and hauled into the cab by the fellow. The cab speedily sped off.

Deji was completely taken unawares. He had assumed the fellow had been inviting him to share the cab only to be physically hauled and dumped in the back seat. 'What is going on?' He yelled confoundedly at them. The two strange men had him sandwiched between them at the back of the car. He was flabbergasted at the turn of events or why these strangers were abducting him in the first place. What had he done to deserve this? He didn't even know who they were. The men restrained him from sitting up by pinning his head down as he struggled to raise his head or sit up. He continued to scream and struggled to wriggle free from their stronghold. 'Help, Help me somebody!' he shouted at the top of his lungs, hoping some one will overhear his pleas or any possible witness will realize he has been abducted against his will.

The men continued to pin him down as he struggled frantically to be free. One of them had his arms forcefully twisted behind him while the other dunked his head down and wedged in between the compact space of the two front seats.   The men and the driver through his ordeal were jabbering angrily. They fact that they spoke in native Hausa dialect didn't stop him from knowing that whatever they were saying wasn't in his favour. He only understood basic pleasantries in Hausa language, same as he had exchanged with Abbas earlier but these men sounded angry. Who were they? What he has done to offend them, warrant abduction or incur their wrath, he speculated fruitlessly and with a growing terror. He couldn't fathom why they were so angry with him. He decided to change his tactics and started to plead with them to set him free.

'What is the matter? What did I do? Take my wallet, please take my wallet, it is at the back of my pants and I promise to raise more money for you if that is not enough.' He pleaded but they ignored him and continued to yak in their malicious tone.

"*Yarinya'* was the only other prominent syllable that he could decipher from their jumbled speech. He knew the word referred to female. What has a girl got to do with his present predicament? He wasn't into women, nor did he dally with any of their wives, daughters or girlfriends so what were they going on about or why couldn't they explain his error so he could apologize. These were not ordinary robbers or they would have picked his wallet from the get go and hauled him out. His heart was thumping with fear and he prayed fervently that Sanni and Abbas could have the prudence to return or any random Good Samaritan for that matter could by timely divine intervention come to rescue him from the hands of these men.

'Please let me go or at least tell me how I have erred.' He pleaded but they continued to ignore him. The fellow dunking his head slammed him into the hard surface of the compartment a few times to silence him. 'I'm sorry, please forgive me.' Deji apologized hopelessly. He grimaced from the sore bump that had emerged on his forehead. 'I will never repeat whatever I have done to offend you. I'll pay you too but please let me go.' He tried to bargain with them again but ineffectively. The men paid no heed to his pleas as the cab driver drove back to the derelict school block.

The three irate vigilante homophobes subsequently hauled him out of the car when the car drew to a stop. They quickly pounced on him before he could make a quick dash to escape after they hauled him out of the car. The driver extricated **kobokos** *(specially primed reeds)*, from the front seat which he handed over to his cohorts and they proceeded to lash at him and also jabbed at him indiscriminately with sharp pointed daggers while one held him down. Deji was begging, screaming and howling for both mercy and help at the same time. The men ignored his pleas and continued to curse at him while brutally beating him up. No help was forthcoming in the isolated area, more so that they had pursued him into the thicket of the surrounding bush while he struggled to extricate himself from their hold or avoid the whip. They pushed him down and relentless pounded him to the floor after he stumbled and fell. The onslaught was vicious and relentless as the men trampled and stumped indiscriminately upon his head and body as Deji writhed and crouched powerlessly for protection. They beat him literally to a pulp until he could no longer offer resistance or protestation. They finally abandoned him, lying prone and limp on the floor. They were significantly exulted in their glorious conquest and having rid mother earth of another abominable homosexual.

Nkiru was apprehensive and waited to hear from Deji the next day after he had left to meet with Abbas the previous night and the following day but to no avail. His phone was perpetually switched off when she tried to call him. She mulled over calling Sanni directly to ask after Deji but didn't think he would take kindly to her queries. Deji hadn't mentioned that Sanni knows that she knew about them. It was not like she had broached a similar topic with Sanni in the past so finally decided to air on the side of caution. She would however confront Abbas if and when she runs into him. She decided to wait till the weekend before confronting anyone else but Deji might well contact her before then.

She reported for work routinely on the third day since Deji's disappearance but wasn't feeling quite right. She had felt unusually lethargic on waking up that morning but couldn't quite lay her hand on what the problem was. She'd been so absorbed in her worries for Deji's safety lately and strange recurrent nightmares of the last two nights whereby Deji was depicted to have met with a dreadful outcome that she assumed the situation was making her physically ill. The previous night for instance, she had had a most terrifying of nightmares. She had seen Deji drenched in blood but oddly happy. He had smiled and waved at her like he was oblivious of his blood-spattered state. She had pleaded with him to stop or tell her what the matter was but he wouldn't. He simply asked her to take good care of herself before disappearing into a light. It was a very strange apparition and heavily shook her up. She promised herself to make that call to Sanni after work.

She still was oddly weak and tired too without undergoing any strenuous activities through the morning. She had however skipped dinner the previous night so ate a heavy breakfast hoping that would quell her bizarre hunger pangs and weakness. She had to hurriedly clutch at a seat while standing in conversation with a colleague from another sudden transient wave of wooziness. She frantically rummaged through her bag in search of a snack and was in luck to find a small pack of biscuits which she guzzled in a rush. She quickly downed a can of soda that the office boy had helped her purchase across the street and it wasn't even midday or lunch time yet. She had ravenously eaten a bowl of cereal, egg and bread sandwich in place of her usual lone cup of cocoa beverage. She just couldn't understand her strange mood or hunger, albeit she was worried sick for Deji.

While reviewing a report with her boss a few hours later, she was overtaken by another wave of light-headedness and subsequently passed out. One minute she was standing and talking and the next, was passed out on the floor. Her boss quick reaction in catching her before she landed on the floor helped to avert a serious head trauma since she could have most likely banged her head on the bare hard concrete floor from her slump. She recovered consciousness a few minutes later as her frantic colleagues were reviving and trying to shake her awake. Her boss insisted that she immediately gets a check up at the clinic; although she felt well save for her confusion over what had happened. She was reasonably recovered by the time she arrived at the clinic.

Nkiru was really baffled by her brief turn. She explained her rather bizarre weakness since waking up that morning and recent lethargy to the doctors but indicated that she was otherwise well. She was exasperated by their repetitive queries. Was she diabetic, epileptic or suffered similar symptoms in the past which she continuously denied? She had never suffered from any similar ailments; this was a first as far as she knew. No, epilepsy did not run in her family either, she repeated for the umpteenth time. A colleague, who had witnessed the episode as well as accompanied her over, attested to the fact that she never jerked her arms or feet during the brief spell. Her strange feeling of dizziness started that morning, Nkiru reiterated, becoming more exasperated at the repetitive cross-questioning before one of the doctors enquired about her last menstrual period. She wondered what that had to do with anything.

Her menstrual period had ceased shortly after she suffered from severe major depression and emaciation but was gradually normalizing. There was still no regular pattern to them but she had spotted blood a few weeks back and it was not as if she was keeping records after all she wasn't in a sexual relationship. She had spotted blood after her return from Obirima which she assumed was a scanty period. The doctors ordered a pregnancy test amongst other tests.

Oh my God, Nkiru exclaimed as soon as pregnancy test was mentioned. What were they going on about? She hadn't been in a sexual relationship since Obinna so couldn't possibly be pregnant, she mulled besides she a period barely two weeks ago. Surely, a pregnancy test will be pointless and negative; she went on to persuade herself as the implications of a possible positive result became evident in her mind. She had called her parents during the ride over to the hospital to notify them of her brief faint. They were very worried and promised to set out to Igbaje to join her at the clinic as soon as they got off the phone with her.

By the time her parents arrived later that afternoon, the pregnancy test result was out and positive. Nkiru was dumbfounded because the only plausible explanation was that she had been raped as she had feared during the spiritual retreat.

Chief Ubaka was raising hell after the full details of his beloved daughter's latest predicament became evident.

'Why didn't you confide your fears to us when you returned home?' Lolo reprimanded angrily.

The uncontrollably weeping Nkiru was shattered by this new turn of events in her life. 'I had no concrete proof that I was raped, Mummy.' She attempted to explain through her freely flowing tears.

'You should have known better than to keep anything from us.' Lolo raged. 'I don't know why you consistently refuse to trust us when you should know better. You are our daughter so we know you better than you know yourself. We would have had no reason to distrust you or judge you even if you were wrong. Nothing will ever change how we feel about you so you should really have known better than keep this from us.' Lolo raged refusing to show any mercy; maybe her brutal frankness will finally jolt Nkiru into trusting them with any worries. She had queried her so many times after she returned from Obirima but she had denied anything was amiss. Nkiru didn't have any excuse not to have trusted them with her suspicions.

Nkiru on her part was very remorseful now, she should have known better in hindsight. The fact that she thought her fears were unsubstantiated notwithstanding, she should have informed her parents. Her main worries then were more related to her fear of losing their trust than anything else. 'I'm very sorry Mum and Dad.' She apologized repeatedly.

'Don't worry my dear; it's not entirely your fault. I'll ensure the Pastor receives his comeuppance even if I have to spend my last penny bringing him to justice.' Her father swore while pacing angrily around the small hospital private room like a caged lion. He doctors estimated her pregnancy was approximately six weeks and urged the family to report the rape assault.

The Ubaka family comprising of Chief Ubaka, Lolo and Nkiru was yet to broach the topic of a termination openly but the idea had occurred to each and every one of them in that room. The thought of an abortion would have been highly inconceivable and wholly against their religious convictions but given the circumstance, they had once again arrived at another impasse. They have had to grapple with and pit their religious tenets against traditional beliefs and now were suddenly embattled with another mêlée. They would have to pit religious conviction against private ethics.

Chief Ubaka bridled with anger at the latest development but his anger was not solely directed at his daughter. Has she made bad choices? Obviously, albeit unwittingly if the truth be told. She had innocently and inadvertently fallen in love with a decent enough fellow who turned out to be an OSU. The upshot of that situation had culminated in not only heartbreak but had also affected her psychological wellbeing. She had only just recovered and misguidedly sought spiritual refuge, only for this to happen, an unwelcome pregnancy conceived in a drug induced rape assault. He feared this latest crisis might induce a relapse or worse in his daughter's state of mind if the situation is not handled carefully. There was also the matter of the unborn child? There were only two options which were either she carries the baby to full term or have a termination.

The tenants of his religion forbade abortion, which was on the same template as murder even though he could argue that a few weeks old foetus was hardly formed as to warrant being termed a complete human. However, was there any moral justification for his daughter to carry a child conceived under such a horrific circumstance? He was at a catch-22 crossroad again, unsure of which was the best decision to make.

Lolo was angry on many counts. She beat herself up for not following her earlier hunch and refused to give Nkiru the permission to attend the retreat. She was also annoyed if not exasperated at Nkiru's inability to trust her with her suspicions or fears. Had they not proven themselves enough to their daughter for her to know that she could trust them implicitly? Nkiru should have told her even if she was afraid of father's probable reaction to the news. She knew something was wrong after Nkiru came back from that retreat but she had relentlessly queried her but to no avail. She was also angry with God. Why the recurrent trials and tribulation being bestowed on her poor daughter, has her beloved little girl not suffered enough already? Why couldn't her life be as simple as those of her mates?

Nkiru was personally tired and completely shattered both mentally and physically. Her tears hadn't failed her this time but her eyes were dried out. She had cried herself dry. Her heart ached like a ton of brick was deposited across her chest and she struggled to shift it. She retrospectively couldn't fathom how she could have ignored the evident signs. Her breast had started to fill out and she spotted blood in place of a full flow menstrual period but how was she supposed to know it was different. It wasn't like her period had fully normalized since her major depression.

She had lost so much weight then that her menses had ceased spontaneously so it was hard to tell it wasn't a proper period since she started to spot or have a light flow. She had also attributed her more rapid weight gain and full breast to a sustained recovery process. She held her tummy but couldn't establish any kinship to the baby that was said to be nestling presently in her womb. She had always longed for a baby but the baby was to be Obinna's. Their baby, conceived by them and with love. Not this unfortunate foetus whose conception was neither with her consent nor knowledge. Was it Pastor Ugo's or someone else's? What happened that night when he must have drugged her? Was Pastor Ugo solely responsible or did he let anyone else to desecrate her body? She shuddered in repugnance at both her defiled body and an unsolicited tot. Oh God, why me, why this trial, especially now that she was beginning to feel that her life was back on track again. Nkiru bewailed helplessly but the next moment was beleaguered by a multitude of open queries. What was it with Life anyway? What was it with God? Why was she unduly overburdened by multiple trials? She raged while lashing out angrily at God and everything.

The doctor re-entered the room as they mulled their respective private thoughts. The confirmation of pregnancy was usually a cause for celebrations but not for this unlucky family at present. 'Hello Nkiru, Chief Ubaka and Lolo,' the doctor addressed them as they looked on glumly. 'The rest of our tests had come back negative except for slight anaemia so there is really no other major problem here. We'll be happy to discharge Nkiru this evening with iron tablets but if you require any other services, please don't hesitate to let us know.'

'Thank you, doctor.' Chief Ubaka replied on behalf of his family. 'We'll let you know.'

'What are we going to do, Nnam?' Lolo directed her question to her husband after the doctor left.

'What do you want us to do, Nkiru?' he redirected the question at Nkiru. 'Let us know what your thoughts are on the matter and be rest assured that we will respect and support any decision you make. We love you my daughter.' He reassured her.

'I'm really confused Dad and Mum. On the one hand I think I should have an abortion given the circumstance. I know that I couldn't bear to have a child under this circumstance. I would never have advocated for abortion under any circumstance until now. I know in my hearts of heart that I couldn't do this, not to the baby or myself. I wouldn't bear to look upon such a baby.' She admitted tearfully and dejectedly.

'My dear, we have to exercise caution. It might be best if we can all go home and think this through over the next few days. I'm sure we'll be able to arrive at a more purposeful decision in that interim.' Lolo suggested.

'That is best, what do you think Nkiru?' her father asked to ascertain her consent.

'Okay.' She agreed.

'I've tried to contact my friend to arrange for the arrest of that Pastor or whatever guise he goes by. I promise you that I'll not rest until he is put behind bars where he rightly belongs.' Chief Ubaka reiterated.

Their return trip to Ubi was very solemn. An unsuspecting stranger would have assumed they were returning from a funeral judging from their grim faces.

Nkiru withdrew straight away to her room when they arrived back home. Her parents prudently let her alone to afford her time and space to dwell on her latest predicament and to make an unimpeded decision. They agreed not to pressurize or influence her decision but to offer her full support whatever she decides to do. She required their love and support now, more than ever. They were also careful and fearful of triggering a relapse if they were to unnecessarily bear down on her.

The next day Chief Ubaka left to consult with his friend, a close associate of the Police Commissioner who could personally lobby for and guarantee Pastor Ugo's arrest. As much as he was enraged at the thought of what the godforsaken ingrate had done to his beloved daughter and was agitating for the fellow's arrest and justice to take its course, he now desired for the case to be handled confidentially. He wasn't sure how he was going to pull that one off. He could well foresee the vicious rumours that would erupt in his hometown, Ubi if it were to become common knowledge that his beloved daughter was raped and pregnant as a result. She'll surely be forever stigmatized if she bore a child outside of wedlock and worst still if it was common knowledge that the baby child was conceived via a rape assault. The potential effects of the sticky situation were plentiful and none of them any more desirable than the other. His experience from their prior quandary had left a bitter taste in his mouth. It was definitely not a place that he wished to revisit again. He was half-broken as he set off on his mission.

Lolo's anger towards Nkiru had significantly abated by the next morning and she was more anxious for her beloved daughter's welfare. She was very bitter towards Pastor Ugo and Uche who had practically led her daughter into the lion's den, more or less. She wondered if any of the other girls at the retreat were raped alongside her otherwise why was Nkiru such a specific target. She had always been a good girl but her luck lately left much to be desired.

'I just didn't believe my fears were founded, I'm sorry Mummy.' Nkiru apologized again to her mother the next day.

'Its okay, what's done is done, Nkiru but please you have to trust us. I pray that we never have to encounter or relive a similar situation but you must feel free to talk to us about anything.' She beseeched.'

I'm still trying to get it round my head that anyone could believe such nonsense as the Sanctification.' Lolo stated after Nkiru had told her about the process. 'How can any one in their right minds believe such nonsense?' She repeated rhetorically. 'I blame myself for granting you the permission to attend that ill fated retreat but I could never have foreseen this outcome.' She lamented.

'It wasn't any of your faults, Mummy.' It was her turn to dispel her mother's guilt.

'I might come off as repetitive but I really need you to understand that you can be open with me, your dad or both of us.' She reiterated once more. 'It doesn't matter how trivial or unbelievable you contrive the matter to be. We'll never stand in judgement of you.'

'I know Mummy and I'm sorry.' Nkiru apologized expressing her deep sense of remorse again. She should really have known better than imagine her parents would have reacted differently than trust and believe in her.

'That godforsaken Pastor will surely receive his comeuppance; Nnam will make sure of that.' The usually charitable Lolo avowed venomously. She was additionally apprehensive that her daughter's present situation could provide another fodder for gossipmongers. Why can't their life just be simply mundane? She bewailed.

Mother and daughter continued to converse about everything else under the sky except addressing the question of an abortion. Lolo played it by the ear and didn't try to affect her decision. Nkiru was an adult and would make her decision, as well as tell them in her own good time.

They both awaited Chief Ubaka's return as nightfall approached while up in the lounge conversing. They only heard his brisk steps hurrying up the stairs to join them and not his car when it drove into the driveway because they had been engrossed in their minor and light-hearted chatter. Lolo immediately rose to greet her husband. 'Welcome Nnam, I hope your trip was successful.' She enquired dutifully after a brief welcoming hug.

'Welcome dad.' Nkiru greeted.

'You'll never believe this,' Chief Ubaka announced eagerly, as he settled down beside his wife on the middle sofa. He was obviously bursting with some exciting news.

'I personally couldn't handle another dose of bad news.' Lolo declared tensely. 'Nnam, please come to the table for your dinner first. I know you must be tired and hungry. Ada, please serve Nnam's dinner.' She beckoned to Ada who was hovering nearby.

'Never mind I'm not hungry, Lolom. Ada fetch me water instead.' He requested. 'Let me tell you what happened first.' He suggested. 'Could you believe that the fool of a Pastor had been incarcerated before I arrived?' He announced dramatically.

Lolo and Nkiru were flabbergasted but pleased.

'Are you serious, who had notified the police to arrest him so soon then?' Lolo asked.

'He'd been in jail for over a week or so, Lolom. The mad man was already under arrest for an unrelated case. He was said to have set his flock ablaze in his mad frenzy. Could you possibly believe that?' Chief Ubaka queried sombrely. 'He set his flock on fire in the name of worship.' He mouthed incredulously. 'The fellow is plain psychotic.' He went on to denounce the Pastor. 'He is presently held without bail and bound to be indicted on numerous charges. He is said to have committed a series of unbelievable atrocities geared mainly against his female flock. I couldn't believe my ears when the Police Chief related the news to us. I didn't even have to delve into our particular case but mentioned that I have a vested interest in the case. I assured him that I was ready to furnish the funds with which to bring the fellow to justice. He reassured me that I was not the only interested party but there was enough evidence to hang the man if it were in the old days. The Police Commissioner indicated that they have an iron-cast case and would successfully bring him to trial. He's bound to get a protracted jail term if not life. A very prominent Army chief's daughter is said to be among his despoiled flock so you can imagine his affront. Surely with the army and police involved, the fellow is doomed'

'That is if he doesn't find a way to bribe his way out to freedom.' Lolo implied cynical. '*Ewo*! **Oh**! Nnam, I can't believe it. They say everyday day is for the thief but one day is for the owner of the house. He will surely receive his comeuppance'

'My dear daughter, God does work in mysterious ways. How this despicable fellow was able to get away with similar crimes and for such a prolonged interval is totally beyond me. The Commissioner confirmed that he had drugged and raped his female parishioners on numerous occasions. The fellow had the gall to record some of his escapades on tape to hawk as pornographic movies and he calls himself a man of God. Can you believe that?' Chief Ubaka raged incredulously at the scope of the fellow's travesty. 'He belongs behind bars.'

'Nnam, I'm not sure you've heard the one about how he whiplashes his flock in the name of sanctification.' Lolo added.

'I heard Lolom, simply mind boggling!' He pronounced with a loud sigh. 'Next he'd have had them crucified on a cross, what drivel? I must admit that I'm equally amazed at his supposed followers. Granted that this fellow is insane but what about them? Have they been indoctrinated into his fallacy to the extent that they had lost the simple ability to think or reason rationally? What has happened to common sense or our society? Have we become so deprived in our lives that we actually have people believing ludicrous fallacies? It is also startling to think that he managed to get away with this travesty for so long while preying on the vulnerability of innocent souls? If one of the girls hadn't escaped with burns to report to the police, the truth would never have come to light until now.'

'The man is sick, mentally ill.' Lolo asserted, echoing her husband's sentiments as they rehashed the appalling details.

'I'll have a termination.' Nkiru announced resolutely but in a quite but decisive voice.

Her parents turned to observe her. She hadn't contributed much to the conversation. They regarded her earnestly and could well detect the firm resolve depicted in her eyes. Who could blame her? Who would want to bear a child for such a monstrous character or under a similar circumstance? They hadn't openly voiced their fears but fervently hoped that Nkiru's image was not portrayed in the warped fellow's pornographic movies, some of which were said to be at large.

Most of Pastor Ugo's cohorts but the tycoon business man from Obirima who had allowed him access and use of his home for the retreat were summarily rounded up and in police custody too. The group were even then said to have received a tip-off from inside of the police before they swooped on them. The Obirima fellow had absconded with vital photographic evidence. It was uncertain to what extent he was involved in the scam because he lived abroad originally and only visited infrequently. A few cameras and photographic apparatus were however recovered and confiscated from other locations. The police were still assessing their value.

Neither Chief Ubaka nor his wife Lolo would have ascribed to abortion under normal circumstances but desperate situations called for desperate measures. Their daughter's present situation was dire and therefore they stood in full support of her decision. They had inadvertently learnt the valuable lesson that life could deal such a hand as to force them to make decisions that would have ordinarily contrasted with their accustomed ideals or principle. They were principled folks but recent tribulations have tested the core of their mettle. However, the welfare and sanity of their beloved daughter superseded any other thoughts.

They were hopeful that her future from now henceforth, would signify an end to the run of misfortunes that had dogged her footsteps lately.

The   present... ...

Twelve

Nkiru was half way through her projected one year Masters Degree program in London and fully acclimatized to her new life in the United Kingdom by then. She had used to visit the city frequently in the past for short term summer holiday breaks when she had felt more carefree, touristy and boarded with relatives.

Her recent first proper winter in the United Kingdom was a rude awakening. She couldn't possibly have envisaged just how bitter and frosty the inclement weather could be, especially for someone like her who was born and bred in the tropics. No one could convince her up till the present moment that she'd ultimately get used to the biting cold weather. She still affirms to this day that there's just no getting used to horrid freezing cold as far as she is concerned. The harsh wintry wind had left her stiff and frozen; she had to practically curl up beside her electric heater for any reasonable warmth besides the central heating. She also found herself quivering in the street irrespective of donning double garments and sweaters or 'padding up' as she designated the process.

She had also had to contend with her primary heartache following the termination of her unfortunate pregnancy. She had grieved for the loss of the baby that she unknowingly conceived before a portent brief collapse landed her in hospital alerting her to the fact. The termination process had concluded without much fanfare after which she had packed up the rest of her belongings and departed Igbaje. She had succinctly succeeded in departing Igbaje for a second time under similar abject circumstance. Her initial enchantment with her beloved Igbaje town had inadvertently turned bittersweet a second time around. She undeniably loved the city yet succeeded in departing again in a miserable state of mind as the first time.

Her first exit was after concluding her Youth Service Program which also coincided with the period when she was gearing for a final showdown with her parents regarding their refusal to sanction her engagement to Obinna. She was offered an opportunity to assume a more permanent post back then but had declined. On the latest occasion, her parents had decided that she'll fare better departing the shores of her country because of the series of unrelenting ill fortune that had dogged her existence lately.

She needed to seek a fresh start in an entirely new environment to help overturn her misfortune in addition to making a fresh start. She had nevertheless bemoaned the loss of her unborn baby but her anguish was in no way comparable to that of losing Obinna, which was still to her, a far more devastating ordeal.

Her grief for the loss of her baby was understandably from the standpoint of pity than any other emotions. On balance, the baby that she lost was not knowingly conceived. She was all the same compassionate and contrite for the tiny foetus, which had unwittingly had to pay the ultimate prize for the whole farce. She recalled returning to the clinic at Igbaje with her parents after she had made the most disheartening decision to undergo an abortion. That option was against everything that she had ever believed in but she was left no other choice.

The whole process had ensued faster than she had anticipated. She was put to sleep after an initial discussion to ascertain that she keen to go through with it and by the time that she woke up, it was over. The baby was gone just as unpredictably as it had been conceived. She was left emotionally drained but not exactly bereft. She couldn't honestly admit to sharing a bond with the baby because there was no affinity between them regrettably. She never experienced its kick nor revelled in either its conception or having it nestled in her womb. She had touched her tummy afterwards in hopes of sensing a residual bond but all she felt was pain, a continuous dull ache in the area of her womb and an aftermath bleed.

She wasn't even sure of the exact identity of the baby's father. She and her parents had decided against confronting Pastor Ugo for the truth of what had happened after much deliberation. Both Pastor Ugo and his cohorts were vile. Her parents were also of the mind that it was unnecessary to pursue a personal vendetta against him. He was already in the hands of the law, languishing behind bars and more likely than not to be successfully convicted.

There would be no end to the scandal that would erupt in her hometown if she was to be linked to Pastor Ugo's unfolding debacle on top of everything else that had transpired lately.

Kelechi was later denoted as the lady set ablaze by the "schizophrenic" priest who unrepentantly entered a "not guilty" plea on all the charges tendered against him so far.

Nkiru wasn't surprised to learn that Kelechi was the tigress that managed to escape from the fire and in the process had exposed Pastor Ugo and his warped ideology to the rest of the world. The lady was untamed and the image of the feisty Kelechi fending off Pastor Ugo and escaping to raise alarm put a smile to her lips. There was also a multitude of other readily available witnesses comprising mainly of Pastor Ugo's old but now turned indignant flock ready to testify against him so all things being equal he was destined to earn his just desserts.

Uche had visited Nkiru just before she embarked on her overseas trip. She informed her of Pastor Ugo's arrest not knowing that Nkiru knew already. She apologized for involving Nkiru in the dubious Sanctification of the Crucifix fold but insisted that she had done so in good faith. She claimed that Pastor Ugo had had her fooled but now she knew him for what he really was. She was also aligned to testify against him in court but admitted that she was yet to fully make up her mind to actually do so. She confided to Nkiru that she had shared his bed, albeit by mutual consent. She surprisingly maintained her old argument that all things said and done, they only ever consented to things at will and were never under duress to consent or conform to any of their doctrines.

Nkiru surmised that Uche wasn't completely persuaded that Pastor Ugo was evil if she was still of the mind that she had mutually consented to sleeping with him. Pastor Ugo had purposefully brainwashed them into a false sense of autonomy whereas he had actually had them dancing to his beat. She could personally grasp how easily one could be ensnared by his guile or fall for his charms. Pastor Ugo was on balance suave, handsome, articulate and attentive to one in such a manner as to make you feel exclusive when in his company. He almost had her falling for him; however all he ever did was betray the trust of the poor vulnerable ladies that had laid their trust in him including her. He was supposed to be a man of God and not defile his innocent flock or prey on their vulnerability.

Uche luckily hadn't readdressed her private session with Pastor Ugo or grill her again even if she now suspected that an indecent act might have occurred. Nkiru on her part deliberately failed to divulge the horrible details to Uche. Uche had never been known to make a good confidante. She was a blabbermouth who could easily blab her own personal secret, much less keep another's. Her doomed pregnancy and subsequent abortion were her private secrets, the lesser number of people let into the secret, the better.

In retrospect, she couldn't imagine how she could have survived the whole ordeal without the full and much needed support of her immediate family members. She hadn't had the courage to confide the details of her latest predicament to close friends before departing abroad. She was sure that Lily must have guessed that there was more to her departure than met the eye when she notified her of her immediate departure from Igbaje.

Lily had actually been taken aback by Nkiru's seemingly out of the blues notice. She hadn't notified her that any such plan had been in the offing beforehand but announced suddenly that she was heading off to England immediately. In as much as she hadn't openly voiced her scepticism, Lily did think that the announcement ranked rather hasty. Nkiru hadn't indicated any prior discontent either with her job or new life in Igbaje but on the contrary, was the happiest that Lily had seen her in the last two years. Lily was therefore befuddled by her best friend's sudden announcement. She was nevertheless happy for her and wished her the best.

Sanni was also surprised on receiving her departure notice. She explained that she had completely taken her mind off the scholarship grant after applying ages ago. She hadn't necessarily thought she stood that much of a chance of winning it; however it had come through unexpectedly. Sanni was ever so his old chivalrous self and helped arrange with her employers to let her off on a 2-year study leave. This would facilitate an easy return to her old job in the future if she were so inclined. She of course hadn't merited vacating service on study leave since she hadn't been employed on the job for long enough. It was a small wonder though what money and affluence can achieve at such short notice.

Nkiru had casually enquired after Deji from Sanni before finally departing. She had fruitlessly waited and hoped for word from Deji but to no avail. She was careful by enquiring after Deji from Sanni in his capacity as Deji's landlord. Sanni sounded evasive in his reply. No, he personally didn't know of Deji's whereabouts and suggested that Deji might have travelled home. He hadn't seen Deji in ages too; moreover he was no longer handling the affairs of the estate so was not in full knowledge of the whereabouts of all the tenants. Nkiru couldn't probe him any further given his offhand reply but hoped that Deji would soon get in touch with her.

She however couldn't, up till the present moment bear to ponder on the true account of Deji's demise that had unfurled lately. That night when Deji had turned up at her door in a panic to inform her of the blackmail threat against Sanni was the last time that she saw or spoke to him.

While she had remained hopeful that he'd contact her sooner than later after she was first beleaguered then embroiled in her personal turmoil and subsequent trip, nothing could have prepared her for the devastating details of his murder. Lily had informed her of the gory details two months ago and she had wept disconsolately for her friend. May his soul find the perfect peace that had eluded him in life, she had prayed.

Nkiru went on to re-evaluate her present situation recalling the not so distant early days when she had initially arrived in the United Kingdom and spent hours wallowing in self pity. She had cried herself to sleep most nights especially after her mother left to return home. Lolo had accompanied and also stayed with her through the first month of her stay while she settled in. The reality of her loss and misery fully kicked in after her mother departed home but she was both mentally and physically stronger now.

She had duly eased into her new studies and life in London. It was a different ball game now that she'd come to stay for a more substantial duration than those short haul holiday break periods. She had used to breeze in and out of the city then, albeit on a guarded rich man's daughter's budget sized mini shopping sprees and on a thrill quest like any tourist. She wasn't oblivious even then to the fact that actually residing in London or overseas generally was tougher than most people back home envisaged. There was nothing like experience to prove it.

She has had to wake up early most mornings to catch a bus to the train station, trivial as it may so sound but a most daunting experience during the cold winter. She had detested rising at dawn when all she desired was to remain cuddled up underneath her warm blankets or beside the heater. The spring and upcoming summer were glorious in comparison. She usually boards the train via Piccadilly line on the Metro Underground to her University grounds at Leicester Square. There was a very cohesive transport system in place for her not to be actually required to own a private car.

Nkiru loved feeding off the energy of the sprawling City of London. No similar feeling beat the palpable buzz of walking across the streets lost in the midst of a distracted teeming crowd. She enjoyed taking in the sights and watching the cross-section of Homo sapiens of different colours and cultures on their various errands and missions around the city especially in the West End area. The scenarios reminded her of a beehive surrounded by swarming bees, buzzing frenetically around or daring to venture afar but yet are gravitated back towards the centre point with a seemingly purposeful intent.

She had always advocated her preference for placid cities with a mix of suburbia which was one of the reasons why she had adored Igbaje. So she was consequently surprised to discover that she also enjoyed the hectic timbre of the heart of the City of London and the West End area. She intermittently felt like she could almost reach her hand out to palpate the throb of the heart of the city with its teeming diverse population and areas.

She loved to absorb the crowd comprising of men and women of different shapes, sizes and colours, all dressed up in assorted garments. There were the perfect gentlemen in Savile Row suits, lugging briefcases to their female counterparts in fancy designer apparels treading the sidewalks of "The City" or financial/business hub of London City. Nkiru also loves trudging past "The Westminster", another segment of the West End with its imposing edifices defining the seat of government. A more youthful generation of men or lads dressed casually smart, some lugging long strap bags strung vertically across their shoulders and could easily pass for either students or workers and dotted around central West End area proper. A similar statistics of female population parades the streets in Topshop and other trendy design apparel and few slobs completing the swarming theme.

She could pinpoint the hardened tourists amongst them. Some of who are easily identifiable by the huge cameras dangling around their necks especially those of Eastern Asian descent amongst the ubiquitous crowd trailing the course of West End from The Strand to Oxford Street in search of entertainment and retail therapy. This eclectic mix also juggles a preppy looking lot, young hippy types, the indie groups and Goths in distinctive dark garments and make-ups, Hare Krishna converts in yellowish-orange-red colourful apparels dancing to the beat of a lone drummer along the street, West Africans and other nationalities in distinctive flamboyant native attires.

She also loved to observe the tacit tussle between the impatient pedestrians, black cabs and inimitable Double Decker London buses cramming the small streets and combating for dominance of the narrow jam-packed roads and alleyways. Not to forget the shrill wail of police sirens in pursuit of an invisible assailant or ambulances on hastened rush to save a soul, all throwing the already swarming cramped streets into slight disarray. She also found herself intermittently marvelling at the ever teeming crowd in the West End; apparently out all year round, come rain or shine. The West End never sleeps.

She occasionally lounged al fresco most especially after lectures and sipping coffee or tea under quirky exterior sheds outside the many cafes or bars scattered in the area in the company of fellow classmates and simultaneously soaking in the crowd.

She was simultaneously part yet detached from the contiguous live crowd. She throbbed along with this heartbeat, yet was secluded because her presence was of no statistical significance. She was still a stranger, foreigner or alien. She wasn't part of the decisive segment of this pyramid but relished her anonymity to an extent.

She was wont to appreciate life more, including its little mercies and derived pleasure from little things including the 15minutes walk or so from her university to the train station which was mayhem on occasions. She equally welcomed the lull when she returns back home to her more subdued Arnos Grove area located at the Northern part of London.

She intermittently window-shopped while leisurely strolling down the streets and gawking at the multitude of designer and departmental shops strewn along the busy Oxford Street area, her spontaneous gasps at the outrageous price tags notwithstanding.

Nkiru was prudent enough with her finances because of the numerous bills that she had to contend with. These include water, electricity and others, even TV required a licence. She had no desire to overburden her parents who had always insisted on bearing her full expenses until she completes her studies. She had intermittently toyed with the idea of securing a part time job. Her parents vehemently muted the idea and encouraged her to finish her studies first. She didn't really need the extra cash because her parents provided sufficient funds to assure she was comfortable.

She hadn't lost contact with her close friends from back home including Lily who had duly informed her of Deji's calamity. She had narrated how his corpse was discovered in a deserted school ground. Deji's corpse was virtually decomposed when he was found but his wallet securely holding his intact particulars helped to establish his actual identify. Rumour had it that he must have attended the secluded area for a dalliance that went horribly wrong. Nkiru couldn't believe the pathetic fate that had befallen her friend. Those rumours were far-fetched because Deji must have gone to the deserted area to meet someone by prior arrangement or else his body was dumped in the bushes afterwards. Did he die on the same night that he was due to meet Abbas or a later date? She had no way of telling or knowing for sure. Who had murdered her unaffected friend whose only crime was being himself? She considered if Sanni had had any hand in Deji's death but decided it was virtually unfeasible from the much that she knew about him. She was in a quadroon for ages wondering how best to deal with the situation or if she were to confront Sanni directly. It was however a difficult situation because he had never previously admitted to her that he knew Deji on a more personal level. She wasn't keen to come off as biting the finger that helped feed her too if she were to accuse him of Deji's murder. She really had no proof except that he was Deji's secret lover. Was the blackmail threat his motive for ordering Deji's extermination? Nkiru was very confused for ages. Sanni has always been an immense help to both her and Obinna. There was no way that she could really contend that the same Sanni might have any hand in Deji's death. Lily was also unequivocal in her belief that Sanni might be anything but incapable of murder when she related her fears. In the end, she decided that Deji had alas met with a very poignant end. She recalled her dreadful nightmare on the night preceding the discovery of her pregnancy. She had visualized Deji drenched in blood but cheerfully waving her goodbye. Was that apparition born out of reality? Deji had seemed unusually calm and happy in the dream so she drew comfort in the thought that he might well be better off in heaven so prayed for the peaceful repose of his soul, Amen.

She had nevertheless remained dejected for a period by her inability to do anything to help in solving the mystery of his death. She grieved for his loss alongside her multitude misfortunes. Her parents consistently updated her on Pastor Ugo's ongoing trial. There was every indication that he would be convicted as well as earn a justifiable jail term. A few eminent dignitaries agitated for justice to be served, more especially because a prominent Army Lieutenant's daughter was involved. The Army Chief was actively clamouring for justice.

Nkiru was making her way to different section after browsing through the lingerie section of Marks and Spencer's departmental store when she glimpsed a rather familiar figure striding along the central aisle towards the exit of the shop. She discerned it was Jude as she fully recognized the fast disappearing figure. She hadn't seen him in ages but there was no mistaking his peculiar stride. He didn't seem to have noticed or heard her when she dared to call out his name aloud. She hurried to catch up with him before he would disappear into the milling crowd on the street. She was elated to find a familiar face from home because she was homesick.

'Hello, Jude.' She called after she finally caught up with him at the exit of the shop. It was truly Jude looking as gorgeous as ever.

'Hello Nkiru, what a wonderful surprise.' He exclaimed, sounding as happy to see her as she was with running into him. 'How are you? It's been ages.'

'I'm fine and how are you?' She returned pleasantly as they stood at a corner of the busy street outside the shop taking in each other's appearance.

She was in jeans pants, black turtle neck top and boots but little make up. She prayed that she wasn't looking worse for wear. Jude was dressed casual but smart in navy blue blazer on a jeans and shirt combo.

'I'm fine. I heard you live here now and had meant to obtain your phone number from your parents before travelling. Unfortunately I didn't get the chance to do so but was hoping to call them from here for your number if I hadn't run into you.' He explained. 'So how are you doing?' he repeated.

'Fine, I'm half way through a Masters program.'

'Congrats. It has sure been ages but you do look well.' He remarked regarding her frame admiringly once more like he liked what he saw.

'So do you.' She returned the compliment. 'Are you here on business or pleasure?'

'A bit of both,' he replied without elaborating further. 'I'll probably be around for another 3 weeks; I've been around for a week so far.'

'Well it's nice seeing you again.' She remarked.

'My pleasure too, we must meet up for a drink or something if you are not too busy.' He suggested.

'That sounds like a good idea.' She agreed and they exchanged phone numbers and addresses.

He was staying in a nearby hotel, located not too far from the swanky shops and restaurants. As they parted to go their separate ways, she reflected on their past history. Both of their parents had been very close friends in their youth and hoped to cement their relationship by encouraging them to get together and possibly wed. She was in love with Obinna and hadn't given Jude the time of the day. He still looked good and she wondered if he was married now. For some mysterious reason he had completely disappeared from her radar lately and she'd barely heard any subsequent gist about him until seeing him now.

She tried to recollect the last time that met which would have be while she was debilitated or suffering from severe major depression. She vaguely remembered him visiting but couldn't exactly recall the exact details of his visit which seemed like an eternity ago.

She had been pretty much on her own lately and was starting to feel like it was time to spread her wings again in the relationship department. She hoped Jude would keep his promise to call or invite her out on a date because she hadn't been on a proper date for the longest time interval. She had invariably attended a few soirées in the company of new course mates and friends but those theoretically speaking, weren't real dates.

She returned to her bed-sit that evening pretending to keep busy by preparing light dinner but barely ate any of it afterwards to pretending to study without taking in a word. She was in all that period anticipating that her phone would ring at any moment. She couldn't have logically predicted such a time would come when she'd be diligently waiting up for Jude's phone call.

He didn't call her that night or the following day and she was very disappointed. She made believe that it didn't matter while actually feeling snubbed. She didn't want to come off eager or would have called him instead.

She was shopping for groceries at Tesco supermarket on the following Saturday, three days after she had ran into Jude when her phone rang displaying his number on the interface.

'Hello Nkiru, its Jude. I'm sorry I hadn't called earlier.' He apologized. 'I had meant to but our conferences concluded so late that I decided not to disturb you by phoning at such ungodly hours, forgive me.'

'It's fine that you've called now.' She assured him. 'How are you anyway?'

'Great, what are you up to tonight?" he enquired.

'Nothing much but I'm presently shopping for grocery so why don't you come over for dinner? I'll cook for you.' She invited impulsively.

'That sure sounds like great fun but I was hoping you can come out to town instead so we can use the opportunity to catch a movie afterwards. I've barely experienced the great buzz of London at night.' He suggested instead.

'Okay then but my dinner invite still stands anytime you want to take me up on it.' She warned.

'Does that mean I'm seeing you tonight then?'

'Yes unless you've changed your mind already.' She teased, unable to believe her open flirtation.

'No, I'll be looking forward to seeing you. I hope to be done by about 6pm. You've still got my numbers or should I repeat them.'

'No, I've got them.'

'Call me then when you set off to expect you.'

'Will do, bye for now.'

'Bye.'

After he hung up, Nkiru sobered up. She was practically flirting with him and what would Obinna think? Oh God, what was she getting herself into, Nkiru pondered? Maybe this proposed date wasn't such a good idea after all. She started to contemplate backing out, despite shamelessly soliciting for it. By the time they have dinner and catch a movie, it would be too late for her to board a train back to Arnos Grove, she anticipated ahead of her. And what if Jude were to invite her back to his hotel to spend the night then what would she say? She deliberated. What could happen if the two of them were to end up in bed together? She critically weighed up the possible outcomes of her proposed rendezvous before realizing that the problem was in her inability to predict her precise reaction in the event of encountering those plausible scenarios.

Obinna was her only significant lover but she liked Jude admittedly. What was there not to like? He was gorgeous, always impeccably turned out and courteous. He was in love with her, at any rate she hoped that he still was. They hailed from the same town so he wasn't a complete stranger and she knew he was principled. Their respective parents had wished for them to wed and maybe that could still come to call, she fantasized.

What of Obinna though? Was she being disloyal or betraying his memory by going out on this date with his old nemesis, Jude? She knew that Obinna would have wished for her to be happy and to find love again but what if that happiness involved Jude?

Nkiru wasn't very excited about the date again at the prospect of betraying Obinna and toyed seriously with the idea of cancelling. She decided to seek advice from one of her new girlfriends, Zola before making her mind up.

Zola was a rather boisterously loud girl from South Africa and they had met two months back while undertaking an elective together. Zola wasn't typically like any of her old girlfriends from her home country but they got on well. Zola had insisted on introducing her to her clique and Nkiru unexpectedly enjoyed hanging out with them. She even sensed a special kinship with Zola, given their African roots.

Zola immediately dismissed her reservations after Nkiru related her reservations and promptly decreed. 'Nkiru my sister, go let your hair down and stop worrying your head. I'm sure Obinna would understand. He is a kind soul and would want you to be happy by all means.'

Nkiru wasn't surprised that Zola would reassure her. She was a free spirit. Nkiru liked to tease Zola, especially with regards to her name, Zola. She was a complete antithesis to the meaning of her name which stood for 'quiet' or 'calm' because Nkiru knew that she was a complete riot. She reckoned Zola's parents must have a good sense of humour for naming her as such after discerning from an early enough stage that she was anything but calm. She liked to suggest to Zola that they must have named her "Zola" in hopes that the name would help calm or overturn her bounciness.

Zola went on to bellow advice over the phone, 'Go have fun, my sister. You've mourned enough besides it's about time you had that engine of yours oiled.'

Nkiru was knocked for six but couldn't help but laugh at Zola's brashness. She should be used to her by now but she found herself laughing so hard that she couldn't stop. 'Zola … … …' She started.

'I'm telling the truth,' Zola declared insolently. 'On a more serious note my sister, I wouldn't worry too much. It's just a simple date.'

'I know,' Nkiru agreed. 'I don't know why I'm acting like a teenager who is about to go on her very first date.'

'It's quite understandable; you haven't been on a proper date in a long time. You are lucky that you are not me because if I haven't had it in a similar duration, there'll be no predicting what could happen on this first date.' Zola divulged candidly.

'Zola, please stop. I'm laughing so hard that I'm crying now.' Nkiru pleaded, wiping happy tears. She knew Zola liked to defy tradition and come out with the most outrageous or suggestive comments but in reality wasn't half as brazen as she made out. While Zola came across as totally emancipated and outgoing, she was however in a monogamous relationship with a rather calm white English chap, David. He was in the same course with them. Zola and David typified attraction between opposites but their relationship worked well as far as Nkiru could see. Zola could drink many guys under the table and smoked like a chimney while David was a teetotaller and non-smoker but the two somehow manage to cohabit harmoniously.

Nkiru had never really interacted with a freer spirited lady than Zola in her whole life so was intrigued by her to an extent. The girl sometimes displayed an almost decadent approach to life and she envied Zola's impiety. She on the other hand couldn't see herself letting go of her inhibitions to the same degree as Zola.

'Anyway you must wear something sexy.' Zola outlined. 'Turtlenecks are sexy but frumpy for a first date, especially when we are trying to make an impression.'

'Okay and is there any other precautions that I must take?' Nkiru jokingly enquired.

'I'm just going to add that you don't forget to take an umbrella along.' Zola suggested mischievously and they both burst out laughing.

"English weather is unpredictable" was a standard maxim between them but Nkiru had recently adopted a modified version stipulating that *"English weather is as unpredictable as its people."*

'I won't forget and thanks for everything. By the way, give my regards to David.' Nkiru added. 'Bye for now.'

'Bye, my sister. Let your hair down, have fun and let us know all the details later. And don't do anything that I wouldn't do.'

'Or maybe you mean the reverse?' Nkiru kidded.

'You get my point either way. Have fun and I'll pass on your message to David.' Zola knowingly added.

'Please do. Thanks and bye.' They were both laughing as they respectively hung up.

David, Zola's English boyfriend who was usually blasé wasn't amused or accommodating of Nkiru's unpredictable English weather/people joke. She'd overheard it somewhere and often repeated it to rile him.

Nkiru was still worrying about her date, even as she started to dress up later that evening. Do I have a special knack for danger or else was jumping the gun? What if Jude isn't remotely interested in me romantically? It might be his polite nature that had prompted this invite, she considered introspectively.

She donned her favourite selection of matching lingerie while chuckling at her own deviousness as she continued to strategize her rendezvous with Jude. She stepped into another favourite, a pair of dressy pants and sexy ruffled red silk top after Zola's jab at her customary turtlenecks. She even left her top more unbuttoned than she would have ordinarily. She subtly dabbed her favourite Estee Lauder "Beautiful" perfume around the ears before lacing up a funky pair of high heel boots and donning a smart fitted black leather jacket. She also packed an umbrella in her bag because jokes aside, London weather was invariably unpredictable. One can metaphorically have the four seasons of the year traded off through a day.

She called Jude to alert him as she started out and subsequently caught a bus en route to boarding the train to the trendy West End. Both bus and train were crammed and for once she felt very much a part of the in-crowd trooping to the centre in time for the abundant weekend entertainment options.

She and Jude ambled past Soho to Chinatown after settling for Chinese meal while taking in the surrounding sights.

'You're still with your old firm?' Nkiru enquired as they chowed through aromatic duck pancakes for starters.

'Yes, same one but I'm contemplating on leaving the firm soon. We're planning to set up ours with a close friend.' He confided.

'Good, so how are your parents, I hadn't seen them in ages.'

'They are fine; dad is still working as hard as ever. I ran into Azu the other day and she looked and sounded so mature that it was unbelievable.' He commented.

'She is a lady now, isn't it true what they say about one maturing to a certain point and waiting for others to catch up?'

'True.' He agreed. 'Do accept my sympathy again with regards to Obinna and his family.'

'Thanks.' She accepted. It was inevitable that Obinna should crop up in their conversation. 'It was a devastating tragedy.'

'I know but you've really been strong.'

'Was I really left with any other option?' She jokily tried to lighten the mood.

'I've always admired you and still do.' He informed her.

'Really?' She replied flippantly but was actually taken by surprise.

265

'Yes.' He bore out. 'I like you a lot and have never stopped.' He repeated gazing earnestly into her eyes.

'Okay, thanks.' She replied, playing it coy but was really speechless.

'I know it might be too soon for you to be considering another relationship but I promise to be patient while we get to rediscover each other again.'

'Mmh...mmh... ... ...Okay,' Nkiru stammered hesitantly. She had sincerely expected Jude to make a move or she would have been disappointed but was still actually taken off guard by his directness. 'So how are your studies going?' He changed the topic, noticing her slight discomfort.

'Not bad at all. I'm almost done with the initial bit and will soon have to contend with writing my thesis.'

They continued to chat and fill each other in on individual and home news through a three course meal. They subsequently ambled down to the Odeon Cinema Theatre in time to catch the last movie showing for the night. It was past midnight by the end of the movie.

'Thanks, I enjoyed our time together.' Nkiru acknowledged appreciatively as they made their way out of the movie theatre.

'The pleasure was really mine. Why don't we go back to my place?' he suggested. 'I'll hate to have you board a cab alone at this time of the day unless you insist.'

Whatever happens to me now is entirely on me; Nkiru self-consciously acknowledged and dithered momentarily for an apt reply that wouldn't sound too obvious. It was relatively unsafe to board unknown cabs at such ungodly hours but if she does willingly return to Jude's base then the resultant outcome was of her own making.

'You know that you are completely safe with me. I'm a perfect gentleman, trust me.' He joked as if he had read her mind.

'I've got no other option than to trust you then.' She grasped the easy way out.

'But of course.' He agreed.

They accordingly walked the short distance back to his hotel suite. Nkiru looked the place over admiringly when they entered. Jude seemed like the neat type as there were no clothes littering all over the place. The suite was considerably spacious and comprised of sitting room area, adjoining bedroom and en suite bathroom.

'Would you like to shower before bed?' He enquired politely. 'There's a bathrobe in the bathroom and you can change into my spare pyjamas. It's clean I promise.' He assured her with a laugh.

266

'Thanks.'

'Let me know if you need anything. We could order food or snacks whichever you'd prefer.'

'No, I'm fine and thanks.' She declined politely.

He afforded her some privacy to shower and change into his pyjama top. She could smell him as she donned the top and was vaguely excited. He showered too before joining her in the roomy bed. They chatted about nothing in particular while watching the television in the background. He suggested a pay per view movie but she declined, fearing she might doze off midway through. It was a long day or rather night already. Jude soon turned off the TV off as they made to retire for sleep.

Nkiru lay on her side of the bed in anticipatory fear and excitement. She hadn't felt this snug with another fellow since Obinna and the situation both frightened and excited her.

Jude drew her into his arms as she lay quivering against him. He kissed her lightly on the lips but she was reluctant to respond initially while contemplating if it was the right or wrong thing to do. Her excitement was however beginning to get the better of her as his kisses deepened. She couldn't resist him any longer but it felt somewhat weird to be kissing another man but Obinna.

Jude started to touch and caress her slowly, gently and was heightening her excitement. She forced them to stop and ascertained that he had protection. She subsequently relaxed and closed her eyes to savour her mounting bliss. Jude was ready to straddle her when she unconsciously whispered, 'I love you Obinna.' He swiftly rolled off from atop her as if his enthusiasm was immediately doused with cold water.

Nkiru on her part cringed in both shock and unwarranted shame. She didn't know where that line had come from; those weren't words that she had deliberately set out to say. She had as a matter of fact attempted to banish thoughts of Obinna from her mind all night but his memory obviously haunted her.

'I'm sorry.' She apologized. 'I swear I really don't know where that came from. I would never intentionally disrespect you.' What else could she possibly say to him under such a weird situation than express her regret? It was not premeditated on her part to utter those words.

'I'd like you to leave.' Jude intoned grimly.

'Now?' she repeated, wondering if he was serious.

'Yes, now.' He repeated without looking her way.

She refused to cry as she rose from his bed and gathered her garments to don in the bathroom. By the time she was ready to leave, he had already booked a cab on her behalf via the hotel front desk.

'I'm really sorry.' She apologized again before departing his hotel room with her bag.

He avoided meeting her eyes as she bade him goodbye and let herself out of his hotel room for the waiting cab. Nkiru barely listened to any of the unsolicited chatter from the cab driver as he drove her home. She quietly let herself into her bed-sit and collapsed into bed fully clothed. She was all the same more sober than tearful; in fact the situation was almost laughable now as she reviewed the sequence more. She couldn't wait to tell Zola and hear her take. Oh, God what was it with her anyway. It was a good thing that the date turned out the way it did. She was in bed with Jude for all the wrong reasons.

She was not in love with him but in lust, as well as vulnerable and looking for love on the rebound. She had needed a change but hooking up or jumping into bed on a seemingly first date with Jude was certainly not her style or the right way to go about it. She had reflexively tried to play someone else. She was never one to kiss on a first date; much less have sex on a first date throwing caution to the winds. Was Obinna reaching out from beyond the grave to reprimand her? He knew her too well. This was not her style. Maybe she and Jude are never destined to be together. In retrospect she wasn't even angry with him for ordering her out of his hotel room at the middle of the night.

She knew the worst thing anyone could do to another was yell somebody else's name in the throes of passionate lovemaking. It was an ultimate insult. She might have happened to be rude to Jude sometimes in the past but she'd never deliberately set out to humiliate him. She prayed that he would understand that it was never her intention to belittle him in anyway and hoped he'd be able to find it in himself to forgive her. She was able to doze off to sleep subsequently after changing into pyjamas.

Nkiru was woken up early the next morning by her mother phoning to have a chat from her home country. Her parents frequently called most weekends and she used the opportunity to talk to her siblings and Obinna's siblings if they were home at the same time.

'How are you dear, did I wake you up?' Lolo asked anxiously, noticing her sleepy voice.

'It is okay Mummy. I needed to have been up already.' She reassured her, sitting up in bed at the same time. 10 O'clock said her bedside clock.

'You wouldn't believe whom I ran into on the streets the other day, Mum?'

'Really, who?' Lolo returned keenly.

'Jude,' Nkiru reported.

'Oh, how is he? I didn't know he was travelling to England or I would have sent a message through him for you. Was he with his new wife?'

'A wife?' Nkiru repeated, startled.

'Oh yes.'

'You mean he wedded in our Ubi town and no one bothered to mention it to me?' Nkiru asked disbelievingly. It was unlikely that a wedding of that magnitude would have gone down unnoticed or unannounced. Jude's father was very affluent.

'Fiancé I should probably say.' Lolo corrected herself. 'They are yet to host the formal weddings but the *iku-aka* ceremony held about a month ago. His betrothed is not from Ubi.' Lolo explained.

That explains it then, Nkiru apprehended. She hadn't been particularly interested in the social activities around her hometown lately but surely Chief Ogele's sons wedding would have been a talk of the town. Jude was ranked most eligible bachelor in town.

'Okay.'

'He didn't mention it when you met?'

'Oh no, we only chatted briefly.' She lied. 'He looked well though.' She commented half wistfully.

'Yes, he's a good fellow.' Lolo agreed. 'I almost forgot the most exciting news. God forgive me that I say that but I'm quite overjoyed.'

'What can that be, Mum? Please tell me.' Nkiru queried expectantly.

'Pastor Ugo is dead.' Lolo announced with a morbid glee.

'True?' Nkiru tried to ascertain with a scream. 'Whatever happened to him?' It was excitingly shocking news.

'My dear, they say that he, who lives by the sword, shall die by one.' Lolo quoted satisfyingly. 'The fellow was found dead in his police cell.'

'Does anyone know how that happened exactly?'

'No one seems to know for sure but rumours are that he was poisoned.' Lolo narrated.

'Okay.' Nkiru whispered with rather mixed feelings. Pastor Ugo did deserve punishment but an untimely death wasn't an outcome that she had envisaged.

'You know that we hadn't mentioned it to you but the case hasn't been going according to plans lately. We all thought this was an open and shut case but as is always the case, corrupt officials let their greed overcome their sense of reasoning. There were rumours that someone was going to help spring him from prison so we are overjoyed this happened. It is jungle justice but he deserved to die.' Lolo declared unsympathetically before changing the topic. 'So how's school?' They went on to converse about other matters.

After she got out off the phone with her mother and the rest of her family members, Nkiru's prior remorse over Jude turned into anger. What was he playing at, blatantly lying about his feelings for her and trying to get her into bed when he was most probably betrothed to another? She became wholly convinced that Obinna had reached out to protect her from beyond the grave.

She was once more reminded of her beloved Obinna and his exemplary dignity. His nobility had known no bounds and she was comforted by the fact that he was definitely looking out for her from yonder. She wasn't going to wallow in self pity, remorse or anger anymore. She had gone full cycle on worthless emotions besides there was so much more to life.

Pastor Ugo's death was another shocker but good riddance! No one ever promised life was going to be a bed of roses. It has turns, curves, hills as well as T's interceding with S's but at the end of the day, what mattered was having that life in itself.

She'll have to live each day now and contend with tomorrow when it comes, Nkiru avowed. She'll trip and fall but rise again she would, to trudge on. She'll also find love, pure and unsullied love, same as the love that she had shared with Obinna. She might have lost the greatest love of her life but there will be another, a love that she deserves and will be deserving of her. While making her new resolve, she contended that she might never be as free spirited as Zola or as gullible as Uche but she was ready to find her old self again. She'll have to rediscover and redefine who and what made her who she was. She felt like a fish taken out of a pond and dumped into a sea but she was determined to adapt and survive.

She'll find herself again and then she would find love. Suddenly feeling like her life was in a greater perspective, Nkiru reached across to her bedside table to turn on her radio. She quickly tuned in to her favourite Heart FM radio station. As providence would have it, Gloria Gaynor's *'I will survive'* was playing. It was a most appropriate anthem and she joyfully rose to her feet and started to sing and dance along to the beat of the empowering anthem in her shorts pyjama.

Her next door neighbour suddenly overheard her singing voice rising melodically above the moderately loud music, '*I will survive for as long as … … ….* He'd never heard her voice previously ricocheting across their thin separating walls much less loud singing or with that much gusto too. Someone sure woke up on the right side of the bed; he mused indulgently as he locked his door after him and stood for a minute listening and enjoying the merry performance.

He had thought that a similar moment indicating his strictly introverted neighbour can unleash her inner wild child would never come. He guessed that she was well on her way to releasing the rest of her inhibitions from the merry chime in her voice. It had seemed to him previously that she had built an invincible wall of silence around her to prevent anyone from penetrating through. She scarcely met his eye in the street and he had seen her galloping up to her flat like she couldn't wait to get away from the rest of the world. If her spirited carefree singing voice was anything to go by then all of that could change now.

He knew her more intimately than she could ever envision after he accidentally came into possession of a video cassette depicting Pastor Ugo defiling her. His Uncle Joe, his father's youngest brother presently on the run from the hands of the law had abandoned a bag containing the videos in his room before absconding.

He had been hugely surprised by Uncle Joe's unexpected appearance at his father's house one faithful night and luckily behind his father back too while he had still lived back in his home country.

His name was Kenenna and he had arrived in the United Kingdom not too long ago. Kenenna's father had vehemently disapproved of his Uncle Joe after he left a thriving law apprenticeship to liaise with a group of dubious friends in perpetrating a colossal 419 scam. The group struck it rich and Uncle Joe flagrantly flaunted his new found well-heeled status with his massive windfall. He constructed a state of the arts mansion in their hometown of Obirima, procured a fleet of cars as well owning a helicopter strip in his compound and was rumoured to be negotiating to purchase a private helicopter. The impoverished villagers of Obirima and rest of the nation practically worshipped at his feet except for his ethical and hardworking elder brother or Kenenna's father.

Kenenna's father had held a prominent public post for years but had little to show for it except for his well educated kids. His outstanding honesty and strong principles was disconcerting to most including his peers, kin and others. He failed to amass significant wealth like his counterparts in a similar position or allow those working under him to misappropriate public funds. He extolled his legacy in the form of his well brought up and educated kids including Kenenna and his four elder siblings as well as his modest home at Isalo. He had also foregone the popular practice of constructing a lavish mansion back in his hometown / Obirima as that was not feasible on his basic pay check. Neither was he able to refurbish his outdated kindred home. His keen and peers were largely unimpressed. Kenenna's father was after all one of the most enlightened indigenes from his small hamlet besides holding a strategic post where he could easily afford to enrich himself and abet others.

Uncle Joe became an instant hero after he helped reconstruct his family's *obi* or kindred home as well as a lavish village villa. He offered to construct a more modest village home for his elder brother and provide funds for him to take a title but Kenenna's father declined both offers. He vehemently denounced Uncle Joe and went as far as disassociating himself from him and forbade his brood also from associating or accepting any proceeds from Uncle Joe's ill gotten wealth.

Much like his father had predicted in propagating the law of karma so did Uncle Joe's receive his appropriate comeuppance. He was presently on the run from both the police and army. None of his relatives had seen or heard from him lately. There were speculations that he might have been robbed and murdered since he had failed to contact anyone since his hasty escape.

His unforeseen demise had emanated from his supposed goodwill after he had unwittingly let his place out to a dubious religious sect. Uncle Joe had insisted that he had no hand in the purported pornographic scam or questionable practices of the sect, yet his carryon bag that he had abandoned in Kenenna's room contained proof to contradict his claim.

Kenenna failed to inform his father of Uncle Joe's unexpected visit or the fact that he had passed the night in his home. Kenenna imagined his father would have personally dragged Uncle Joe to the Police Station or ejected both of them.

He had hosted Uncle Joe overnight but dreaded his father's wrath if he should find him out. Uncle Joe absconded the following night but in his haste forgot his sizeable holdall after his contacts scheduled to smuggle him across the border had arrived to whisk him off.

The bag contained 3 video tapes, clothing and other knick-knacks. Kenenna couldn't believe his eyes when he had watched the movies out of curiosity. He was shocked at the sight of visibly drugged and dazed ladies coerced to participate in the picture. He was enraged and repulsed at how any one could possibly derive any pleasure from watching such vile movies. He was however mostly drawn and taken in by a particular lady in one of the video cassettes. There was something different about her in comparison to the other ladies. She had an unforgettable quality about her and he just couldn't bear to dispose of the reel as he had done with the rest. He had watched her countless of times, admiring her exquisite body even as she laid limp and drugged out in another man's arms.

He found himself falling for her even as he watched another man defile her. He felt that she possessed a certain vulnerability and haughtiness, even as she had lain limp in Pastor Ugo's arms. She was special and he just couldn't get her out of his mind. He had felt attracted and protective towards her without knowing who she was.

So fancy his greatest amazement when he finally secured a flat to move into a fortnight ago and saw her for the first time in person.

He had arrived in the United Kingdom about six months ago to pursue a Masters degree at the prestigious London School of Economics. He was initially staying with his sister and brother-in-law but then decided to secure his own place.

He almost tripped up on the stairs in shock when he stumbled upon her as he left his new digs. They were next door neighbours. If that wasn't destiny then he wouldn't know what to call it. He destroyed the video tape same day.

She was everything that he had imagined and more. There was however an aura of sadness and gloom hovering around her. She also looked vulnerable and broken and he wished that he could enfold her in his arms and shift her blues. He had watched and waited, hoping to find a forum to break through her ice and that façade enclosing her.

Kenenna stopped briefly to appreciate her happy, carefree voice which reminded him of the cheerful chirpings of an entrapped bird that was unexpectedly set free.

He was excited because she was considerably cheered up now.

Author's Profile

Dr Ejine Okoroafor–Ezediaro was born in Enugu in 1968 but hails originally from the illustrious town of Oguta, Imo State, Nigeria.

She holds a B.Sc. in Physics from University of Port-Harcourt, Nigeria and MBBS from Vinnica State Medical University, Ukraine.

Ejine presently divides her time between the United Kingdom where she practices Medicine and New York, USA where her spouse resides until she can secure a substantive post in the USA after securing her ECFMG licensing certificate.

Ejine's flair for prose and poetry was evident from childhood. She attributes her love for literary arts to an early exposure from her late mother, (a dynamic literature and French tutor) that kindled a great interest in books in both herself and her elder sister.

She wouldn't wish to rest on this laurel but hopes to produce more literary works. She is presently working on a number of new projects.

She also promises that the best of her is yet to come!

Dr Ejine Okoroafor-Ezediaro

Other books by the same author

Whimsical Rhapsody is a delightful collection of freestyle poems, available on www.lulu.com/contents/1091343 as well as other internet sites and numerous bookstores.

A ROSE IN BLOOM
A CONTEMPORARY AFRICAN TALE

Dr. Ejine Okoroafor-Ezediaro

About the Book

A Rose in Bloom is the prequel to **Pathos of a Wilting Rose.**

-An initial glimpse of young and idealistic Nkiru venturing into adulthood.

Ancient beliefs and tradition nearly derail her wedding plans, her modern outlook notwithstanding.

This book also explores and showcases the dichotomy between tradition and modernity.

It's available on www.trafford.com/**06-1468**, Amazon, other sites and bookstores.

Acknowledgment

My foray into writing was never on a whim. I give thanks and praise to God for the inspiration.

My love and gratitude goes to Ikenna Ezediaro, my hubbilicious for holding the fort et al.

I also dedicate this book to my beloved father whom I love and cherish dearly. I salute my lovely Big Sis, Agboma Okoroafor and nephew, Chukwuma Nwadike.

My sincere gratitude goes to Anthony Chukwuma Animba, Dr. Emeka Efobi, Dr. Eze Ugwueze and Valentine Okoroafor-Anene for their time and constructive comments. Thanks to my cousin, Ike Francis Okoronkwo for providing the cover picture.

I'll use this opportunity to shout out to the entire members of the Okoroafor family of Abatu village, Ezediaro family of Umunkwokomoshi village and Agorua family of Okichi village, all of Oguta, Nigeria.

Special mention of Ogbuagu Newton Okaru & his delightful wife, Aunty Val, Dr. & Mrs. Ike Okam, Dr. Nicholas Oforka, Mrs. Vicky Nsofor, Uche Best Ibuaka, Broken Okoroafor, Ben Okonya Okoroafor, Samuel Ifeanyi Okoroafor, Ikenna Kennedy Okoroafor, Ikechukwu Okoroafor, Emmanuel 'Manny' Ezediaro, Nkeiru Henrietta (nee Okoroafor), Sylvester Nwakuche, Ngozi Obikwere-Bell, Dr. Emma Nwapa, Dr Mike Okorie, Clement Aguiyi, Stella Obodo, Dr. Uju Oyolu.

I salute y' all!